When Mary Margaret opened her front door, her mouth fell open. "What are you..."

Kevin pounded the Christmas tree trunk on her porch. "It's pretty, isn't it? Nice shape. Manageable size. My son and I picked it out for you."

Mary Margaret opened the door wider. "You better come inside before someone sees you."

Not, *Thank you, Kevin. You're so sweet.*

"You really didn't have to do this," she said. But there was a crack in her defenses; he could feel it in the way she ran her fingers over the needles on one branch. "Thank you. It smells so good."

"I see someone dropped off a bit of mistletoe." He nodded toward a wilted bag on her counter.

"Don't get any ideas, *friend*." She crossed her arms over her chest. "That's not happening."

"Okay, then. I guess that's my cue to leave." He hesitated on her porch.

"Kevin." Mary Margaret stared at him with what he'd swear was longing in her eyes. "Thank you for the tree and...and your friendship."

"Friendship is a solid basis for a relationship." *That was both boring and lame.*

"I'm closing the door on you now." True to her word, she shut him out.

ALSO BY MELINDA CURTIS

A Very Merry Match

MELINDA CURTIS

FOREVER
New York Boston

Forever
Hachette Book Group
1290 Avenue of the Americas, New York, NY 10104
read-forever.com
twitter.com/readforeverpub

First Edition: September 2020

Forever is an imprint of Grand Central Publishing. The Forever name and logo are trademarks of Hachette Book Group, Inc.

The publisher is not responsible for websites (or their content) that are not owned by the publisher.

The Hachette Speakers Bureau provides a wide range of authors for speaking events. To find out more, go to www.hachettespeakersbureau.com or call (866) 376-6591.

ISBN: 978-1-5387-3345-5 (mass market), 978-1-5387-3344-8 (ebook)

Printed in the United States of America

OPM

10 9 8 7 6 5 4 3 2 1

To Mr. Curtis, who intuitively understands that sometimes a woman feels like getting dressed up and going dancing, and sometimes she just wants to lounge in her pajamas on the couch. Thank you for being yin to my yang.

Acknowledgments

I'm a giggler. My husband says I hide it well, but it's true. Life makes me laugh even when it's not always appropriate to do so. Like during our wedding ceremony (the minister referred to me as Susan). Or during labor (when I transitioned before they could administer pain meds). That's why I'm thrilled to be writing the Sunshine Valley books for Forever Romance. In them, I get to sneak in life's funny moments while a couple falls in love.

Writing is a solitary endeavor but it isn't always a one-person show. Many people had input into this book from the idea phase to my getting over the my-book-sucks phase to the you-can-finish-it-because-it's-awesome phase to the editing phase to the marketing and selling phase. Everyone who touched this book helped me find the yellow brick road and persevere to the end. With that in mind, I'd like to thank my family, Cari, Sheila, Pam, Alex, and all the folks at Forever Romance.

So, whether you were looking for a little giggle over life's sometimes silly moments or for a little sigh when a couple finally earns their happily-ever-after, thank you for visiting Sunshine Valley.

Prologue

✳

I want to match Darcy Harper."

"*Edith!*" chorused the three mature females who made up the Sunshine Valley Widows Club board.

"Why are you upset?" Edith Archer demanded, trying to sit as tall as she could at the card table, height not being one of her assets. "I thought we were here to choose someone who needs help falling in love."

She'd overheard her three friends at a Widows Club Thanksgiving potluck yesterday discussing their intent to give Cupid a helping hand this holiday season. Since it sounded like something she'd be interested in, Edith had dropped by because Mims, Bitsy, and Clarice often forgot to extend an invitation her way.

"You can't choose Darcy." Bitsy's head shook so hard her black velvet hair bow slid lower on her bobbed blond hair. "For one thing, she's married. And if you must know, we give priority to matching widows and widowers."

"That's a rule." Clarice shouted, having left her hearing aids at home. She shuffled a deck of cards. "Like having to be on the Widows Club *board* to participate in the matchmaking."

"I come to all the board meetings." Edith shifted in her seat, wishing Mims had cushioned folding chairs. "Therefore, I'm on the board."

There was another uproar. Clarice's cards spewed like a fountain across the table. Bitsy's bow fell to the floor. Mims stared up at her husband's tall, hand-carved gun case, mouth moving as if having a silent conversation with Hamm.

Edith sat patiently through it all. If possession was nine-tenths of the law, then attendance should count the same. When her husband died last winter, she'd needed an anchor. The Widows Club board had helped keep her grounded. Yes, they sometimes overlooked her but their hearts were in the right place. And she'd been tickled to learn they had a secret purpose and a code name—the Sunshine Valley Matchmakers Club. They were a club, Sunshine Valley's version of the secret society in *The DaVinci Code*. Only they operated for good, not greed.

"Edith," Mims said in her firm voice, pausing to chew off more of her lipstick as she tried to fluff her white, short, flat curls. "Some may question Darcy's choice in husband." Darcy was in her early twenties and had married Judge Harper, who was pushing eighty. "But that's not why we're here."

"You can't mean to let Edith have a vote." Bitsy stopped trying to fix her hair bow. She was always perfectly coiffed, even if stuck in '80s fashion trends.

Leg warmers had never been Edith's thing. But Bitsy's words...

Edith experienced a rare moment of gut-shaking doubt that things wouldn't go the way she wanted them to. She stared at Mims pleadingly through eyes filling with unexpected tears.

"Listen closely, Edith." Clarice used her outdoor voice and pointed at Mims and her neon orange camouflage sweatshirt. "*President.*" She pointed at Bitsy and her red, silk-covered, linebacker shoulder pads. "*Treasurer.*" She jabbed a thumb at her pink and yellow paisley blouse. "*Secretary.*" And then she faced Edith. "Which means you're—"

"Vice president," Edith interrupted with a relieved laugh. Thank heavens. She'd found a slot to fill. "Boards always have a vice president." A second in command. Edith's chest swelled with importance.

Her pronouncement was met with silence. They were probably all stunned they hadn't seen this before.

"I vote we table the issue of vice presidency to a later date," Mims mumbled.

"Second." Bitsy went back to her hair bow and then shouted at Clarice. "Deal the cards. We'll figure things out later."

Clarice frowned. As a flower child, she'd seen a lot of sun in her day, and when she frowned, her thin face thickened with sun-spotted wrinkles. "There are rules."

Mims waved her hand the way she did with the board when Edith got her way.

Frowning, Clarice settled her long gray braids over her shoulders. "You have to win a game of poker before you can propose a name."

"Preferably the name of a widow or widower," Bitsy said, hair bow in place.

"Who's been widowed at least a year," Mims added, gaze drifting back to the locked case of hunting rifles.

"That could almost be me." Suddenly, Edith had mixed feelings about the game. She'd practically earned a coveted seat on the board. What if the winner of the poker game chose to match her?

"We tend to focus on the younger widows," Mims explained.

"Oh." Edith blew out a relieved breath.

"We could make an exception," Bitsy murmured.

With a snort, Clarice began to deal. "Ante up."

Each of the widows had ten pennies in front of them.

Edith laid two pennies in the middle of the card table. *Clink-clink.* "One, two. Buckle my shoe." The mood in the room was too serious for her liking.

After a moment's hesitation, Mims slid out two pennies.

"Three, four. Shut the door." Edith beamed.

Clarice stopped dealing cards to stare at Mims and Bitsy. "This is a bad idea."

"You're right," Edith said, grateful the conversation had turned. "Gambling is never to be condoned. My grandson-in-law did a good bit of it before he died."

"How is Mary Margaret doing?" Bitsy sorted her cards.

"The first holidays are always tough." Mims directed her soft words toward Edith.

Who nodded, thinking about the empty side of her own bed instead of her granddaughter's. "I'm lucky to have such good family and friends around, especially the

Widows Club." Edith turned a warm smile toward Bitsy. "Did you forget to ante up?"

Bitsy contributed her two cents. "Widows roll with the punches."

"Five, six. Pick up sticks," Edith sing-songed.

"I'm afraid of what comes next." Clarice finished dealing. She set the deck of cards aside and tossed her two pennies on the pile.

"Seven, eight. Lay them straight." Edith beamed at her friends. And then she beamed at her cards, splaying them on the table. "Four queens. Who can beat me?"

The original three board members groaned.

"That's not the way poker is played." Mims exhaled, long and slow. "This isn't going to work."

"Agreed." Bitsy crossed her arms.

"Yep. Can't play without protocol." Clarice stood, reaching for her wooden walking stick. She'd been using it since her double-knee replacement last year.

"I have to go." Bitsy got to her feet, adjusting her listing shoulder pads. "I forgot I have a...a...*thing*."

Mims had no excuse to leave since they were at her house. She stood anyway.

"I win?" Edith happily raked in her coins. She should have known she'd prevail. Edith had always been lucky. "I thought we'd play until someone had all the pennies. But if not, I'll choose Mary Margaret." Because the anniversary of her granddaughter's husband's death was Christmas.

"You can't choose," Clarice said in her loud voice. "It goes against the rules." And being secretary, Clarice was a stickler for the group's rules.

"All right. Then who will we match?" Edith looked at

each of the board in turn, hoping they wouldn't point to her. "I thought Mary Margaret was the perfect choice."

The rest of the board fell silent.

And in that dead space, Edith realized it didn't matter who won their forty-cent game of poker. They'd all had Mary Margaret on their mind.

Chapter One

❄

Mary Margaret Sneed was going to find some holiday spirit if it killed her.

It had been a rough year. Her husband, Derek, had died last Christmas after a second bout with cancer, leaving her with an unexpected pile of debt, no life insurance policy, and only her kindergarten teacher's salary to set things right.

Fulfill your obligations.

Mary Margaret hadn't heard her father's voice anywhere but in her head in more than five years. It still had the power to chill her. She shut him out by humming the chorus of "Grandma Got Run Over by a Reindeer."

Memories might not be doing much to bolster Mary Margaret's spirits but Mother Nature was. It'd been snowing for three days in Sunshine. There was two feet of snow on the ground, more alongside the road where the plows had run. It was only two days past Thanksgiving but it looked like Christmas.

Mary Margaret shoveled her walk, made a small snowman, and got out the rickety wooden ladder to string colorful lights along the eaves of her small rented bungalow. Her street was lined with historic Craftsman homes painted everything from light blue to forest green to sunny yellow and would soon be decorated with lights and lawn displays. Small town life in high plains Colorado was all about heritage and tradition, even if you were only going through the motions.

"Good to see you, Mary Margaret." Kimmy Easley waved from across the street. She was going all-out with a nativity scene and spotlights. "If you need help setting up your tree, let me know."

"Will do," Mary Margaret said. She didn't think she was up to indoor cheer, not when she'd decorated for Christmas around Derek's hospital bed last December.

"Now that's going to look pretty at night."

Mary Margaret contorted herself on the ladder to see who was coming up the walk.

Two men wearing black leather jackets approached. One man was tall, thin, balding, and chewed a plastic coffee stir stick the way cigarette smokers did when they were trying to quit. The other man was Hardy to his partner's Laurel. Shorter, stockier, and with the kind of features that said he hadn't had enough to smile about in life.

Neither was a local. Mary Margaret may not have grown up in Sunshine but, as a five-year resident, she knew everyone in town, at least by sight.

"Are you Mrs. Sneed?" Mr. Hardy asked with the narrow-eyed look of an amateur detective.

At her nod, Mr. Laurel said, "Sorry about your loss, ma'am. Derek...He was..."

Mary Margaret's chest locked, refusing to take in air.

Over the past eleven months, she'd learned the lack of words to describe her husband usually meant he'd borrowed money and hadn't paid someone back. Derek had faced his mortality armed with the balm of retail therapy. He hadn't just bought things online, in stores, and at dealerships. He'd bought things from friends in town, promising to pay later, knowing full well that he'd never see a later date.

Drawing a deep breath, Mary Margaret climbed down the ladder, took a stand in the snow, and pushed up her sweatshirt sleeves. "Gentlemen, I hope you're here to tell me Derek had a lottery ticket he never claimed."

She could tell by the lack of change in their expressions that this wasn't the case.

Hardy planted his feet wider than his shoulders on her walk and hinged his hips from side to side. "We represent a company that floated your husband money."

"*Loaned*," Mr. Laurel clarified, swiveling the red stir stick from one side of his mouth to the other. "Derek had a line of credit."

"*Fellas.*" They'd dropped in her estimation from gentlemen to random dudes. "My husband has been gone nearly a year. In all that time, I've received many invoices for his debt. Have you billed me already? What's the name of your company?"

Shrugging deeper into his jacket, the tall Mr. Laurel gestured toward the front door and the plastic holly wreath hanging there. "Can we go inside and discuss this?"

"No." The rejection was instinctual. Her creep-o-meter was pinging off the charts. These weren't your average bill collectors. Their tans and thin jackets said they'd come from a warmer climate. "So, here's the thing, guys.

If my husband owed you money, you need to prove it with receipts, contracts, or invoices." She'd learned that in the early weeks after Derek passed.

"Mrs. Sneed." Mr. Hardy's hips did that unsettling side-to-side mamba. "Last December, your husband lost one hundred thousand dollars to our online gambling casino."

Mary Margaret gripped the ladder, trying to steady herself in the shifting snow.

"We've been trying to get in touch with him through the usual channels," Mr. Hardy continued. "Cell phone." Which she'd canceled. "And email." Which she didn't have the password to.

"That can't be true. My husband only gambled at the Indian casino down the road." But she could tell by their expressions this wasn't a joke.

Mr. Laurel swiveled the red plastic stick in his mouth and handed her a stapled set of papers.

Black Jack Online Gaming. Account for Derek Sneed.
  Debt Validation Notice.

No physical address was listed for Derek, just his email. There were fourteen days of transactions listed in December of last year. That alone didn't mean much. It was the Debt Validation Notice that legitimized their claim in Mary Margaret's eyes.

The bottom of her small world fell out.

Oh, Derek.

Her husband hadn't handled cancer well. At the news of his first diagnosis three years ago, Derek had said he didn't want to be married anymore. He'd taken Carina

Snodgrass, his high school sweetheart, to Las Vegas with no indication that he was ever coming back. After two weeks, he'd returned to Sunshine without Carina, and Mary Margaret had taken him back because it was the right thing to do.

Marriage is a sacred bond.

But things hadn't been the same. Mary Margaret rubbed her temple, trying to get her father's voice out of her head but, as usual, he slipped in the last word: *Always fulfill your obligations.*

A little over a year after his cancer all-clear, Derek had been diagnosed with a brain tumor. This time, he swore his love for Mary Margaret. That hadn't stopped him from going on a spending spree the day they'd diagnosed him as terminal. Among other things, he'd bought a seventy-inch flat screen, a fancy laptop, an all-terrain quad, a fishing boat, and a new pick-up truck. And then when his body began shutting down, he'd coerced his friends into taking him gambling, betting big in the hopes he'd win enough to square Mary Margaret away.

Derek had been as unlucky in the casino as with his health.

She'd tried to return and sell everything after he died. The truck and fishing boat had been returned with what she'd felt was an unreasonable re-stocking fee. The all-terrain quad had been sitting in the driveway with a FOR SALE sign for nearly a year. And now this...

"Here's the thing, Mrs. Sneed." Mr. Hardy was glee-fully fidgety. "We tried in good faith to contact your husband. We aren't completely heartless regarding your loss." He tried to look sad. Tried, but failed. "Do you own this place?"

"No." Some of the bitterness she tried not to feel toward Derek slipped out. She'd had to sell their starter home last spring. "How much will it take to buy his debt down?" She'd learned that debt collectors would settle for less than the full amount just to get it off their books.

"This isn't a sale at Macy's, Mrs. Sneed." Mr. Hardy's good humor evaporated. His words were as chilly as the thirty-degree air. "We want our hundred grand."

Mary Margaret twitched so hard that the ladder fell sideways into the snow.

"We'll be needing a good faith payment today." Mr. Laurel walked a few feet into the snowdrift and righted her ladder.

Mary Margaret cleared her throat. "Gentlemen..." She decided to upgrade their status in the hopes of leniency. "I've spent months consolidating Derek's debt. I'm on a very strict payment plan. I could maybe add fifty dollars a month for you." She was grasping at straws.

Their heads swung slowly from side to side.

"We'll be needing a good faith payment today," Mr. Laurel repeated.

Mary Margaret only had two hundred dollars in her checking account. But she wasn't the most beloved kindergarten teacher in Sunshine for nothing. She was a quick thinker and had a winning smile. "Can I interest you in a quad?" She gestured to the vehicle to the side of her driveway. The one with the faded FOR SALE sign.

They shook their heads.

"We plan to stay in town until a sizable portion has been paid," Mr. Hardy said. "Our boss wants us back in the office before Christmas." He stared at her blue jean–clad legs.

And it wasn't the admiring kind of look a man gave a woman's gams.

It was the kind of look a kindergarten boy gave to a Popsicle stick before he tried to snap it in half.

❋

"Daddy, are you sure Santa likes Christmas trees with toy cars?" Five-year-old Tad wrapped a red sports car with a white pipe cleaner and hung it on the ficus in Kevin's office. "I never see trees with cars." His small brow wrinkled. "Or ninjas." His role-playing favorite.

Sunshine Mayor Kevin Hadley stopped working on the road-repaving budget and turned his chair to face his son. "Do you know what Santa likes?"

Tad solemnly shook his head.

"Santa likes Christmas to be fun and full of surprises." Surprises weren't so fun to politicians.

Like the news that your wife had been unfaithful. Or that she considered you boring, in and out of the bedroom. Or that, despite all that, she still wanted to be married to you. As if your shared aspirations of climbing the political ladder to Washington, DC, could survive that.

Their divorce was final. Ironically, that had coincided with his party floating an invitation to run for state assembly from his district. All Kevin had to do was tell them he was ready and pass a few background checks and interviews to earn their support. Not one to leap before he analyzed the situation, Kevin hadn't told anyone about the conversation, not even his parents.

"What are you going to get me for Christmas?" Tad

brought a fire truck over and stood at Kevin's side, trying to look innocent and reinforcing all the love Kevin had in his heart for him.

I'd do anything for Tad.

On the outside, Tad was a precocious, sturdy kid, big for his age. On the inside, he was made fragile by his parents' divorce, struggling a bit at school and seeking attention more than he had in the past.

"All I can tell you is this, Tad." Kevin leaned down and whispered, "The present you'll get is a surprise."

"Daddy." Tad climbed into Kevin's lap, continuing to wrap the fire truck with a pipe cleaner.

Footsteps sounded on the staircase from the first floor of the town hall. His father filled the doorway, still looking vital and hale at sixty years, despite his white hair. "Kevin, I need a moment."

"Grandpa!" Tad tumbled to the floor and scrambled across the room to hug him before returning to decorate the ficus.

"I've only got a minute, Dad. I have a meeting with Everett." He and his city manager had decided to convene on the Saturday after Thanksgiving to speak their minds on the controversial development project they were supporting. "How did you get in?" Kevin was sure he'd locked the door downstairs behind him.

"I used my key." Dad shrugged. He'd once been mayor too. Politics and furniture-making had been family businesses for three generations. "Listen, about this distribution center you're considering…"

Kevin sighed. Since he'd been elected nearly a decade earlier, everything about his public service had been smooth sailing, approved and embraced by almost everyone. And then came the dissolution of his marriage and JPM Industries' proposal to build a distribution center on the outskirts of town. Now everyone had an opinion about his life and his leadership.

"It's the wrong choice for Sunshine." Dad moved his hands as if smoothing a tablecloth one final time before company arrived.

End of story, Dad meant.

It was far from the end for Kevin. "Do you want to elaborate on that?" Because everyone in Sunshine was telling Kevin it was the wrong thing for the town but no one would articulate why.

"We're a small ranching community." Which was essentially code for Dad not liking change.

The distribution center would bring much-needed jobs and tax revenue to Sunshine, not to mention it would look good on Kevin's political résumé. He'd need that to make the move to the state level.

"Thanks for your input, Dad." Before his father could accelerate his DEFCON level to emergency mode, Kevin turned the conversation in a new direction. "Are you out shopping with Mom? You know, I told her not to spoil Tad." Their only grandchild.

"I wrote a long list to Santa," Tad said, right on cue. "Ms. Sneed mailed our class letters to the North Pole last week."

Kevin made a mental note to ask Mary Margaret what had been on Tad's long list, although something ninja-related was a safe bet.

"Grandma was going into the pet store." Kevin's father ruffled Tad's dark brown hair. "She promised not to buy anything."

A twinge of worry plucked a muscle in the shoulder of Kevin's throwing arm, threatening to cramp. "Rosalie had poodle puppies for adoption in the window." And she was one of the best salespeople in town. "Given I'm never home during the day, any pup she picks up will be living at your place from eight to five."

"Your mother knows my rules about dogs," Dad said with the blind confidence of a lord who thought he ruled his castle. The elder Hadleys were a one-dog household. And Chester, their Labrador, had many years ahead of him. "Now, about the distribution center..." Dad's cell phone chimed with a message. He stared at his phone, swore, and hurried out the door, mumbling something about Chester being his only fur baby.

Kevin chuckled, confident Dad would stop Mom from getting a puppy. They were all too busy for new household members, especially this holiday season.

Tad hung another car on the ficus next to a twinkling white light. "Can I have a puppy for Christmas? All ninjas have puppies."

"No."

"But, Daddy." Tad returned to Kevin's side and leaned on his thigh, digging his elbows in and smiling for all he was worth. "I'll keep it at your house and take care of it always."

"No puppies." At least he and Barb could agree on that.

Another set of footsteps sounded on the stairs.

"Merry Christmas." Everett, his city manager, said hello to Tad and sat down across from Kevin, shedding his jacket and red knit scarf. He was a rangy man, a decade older than Kevin. His brown hair was always shaggy, and his clothes were always rumpled, but he was as good as, if not better than, Kevin when it came to running Sunshine. "Rosalie is having a huge sale, plus the rescue shelter is running an adoption fair, and I promised her I'd only be gone for thirty minutes." He and his wife were a unified team.

Like Barb and I used to be.

Or perhaps that had been a lie too.

"Let's get to it, then." Kevin reached for the folder with his notes on the development project.

Heeled footsteps struck the wooden stair treads.

"I'm sorry I'm late." Barb walked through the door to Kevin's office as if she owned the room. His ex-wife looked as if she'd stepped out of a fashion magazine. A hair stylist by trade and the owner of the town's only beauty salon, her blond, tailored appearance was designed to wow. "Funny how no one told me there was a development meeting today."

Kevin swallowed his annoyance.

"Mommy, look. *Look-look-look.*" Tad grabbed Barb's hand and tugged her over to the ficus. "I'm making Santa a surprise tree."

"You are indeed." Barb hugged their son and wisely handed him another toy car to prep for hanging. "It looks fabulous. But it's not finished, is it?"

"This isn't your meeting, Barb." Kevin suspected she'd been shopping downtown and had seen Everett enter the town hall. He couldn't imagine how else she'd have found out about their appointment. "How did you get in?" For his own sanity, he was going to have to change the locks on the doors to town hall.

Barb didn't bother narrowing her eyes or tossing her hands. She sat down next to Everett and set her ginormous pink leather purse on the floor, slipping out of her thick wool coat. "Don't be stubborn, Kev. You're facing a huge issue before Christmas with an election year looming. One wrong choice and you become replaceable, sending our dreams of higher office down the drain. You need me here."

"The city won't make a wrong choice." But Everett pressed his lips closed at Barb's cold stare.

"My career *and* I are fine on our own," Kevin reassured his ex-wife.

"Ms. Sneed asked us what we want to be when we grow up." Tad had wound so much white pipe cleaner around a car that nothing but the grill and taillights were visible. "I'm going to be the mayor." He stretched to hang it on the highest branch. "Or a ninja."

"Honey, you can be anything you want to be." Barb swiped Kevin's paper calendar from his desk and perused December. "But if you're going into politics, dream about being president of the United States." She dropped the calendar back on the oak surface. "Kevin, really. You've allocated too much time to events hosted by the Sunshine Valley Widows Club. Everyone knows that's the local dating mart. You need to look above all that."

"Above all what?" Kevin said in a hard voice.

Barb rolled her expertly lined eyes. "Romance."

"Here comes the kettle," Kevin mumbled, finding a small mint in his desk drawer and taking his time to unwrap it. "I'm supposed to be celibate because you couldn't honor our wedding vows?" Not that he'd had romance on his mind when he'd agreed to help the Widows Club. "Besides, it's only two events." He'd agreed to judge a poetry slam at the retirement center and act as emcee for a formal ballroom dance. Widows Club events were good for mingling. And mingling earned votes.

Barb blinked false eyelashes. "Your voting public expects you to be above reproach, like a much beloved priest."

Everett adjusted his glasses, looking like he'd rather be anyplace but in the audience of this post-marital showdown.

"You're not a priest, Daddy." Tad turned to look at Kevin. "You don't have a white collar."

"From the mouths of babes," Kevin murmured, allowing a Cheshire cat smile to grow on his face.

"You know what I mean." Barb huffed. "Don't give the public a reason *not* to vote for you."

"I always followed your advice regarding my political career." Kevin hoped his gaze was turning as hard and closed-off as his heart. "You've always told me to avoid gossip and bad press, which is why I divorced you."

Barb gasped but it was a princess intake of breath, meant to warn those in her immediate vicinity that she was displeased and that reparations needed to be made.

Kevin was done bowing down to Barb.

"Tad, you and Mommy need to leave. I've got lots of work to do." Kevin closed his calendar. "I think Mommy should take you to the Saddle Horn for a mile-high whip." The diner's signature hot chocolate was served with inches of whipped cream on top.

"Daddy." Tad slid a guarded glance toward his mother. "You know mile-high whips are only on Sundays."

"Tad," Kevin teased, "you know they serve them every day on Thanksgiving weekend. You should get one."

"Ninja mile-high whip!" Tad wrestled himself into his jacket.

"You know we need to limit Tad's calorie intake." Barb didn't budge, not her butt and not her businesslike expression. "You can't get rid of me that easily."

"Mommy!" Tad ran out the door and down the stairs. "Thanksgiving is special!"

Kevin shrugged. "If you don't want to take him to the Saddle Horn, you might want to check on my parents at the pet store. I think Mom sent a picture of a puppy to Dad via text. And she was shopping for Tad."

"Oh, for cryin' out loud. Your mother is too impulsive." Barb hightailed it out of there, leaving Everett and Kevin to get down to business in private.

Chapter Two

❇

I knew you'd be in soon." Ricky Parker, the thrift store manager, had been slouching on a stool behind the counter, but when he saw Mary Margaret enter the store he sat up. "Haven't seen you in three weeks."

His greeting didn't lift Mary Margaret's spirits. Nor did being in the secondhand store, which had aisles packed with a jumble of used merchandise and competitive bargain shoppers.

"Time is a commodity I'm very short on." Mary Margaret dodged a family of five and made her way around an inflatable snowman. She set her purse on the counter and unloaded what she'd brought to sell. "I've got my wedding ring. Derek's wedding ring." Had she been wrong not to bury it with him? "My great aunt Bunny's ruby earrings. An old iPod. A flip phone. And…"—she dug around the bottom of her bag—"a personal metal detector."

Ricky's eyes lit up. "Are you looking for your usual? To sell?" Not pawn.

"Yes." She hated that she'd become a regular, selling off possessions to make good on Derek's debt.

Material possessions don't define you. Her father's words sounded like they were being delivered from the pulpit.

But a few material things can give you comfort in dark times, Dad.

She was running out of things to sell.

"You've been holding out on me," Ricky said on a gasp-wheeze. His emphysema made him a man of few words. He placed her jewelry on a scrap of red velvet and thrust his brown-checked shirttails behind him as he leaned over for a closer look. "This is better than what you brought me last time." *Gasp-gasp.*

Good-bye, plain wedding band. Good-bye, princess-cut diamond and ruby chips. Good-bye, vestiges of a former life.

Mary Margaret drew a breath as labored as Ricky's. "How much?"

"Gee...I don't know." Ricky regarded her with the same intensity he'd given her possessions, as if trying to suss her level of desperation. "Flip phones are actually being made again. The earrings are clip-ons. And your battery's dead on the iPod."

"It works. I swear." On her husband's grave. Ugh. She sounded in dire need of cash. *Take a breath, Mary Margaret.* She did. "Those earrings are bound to move at the holidays. And the new flip phones open like a book and cost a fortune."

He *tsk*ed. "I can give you a thousand bucks."

"A thousand? That's all? I could make more than that in one night..." *Dancing.* She'd financed her college education dancing in a burlesque revue at a club outside of Denver. She ran a hand beneath her hairline at the back of her neck, tracing the scar there, hearing her father's damning words.

Wicked. Sinful. Her father wasn't shutting up today.

I kept my clothes on, Dad. And being good at burlesque is an art form.

It was easier to argue years later, especially when she'd only seen her father one time since her college graduation. Mary Margaret rubbed the back of her neck. Performing burlesque was no more risqué than the dancing done in most music videos. The moves were suggestive, the costumes cheesy, and some pieces removable. But there were no private parts revealed.

Being a burlesque dancer...

Those were the days when she hadn't worried about making her money stretch to the next paycheck, when she'd dreamed of building a life with Mom, away from her controlling father.

Burlesque. Was that even trendy anymore? She'd heard about a club opening in nearby Greeley.

Ricky stared at Mary Margaret, waiting for her to complete her sentence.

She wasn't going to give him the satisfaction of gossip fodder. "I mean, I could make more than that in one night waiting tables at Shaw's Bar & Grill."

"You wish," Ricky scoffed, knowing that wasn't true. The local bar and honky-tonk appealed to conservative-tipping clientele. He sat back on his stool. "Twelve hundred. That's my best and final."

"Fine, but I'm taking back my flip phone." In case she ever needed to disappear, it'd make a good burner phone. "Are you sure you don't want to buy a quad?"

"I keep telling you." *Gasp-wheeze.* "I've got no floor space." *Gasp-gasp.* "Maybe Santa needs one."

She walked out of the thrift store with shoulders slumped. Where was she going to find ninety-eight thousand, eight hundred dollars?

With the hundred-year-old brick buildings blanketed in snow, downtown Sunshine looked charming, challenging Mary Margaret to find some holiday spirit.

"Watch out!"

The Bodine twins ran past her on the covered sidewalk toward a cluster of teenage girls at the movie theater. The teens wore Santa hats and sang snatches of Christmas carols as they joined the girls in line for the latest Disney cartoon feature.

Bah, humbug.

Mary Margaret hurried to her car. The wind was picking up as the sun was setting. She wanted nothing more than to go home, cuddle up in front of the television, and wait for the holidays to end. She passed the three-story brick shopping mall, which had once been an apartment building with an atrium. They were behind on their holiday prep. Eighties pop boomed from their speakers.

The dark of night. Music that moved people. Show time!

Her steps slowed. She could dance her way out of this. A grand a night at a big club. Ninety-nine nights. It would take her three months—four, max—and she'd be free and clear. If the thugs were patient.

Her gut clenched.

Laurel and Hardy didn't strike her as patient types. Besides, she couldn't risk moonlighting as an exotic dancer. If anyone in Sunshine found out, she'd lose her teaching job. There was a morals clause in her contract.

"Ms. Sneed!" Tad Hadley burst out of the town hall and ran over to Mary Margaret with the awkward steps of a growing boy. He hugged her leg and beamed up at her. "I miss you."

"I miss you too, honey." She smoothed his brown curls. "Did you have a good Thanksgiving?" Tad was in her kindergarten class and a rascal, like Becky Taylor had been last year. Mary Margaret was partial to rascals.

Tad patted his stomach. "I ate so much pumpkin pie, I almost burst!" His jacket was unzipped, ends flapping in the wind.

Mary Margaret kneeled to zip him up.

"When you rack up calories one day, you pay for it the next." Barbara Hadley appeared behind Tad, catalogued Mary Margaret's outfit and sniffed her reluctant approval. She was a stuck-up pill but she was Mary Margaret's room mother this year, not to mention her beautician and the town's queen bee, a position not lessened by her recent divorce from the mayor.

"Calories?" Mary Margaret couldn't leave Tad undefended. "Pumpkin pie has no calories." She tweaked Tad's nose. Kids his age shouldn't worry about things like that. "Hey, Barbara, I don't suppose you'd be interested in buying someone a quad for Christmas."

Tad gasped. "Is it Tad-sized?"

It wasn't. Mary Margaret shook her head.

"You asked me that already, Mary Margaret. The answer is still no." Barbara managed to look disapproving without frowning. Plus, her hair didn't move much in the wind, making her appear above mundane emotions, like worry and grief. Barbara took Tad's hand. "Come along, Tad. We've got to find your grandparents."

"And then we can go to the Saddle Horn?" Tad asked hopefully.

"We'll see."

Mary Margaret walked with them around the corner, wishing them a Merry Christmas when she reached her car. The pair continued around the next corner in the direction of the pet store.

Mary Margaret opened her car door just as her phone buzzed with a text message from Lola Taylor, asking if she wanted to meet at Shaw's for a drink. The answer was an immediate yes and included the wine glass emoji. When creating her payment plan, Mary Margaret had budgeted for two wine glasses a week because kindergarten teachers needed to unwind.

A few minutes later, Mary Margaret was sitting in a booth at the back of Shaw's with her friends Lola, Darcy Harper, and Avery Blackstone. When she was in Shaw's with her besties, she could pretend that her life was normal and that terms like "interest compounded daily" didn't scare her.

Shaw's had a big stage and a dance floor on one end with padded booths and large wooden tables on the other. A long, narrow bar sat in the middle of Shaw's with stools on both sides. There were license plates on the walls instead of photos or mirrors. Old saddles were mounted on the high rafters. And on Saturday nights, the shells from free peanuts littered the floor.

Classy, it was not.

Mary Margaret and her friends occupied a booth near the pool table.

"I'm so tired of studying for the bar." Blond hair in a bun at her nape, Darcy clutched her beer stein, her single karat wedding ring glinting in the dim fluorescent light. "I took the test weeks ago and George still grills me at every opportunity during the day and every night after dinner. I feel like I'm in law school all over again."

"Trouble in paradise?" Avery tossed her straight black hair off the movie theater logo on her navy polo, narrowly missing Mary Margaret. "Is the honeymoon over?"

There was an uncomfortable silence. Avery had broken the unwritten rule of the group. They weren't supposed to ask Darcy intimate details about her unorthodox marriage.

Darcy was too young to have married the nearly eighty-year-old judge on a whim last spring. He seemed more determined to help Darcy pass the bar than to make her happy. Plus the judge had purged Darcy's wardrobe of anything too feminine or fun.

Mary Margaret's chest ached at the robbing of Darcy's independence. But what could she say?

"I can tell you how a newlywed sounds." Lola picked up the thread of conversation with a purr and a satisfied smile. Her thick brown hair was braided with strands of tinsel, most likely a product of her stepdaughter's whimsy. "I've never been happier."

Darcy chugged her beer.

"You've never been happier?" Avery teased, elbowing Mary Margaret. "Even when Drew works on Saturday nights?"

"He doesn't work on Sunday mornings." Lola hugged Darcy. "Oh, sweetie, don't worry. You'll work it out with the judge. How could you not? It's practically Christmas."

Avery and Mary Margaret were quick to support that sentiment.

"The holiday can't fly by fast enough." Noah Shaw, the bar owner, was taping sparkly red garland around the edge of the pool table. "My business is down during the holiday season."

He had a point. Other than Mary Margaret and her friends, the only other person in the bar was Kevin Hadley, the town's recently divorced, gorgeous-as-sin mayor. His thick, dark hair was longish on top, tousled as if a woman had tangled her hands in it. Since his divorce, he'd been sporting a stubbled beard. Just the thought of it scraping across her neck was delicious.

Since when do I look at Tad's father and feel delicious?

Mary Margaret felt a blush coming on. She looked away and drank her wine.

"If business is so bad, why bother decorating?" Avery managed her family's movie theater and had spent all last weekend decorating the lobby.

"Because if I don't decorate, I'll get a visit from the Widows Club." Noah stood, looking one hundred percent Colorado cowboy bachelor with his checked shirt, blue jeans, and boots. "And I like being a bachelor operating under their radar."

The Widows Club. Mary Margaret had forgotten about them. They'd visited her after Derek died, asking if she needed anything, telling her they'd extend a formal invitation to join their ranks six months after Derek's death, but she'd put them off another six months. They were a well-intentioned organization, and she shouldn't care that the average age of their membership was sixty.

But she did care. "I feel old." Mary Margaret's shoulders drooped lower than Darcy's.

"What's wrong, Mary Margaret?" Lola reached across the table to give her hand a squeeze. "Oh, I know. It's your one-year widow-versary, isn't it? I completely freaked out when mine rolled around."

"That was the day you discovered Randy had been cheating on you." Avery chuckled. "The day we found your husband's blow-up dolls and put them on display in your window."

"That display drove Drew crazy." Lola's smile turned wicked.

Those blow-up dolls had caused an uproar. Small town Sunshine had freaked out over what would essentially have been a ho-hum window display in Denver. That's why Mary Margaret couldn't dance her way out of trouble this time. This wasn't Denver.

"Rest assured..." Mary Margaret held up her wine glass for a toast. "My widow-versary will pass quietly. I'm one of the most invisible residents in town." She'd learned long before she moved to Sunshine that a quiet life was the way to go.

Thank you, Dad.

They clinked their glasses.

"But you seem distracted." Newlywed Lola wanted everyone to be as happy as she was. "You aren't thinking of Derek, are you?"

"No. I'm not still grieving, if that's what you mean." Thinking about Derek separate from his debt created a dull ache in her chest and the threat of tears in her eyes. Unfortunately, she was more likely to think about him *and* his debt than just him. "I just..." Mary Margaret swallowed back the unsettling feeling of trouble on the horizon. "I suppose I can tell you..." *A little of the truth, at least.* "I received a new collection notice today."

Her friends sat back in shock.

"Almost a year after he died?" Avery frowned.

On a positive note, Darcy looked less glum. "Derek shouldn't have opened so many lines of credit in your names."

"Do you want to head out to the cemetery and rail at him?" Lola raised her wine glass. "If you do, I'm riding shotgun."

"Thanks but..." Mary Margaret was touched by their support. "Every time I think I've made peace...Every time I think I've finally laid Derek to rest..."

"What did he buy this time?" Avery was intrigued. "A fancy gun? A timeshare?"

"It doesn't matter." She didn't want to draw them into her Laurel and Hardy nightmare. "I just need to make extra cash."

The club in Greeley came to mind once more.

Widows don't dance in clubs.

Three weeks ago, Barbara had plucked a gray hair from Mary Margaret's head as she sat in her salon chair. Mary Margaret's shoulders hunched once more.

Across from her, Darcy's gaze drifted to a cowboy on crutches coming in the door. Her features closed down tighter than a summer cabin's shutters in winter. It was her ex-boyfriend, rodeo star Jason Petrie. A bull had busted his leg, which was fitting since his womanizing had busted Darcy's heart and propelled her into matrimony with the elderly judge.

"Let's finish these drinks and get out of here." Mary Margaret slurped her wine.

"No. Not yet." Darcy caught Mary Margaret's gaze. "I heard through the grapevine that Jason's stud business is looking for part-time help while Jason recovers."

"Manure and bull semen?" Lola drained her chardonnay. "Ugh."

Darcy rolled her eyes. "This from the woman who does hair and makeup at the mortuary." Her expression turned speculative as she looked at Mary Margaret. "I know you have a full schedule with teaching but your nights and weekends are free. And I heard through the grapevine—"

Truly, Sunshine had the best grapevine ever, as long as the gossip wasn't about you.

"—that Jason's business partner Iggy needs someone in the late afternoon and evenings."

"I don't know." Mary Margaret had promised to help with the elementary school's Christmas pageant, not to mention she had to watch out for Grandma Edith, who'd been taking Grandpa Charlie's death pretty hard.

"Go on," Lola encouraged. She waved her empty wine glass in the direction of Jason, who was hobbling toward a seat at the bar next to Kevin. "Ask Jason for a job. What have you got to lose?"

❋

Kevin sat in Shaw's watching a college football game on television. He'd played quarterback in high school and college. He enjoyed the strategy of the game. What he didn't enjoy was being outwitted.

Blindsided, the quarterback on TV missed a defensive read and was sacked. Kevin may have been blindsided by Barb's infidelity but he was going to be bulletproof when he ran for state office. That is, if the distribution center lived up to expectations and raised Sunshine's standard of living.

A memory of his grandfather returned: the summer Grandpa had run for governor. They'd stopped in a poor suburb outside Denver and barbecued hot dogs during a meet-and-greet. The line had been down the block. And it had been a long block.

"Why are there so many people in line?" eight-year-old Kevin had asked. "It's just a hot dog."

"For some of these people, that hot dog is all they'll get to eat today." His grandfather had knelt in front of Kevin. "Those of us lucky enough to have a full fridge need to help those who aren't so lucky. It's a responsibility, just like you being Vanessa's older brother and watching out for her."

Those words and their meaning had stuck with Kevin—the more you had, the bigger the responsibility to give back. Now that Grandpa was gone, it was more important than ever to carry on his legacy.

The stool next to him listed to one side as Jason Petrie tried to belly up to the bar with his broken leg. A clatter of crutches, a scrape of stool footings, and the blond, blue-eyed cowboy had half his butt on the seat. His casted leg rested gracelessly to the side.

Noah had a beer in front of Jason before the cowboy released a put-upon sigh or had time to glance over his shoulder at his ex-girlfriend Darcy.

"Before you start off with your smarmy metaphors and clichés, Kev." Jason paused to sample his beer. "Remember that I'm the only guy in town who shows up to drink with you."

And wasn't that a sad state of affairs?

Kevin signaled Noah for another whiskey. He'd been nursing his first for thirty minutes, and he was walking home. "I have no life."

"Good mayors rarely do." Jason drank some more beer. "You're like priests. Nobody trusts priests who get out there and have a life either."

Kevin scowled at him, annoyed that Jason's opinion mirrored his ex-wife's, doubly so when he realized they were both right.

If he was ever going to re-activate his social life, he needed a steady girlfriend, someone as boring as he was, someone who was never the talk of the town, someone who wouldn't ruin his political chances.

"Excuse me." Mary Margaret Sneed picked up Jason's crutches and leaned them against the bar. She wore blue jeans, tall black boots, and a chunky fisherman's sweater that hinted at her curves. She had a full mane of red hair, a pair of tender blue eyes, and was like the Pied Piper when it came to making children behave. "I hate to interrupt, Jason, but...I heard you might be hiring part-time workers."

"Yep." Jason patted his walking cast beyond the fringe where he'd cut off one leg of his blue jeans. "The logistics of bull semen collection, storage, and order fulfillment are not what the doctor ordered for another few weeks."

"Whereas drinking beer is," Kevin murmured.

Mary Margaret and Jason both paused to look at him. Kevin stared into his whiskey glass.

"I'm looking for a part-time gig," Mary Margaret continued in that church-girl voice of hers. "But I can't work until after school during the week."

"Ahhh." Jason gave her another once-over. "Didn't you know? Iggy is a vampire. He and the bulls do all their best work after happy hour." While Jason explained the horrors of collecting bull semen, storing it with proper labeling in cryogenic units, and shipping it out, Kevin studied Mary Margaret out of the corner of his eye.

She was the complete opposite of his ex-wife. Soft-spoken. Openly kind. Stable. The type of woman a man who was one step from the priesthood would date. It didn't hurt that she was beautiful or that she knew how to dress well enough to fit in but not loud enough to stand out. He'd seen her circulate in a crowd and not steal the limelight from anyone. She checked a lot of boxes.

And if he looked at the soft bow of her mouth, he could imagine kissing her. And if he imagined kissing her, he could imagine pressing the length of that long, tall body of hers against his. And if he could imagine that…

Kevin sipped his drink, unused to envisioning getting physical with one of his constituents, especially his son's kindergarten teacher.

He snuck another glance at her. At that thick curtain of red hair, at her creamy skin, at the delicate way her fingers interlocked and squeezed intermittently as she listened to Jason.

Kevin swallowed thickly. With all this talk of the priesthood, a switch had been flipped inside him. It'd been months since he'd burned the sheets with a woman. He could probably look at any single woman and imagine…

He glanced over his shoulder at Avery. She was single and his age. Mary Margaret's conservative work clothes didn't vary much from the outfits she wore to Shaw's. When Avery wasn't wearing her theater uniform, she chose clothes that showcased curves and skin. But as much as he stared, he couldn't imagine getting busy with Avery.

His attention shifted back to Mary Margaret, to intelligent blue eyes and a soft laugh. She shifted her feet, and then he couldn't stop thinking about her long legs.

"Noah," he croaked, a dying man in need of a sanity-leveling drink. He held up his empty glass.

What was taking Noah so long?

Maybe this awareness of Mary Margaret was a good thing. She was a conservative member of the community, never any trouble to anyone. Dating her would be better than drinking at Shaw's with Jason.

Noah topped off his drink.

Kevin took a sip, forcing his gaze to the football game on television.

Mary Margaret and Jason finished their job discussion but she lingered.

"Just by chance..." She gave the men a hopeful smile. "Can I interest any of you in the purchase of a quad?"

That was a triple no. Not Kevin. Not Noah. Not Jason.

"Never hurts to ask." With a self-deprecating smile, she returned to the back booth.

"I heard a new club opened in Greeley. I need some action," Jason said, without specifying what kind.

Me too.

Kevin downed his whiskey and said, "Let's go."

✳

"Hey, are you interested in the mayor?" Lola pulled Mary Margaret aside in Shaw's parking lot as Avery and Darcy continued toward their SUVs.

The snow clouds had moved on but the air remained cold enough to chill Mary Margaret's throat. It just wasn't as chilling as Lola's question. "I'm not interested in Kevin. Why would you ask?"

Lola shrugged. "When you were talking to Jason, Kevin was looking at you like..."

"Like I'm his kid's teacher?" Which she was.

"No."

Shoot. "Like I'm one of his loyal voting public?" Which she was.

"No." Lola grimaced. "It was just a look, all right. And I just got this vibe."

"I would never..." Kevin was handsome in a white bread politician kind of way. Or at least, that used to label his look. He had more of an edge to him now that Barbara wasn't cutting his hair, and yes, Mary Margaret occasionally let her mind wander in that direction when she saw an attractive man but it was never a serious veer from the celibate widow in financial trouble path. She didn't have on her guy-finding glasses. Besides..."Barbara cuts my hair." By that fact alone, Mary Margaret was Team Barbara.

"Exactly." Lola nodded. "And Barbara doesn't act like she's over Kevin. She dogs his every step around town."

"I know." Most everyone knew.

"You don't want to cross her." Lola shivered and hugged herself. "I'm just saying."

"I didn't pick up on signals from Kevin the way

you did. I was talking to Jason about the job." Which seemed to involve labeling vials of collected goods and making sure they didn't spoil in storage or shipment. It was practically postal work. Right up Mary Margaret's alley, if not for being mere pennies in the bucket of Derek's debt.

Down the block, a few holiday lights outlined the gables of some houses, trying to convey holiday cheer. Mary Margaret wasn't heartened. She imagined casino thugs waiting outside the glow of twinkle lights, perhaps even in the shadows of her front porch.

She shivered.

"Okay. I'm just looking out for you, Mary Margaret." Lola's smile turned mischievous. "Besides, if you do date him, I can be your hair stylist."

"She really will kill me then." There was nothing Barbara hated more than losing a client.

"No doubt." Lola chuckled. "When Avery switched, Barbara tried to get the town to boycott the movie theater." Lola gave Mary Margaret a hug; the good kind between two women who'd buried husbands and knew nothing in life was guaranteed.

Not even next month's rent.

Chapter Three

When Mary Margaret got home, she locked the knob on her front door, slid the dead bolt home, and set the chain. Finally, she felt safe.

"I was wondering when you'd get home."

Mary Margaret jumped half out of her skin, whirling around. Too late, she registered it was her auburn-haired grandmother. "Grandma Edith, how did you get in here?"

"You gave me a key, remember?" Edith held it up next to her grin. She stood at the kitchen counter, wearing pink snow pants and a pink sweatshirt. Her white snow boots were tucked in the cubby near the front door, which was why Mary Margaret hadn't seen them.

Mary Margaret sucked in much-needed air. "You can't just come into my home without telling me."

What if Laurel and Hardy broke in and found her here?

"Why not? I brought you dinner." She started the microwave, rising on tiptoe to reach the buttons. "Turkey mixed in with my leftover green bean casserole. And I brought in some of your Christmas boxes from the garage so you can decorate."

It was pointless to argue with her grandmother. Edith pretty much did whatever she wanted to, and since she was a well-meaning little dear, Mary Margaret let her.

Mary Margaret's rented one-bedroom bungalow was only six hundred square feet. The Christmas boxes were stacked next to the couch because there was no room for them elsewhere. She opened one. It didn't contain Christmas decorations. The box was full of her burlesque costumes. Red-sequined polyester glittered in the light.

The lights, the music, the sense that she owned the crowd.

"*How could you?*" Dad had demanded, red-faced, drawing back his fist to strike.

Mary Margaret closed the box, shutting out the painful memories.

"Turn on some music." Grandma Edith did a little shoulder shimmy. "Let's dance."

"I don't think so." Mary Margaret eyed the box with the costumes.

"Ah, come on." Grandma Edith added a grapevine to her shimmy. "Remember how we used to dance? Like no one was watching? You and I have moves."

That might have been an overstatement. Grandma Edith had rhythm and enthusiasm, rather than pop and soul. The only reason they'd started dancing together was because Grandma Edith had used her key shortly after Mary Margaret had moved to town. She'd stumbled upon Mary Margaret going through the general motions of a burlesque routine. Instead of being appalled, Grandma Edith had joined in. It'd become their thing. They'd danced while cooking holiday dinners and baking cookies for fundraisers. They'd danced when Grandpa Hamm went hunting or fishing with his pals. They'd danced any time they were happy.

"I haven't felt like dancing in a long time," Mary Margaret admitted, trying not to look at the box of costumes.

"I know we haven't danced in over a year." The microwave finished, and her grandmother halted her simple moves. "But that needs to change. We have that Widows Club ballroom dancing fundraiser coming up."

Edith had mentioned Mary Margaret's dance skill to Mims, who'd recruited her to teach people the waltz and tango in the hour prior to the Christmas Ball's official beginning. Ballroom didn't require the all-out joy of burlesque, not for Mary Margaret, but she'd done her duty and agreed to their request.

"After I teach, I'll probably be a wallflower at the ball," Mary Margaret said, skating the edge of self-pity.

"You and I aren't wallflowers," Edith replied with certainty. "And we will dance again someday."

They ate in the small dining nook adjacent to the equally small living room. Derek's seventy-inch television sat on the floor and occupied the entire living room wall. She'd been unable to return it or sell it for anything close to what Derek had paid for it.

"I'm proud to announce I'm officially on the Widows Club board." Grandma Edith fidgeted, as if she was bursting with the news. "And as your vice president, I'm sure I'm going to need your help."

Uh-oh. "I don't know if I can spare the time." Mary Margaret speared a green bean. "I'm trying to land a part-time job."

"Oh, honey. You don't need to save up to buy me

anything special for Christmas." Grandma Edith was a bit self-centered, living life with blinders on like some of Mary Margaret's kindergartners. She'd probably forgotten all about Derek's debt. "Although I did see a lovely pair of ruby earrings just like Great Aunt Bunny's at the thrift store this afternoon. Wouldn't it be great if we had a matched set?" She sighed dreamily.

Guilt stabbed at Mary Margaret's chest.

"Or you can just regift Bunny's earrings to me." Edith grinned. "I don't think you've worn them more than once since Lola found the missing one last spring."

If Mary Margaret went back to Ricky, he'd charge her retail for those clip-on earrings and their ruby chips.

"You need a Christmas tree in here." Edith's gaze roamed over the small space. "And mistletoe. That'd give a man an excuse to steal a smooch."

Mary Margaret thought of Kevin and that scruffy stubble. "Smooch" wouldn't describe that man's kiss.

"I miss your grandpa." Edith sat back in her seat and hugged herself, her smile one of rare melancholy. "Don't you miss Derek?"

Mary Margaret turned her gaze toward her wedding picture on the wall, toward joyful smiles and warm embraces. She and Derek had just been starting out their lives together, crazy in love, a clean slate between them and the future. "I miss the man in the picture." She missed the promises he'd made to her.

In sickness and in health. For richer or poorer.

Something inside of her pinched at a memory.

"*You forgive me, don't you?*" Derek had rasped on his deathbed.

She'd assured him she had, thinking he was asking

for absolution for running away with Carina. She'd had no idea what was to come. Nearly a year later, that forgiveness was being tested.

But at least I forgave him.

Her parents—a preacher and his wife—hadn't forgiven Mary Margaret for dancing during college. But it wasn't as if anyone in her father's congregation knew about it, unlike Derek's indiscretion. His trip to Vegas had fueled the town grapevine for weeks.

"I miss Charlie," Grandma Edith said. "But sometimes I wonder..." Dramatic sigh. Dramatic pause. Dramatic use of sorrowful eyes.

Grandma Edith is up to something.

This was nothing new. Grandma Edith was always up to something.

"Do you think that I..." Vulnerability lined Grandma Edith's eyes, along with tentative excitement. "Do you think I should date again?"

Grandpa Charlie was nearly ten months in the grave, and Derek nearly twelve. Was dating even appropriate yet?

Mary Margaret set down her fork. "Define 'date.'" Because with Grandma Edith that could encompass anything from sitting next to a widower at a Widows Club meeting to running off to Reno tomorrow to get married.

"You know." Grandma Edith's mouth worked into a wobbly line. "Go out places. *With a man.* Sit in front of the fire at home. *With a man.* Be given flowers and chocolates and taken to nice restaurants for dinner. *By a man.* Just the other day, Mims told me that eventually the complacent solitude of being a widow will give way to loneliness. Aren't you lonely?"

Again, Mary Margaret thought of Kevin and his stub-bled, chiseled chin.

"Mary Margaret?" Grandma Edith was impatient for her answer.

"No. I'm not lonely." And that wasn't the point. No-where in her grandmother's definition had she mentioned love. "If dating fills your day and makes you happy, go right ahead." Although the dating pool was rather thin for men Edith's age in Sunshine.

"There's a difference between the solitude of being a widow and ready-to-date loneliness, don't you think?" Again, Grandma Edith's gaze was the curious mix of vulnerability and excitement. But then she scoffed. "All this talk of my dating." Edith took Mary Margaret's hand. "I bet you're ready to put yourself out there."

"No." Mary Margaret didn't have to think twice. "Not now. I'm still cleaning up the financial mess from my marriage." Trying as hard as she could to avoid bankruptcy and broken legs.

"Derek broke your heart completely." There were tears in Edith's eyes.

"Derek broke something," Mary Margaret muttered. He'd nearly broken her. She'd loved her husband but now it was hard to remember being *in love* with him.

Edith flipped the grumpy switch. "It'd be nice if we two widows tested the dating waters together. I thought going on a double date would be fun."

"No." Mary Margaret repressed a•horrified shudder mid-spine.

But her grandmother wasn't done. "I thought we could help each other through this holiday. Go the party rounds together. Join the Victorian choir that sings in the town square. Get our nails done at Pretty Toes." Edith got to her feet. "I guess I'm as alone as I was the day I buried your grandfather."

Guilt made another stab at Mary Margaret's chest. "That's not fair."

Grandma Edith stomped toward the door. "I was going to ask you to go to the poetry slam with me at the retirement home on Tuesday but I guess—"

"How much is a ticket?" Mary Margaret asked before she could stop herself.

"Five bucks." Edith thrust her arms in her jacket. "Pick me up at six-thirty. I'll pick up the toys to donate at the event and get you some mistletoe. Mims says the best way to move on is to find a new man. And you can't just open your door and find one waiting on the stoop." She stepped into her snow boots and then opened the front door. "Who are those men parked in front of your house?" She pointed at Laurel and Hardy in their big sedan. "They look like undercover cops."

"Ignore them." Mary Margaret was going to as soon as she handed over a check with her first payment.

She closed the door and watched through the peephole as her grandmother walked away. Only when Grandma Edith was out of sight did Mary Margaret go outside and approach the Town Car.

Mr. Laurel rolled down the passenger window, red stir stick protruding from his mouth like an unlit cigarette. "Was that your granny or your housekeeper?" There was something lilting about his words, a trace of a long-forgotten accent.

"My grandmother." She passed over her check.

"Ha!" Mr. Laurel tossed her payment toward his

partner and then punched the man's shoulder. "You owe me twenty bucks."

Mr. Hardy rolled with the punch and scrutinized Mary Margaret's draft as if it might be a forgery. "How soon can you make another payment?"

"Maybe next weekend? I'm trying to find part-time work."

"Have you tried cleaning houses?" Mr. Laurel seemed sincere in his suggestion.

"No. I have a job interview Monday with a local breeding outfit."

"You should try cleaning houses." Mr. Laurel wasn't giving up on his idea. "You can steal things to fence. You have a trusting face and could probably get by saying they must have misplaced something."

Mary Margaret choked on cold air.

Mr. Hardy snorted and started the car. "Make sure the next payment is more substantial."

Or what?

Mary Margaret returned to her house under a heavy drape of fear. Even if she got the job with Jason and Iggy, even if she asked for an advance on her salary from them, she wasn't going to make more than a thousand dollars in a week. She wasn't going to satisfy Laurel and Hardy.

She huddled on the sofa wondering what to do.

Dancing had kept her on her feet before.

And estranged her parents.

She shouldn't do it but... Could she?

She was cold, iced over by indecision. But she had to do something.

Mary Margaret stared at the box of costumes, losing a debate with herself.

✳

"Now, this is more like it," Jason shouted in Kevin's ear.

Kevin preferred the relative quiet of Shaw's. The two men had gone out looking for action and ended up at a small circular table next to a wall in the recently opened burlesque club in Greeley.

The pop music was loud. His vodka tonic was watered down, and it didn't even have ice. The woman on stage wore a neon yellow bikini and struck poses beneath a strobe light. She looked like she should be home studying vocabulary words for her college entrance exams.

Fighting a headache, Kevin stared into his drink. When Jason had proposed coming here, the cowboy had said he'd been to burlesque clubs in other cities. He'd said the dancing was good, and after the show was over, the audience got to grooving together on a dance floor. Not that Jason and his broken leg were going to be cutting a rug. Not that Kevin planned to dance either. He wasn't the kind of guy who danced in public, preferring to sit on the sidelines and watch.

The Hanky Panky was the only nightclub of any kind for a hundred miles. It was busy but not packed. In the far corner, a group of women wearing pink "I'm with the bride" T-shirts were served a tray of blended piña coladas. Among the men, there was a mixture of cowboy hats, tractor logo caps, and business haircuts. How many of them were here unbeknownst to their spouses?

The thought brought him up short. Barbara's infidelity had left him jaded toward relationships.

So, no. He wasn't going to cruise the club looking for female companionship. It looked like the best thing about this spur of the moment trip was that Kevin had gotten out of Sunshine and the watchful eyes of Barb and her beauty shop minions.

Jason was bobbing his head to the beat and tapping his fingers on the table as if he was into the pose-performer's strobe dance. But then again, as a rodeo bull rider, he'd probably suffered a concussion or three, and it wouldn't take much to capture his attention.

"Let's give it up for Didi. First times are tough, aren't they?" The announcer stood just outside the wings of the main stage. "We've got another Hanky Panky newbie coming up. We all 'Wanna Be Starting Something' with *Fox-xy Rox-xy!*"

Foxy Roxy? Kevin groaned. That had to be the worst stripper name ever. Or it would've been if this had been the type of establishment where women stripped. The removal of clothes might have made the experience better.

Kevin downed his drink and nudged Jason's shoulder. "Come on. Let's go."

The beat of the song shook the walls, and then a woman thrust the red center stage curtains aside and stood there as if waiting for her due.

Notice me.

Kevin did. And so did the rest of the crowd.

There had been attractive women on stage earlier but none of them had owned the audience the way this woman did with just one pose. Which made no sense because she wore a short red dress trimmed with white fur that covered the essentials. Sure, she had on the requisite towering heels, also red, and yes, she had on a black superhero mask that concealed her identity. She didn't

move, unless you counted her gaze, which assessed the
audience members one by one.

Her inspection reached Kevin.

He held his breath and leaned forward in his seat, along
with every other person in the room she'd connected that
intense gaze with.

Watch me.

Foxy Roxy strutted forward, lifting her knees and
swinging her hips and hands. She was more animated
than a runway model and less in-your-face sexy than the
last dancer, but she was smokin' hot. She reached the
pole and did the standard circuits—swinging her feet
around in the air, swinging her hand close to the men
sitting in a ring around the stage. Her hand flattened
around green bills, which she slowly tucked into her
cleavage the way a man copped a feel.

Kevin's mouth went dry.

She slid to her heels with her back to the pole and then
straightened her legs, keeping her back flat and parallel
to the floor. Again, a standard stripper move. Again,
she owned it differently, turning in small increments and
capturing the gaze of every person in the audience as she
rotated around that pole.

Kevin reached for his wallet even as Jason produced
a twenty.

But neither of them had to approach the stage.

With a high kick, she was off the platform and dancing
through the crowd. Her hands outlined her curves as if
showing how she wanted to be touched. And then she
did the same to every member of the audience. Tracing.
Touching. Teasing. Possessing.

Possess me.

The high plains Colorado crowd had never seen anything like Foxy Roxy. She accepted her due with hands that never dropped a dollar. Not that she was given any George Washingtons. Kevin registered a lot of twenties and fifties.

And then she was at his table, arching her back, lowering to a crouch, swiveling provocatively. She straightened and moved behind Kevin before he could blink, running her palms over his shoulders, to his elbows, reaching for hands as her breath wafted over his ear. She tucked his fifty into the stiff red fabric holding her cleavage and moved on to trace Jason's face with her hands. And then she stepped around behind him, fingertips pausing on Jason's neck, as if she were taking his pulse.

Kevin's was through the roof.

What's happening to me?

She was touching another man, and Kevin was turned on.

Their gazes connected over Jason's straw cowboy hat, hers a surprising blue. Her eyes widened slightly, and then she strutted her way to the stage with a swing of white blond hair streaked with one strand of red.

The roar of appreciation was deafening. The bridal party in the back was howling for an encore.

Several of Kevin's body parts clenched. Sweat broke out on his forehead.

What just happened?

He felt as if he were a teenager and had just had a hot make-out session in the backseat of his car only to be busted by the cops before—

A voice inside his head—one that sounded a lot like

Barbara's—said, *What are you doing in a club like that? What if someone recognizes you?*

The deejay began to play dance music. The women in the bridal party were snatched up like free food at a golf tournament. Neither Jason nor Kevin was going home with a woman tonight, certainly not the masked and mysterious Foxy Roxy.

But what would it be like to take that woman home?

Kevin sucked in air, reminding himself he was the chaste mayor, the proverbial minister of town hall, the man with political aspirations. Just being here was risky. Taking a woman like that anywhere? Political suicide.

"Time to go, Jason." Kevin did his best to be invisible, to gather Jason and try to inconspicuously walk out the door—impossible when escorting a cowboy on crutches, especially one who wouldn't shut up.

"Dang. The look on your face." Jason laughed. "You've never seen porn, have you? Watching you watch *Fox-xy Rox-xy* was like watching a virgin get deflowered."

It was all Kevin could do not to sweep Jason's good leg out from under him.

And then a voice inside his head—one that sounded like his father's—said, *If you want to serve the public, you need a woman who won't be like a rock tied to your ankle in a deep pond.*

Kevin wanted to be a politician. He wanted to help communities live better lives.

But he also wanted…platinum blond hair and black bustiers…what he couldn't have.

Clearly, he needed female companionship, to date but not play the field. That would only earn him a reputation like Iggy King.

Clearly, he needed to date a woman above reproach, someone who'd keep him at home watching movies on Netflix instead of going to burlesque clubs.

He didn't need Foxy Roxy or a reputation. He needed someone as boring as Barb thought he was on the outside, someone who'd be an asset to his political career, someone who didn't have aspirations of her own.

Kevin reminded himself of a woman he knew that would fit the bill.

Mary Margaret Sneed.

＊

"What was that?" Ned, the club owner, followed Mary Margaret back to the dressing room.

"I told you. It was one of my routines." Mary Margaret hurried down the hall, planning her escape.

Kevin and Jason had been in the audience!

I could've been made!

Kevin had given her money!

And she'd almost dropped it when she'd realized she'd been about to nibble his ear.

Amateur.

"I'm not complaining." Ned dogged her steps. "What I meant was, you told me you could dance but you didn't tell me you're a pro. Do other burlesque clubs have their dancers go out in the audience?"

"Yes." Mary Margaret burst into the small dressing room and closed the door behind her, shutting Ned out. In a few seconds, she had her cash in her purse and her Santa dress off. It took a bit longer to remove her mask and blond wig, and to tug on her jeans and sweatshirt.

What if Kevin or Jason recognized her car out back?

Mary Margaret's stomach dropped to the floor.

Meanwhile, Ned was shouting through the door about return engagements.

"Were they applauding you?" Didi had a science book open on her dressing table. She was studying to be a vet tech.

"I guess I just lost top billing." Angie didn't look like she cared much. She had a baby and a second job waitressing at the nearby diner.

Both their performances had been uninspired, as if they were strippers who'd decided to keep their clothes on.

"I'm not sure I'm coming back." Not if Sunshine residents frequented the club. Mary Margaret slung her purse across her body, put on her black jacket, and crushed her pinned hair beneath a black knit cap.

"*What?*" Ned shrieked when she opened the door. "You can't dance like that and then *not* return." He followed her toward the back door. "I'll pay you double."

"Fifty bucks a night?" It killed her to say, "I don't think so." She'd thought this might solve her problems with Laurel and Hardy but her teaching position was at stake. "Your acts are all wrong. Burlesque is more tease and less in-your-face sex-me-up. You have no group dances, no comedian, no grand finale."

If Kevin recognized her . . .

Her steps slowed. What was the mayor of Sunshine doing in a dance club?

Well, duh. He was recently divorced and had every right to a night of fun.

"Listen." Ned caught her arm and lowered his voice. "If you become a regular dancer, I'll give you a hundred bucks a night. Seventy-five people paid to get in tonight. With you dancing, the gate doubles."

His drink sales would double too.

The neon P in the Hanky Panky sign on the street sizzled, and shorted.

Her father would have said that was a sign from above.

Of course, he would've slapped her for even stepping foot inside the club.

But I made five hundred bucks.

Mary Margaret hesitated, rubbing the scar at the back of her neck.

"Sinner," Dad hissed, holding one of her flimsy black costumes in his fist and shaking it to the heavens. "You're a betrayal of everything I stand for. I must cast you out before you infect your mother."

Cast her out. Like Mary Margaret was diseased.

"What's this about group dances?" Ned demanded. "Do people like that?"

She blinked, coming back to the present—the dingy hall, Ned's powder blue velvet smoking jacket. "People love a good burlesque revue. It becomes theater. It earns respectability." Well, that was a stretch in a small town like Sunshine, and maybe even for a bigger small town like Greeley. She faced him. "Is that something you're interested in?"

"I'm interested in making more money," Ned grumbled, face reddening. "I opened this club to make my girlfriend happy but she left me for our bartender before we opened. Merry Christmas to me."

"You were left in a lurch." Mary Margaret nodded, seeing Ned's plight in a new light. She'd been a business major for a year before turning her focus to education.

She clutched her backpack strap and faked confidence. "I'll dance two nights a week for one hundred per night and a cut of the gate. I'll train your dancers two nights a week for the same deal."

Ned scowled. "I can't afford that. My cover is only five bucks."

He really was in over his head. She snapped her jacket closed. "You should be charging ten. And if the revue is a success, you can charge thirty-five for reserved tables in front." She had his attention, although he still regarded her with disbelief. "And no one would complain if your booze wasn't watered down." Ned never should have offered Mary Margaret that shot of vodka to toast her inaugural dance. "Charge ten. I'll take four, plus my hundred. Two nights a week."

She offered her hand.

Ned's scowl turned into a thoughtful frown. She had no idea what he'd done before opening this club but he might have the skill to turn it around if she gave him the know-how.

"Three from the gate," he said. "Choreograph two nights a week. Dance three nights a week. Two dances a night." He shook his finger at her. "And I want some of those group dances."

"You forgot my hundred." Mary Margaret decided a little leverage was in order. Pretending to leave, she pushed through the back door into the crisp, cold night air.

At the far end of the parking lot, Kevin was walking a slow-moving Jason to his truck. He looked their way.

Slouching, Mary Margaret turned her back on him.

What am I doing? I can't get away with this.

"You're killing me." Ned had followed her out. "What am I going to say to my regulars?"

His words reminded her of the muscle the online casino had sent to collect Derek's debt. She was backed in a corner. Still, she wasn't prepared to leap at the first chance of escape.

"Why not tell them at the holidays they should enjoy special shows?" That was a stretch.

Ned blew out a long breath. "Okay. I throw in the hundred every night you show, whether you dance or not. You can start on Tuesday. Be here by nine."

Mary Margaret glanced over her shoulder.

Kevin still stared her way.

He's going to come back. He's going to unmask me.

She tried to suppress the feeling of excitement that idea created, because it should be fear making her heart trip, not awareness of broad shoulders and a dangerously stubbled beard.

"Well?" Ned was impatient.

"I'll have to get back to you." She couldn't pull the trigger.

The risk of discovery was too great.

Chapter Four

"Tad, don't eat paste." Mary Margaret's words drifted to Kevin before he reached the open door to the kindergarten classroom on Monday morning.

Uh-oh. He wanted to ask Mary Margaret out. His son's behavior didn't exactly smooth the way. Kevin hesitated in the doorway, struck by the idea that this was a calculated move when romance should be spontaneous.

Green triangles of paper were scattered on Tad's desk waiting to be pasted on his paper.

"Spit it out, Tad." Mary Margaret held a brown paper towel beneath Tad's chin. She looked almost amused, as if this happened more often than not.

Given this was Tad, Kevin was willing to wager on more often.

The white paste came out of Tad's little mouth in slimy chunks. *Plop-plop-plop.*

Tad gagged. "Ninjas don't like paste."

Kevin fought a grin.

Mary Margaret whisked away the globs of paste with one hand while rubbing Tad's little back with the other.

"Nobody likes paste, Tad. The taste won't be different, no matter how many times you try it."

She understands my kid. Bonus points.

Tad's gaze lit upon Kevin. "Daddy!" He wiggled out of his seat and ran to give Kevin a hug. "Did you come to help me with my holiday book?"

Kevin knelt down, arms outstretched. There was nothing as good as one of his kid's hugs.

"The holiday book is a surprise," Mary Margaret murmured demurely. She wore a green tunic sweater, skinny jeans, and blue Keds. It was nothing as tantalizing as red, sky-high heels, a brassiere shaping breasts like missiles, or an attitude that said she could handle any man.

He stood and swung Tad into his arms. His son had paste in his hair and a smudge of something red on his cheek.

Mary Margaret swooped in, wiped Tad clean, and then retreated.

Kevin's breath caught in his throat. She was perfect, so compassionate and caring. Kevin tried to give her a smile that said he knew it but she busied herself with another student, Elizabeth Franklin. Her mother was one of Barb's close friends.

"Are you taking me to work with you after school, Daddy?" Tad frowned. "It's Monday."

Barb had Tad on Saturday, after the salon closed, through Tuesday morning. Kevin had him the rest of the time, and if he had events that ran late, his parents took Tad.

"No, buddy. I..." Kevin shouldn't have come during Mary Margaret's working hours but it had been over a decade since he'd asked a woman out and he'd forgotten all the unwritten rules. Now that he was here, he couldn't just leave without an excuse for stopping by. "I wanted to talk to your teacher about something."

Tad's teacher moved quickly on from Elizabeth and knelt next to a little girl with thin blond hair who was coloring far outside the lines but didn't look like she cared.

Mary Margaret half-glanced over her shoulder. "Mr. Hadley, my meeting times are before and after school."

Blocked, Kevin set Tad on the floor.

His son gave him a once-over. "Daddy, did you get a hall pass from Ms. Adams in the office?"

"No." Kevin was blowing through protocol right and left—he had no appointment or hall pass. He tried the smile on Mary Margaret again, the one that said he admired her people skills more than her beauty. "If I could just have a quick word…"

Mary Margaret relented and led him to the door, looking as if she were about to be led to the gallows. "Class, I'll be right back."

They stepped into the hallway. The sound of the door closing echoed around them like a water drop in a large, empty cave.

"Well? Go on. Say it." Mary Margaret settled her hands on her hips the way Foxy Roxy had the other night. The effect wasn't as jaw dropping or as mesmerizing but it made him want to smile. There was an interesting personality beneath that cool exterior, just waiting to be discovered.

Just like me.

"I was wondering if…" Kevin's words echoed down the hall. Other classroom doors were open. Someone was lecturing about basic subtraction. If he asked Mary Margaret out now, everyone in school would hear. "This is difficult." And awkward. If only he had an excuse to see her. If only she was an active citizen. A volunteer.

Of course!

Kevin cleared his throat and lowered his voice. "You know, the town has a big decision regarding the company that wants to build a distribution center near the interstate."

"I thought you..." Her brow furrowed. "Are you asking my opinion?"

"Yes. I'm assembling a special group of residents to discuss town issues, and I'd like you to be on the panel." That was a complete and total lie. He hadn't thought of the panel until just now.

Mary Margaret's gaze did a circuit of the hallway, passing over his face with barely a pause. "I'm very busy, especially this time of year. And I'm...trying to fit in a second job." She looked embarrassed to admit this fact.

"It won't take up much time, and it would mean so much." To Kevin, as a way of getting to know her better.

Talk about abusing executive privilege. His shoulders bunched at the base of his neck.

He was considering apologizing for bothering her when she spoke. "When does this committee meet?"

Criminy. He still had a shot. "I haven't ironed out all the details," he said hurriedly. "If you could just give me your number..." He pulled out his cell phone and waited.

She seemed to hold her breath, deciding. He liked that she contemplated her decisions carefully.

His cell phone buzzed with a message from Barb:
Where are you?

He made a disgusted noise, which echoed and re-
bounded, filling the hallway.

"Good thing you didn't cuss," Mary Margaret whispered in a teasing voice. "Curse words have a special
echo in the school hallway."

Bless her for having a sense of humor. The tension in
his shoulders eased. "Is that so?"

"Yes. Especially curse words about ex-spouses." Her
gaze shuttered. "That was out of line. I'm sorry."

"No need to apologize." He swiped the message noti-
fication from his screen. "The court may have declared
us through but Barb's having a hard time with the
concept."

Mary Margaret nodded, reaching for his phone. She
created a contact and returned his device. "Let me know
when you're meeting but I can't promise anything." She
returned to her charges, leaving him standing in the hall,
proud of himself.

For obtaining a woman's number under false pretenses.

He berated himself all the way back to the office.

In between mentally patting himself on the back.

✳

Mary Margaret smelled like paste when she showed up
after school at the Bull Puckey Breeding facility for her
job interview with Iggy King.

But it wasn't Iggy she'd been thinking of on the
drive over.

It was Kevin.

When he'd shown up in her classroom, she'd been certain he was going to call her out on her performance as Foxy Roxy. She'd had to kneel next to Louise's desk because her knees had given out.

Apparently, Kevin hadn't recognized her at the Hanky Panky. She should have turned down his invitation to be on the development committee. Serving would make it even riskier to dance her way out of trouble. The threat of exposure might just give her a heart attack.

And yet, Kevin…

Maybe it was her widow-versary on the horizon, or maybe Grandma Edith's talk about dating and loneliness had penetrated her twenty-seven-year-old brain, but she was looking at Kevin in a different light. One that was just as dangerous as the Hanky Panky stage spotlight, because *wow*, he was datable—handsome, financially stable, beloved by Tad.

Get a grip. A man who'd marry Barbara isn't my type.

Amen. Dad's disapproving voice.

Besides, whoever dated Kevin next was going to have a fight on her hands with Barbara. If she didn't like you, that woman would rummage around in your closets until she unearthed all your dark secrets and bad fashion choices.

Mary Margaret's empty stomach did a slow churn.

She got out of her car and greeted Iggy in the gently falling snow. He was about her age, a regular at Shaw's, and what she'd consider a caution. He didn't seem particular about the women he slept with and he was the type of man whose volume amplified as his beer intake increased.

Iggy was unloading boxes from the back of his big

black truck, made harder because he had a lift kit which added a good two feet to the height of the vehicle. He wasn't as tall as Kevin, as broad-shouldered as Kevin, or, in fact, Kevin.

Mary Margaret gave herself a mental head thunk.

"You here about the job?"

"Yes." Mary Margaret had to stop thinking about Kevin. She had her résumé in hand and was wearing blue jeans, a thick green cable-knit sweater, and cowboy boots with a paisley pattern and silver trim. She'd put on the boots after school to make a good impression.

Iggy looked her up and down and then gave her a half smile.

Impression made.

"Can you start now?"

"Yes." Her smile came more naturally.

"Great. The Bodine twins called in sick." Iggy transferred a cardboard box that clinked into her arms. "They have a bad case of high school senior-itis." He slid another box out of the back. "Follow me."

He led her into a large, aluminum-sided barn with an unadorned wreath on the door, as plastic as her own. They passed bulls of all different breeds and colors in large stalls. Most were taller than she was.

That was saying something since Mary Margaret was nearly six feet tall.

Iggy unlocked an office in the back corner, and they set their boxes inside.

The office was very large. There were a couple of cluttered desks and several waist-high containers that hummed with electricity like overworked refrigerators.

"We have cryogenic units here to freeze the product." He took another critical look at her. "Nice boots."

"Thanks."

"I wouldn't wear them to work again." He picked up something from the floor in the corner and shook it out. "Here's a pair of coveralls."

She accepted the workwear with the tips of her fingers. The coveralls were stained and smelled worse than paste. "I thought I was helping you pack up *goods* for shipping."

"You are but I need to collect the goods first." He picked up another pair of coveralls, removed his boots, and stepped into a similarly stained garment. "And as I mentioned, the Bodine brothers are a no-show."

Mary Margaret's purse fell off her shoulder at the same time her jaw fell to the floor. "You don't expect me to…"

Iggy heaved a sigh. "I do. Everyone chips in where needed around here. But Samson is just a big kitten, and Jason said he'd be here despite his doctor's orders. I usually give whoever helps me a buck a straw. Samson is young but he can produce a couple hundred straws at a time. Do the math."

"I guess this isn't an hourly job." Mary Margaret slipped off her boots and stepped into the coveralls, trying not to think about where the stains had come from. She zipped up and put her fancy boots back on.

Iggy scribbled something on a clipboard. "I'm assuming, since you haven't run screaming from the room, that you're interested in the job."

She nodded. Thanks to Derek's gambling, she had no choice.

A few minutes later, Mary Margaret stood next to the largest creature she'd ever been up close and personal with, feeling like a rookie Ghostbuster missing her proton pack. "What kind of bull is this?" She'd only ever seen bulls on television and that one time she'd gone to the rodeo with Darcy to watch Jason ride. "Has Jason ever ridden him? Is he dangerous?"

Samson was black and more fidgety than Mary Margaret, refusing to stand still.

Before Iggy could answer, someone came into the room behind her.

Samson huffed and shifted so he could see around her.

Jason hobbled in using one crutch. His free hand held the lead rope to another bull, this one brown. "Hey, Mary Margaret. Glad you could step in and help."

Iggy rubbed Samson's big ears. And then he explained the process and Mary Margaret's role. Unlike Jason at the bar, he didn't use words like equipment or goods.

Mary Margaret drew back, stomach readying a protest. "You want me to hold the artificial..." She swallowed, reluctant to say the term. "You want me to hold the artificial *va-jay-jay*?" She peeked at Samson's equipment and tossed her hands. "I'm out." She'd sell some of her shoes online. She had lots of shoes.

The two cowboys protested and tried to reassure her of the procedure's safety. Samson continued to be restless.

"It's not my safety I'm concerned with." *Although perhaps it should be.* "It's the ick factor." All those stains on her coveralls. "Can I bow out gracefully and interest your business in a low-mileage quad?"

"No." Iggy repeated how much money she might make.

"We're in a bind, and so are you." He smirked. "You know, thanks to Derek."

Jerk.

Not Derek. Iggy.

Mary Margaret was stuck, and not just with a quad. "Why can't I hold Carl?" The smaller, brown bull.

"Because I have no mobility." Jason leaned on his crutch, proving his point. "Full leg cast. I could be trampled if Samson lurches to the side. Having already been trampled once this year, I'll stick with Carl here." He patted the smaller bull's neck.

"You get around well enough," Mary Margaret mumbled, thinking of him being at the Hanky Panky. "I need more money than a dollar a straw."

"I'll pay your bar tab at Shaw's for a month," Iggy offered, earning a double-take from Jason.

"Are you sure, Iggy?" She wasn't. "I have a feeling I'm going to need a lot of drinks to forget this."

"We can't delay anymore." Iggy brought Samson forward. "Samson's ready. It's a buck a straw and your bar tab. Man-up, girl."

She didn't want to man-up. Quite the opposite. She wanted to be pampered and cared for. But those days were long gone.

Mary Margaret held out the receptacle and turned her head. "I can't look."

"You have to look." Iggy was the kind of guy who'd probably been a bit of a bully in high school, always quick with a snappy comeback or snarky reality check. "You're being paid to look."

Mary Margaret snuck a peek at Samson's equipment from the corner of her eye and tried to line things up.

The bull lurched forward and stepped on her foot. She screamed. The bull grunted. Iggy and Jason's much-needed product spilled on Mary Margaret's other foot. She heaved.

And just like that...

Her boots were ruined.

And she was fired.

*

"Is she ready to launch?" Clarice pulled her shopping cart even with Edith's at the sweet onion display in Emory's Grocery.

The chorus of "White Christmas" almost covered the pleas of the McEwen children for ice cream one aisle over.

"Is who ready?" Edith glanced around, clutching a yellow onion to her chest. "*Me?*" She had no idea what Clarice was talking about.

Frowning, Clarice fiddled with her hearing aid. She wore bell-bottoms that seemed to be held together with seam binding tape embroidered with green apples. Her gray braids fell over the front of her bright yellow jacket like service bell pulls, and her wooden walking stick thrust out of her cart like a jousting pole. "I said, is she ready to launch? *She.*" Clarice glanced about but they were alone in the produce section. "*Mary Margaret*," she whispered.

"Mary Margaret?" Edith quit squeezing her onion. "Ready for what? She's been looking for a part-time job."

Clarice gripped her shopping cart handles as if they were throttles on a motorcycle and she was gunning it. "Is *she* ready to date? You're supposed to be greasing the wheels to the idea of a new man."

"Oh. That." Edith bagged her onion. "Of course. I bought her mistletoe for her foyer." Edith was rocking the vice presidency. "Mary Margaret said she didn't want to date—she's got the idea in her head that she needs a part-time job more than a man—but all I need to do is find her a man or two at the poetry slam and—"

"*Edith.* That is *not* the way it's done." Clarice shook her head. "The success of our *endeavors* hinges on careful prep work. Testing the waters discreetly. Uncovering any objections Mary Margaret might have to loving once more. Dating is irrelevant." She gripped Edith's shoulder and leaned down to whisper. "You can't be on the board if you don't do the work."

Can't be on the board?

Panic tingled its way up Edith's legs. "No one told me any of this." And her granddaughter had been acting oddly, perhaps an indication that she really wasn't prepared to test the romantic waters. Mary Margaret hadn't put up the mistletoe Edith had brought her. For heaven's sake, the wreath on her front door was plastic. "Oh, my goodness. She's not ready."

"I figured as much." Clarice pushed her cart to the prepared salad section, mumbling incoherently along the way to a bag of cut kale.

"What do I need to do?" Her position on the board was at stake. And she'd told everyone she was on the board. *Everyone.*

"Find Mims." Clarice tossed the salad bag in her cart. "She'll know what to do."

"Of course." Edith texted Mims a quick: Where are you? And then hurried to finish her shopping.

Darkness had fallen, and it was snowing outside. Edith flung her groceries in the trunk of her car, trying not to connect Elvis crooning "Blue Christmas" through Emory's outside speakers with her fate. She'd be blue if she was kicked off the board.

Edith plopped into the front seat and called Mims. It had been nearly ten minutes since she'd texted, and Mims hadn't answered her.

She didn't answer the phone either.

Edith had many friends but her absolute best friend was Mims.

Edith often overlooked the fact that they'd both been in love with the same man, mostly because Edith had won that contest by marrying Charlie and Mims had found a man of her own. But both their husbands were dead and buried. They were back to being friends who relied on each other.

Good friends.

The best of friends.

They shared everything, except…

Mims was keeping something from Edith. She hadn't been coaching her in matchmaking. And she hadn't gotten back to Edith in the past few minutes. Not a peep.

Maybe Mims had suffered a stroke. Maybe she'd fallen and couldn't get up.

Edith drove to her house.

No Mims. Her Subaru wagon was gone.

Edith drove around town—past the movie theater, past the Saddle Horn coffee shop, past the emergency clinic, past Prestige Salon. Finally, she drove to the mortuary because, if Mims wasn't answering, someone might have died. Maybe even Mims.

No luck. The funeral parlor was dark. The parking lot empty.

They're going to kick me off the board for not doing my job.

Edith's heart raced. This wasn't something she could just sit and ignore, an objection she could outlast. Edith had to produce or there'd be no more Sunday morning breakfasts with the board, no more weekday breakfasts with the board, no pre–Widows Club meeting conferences. She'd be...

Just like everyone else.

Or worse—the woman no one wanted to sit with, the woman who never fit in without a popular man on her arm. It was high school all over again.

"Where are you, Mims?" Edith wailed because her one friend must have driven off the road somewhere. She'd be stuck in a ditch, helpless, crying out for Edith to come save her. Edith sat behind the wheel of her car, working up the courage to contact the sheriff and report Mims missing.

And then, like the proverbial light bulb, the Christmas lights at the retirement home up the slope flickered on.

There she was! There was Mims in the retirement home parking lot, carrying a picnic basket, practically skipping toward her car in black snow boots and a camouflage jacket, looking like Dorothy if Dorothy had been heading down the yellow brick road during hunting season.

She's fine.

Happy, even.

Edith heaved a sigh of relief. Her pulse slowed.

And then she wondered: *Why is Mims picnicking in*

the winter? During the dinner hour? At the retirement home?

Edith narrowed her eyes, remembering an afternoon last week when Mims hadn't answered her phone at all. And Edith had tried—repeatedly—to get her on the phone because she couldn't remember what worked best as a substitute for butter in a low-fat oatmeal cookie recipe. Mims had been at the movies. A cartoon movie, no less. Mims wasn't the cartoon movie type. She packed heat. She appreciated a good shoot-'em-up, happy ending optional. And now she was incommunicado at the retirement home?

Something wasn't adding up.

The retirement home had three levels of residents— independent living, acute care, and hospice. No one came skipping out of there after visiting the sick or the dying. That meant Mims had visited someone in independent living.

But who?

Edith remained idling in the mortuary parking lot until Mims left. And then she drove over, parked in a visitor's slot, and marched inside. "Gosh, Beatrice. What are you still doing here? It's late." But thank heavens she was still here to help Edith solve the Mims mystery.

"I know." Beatrice was a wiry woman with two kids in college down in Denver and a fondness for tacky holiday sweaters, if Rudolph's blinking red nose on her chest was any indication. "I was decorating the rec room for your club's poetry slam this week and lost track of time."

My club...

The mourning for Edith's vice presidency began.

"To that end..." Edith drew a deep breath and considered her fibbing options. "I was supposed to meet Mims here. Do you know where she is?"

"She was with David Jessup." Beatrice dug in her purse for her car keys. "But you just missed her."

"Oh, that's right. David Jessup." Edith drew another breath. "I should stop by and apologize for being late."

"That'd be nice." Beatrice provided Edith with directions to his room and bundled up to leave.

Edith marched down the nearly deserted halls of the residential section. Televisions blared from behind closed doors. Walkers and mechanical wheelchairs were parked here and there along the way.

David Jessup. His wife had passed around the same time Charlie had died. His adult kids lived in Greeley. He'd refused to move there but they'd convinced him that moving here would make his life easier because he wasn't good in the kitchen.

And there had been Mims's picnic basket.

How nice of her to bring David a housewarming gift. *How nice...*

Edith didn't believe that for a moment.

She reached David's apartment and knocked. He didn't have a television on at full volume. He didn't have a walker or a scooter waiting next to the door. There was a small bulletin board above his unit number. It was filled with greeting cards welcoming him to the neighborhood. Someone had even made him a heart from pink construction paper. It looked like it wasn't just Mims who was courting him.

David opened the door, and Edith forgot all about Mims.

He was taller than most men in their seventies. He didn't have hunched shoulders or a ski-slope belly. His eyes were still a sharp blue, and his tightly curled hair wasn't completely gray. He wore a crisp green turtleneck and khakis. But most importantly, he wore fine leather loafers that weren't orthopedic. "Edith. What a surprise."

He was the surprise. Just the sight of him tugged a string connected to the flutter fan in Edith's chest. He was handsome. He had all his marbles. And he wasn't deaf.

He was a catch!

Edith's smile felt soft and warm. She stepped into the doorway, smile broadening when he didn't step back. "I was just in the neighborhood and remembered I'd never stopped by to see how you were doing. I know how lonely it can be to lose"—*the love of your life*—"your spouse."

Something akin to guilt tried to smother the flutter in her chest. It was the memory of Charlie. She ignored it, darting past David and inside. It was a lovely little unit with a kitchenette, a small living area, a bedroom and bathroom. Everything looked modern and new. The countertops were granite. The floors oak. Who knew people could live like this?

David knew.

He was smart, probably smart with his money too.

Edith turned and smiled at David some more, wishing she'd remembered to freshen up her lipstick. "We should get together sometime. Have coffee or…catch a show."

Thankfully, he'd probably already seen the cartoon movie playing downtown—with Mims.

Competitive outrage tried to smother the flutter in her chest. Mims had identified David as a catch before she had. Edith ignored her annoyance. Colorado winters were long and cold. Men needed to warm up. Food...food they could get anywhere, including down the hall in the cafeteria. The holiday season was always busy, and she had matchmaking duties to fulfill. But David...He was popular, like Charlie had been. Whatever woman landed him would belong wherever he belonged.

She ran her hand over the cool, smooth granite. She was living on a single income in a run-down bungalow she and Charlie had purchased a few years after their marriage. She didn't think she could afford an apartment like this, even if she sold her house.

She wanted to be in the Widows Club but, if she couldn't be on the board, she'd take David.

Edith smiled harder.

※

"There you are." A few days after Iggy fired her, Mary Margaret entered Olde Time Bakery and came to stand by her grandmother. "You had me worried. You said you wanted to talk and then you didn't answer my calls."

In the morning, the bakery catered to harried moms who needed treats for work and school. In the afternoon, its business relied on weary workers, harried families, and high school students. Shy little Louise was at a nearby table with her mother. The Bodine twins sat at a table in the back sucking down iced coffees and smiling at teenage girls behind the counter. A Christmas tree stood in the corner, covered in twinkle lights and white crocheted snowflakes.

"I've been catching up on my research." Grandma Edith flipped through *Cosmopolitan* magazine in between bites of strudel. She paused on a feature about what men really wanted, which seemed to involve lots of lacy lingerie and chocolate-covered strawberries. "This will be helpful as I re-enter the dating scene. I can't rely on Mims for advice."

Mary Margaret escaped the image of her grandmother dating and needing sexy underthings, and stood in line for coffee. On impulse, she also ordered a small chocolate cake pop because she deserved a treat and it was in the day-old case.

Laurel and Hardy entered, immediately making Mary Margaret feel guilty for her one-dollar cake pop splurge. It was snowing outside, and as usual, the two out-of-towners looked cold in their thin, black leather jackets. That cold spread to Mary Margaret's veins.

Sour Mr. Hardy rubbed his arms and headed straight for the counter, shouting for a hot black coffee.

Tall Mr. Laurel paused just inside the doorway, took in Grandma Edith and her magazine, took out a much-bitten red stir stick from his mouth, and grinned. It was an *I'm-interested-in-you* smile.

Now Mary Margaret was afraid for an entirely different reason. Grandma Edith was too friendly for her own good. And Mr. Laurel wasn't good enough for her grandmother.

"Stop that," she told him, having reached deep and found her spine.

Grandma Edith glanced up to see who Mary Margaret

was speaking to. Edith had at least fifteen more years on her tires than the taller half of the debt-collecting duo but she blushed under his grin. "You're never too old to brush up on new tricks." She slid the open magazine in front of Mary Margaret. "Thanks for letting me have a look-see."

Mr. Laurel joined his partner in line, humming to the cheery Christmas carol filling the air.

"That is a hard no," Mary Margaret told her grandmother, nodding toward Mr. Laurel.

"Young lady." Grandma Edith squared her shoulders. "I haven't let anyone tell me a boy is off limits since high school."

"*Boy?*" That man could break both their legs.

As if privy to her thoughts, Mr. Laurel snapped the remains of his chewed stir stick in half and tossed it in the trash.

Mary Margaret gripped her grandmother's forearm. "I still say no."

Kevin entered the bakery with Tad. "It's not a mile-high whip, buddy, but a cold day like today deserves a hot chocolate." His gaze lit on Mary Margaret, the magazine, and the cake pop, which she had yet to eat. He grinned. "Now that's living dangerously."

His sly smile didn't get past Grandma Edith. "I must be doing something wrong with you," she muttered, studying Mary Margaret. "If it was any of my business who you date"—she sniffed—"I'd tell you to date that one." She jabbed her finger in the direction of Kevin's retreating back. "Aren't you the least bit interested?"

Mary Margaret stuffed the entire cake pop in her mouth and shook her head.

Laurel and Hardy sat at the next table with giant cups of steaming coffee.

Mr. Laurel had swiped a fresh stir stick. He also swiped Grandma Edith's *Cosmo*. He read the headline out loud. "'What a man wants'?" He smoothed out the pages and scanned the article. "They've got it all wrong. They don't even have a warm bed and a foot massage on the list."

"My husband used to love foot massages," Grandma Edith said in a dreamy tone of voice. "Whatever made him happy, made me happy."

Mary Margaret choked down her stale cake. "I don't want to be part of this conversation."

"I like a woman who speaks her mind." Chuckling, Mr. Laurel slid the open *Cosmo* back onto their table.

Mary Margaret flipped the magazine closed, cover face down on the table. "What did you want to talk to me about?" She had a dance number to practice and worksheets to grade.

"Do you come here often?" Mr. Laurel asked Grandma Edith.

"Do you mind?" Mary Margaret scowled at him, pulled her table farther away from him, and then tugged her grandmother's chair to her side.

"Have we met?" Grandma Edith's brow furrowed as she eyed Mr. Laurel. "I feel as if I've seen you somewhere."

"You haven't met. He's a stranger. Eyes on me, Grandma. Have you forgotten why you wanted to talk to me?"

Her grandmother's frown deepened.

Tad skipped over to lean on Louise's table, gushing

toward his crush. Someday it'd be Tad and Louise with the teen crowd at the back of the bakery. Maybe he'd remember his kindergarten teacher fondly. Maybe he'd recall how she'd mysteriously disappeared one Christmas, body found in the woods years later.

Maudlin! Maudlin! Stop being so maudlin!

Kevin came to stand near Mary Margaret with a cup of coffee. He studied the pair of cold debt collectors. "Have we met?"

"No." Mr. Hardy held his open coffee cup beneath his nose, as if the steam was needed to warm his face.

Grandma Edith warbled with the carols piped through the speakers. She was off-key and off-tempo but her heart was in it. She never did anything in half measures.

"She's good," Mr. Laurel commented. "Do you sing in a choir, honey?"

"No, but I should." Grandma Edith had the kind of confidence and thick skin Mary Margaret could only dream of. If only her grandmother had better taste in men.

Mary Margaret tried to reach through the mist of her grandmother's attention again. "If I step outside and call you, will you pick up the phone and tell me what you wanted to talk about?" That earned her a no-nonsense smirk from Grandma Edith.

Pearl Conklin marched in. She was the head waitress at the Saddle Horn diner and was spry for her age, not that anyone had the audacity to ask her age. "Mayor Hadley. Just the man I was looking for. You've got to put the kibosh on that distribution center nonsense. We're not that kind of town."

"What kind of town?" Kevin watched Tad run over to pick up his hot chocolate from the counter. He doted on that rascal. If Mary Margaret wasn't so stressed about her financial situation, her heart might have melted a little.

"The kind of town that grows into a city." Pearl white-knuckled her grip on the slim strap of her white purse. Her puff jacket was also white and matched her white snow boots. "The next thing you know, we'll be building a sports complex and a foreign car dealership."

"Would that really be so bad?" Kevin asked her, weary yet serious, gaze still on his son.

Pearl clutched a hand over her chest. "You joke but these are dangerous times. Mark my words. The day we get a frozen juice bar is the end of mile-high whips." She stomped out.

Tad gasped. "No more mile-high whips." He gave his father a look that said, *Say it isn't so.*

The bakery fell silent. Even the Bodine boys were quiet. And everyone was looking at Kevin the same way. Like he was the town fun-killer.

Mary Margaret turned to Grandma Edith. "Where do you stand on the distribution center?" Her input might be useful when she showed up for that panel Kevin was forming.

"I don't care." Her grandmother shrugged. "By the time things change around here, I'll most likely be dead. I'll save my energy for more important endeavors." Her gaze drifted toward Mr. Laurel.

"I think it's a good idea," the object of her interest said. "Think of all the good the extra tax revenue will bring."

A thug with an understanding of economics?

Grandma Edith leaned closer to whisper to Mary Margaret, "Why do these two look so familiar?"

"Miss Pearl's right, you know," Mr. Laurel said to Kevin. "A significant influx of jobs means a significant influx of chain restaurants."

That earned him a scowl from Mary Margaret, Kevin, and Mr. Hardy.

"I hear those fancy coffee shops are good places for first dates." Grandma Edith rifled the pages of *Cosmo* as if preparing to reference what men wanted once more.

"I can take you to the Starbucks in Greeley if you're interested," Mary Margaret offered. "And we can talk about…whatever."

"Can't you take a hint?" Grandma Edith frowned at Mary Margaret. "I was talking about fancy coffee shops being good for you. First dates *for you*."

Mary Margaret didn't believe that for a minute. "Then why are you brushing up on your man skills with this magazine?" She tapped the back cover.

"It pays to be prepared when you do start dating." Her grandmother's cheeks flushed with color.

Mr. Laurel grinned so hard that Mr. Hardy swatted him on top of the head with a real estate brochure.

"Are you in town visiting someone?" Kevin asked the two men.

"No." Mr. Hardy drained his coffee and stood, heading for the door with his partner.

Across the room, Tad tried to take the lid off his hot chocolate and spilled it. It was a small splash but Kevin rushed to his aid, as did Louise's mom.

"Finally, we're alone." Grandma Edith reached into her purse. "I heard from your mother today."

Mary Margaret had been about to take a sip of coffee. She set her cup back down. "She called?"

Grandma Edith shook her head. "Christmas card. She says she's fine but it included a holiday letter from your father's church." She shook her head some more, her words turning uncharacteristically vicious as she placed an envelope on the table. "Like that man she married has a Christian bone in his body. After what he did to you..." She laid her petite palms on Mary Margaret's cheeks.

Mary Margaret covered her grandmother's hands with her own. "He was angry. Haven't you ever been angry and done something you regretted?"

"Don't say you deserved what he did." Grandma Edith pressed her palms deeper into Mary Margaret's cheeks when she didn't immediately answer. "What he did—"

"What who did?" Kevin sat down. "Sorry to eavesdrop."

Mary Margaret rolled her eyes, leaning back so her grandmother's hands dropped away. "You're not sorry."

"You're right." He grinned, unrepentant.

Something had happened between them the day he'd asked her to be on the development committee. Perhaps it was the shared moment when they'd joked about unfortunate echoes in school hallways. Regardless, suddenly they seemed more comfortable with each other, which wasn't wise.

Grandma Edith was considering Kevin the way she considered long menus with high price tags, which usually meant she was going to say something inappropriate like, *My granddaughter was physically abused by my son-in-law*. She wouldn't qualify her statement that it had been one time.

"It's no big deal," Mary Margaret blurted before her grandmother could speak. The back of her neck tingled. She took the Christmas card and slid it into her purse.

"Water under the bridge with my dad. He was always fire and brimstone, a strict disciplinarian, a devout minister. He...uh..."

She didn't want to admit it but felt she had no choice. If she didn't say it, Grandma Edith would. "We argued. You know how it is with parents when you're out of high school and pushing for independence. I said something...I took him unawares. He lost his temper and hit me." She'd boiled it down to a no-big-deal event. She didn't mention the ambulance ride to the hospital and the surgery to her neck. "We haven't talked since."

Except in her head.

Kevin's expression turned thunderous. "Don't make light of it. I'm assuming your mother divorced him." He turned his dark look on Edith.

"No. My Rinnie assures me he's never been violent with her," Grandma Edith said in a small, worried voice. It was why they poured over the annual Christmas card, looking for any clue that things weren't as they seemed. She gestured weakly to Mary Margaret. "And this one is convinced it was her fault."

"He was angry," Mary Margaret insisted but her words were hollow. "I was raised to forgive."

"If he was a good man...a just man...he'd have apologized by now, and you could forgive him in person." Grandma Edith frowned, reaching for Mary Margaret's hand under the table.

Kevin's forehead smoothed. Wheels seemed to be spinning in his head. "Have you considered sharing your story?"

"No." Mary Margaret clutched her grandmother's hand. "It was one time. I'm sure, when you were younger, you got in a fight and exchanged blows, maybe with one of your friends. And then you moved on. I wasn't abused. Abuse is such a...such a harsh word."

Besides, what good did labels do her? Other than to make her feel like she was weak and vulnerable?

"Honey," Grandma Edith said, "he put you in the—"

Mary Margaret shushed her.

"Your father wasn't a kid." Kevin leaned forward, lowering his voice as if aware of her need for some privacy. "He was a parent. A minister." And then he added in a whisper, "He knew better."

Mary Margaret couldn't argue with that.

"Whatever happened to you," Kevin said, still in that soft, understanding voice, "you've prevailed. You've grown stronger. You've moved on."

Mary Margaret nodded. She liked the sound of that.

"Have you ever considered telling your story?" Kevin's gaze swung to her grandmother, missing the recoil that had stiffened Mary Margaret's body. "I bet it's inspirational."

"Mr. Mayor..." Grandma Edith glanced down at Mary Margaret's white knuckles gripping her hand. "*Kevin.* This is a personal family matter. I'm sure you understand that we don't want it spread around town."

Kevin nodded. He stroked his hand down Mary Margaret's arm.

But he looked at her differently than he had before, with less manly interest and more gentlemanly care.

Chapter Five

✳

As mayor, Kevin judged a lot of events—art shows, bake-offs, float competitions. He wasn't qualified to judge most of them but he tried to be a good sport; he tried to be a good person.

He hadn't felt like a good person when Mary Margaret confessed that her father had hit her. He'd felt like a man who needed to howl about insensitivity and injustice. He'd wanted to shout, to punch, to push her father to the ground and tell him mistakes like that weren't to be tolerated.

And then...

A corner of his brain, a dusty, cobwebbed corner he hadn't known existed, had whispered about the value of a woman triumphing over adversity, allowing Mary Margaret to feel like a survivor rather than a victim.

So he calmed himself down and thought about her feelings rather than about punishing her father.

Tonight, he was part of the judging panel for the poetry slam at the local retirement home. And because he'd been assured it was a night of holiday poetry, Tad sat on his lap as an honorary judge.

So far, only one person had channeled Scrooge and told Kevin he'd be a fool to support the distribution center being built. But it was a small crowd and not everyone had had a chance to speak to him yet.

The retirement home's rec room had been decorated for Christmas with a large tree, wreaths over the windows, and red bows on the chairbacks. A small area had been cleared to serve as a stage. Kevin, Tad, and Clarice, the other judge, sat at a table near the windows.

"I love poetry with deep meaning, don't you?" Clarice nudged Tad with her elbow.

"I like rhymes." Tad had taken two sprinkle cookies from the refreshment table. He was breaking them into bite-sized pieces. He offered the point of a star cookie to Clarice. "And I like Santa poems."

A flash of red hair had Kevin lifting his head. Mary Margaret had arrived. She escorted her grandmother to a seat and brought her refreshments, gracefully weaving in and out of the crowd.

Tad waved madly to get her attention. Kevin fought the impulse to do the same.

Mims asked for everyone to take their seats. She usually favored blue jeans, lugged-sole shoes, and sweatshirts, but tonight she wore a black blouse over a pair of burgundy velvet slacks. "This is our third annual Holiday Poetry Slam, co-sponsored by the Sunshine Valley Widows Club and the Sunshine Retirement and Rehab Center. Tonight's event benefits our annual toy drive. Thank you to everyone who brought a new toy."

Kevin and Tad had brought a set of Hot Wheels and a

baby doll that wet its diaper, both purchased by Kevin's assistant Yolanda.

"Do you take last-minute poetry entries?" Edith Archer got to her feet. She'd also dressed up for the event in a flowing black dress, ruby red lipstick, and sky blue eye shadow. Her short, unnaturally auburn hair was almost completely hidden beneath a red Santa cap.

"All entries must be in writing," Mims said with a slight hint of impatience. She turned her back on Edith and faced the judges. "We have poets of all ages tonight, and all poems must have a wholesome holiday theme." Hence the written pre-screen.

"*Written?*" Edith frowned. "I thought there'd be back and forth."

"Grandma." Mary Margaret grabbed Edith's hand and tugged. "That's a rap battle."

"No." Lola Taylor twisted around from her seat in the front row. She sat next to her husband, the sheriff. "You're thinking of a riff-off for a capella singers."

Sheriff Drew and Lola. They'd become a happy couple about the time Drew's marriage imploded. There weren't many happy couples in attendance. The Marleys frumped next to each other. The Smiths weren't even sitting together.

"If you're just reading poetry, where does the slam come in?" Edith surveyed the crowd, looking for answers.

No one responded, although Mims frowned.

Mary Margaret tried to pull her grandmother back into her seat but the little old lady resisted.

Kevin jumped into the void in an attempt to smooth things over. "I think *slam* was used in the title to make it sound cool. A poetry slam sounds better than a poetry reading."

"You're right." Appeased, Edith sat down. "Thank you. I'd never be caught dead at a poetry reading."

"Did you want to leave?" Mary Margaret looked like she was biting down on a smile, more so when her grandmother insisted upon staying.

Kevin caught Mary Margaret's gaze. His grin earned him a hesitant smile, one that took hold like a shake to the shoulders and said, *Foxy Roxy who?*

Edith leaned in front of Mary Margaret and winked at Kevin, which made the object of his interest blush.

The first poet took the microphone. It was Augie Bruce, who owned the mortuary. He slapped a slow beat on his thigh. "Old man Santa. Went to Atlanta. Drank some Fanta. Old man Santa."

"Two Santas," Tad murmured, awed.

"Everything rhymed." Clarice smoothed a gray braid and leaned over to murmur, "Winner, winner, chicken dinner, Tad."

"Careful, that's only the first contestant," Kevin whispered, before asking Augie to perform his poem again.

The next contestant was David Jessup, who nodded when Edith and Mims waved at him, and again when a trio of retirement home residents hooted their support. "Christmas in Sunshine." He paused dramatically, smoothing his reindeer tie. "Snow." Another pause. "Pretty lights." Another pause. David used those breaks to make eye contact with different women in the room. "Love takes flight." He smiled, accented with a sweeping head nod that managed to encompass all his female admirers. "Christmas in Sunshine." And then he bowed.

The elderly ladies in the room gave him a standing ovation, including Clarice.

Kevin thought David's delivery was a little heavy-handed.

"Why did Mr. Jessup talk so slow?" Tad asked.

"That's haiku." Kevin had done a cursory poetry search before showing up tonight. He asked David to recite his pick-up lines once more.

"He's good," Clarice murmured when David glanced her way during the second recitation. "This is going to be tough."

Wendy Adams, the school secretary, claimed the mic next. She was dressed in black from head to toe and had put a black beret over her short blond hair. "Christmas is red and green, it's true. Christmas is fun, fun-fun-fun for me and you. Christmas is shiny and sparkly, you bet. But under the mistletoe, Christmas is the best."

That received heartfelt chuckles and strong applause.

"I don't get it." Tad twisted in Kevin's lap. Green frosting ringed his lips.

"She referenced a kiss under the mistletoe." Kevin cleaned Tad's face with a napkin and asked Wendy for a second run-through.

"Amusing." Clarice chuckled and made notes. "But not the best rhyme."

The poetry continued. Who knew so many residents were interested in verse?

Kevin's mind drifted to Mary Margaret, to curiosity about the texture of her hair and the softness of her lips.

When the winners had been announced and a grand prize trophy awarded to Augie, Kevin sought out Mary Margaret while Tad went for more refreshments.

"That was an amusing evening," Kevin said when he reached her side.

Edith had been craning her neck, presumably searching for the catch of the day, David, who was ringed by his many single admirers. At Kevin's arrival, she turned to look him up and down. "I...I...I don't know what to do." Her gaze turned toward the throng around David and then back to Kevin. "I'm torn between my vice presidential duties and..." She put David in her sights again.

Mary Margaret chuckled. "I've never known you to hesitate in going after what you want, Grandma."

"You're right." Edith took Mary Margaret's hands. The white pom of her Santa hat swung across her cheek. "Even though you haven't put up your mistletoe, you're ready to date again. I just know it." She winked at Kevin. "You both deserve a second go-round, as do I." She squared her shoulders, lifted her chin, and plowed her way into the throng of David Jessup worshippers, who congregated by the Victorian choir practice schedule.

"Ignore my grandmother," Mary Margaret said apologetically, cheeks blossoming with color.

"I'll try." With Edith, that was sometimes a Herculean task.

Mary Margaret was just the distraction the divorce doctor ordered. She was tall and had intelligent blue eyes and that mane of long, thick red hair that begged to be touched. Kevin could barely remember what Foxy Roxy looked like.

Mary Margaret cleared her throat. "Why do I feel like everyone's staring at us?"

Kevin scanned the crowd. Hardly anyone was paying

attention to them. And why would they? The retirement crowd was focused on its most eligible bachelor. Kevin was just the boring mayor, and Mary Margaret was just the sweet kindergarten teacher.

"No one's looking at us." Still, they couldn't just stand there like seventh graders at their first dance.

Her gaze drifted to his mouth—*hallelujah!*—but there was a wrinkle to her brow.

"Did you want to ask me something?" he prompted.

She sized him up, lips parted, hesitating.

He recognized the need for small talk. "What's it like working for Jason?"

She looked stricken.

"Oh, I'm sorry. You must not have gotten the job." What a shlub he was for even bringing it up.

"Don't be sorry." Something opened in Mary Margaret's otherwise closed-off expression. "I was fired. Although it wasn't completely my fault. I can do clerical work but not handle *product* collection." She grimaced. "If you get my meaning."

He did. The line for the refreshments had dwindled to manageable. Tad was admiring Augie's trophy, a Snickerdoodle in each hand. "This calls for a cookie." If there were any left.

"I shouldn't." But there was a smile teasing the corner of her lips.

He wanted to kiss that smile into full bloom.

"You should." He began walking, pausing when he realized she hadn't followed. "What? You think you're the only person to ever be fired or lose a job over a mistake?" He waved her toward his side. "In college, I lost my job as a pizza delivery boy when my car broke down and my cell phone died. Trust me. You need comfort food and the kind words of a commiserate *firee*." When she dragged her feet, he had to probe. "Don't tell me you're hesitating because you count calories."

Mary Margaret's smile took its full shape. There was no more hesitation as she accompanied Kevin to what remained of the treats. "If you knew how many parents send cookies to school for snack time, you wouldn't ask that question."

"And now we're in the season of candy canes." Kevin gestured toward the tree, which was decorated with several large ones.

"I have no will power." She picked up a chocolate chip cookie and took a big bite.

"Me either." Before Kevin knew what he was doing, he chose a boring, round sugar cookie. He should have taken a frosted star or a piece of baklava.

"You ate the last plain sugar cookie," Mary Margaret said accusingly. "Those are my favorite. Some people think they're boring but I love them."

Smiling, Kevin took a bite. The cookie was perfect. The moment was perfect. *She* was perfect.

He opened his mouth to ask her out and—

"Kevin." Disrupting perfection, Barbara's loud voice had the entire room turning.

Everyone, that is, except Kevin.

The sheriff and Lola took that as their cue to leave. Understandable, since Barb had been having an affair with Lola's first husband before he died.

"Maybe we should step away from the cookies." Mary Margaret's smile faded from her expression as her cookie crumbled in her fingers.

Kevin clasped Mary Margaret's elbow. "Please, don't."

She made a miniscule move to free herself and then shrugged her shoulders into a more relaxed position. Her gaze flickered over his shoulder. "There's a storm blowing in."

"Hurricane Barbara," he confirmed, battening down the hatches where his temper was stored.

"Kevin." Barbara stopped next to them and crossed her arms. "I'm here to pick up Tad so I can take him to the dentist first thing in the morning."

"He's practicing rhymes with Ms. Adams and Augie." Mary Margaret pointed across the room.

"Go get him for me, Kev," Barbara said in a hard voice, staring at their son's teacher.

And leave Mary Margaret to you, the she-wolf? Not a chance.

Kevin called Tad over and lifted him into his arms when he arrived. "Did you have a good time, buddy?"

"I was the best judge ever, wasn't I, Ms. Sneed?" Tad tilted nearly sideways to reach for a cookie, trusting Kevin to keep him out of harm's way.

"You were The Awesome in the judging sauce, my friend." Mary Margaret had moved to the end of the table, ostensibly to pour herself a glass of punch, but her gaze darted from Edith to the door.

"Let's go, Tad. It's a school night." Barbara snatched him from Kevin. "You've had too many cookies, I bet." Barb's frown was meant to censure Kevin. To Barb— someone who'd always been rail thin—her son was obese and imperfect.

That broke Kevin's heart more than their divorce had, which Kevin suddenly realized told him a lot about the depth of his love for Barb. "It's the holiday season," Kevin told her. "A few extra cookies never hurt anyone."

"Extra cookie eaters grow up to be extra beer drinkers." Barb arched her penciled brows and hugged Tad closer. "You're getting a reputation as a drinker, Kev. That won't help you in an election year. Remember what I told you voters want. The scrutiny will be worse at the state level."

Kevin pressed his lips together, refusing to be baited.

His ex-wife decided she'd won this round and turned, carrying Tad away.

Kevin's heart panged, the way it did every time he had to let Tad go.

"Good night, Daddy." Tad waved, smiling. Like Edith, it took a lot to get him down.

"Good night, buddy."

When Kevin turned back around, Mary Margaret was gone.

*

"Why did we have to leave?" Edith was still putting on her jacket when they exited the retirement home. The wind blew her Santa pom straight back. "David was just about to ask me out, I think." She gave Mary Margaret one of her grandmotherly huffs. "Did you forget to record one of your TV shows?"

"No." Mary Margaret had let Kevin's sexy stubbled chin and sultry smile breach her resolve against bad decisions. She had no time for romance.

Snow was falling, stirred about on a chilly wind that sought bare skin. On the other side of the road in the town proper, Christmas lights glowed a welcome on nearly every street and building. Mary Margaret refused to be cheered.

"Did you get an inappropriate touch from the mayor?" Edith clutched her coat closed, still digging for the reason behind their hasty departure. "I can find you someone else."

"No." Mary Margaret towed her grandmother along, their steps crunching through a thin layer of snow. "Please stop trying to fix me up."

"I bet the two of you ignored my dating pep talk," Grandma Edith grumbled. "Here I am, trying to do my duty…"

Two figures separated themselves from the shadow of the minivan that was parked next to Mary Margaret's sedan.

She pulled up short, cold air biting the back of her throat, fear freezing her from the inside out.

"Hello, Mrs. Sneed." Mr. Hardy had his hands in his leather jacket pockets and his feet spread shoulder width apart. His hips moved side to side, like those plastic hula dolls they sold every summer at the dollar store in Greeley.

"Evening." Mr. Laurel had succumbed to mountain temperatures. He'd added a knit cap and thick blue scarf to his thin leather jacket. The red stir stick he chewed was crinkled, possibly bent out of shape by chattering teeth.

Mary Margaret muttered a greeting. She should've threaded her keys like extended claws between her fingers before they'd left the retirement home. But she hadn't. And now Derek's trouble was putting her grandmother at risk.

"If we're going to keep meeting like this, I feel we should be introduced." Edith's comment lacked her normal bluster.

"Laurel. Hardy. Meet my grandmother." Mary Margaret stood in front of Edith and tried to pretend the two men were an annoyance, not a threat. "What do you want, fellas?"

"An update." Mr. Hardy's hips rocked faster. "You don't seem to be working all that hard on meeting our payment demands."

The cookie in Mary Margaret's stomach shattered into sharp shards of distress.

"Good paying employment is hard to find," Mary Margaret said, not without feeling a bit guilty. She hadn't given Ned at the Hanky Panky her answer regarding his job offer.

"Glad to meet you, miss." Mr. Laurel removed the stir stick from his mouth and smiled at Grandma Edith, who didn't seem to know what to make of him. "I believe we already gave you advice in the employment quarter."

"Advice rejected." Mary Margaret wasn't stooping to robbing from her neighbors while she cleaned their toilets.

"Honey." Grandma Edith gazed up at Mary Margaret. "Did you sign up for a pyramid scheme? Is that why they want money?" She lowered her voice. "You know that's illegal."

Mr. Hardy frowned.

Mr. Laurel swiveled his stir stick from one side of his mouth to the other and regarded Grandma Edith with continued interest.

Heaven help them, her grandmother didn't back down.

"I've seen these men before. At the bakery and . . . outside your house? Did they show up at your door and ask to see your utility bill without proper identification?" Edith's voice was still low but loud enough for the two men to hear. "You know AARP says that's a scam."

"That's not it, Grandma." Mary Margaret didn't take her focus from the two goons.

Snow swirled around them, the flakes getting larger, the flurries thicker, blocking out the cheerful Christmas lights in Sunshine proper.

"And then there's the predators who pretend to be policemen," Grandma Edith continued. "They buy old cruisers and put a flashing light on top to pull you over." She surveyed the parking lot. "I don't ever get pulled over, but if you do, AARP says you shouldn't roll your windows down for anyone without a uniform and identification."

Mr. Laurel tried to cover a laugh by coughing.

"You won't see these two in a police cruiser." At least not in the front seat. It was Mary Margaret's turn to shiver.

Mr. Hardy's thick dark brows lowered dangerously on his broad forehead, as if he was unused to Edith's babbling.

"Good evening." Kevin came up behind them, looking too good for gambling debts and shakedowns in his long, camel-colored wool coat.

Mr. Hardy stared at Kevin's legs, as if he was calculating how much force would be needed to break them.

Mary Margaret thought she might faint.

"Mr. Mayor." Edith turned to Kevin. "I think these scammers are trying to get money out of my granddaughter."

Without a word, Mr. Laurel faded into the shadows on the other side of the minivan.

"We'll be in touch," Mr. Hardy said, before following suit.

The snow turned as thick as whipping cream, surrounding them in a cold, wet bubble, flakes hissing louder than the alarms ringing in Mary Margaret's ears. Or maybe that was the air in her tires. Her car began sinking lower on the far side.

"Mary Margaret?" Kevin's hands gripped her shoulders. "What is it? What's wrong?"

They slit my tires.

She clutched her throat.

Being Derek Sneed's widow was turning out to be more dangerous than a sideline job as a bull sperm collector.

"I'm going to start packing heat, like Mims does." Edith scowled. "I'll need a bigger purse. Sunshine is no longer safe." She looked Kevin up and down. "Aren't you supposed to do something about this? Call the cops? Arrest them for harassment?"

"I . . ." Mary Margaret cleared her throat. The last thing she needed was her grandmother getting a gun. "They didn't actually do anything, other than be creepy. My tires . . ." Her slit tires. "They haven't been holding air."

"I'm going to call the sheriff and drive you two ladies home." Kevin ignored Mary Margaret's protests and did just that, hustling them into his fancy SUV. "Drew said he'd keep an eye out for those men, but until they break the law . . . you ladies should be careful."

"Careful requires thought. You put me in the front seat, Kevin." Edith harrumphed, clearly unhappy with her mayor. "I take back what I said earlier. You two aren't ready to date. You didn't even think through our seating assignments."

"Haven't you ever heard of age before beauty?" Kevin took Edith's attitude in stride. "Besides, I'm dropping you off first."

"But then Mary Margaret will be in your back seat all alone." Edith angled to face the evening's hero. "You can't steal a kiss that way."

Kevin chuckled.

"Drop me off first," Mary Margaret pleaded, grateful to be in the back seat.

"No," the pair in the front chorused.

After they dropped Edith at her house, Kevin pulled up in front of Shaw's Bar & Grill.

"What are we doing here?" Mary Margaret's hands were tucked between her legs. They'd just stopped trembling.

"Earlier...back at the cookie table...I wanted to ask you something." He turned to face her. "But there's something about you that takes my breath away."

The lights in Shaw's parking lot illuminated the dark whiskers on his sculpted chin. And wow. She could practically feel the scrape of his dark stubble across her skin as he nibbled his way around her throat to that sensitive spot below her ear.

"I wanted to ask you out," he continued with that seductive smile of his. "But confrontations with men in dark parking lots require nightcaps with *friends*."

"I..." *Am so disappointed*. Until she realized she shouldn't be at the bar alone with him. But she didn't want to be at home alone either. "*Friends*." She latched on to the word. "I could use a drink with a friend."

Friends? Who was she kidding? Her heart was playing the *hubba-hubba* sing-along.

"Friendship is a good place to start." Kevin smiled, which seemed to be the key to loosening her shoulders, despite the danger any kind of relationship with Kevin might cause. "And a drink with me will have the added benefit of annoying Barb."

"That alone should be a reason I *don't* go inside." But Mary Margaret was already boots on the ground. She needed a bit of liquid courage if she was going to sleep alone in her bed tonight.

They sat at the booth Mary Margaret usually occupied with her friends. The familiarity and Noah's skimpy Charlie Brown tree decorated with sparkly red garland helped ground her. Unlike Mary Margaret, the bar owner was unapologetic about his lack of holiday spirit.

Kevin waited until he had a beer in hand before asking the inevitable. "Who were those guys? Weren't they at the coffee shop the other day? The truth please, since Edith isn't around to hear."

Mary Margaret shrugged. She'd ordered a cheerful strawberry daiquiri. She wasn't the cheerful strawberry daiquiri type, and Noah had given her a worried look when she'd ordered. And then she might have snapped at him to turn off the Christmas music. He'd obliged and was now playing country.

"Oh, you know…" Mary Margaret ate the cherry off the red plastic sword in her drink. "Derek and his debts. Those guys haven't accepted the fact that there's a long line of creditors I'm working through."

They'd never accept they weren't first in line to be paid.

She clasped her hands beneath the table to stop them from shaking.

"Hence the need for a second job." Kevin nodded in understanding. "You know, I could—"

"If you say loan me money, I'm going to walk home." Without finishing her drink, which would be a shame, because on the eve of her widow-versary she'd forgotten how good the youthful, cheerful drink tasted.

Kevin *tsk*ed. "I was going to say that I could ask around to see who's hiring." He scratched that stubble. "Have you considered tutoring? I heard the Bodine twins might not graduate high school."

"Very few people hire a kindergarten teacher to tutor their kids in geometry." Ned's offer to dance was looking like her only way out. She slurped daiquiri through her straw and then glared at Noah behind the bar. He'd gone light on the rum.

"Okay." Kevin's optimism drew her attention back to him. "You could work as Santa's assistant at the mall in Greeley, picking up babies and positioning them in Santa's lap."

"Santa deserves someone with more holiday sparkle." That wouldn't be her this year.

"Or you could offer to house sit someone's ranch over the holidays. You know, feed cattle, make sure their water supply isn't frozen."

Mary Margaret slurped her daiquiri too quickly. It gave her brain freeze. How appropriate. She massaged her temples. "In the scheme of odd jobs, I've already tried being a bull sperm collector." Was that even a term? She rubbed her forehead. "Tried and failed. So any type of farm job is out."

"Ranching," Kevin corrected.

She blinked at him. At handsome him.

On the one hand: *Falling for the handsome, newly divorced mayor isn't going to help me.*

On the other hand: *Falling for the handsome, newly divorced mayor could be just the distraction to help me sleep tonight.*

Mary Margaret stared at the melting little squares of ice in her drink and slurped some more, avoiding temptation on the other side of the booth.

"There aren't any farms out here," Kevin explained, oblivious to her fatal attraction. "We call them ranches."

"I knew that." She'd been here for five years, after all. She just didn't much care. She risked another peek at Kevin.

He grinned.

Mary Margaret took a steadying breath. She liked that grin. She liked it a lot.

She liked her job a lot too. If she let that grin win her over, Barbara would see to it she was fired. Barbara was president of the school board.

Mary Margaret slurped to the bottom of her drink and slumped against the wooden back of the booth where it was all too easy to take in Mr. Handsome and that touch-me hair.

Mary Margaret swallowed. Anyway she looked at it, she was in trouble. "Just my luck. I never thought of you as dangerous before."

Kevin's grin morphed into a killer smile, more than ready to slay her defenses.

"I mean, you're the mayor," she babbled. "Super nice. Always well-groomed." He smelled nice too. "I've never

seen you dance a woman into the shadows at Shaw's."
Now there was a tempting thought. "I've never seen you
tell Barbara off either." And boy, if anyone deserved to
be put in her place, it was Barbara.

Mary Margaret ran her fingers over the scar at the
nape of her neck and frowned. Powerful people hurt
little people all the time. "Please do me a favor. Don't
censure your ex around me. Barbara cuts my hair, you
know." And she'd been known to take out her slights
on her customers. "Just last July, Wendy Adams made
the mistake of asking Barbara why she was still wearing
her wedding ring. Barbara gave Wendy a pixie cut." The
style hadn't complemented Wendy's face. "And growing
it out…"

Kevin chuckled.

Mary Margaret liked his laugh. It was deep and throaty,
emanating from a heartfelt, special place.

Uh-oh. It was possible that Mary Margaret was a little
tipsy off the limited rum Noah had given her.

"No one ever told me about Wendy," Kevin admitted
with an honesty she found endearing. "I'll give her a kind
word about her hairstyle the next time I see her."

"I take it people don't flat-out tell you about
Barbara's…*activities*." Mary Margaret was definitely
tipsy or she wouldn't be bringing up his ex-wife quite
so much.

Kevin shook his head but his carefully neutral expression indicated they didn't have to tell him. He knew
Barbara was the town's self-proclaimed queen bee. "Did
you vote for me in the last election?"

Good conversationalist that Mary Margaret was, she
nodded.

"Why?"

"Because you seemed nice and my grandfather recommended you."

"A politician can't really build a reputation off likability alone." His voice lost every note of lightness. "I want people to vote for me because I make a positive difference in their lives. I want people to say, 'That Kevin. He really turned things around.'"

That Kevin. He was wound up tighter than a fresh spool of kite string.

"But I can't seem to make people realize, if we don't make a change now, things will get worse."

"Does this have anything to do with the proposed development by the highway?"

He nodded. "It's a problem for the town and my career."

"I could be a problem for you." For his career, what with bullying debt collectors and a possible stint as a burlesque dancer.

"I doubt that." Some of his tension unwound. Some of his sex appeal returned.

Mary Margaret tried to laugh, pressing her lips together almost immediately because she was rapidly turning into that pathetic woman who drank too much and used it as an excuse to dance between the sheets with a handsome guy she barely knew. She had no routine for this. "I can't solve any of your problems."

And he couldn't solve any of hers; more's the pity.

"We skipped over an important point in the conversation." Kevin drank his beer and studied her. "Why do you think I'm dangerous?"

"Because…" Mary Margaret cut herself short. She couldn't tell him the truth. But she couldn't tell him nothing either. He was only halfway through his beer, and the thought of walking home with Laurel and Hardy on the prowl chilled her in more ways than one. "Because although we've greeted each other before, I've never..."

Acknowledged your hunkiness.

Don't say that!

She tried again. "You've always been the mayor. The *married* mayor," she amended.

"And you've always been Mary Margaret Sneed, kindergarten teacher, and possibly good Catholic girl, seeing as how you have two first names." He was back to teasing her.

She sighed, liking the smiles, the flirting, the feeling that she was interesting. "I'm not Catholic. My father has his own ministry. I think he liked the idea of a daughter following Mary Magdalene's footsteps."

"We all disappoint our parents at one point or another," Kevin said cryptically. "I think your grandmother was wrong." His gaze was warm and heated her in places that could only lead to more trouble.

"If you think Grandma Edith was wrong about Laurel and Hardy, you're right." They weren't your average door-to-door scammers.

"No." He shook his head. "She was wrong about us *not* being ready to date. I'd like to take you out to dinner sometime."

The air was sucked out of her lungs.

"That's my cue to leave." Mary Margaret gathered her jacket and purse. "Finish your beer. I can walk home."

He made no move to get up or make a scene, not that there was anyone but Noah in the bar to witness it. "You'll go out with me."

"You're wrong there." It took her three times to find the armhole of her jacket.

"I don't think so." She really wished he wouldn't flash that grin. "I have a feeling you're attracted to danger."

"Sinner!" Her father drew back his fist to strike.

"This is as much danger as this girl can take." Mary Margaret didn't bother fastening her coat. "I've learned the hard way that a walk on the wild side isn't worth it in the long run."

Chapter Six

✳

Edith shimmied happily into the Saddle Horn the next morning for breakfast and coffee, singing to the radio in the kitchen. "I saw Mommy kissing Santa Claus."

Kisses. How appropriate.

There were men on the horizon for both herself and her granddaughter. Last night, David had sent her a good night text, and Kevin had driven Mary Margaret home.

"Why are you singing and dancing?" Mims grumped when she saw Edith boogying toward the corner booth where the Widows Club board sat. She wore a frumpy hunting hat that covered most of her hair and a frumpier camouflage sweatshirt, which might have explained her foul mood.

Or it could be that she'd left the poetry slam without another date with David.

"For the first time in a long time, I feel like a woman who isn't past her prime." Edith swiped a prune from Mims's plate. "*Boo-yah!*" She slid into the booth. Her rump on the cushion created a current of air that gave Mims, Clarice, and Bitsy a ride. "Isn't it a glorious morning?" She passed her jacket to Bitsy to add to the pile in the corner and then waved the waitress over. "Pearl, I'll have the special."

Pearl slid a cup of coffee with room for cream in front of Edith. "Hold the mushrooms, the tomatoes, the cheese, and the onions?"

Edith nodded, beaming at the world. "I feel loved."

"Scrambled eggs coming right up." Pearl hurried off.

Frowning, Clarice closed her notebook, dropped her pen, and then picked up the end of one pale braid, brushing it beneath her chin. "Why can't you just order scrambled eggs?"

"Because the special is one dollar cheaper." Edith dug French vanilla creamer pods from her purse. "I'm on a fixed income."

"Aren't we all?" Bitsy sipped her hot tea. "And so, it seems, is the rest of the town. Ticket sales for our Christmas Ball are slow."

"How slow?" Mims asked, tucking more gray curls under that hideous hat.

"We've sold ten, and that includes the four of us, Mary Margaret, the mayor, and his parents."

"Remind me." Edith stirred her coffee, trying to transition from the power of a natural woman to that of club vice president. "What does this ball benefit?"

"Us." Clarice laid a hand on her neck. "Our club."

Edith sipped her coffee and decided it needed more creamer. "Huh. Why is the stodgiest event of the year, during the busiest time of the year, ours?"

The board quieted.

"I mean..." Edith added more flavored cream. "There's the bachelor and bachelorette auctions. The bake sale competition. The wrapping booth. The fashion show. People—okay, let's be honest—*men* don't want to rent a tuxedo at the holidays when they stress about buying gifts for the women in their lives."

"I hate it when she makes sense," Clarice mumbled.

Mims stared at Edith with resignation in her eyes. "Edith comes up with more good points than you'd expect."

"Thank you, fellow board members." Edith beamed at the women and then at the sparse crowd of customers in the Saddle Horn.

"We can't just change the theme." Bitsy set down her tea mug. "We've been promoting it as a formal."

"To no success," Edith pointed out kindly. "On a more important note, Clarice, what are the rules for the board's holiday gift exchange?"

Clarice seemed at a loss. She tugged one long braid. "We don't exchange gifts."

"Oh." Edith stared out the window. "I hope they take returns."

"Who?" Bitsy touched her hairband. In an ode to the eighties, it was velvet, of course, but today it was red to match her sweater.

"I can't say." Edith was disappointed. She'd thought as board members they were a close-knit group. And close-knit groups always exchanged gifts. "It would be impolite and make you all feel bad. But, oh..." She perked up. "I think we should hire a deejay for the dance and give it a new title. Something hip, like you did with the poetry slam. How about Santa Jam?"

"That's actually not a bad idea." Bitsy stopped fiddling with her hairband.

"Really?" Clarice mumbled something about *Robert's Rules of Order*.

"It's okay." Edith didn't want Clarice to feel bad. "I'm just a natural as vice president. Now, about Mary Margaret's matchmaking." Edith had made a mental list of topics she wanted to discuss, and she intended to check off every item before her breakfast special arrived.

"Slow down." Clarice tapped her notebook. "We have an agenda for this meeting."

"What's on it?" Edith sipped her coffee.

Opening her notebook, Clarice ran her finger across her chicken scratch. "We've covered everything except... Mary Margaret."

"Right." Mims scrutinized Edith's face.

"I think we can cross that off our list." Edith wiped her mouth with her napkin in case Mims's stare meant she had a coffee mustache. "The mayor drove Mary Margaret home from the poetry slam. I think he's a fine catch. So tall and debonair."

Movement at the front of the restaurant caught her eye. The tall man with the unclear motives regarding Mary Margaret removed the red stir stick from his mouth and tipped it her way as if it were a hat.

Edith didn't know whether to shoo him off or give him a smile. Apparently, she'd gotten her mojo back. As a young lady, she'd never had a problem attracting men. It had been her superpower.

"I always liked my men tall," Bitsy said wistfully, admiring Edith's admirer.

"Hang on." Mims pointed her finger at Edith. "I don't think Kevin is the right choice for anyone yet."

"How can you say that?" Edith snuck another glance at the tall man settling up his bill. "Kevin is our mayor."

"Because of Barbara." Mims looked at Edith as if she'd missed identifying a transitive verb on a grammar test. "We try to steer our projects from choppy waters."

"Are you just saying that"—a pit formed in Edith's belly—"because it would mean that I failed?" That they could give her the boot from the board?

"Listen to me," Mims began. "If Barbara were a widow—"

"Which she's not," Clarice interjected.

"We wouldn't consider her ready to move on again."

"She still wants to be with Kevin." Bitsy nodded.

The trio often talked like that, finishing each other's sentences, making Edith feel like the odd man out, bringing back painful memories from her youth.

"Barbara can't still love him." She'd stormed the poetry slam with annoyance in her eyes.

"No. It's worse." Mims sat back while Pearl topped off her coffee. "Barbara still considers Kevin her property."

"It has nothing to do with love." Bitsy's gaze turned mournful, almost as if she was pining for her three lost husbands.

"And you know Barbara can be as troublesome as poison oak to get rid of." Clarice closed her notebook.

The finality of the moment—of Edith's tenure on the board—spun in the ensuing silence like an out-of-control carnival ride. "So? Where does that leave Mary Margaret?"

"Out of luck." Clarice sniffed.

"Out in the cold." Bitsy cradled her tea mug with both hands.

"We should brainstorm a list of single men, I suppose," Mims said.

A big truck drove past. Tom Bodine sat behind the wheel.

"Didn't someone mention we match *widowers*?" Edith was super pleased with her idea. "What about Tom Bodine? His teenage boys could use the calming influence of a mother."

And bonus: Tom was the wealthiest man in Sunshine. Mary Margaret could use an influx of cash.

✳

"Ms. Sneed, don't you like Christmas?" Elizabeth Franklin skipped alongside Mary Margaret toward the office after school.

"Who doesn't like Christmas?" Mary Margaret attempted a jovial laugh.

"You don't wear Christmas sweaters." Elizabeth eyed Mary Margaret as critically as her mother had done during their Halloween party when Mary Margaret hadn't dressed up. Elizabeth was the opposite of her cousin Louise in every way, including her tendency toward bossiness. "Ms. Birchswallow wears Christmas sweaters every day." Linnie Birchswallow was her older brother's sixth grade teacher.

"I haven't dug out my holiday sweaters yet, honey." Did she really have to this year?

"But you will?" Elizabeth's tone mirrored her mother's in self-importance. Her mom was one of Barbara's close friends. "Promise?"

"I promise." Mary Margaret answered begrudgingly,

then opened the rear office door and led Elizabeth inside where Wendy, the school secretary, was decorating a small Christmas tree. "Look, there's your mom."

Sandy Franklin was pinning an announcement for the Parent-Teacher holiday party on the bulletin board.

Elizabeth ran around the front counter to her mother. "You don't have to worry about Ms. Sneed's holiday spirit, Mommy. She just has to unpack it."

Mary Margaret feigned hearing loss and checked the papers in her box as the Franklins left.

Tom Bodine walked into the school office and directed his twin teenage boys to sit in the chairs normally reserved for sick or misbehaving elementary children. "Mrs. Sneed, I hear you're available for tutoring." Tom didn't look at Mary Margaret as if she came highly recommended.

The Bodine twins slouched in the blue burlap chairs behind their father, backpacks at their big feet.

"I... Did the mayor put you up to this?" Mary Margaret stayed behind the school counter, hands folded primly on the green Formica.

Kevin wasn't just dangerously handsome. He was meddlesome and overstepping his slim-fitting khakis. Mary Margaret was in no mood for referrals or charity, even though she'd been forced to buy two new tires because of Laurel and Hardy's tire slashing.

"Nobody forces me to do anything." Tom sized up Mary Margaret the way she imagined he sized up a steer for sale. He owned the largest ranch in Sunshine County. He was a hard man, from his scuffed black boots to the sharp angles of his face to his absolute determination to live his life by his rules. "Two different parties recommended you. I'll pay five hundred dollars if my boys pass all their classes in two weeks."

Tempting, but Derek wouldn't approve of the odds. The Bodine boys had a reputation as slackers. And they hadn't shown up for work the day she'd been fired by Iggy.

Still, Mary Margaret was always up for a haggle. "Two weeks left in the term for them to pass every class? Five hundred seems low."

Tom smirked. "You've got a leg up. One of their classes is PE, and their basketball coach assures me they'll pass if they show up."

The twins stared at Mary Margaret with teenage detachment. They had no desire to pass anything but time.

Mary Margaret decided to toss them a bone, pricing herself out of the running. "My tutoring fee in this situation is two hundred per class."

"Two hundred?" Tom sputtered, tipping his black hat back.

"Per student," Mary Margaret clarified, ignoring the breathy, "Wowzer. That's ballsy," from Wendy.

Linnie Birchswallow opened the rear office door, spotted Tom's red face, and immediately closed it again.

"Mr. Bodine, the success of tutoring requires the student to want to learn. And..." Mary Margaret encompassed his sons with a sweep of her arm. "Sometimes it's best to let children fail. What harm would be done in the long run by making them repeat their senior year?"

The twins exchanged wide, reality-laden glances, as if they hadn't considered the ramifications of failing.

"They're not children," Tom roared. "They're *Bodines*! If they don't pass their classes by year's end, I'm taking them out of school. No sports. No dances. They'll work for the roof over their heads, just like I did."

If Mary Margaret hadn't been raised by a blustering father, she might have been cowed.

"Geez, Dad," said one identical twin, scratching his head beneath an unruly dark curl. "Tone it down."

"Yeah, Dad," said the other, scratching a similar itch. "This is the elementary school, not the ranch."

"Besides," said the first twin, "we'll take Ms. Sneed as a tutor."

"Yeah," echoed his brother. "She's cool."

Tom made a sound like a trapped, wounded lion and stalked out. The heavy door closed behind him with a thud.

"Wait!" Mary Margaret called after him. She hadn't wanted the job.

"It's okay, Ms. Sneed," said Twin One, shrugging. "We know how to get our grades up."

"Yeah," said Twin Two. "We just waited a little too long to start catching up this term."

They gathered their backpacks and headed for the door.

"*Boys*," Mary Margaret warned. "Come back here."

They ignored her.

"I promised Jami I'd take her to the winter formal next month," said Twin One.

"Boys!" Mary Margaret said, louder this time but to the same effect.

"There's no way I'm sitting out the basketball game against Highland High," said Twin Two.

They left the office.

"I don't get it." Wendy fluffed her short hair. "Are you their tutor or not?"

Tom had referenced two recommendations. Kevin and...? "I have no clue." But what she did know was that tutoring those boys wasn't a sure thing.

She picked up her cell phone. The date of her next payment of Derek's online debt loomed. She was going to have to call Ned and accept the job.

A sure thing involved a mask, a wig, and the Hanky Panky.

※

"Thanks for making time for me today." Cray McDonald sat down across from Kevin. He'd played center at Western Colorado University to Kevin's quarterback, but had traded football pads for fine wool business suits. Cray had slimmed down since then but he was still a presence to be reckoned with, blocking for shot-callers. "My boss is wondering why you haven't forced a vote on the distribution center yet."

"Funny you should mention forcing a vote." Kevin paged Everett to his office and then picked up one of Tad's cars that had fallen from the ficus. The car made him think of Tad, which made him think of Mary Margaret, which made him want to smile. *She thinks I'm dangerous.* "I believe we've garnered support from all but one town councilman."

"That's great." Cray rubbed his big hands together. "Vote already. We can break ground at spring thaw."

"Not so fast." Kevin instructed Everett to enter and close the door behind him. "The problem is with our residents. They're resistant to change. We were wondering what you could do to sweeten the pot for the community."

Cray frowned.

Everett sat next to Cray and placed a sheet of paper in front of him. "These are our ideas."

"Fund the remodeling of the high school football stadium snack bar," Cray read. "Pay for a war memorial bench at the cemetery. Sponsor a float in the Christmas parade." His frown deepened as he tossed the paper back toward Everett, several line items still unread. "I don't have the budget for this."

"Do you want to win the community over?" Kevin picked up the list.

"We're offering jobs. Shouldn't that be enough?" Cray sat back in his chair and gave them a disparaging look. "If you rezone the property, they'll see the impact like that." He snapped his big fingers. "Demolition crews. Construction workers. Staff to run operations."

"We're a close-knit community." Everett took a moment to adjust his glasses, as if he wanted to see Cray more clearly. "We don't want to be a town divided."

Cray huffed. "You mean if people are upset, Kevin might not be re-elected, and you might get fired by the new administration."

"It's not beyond the realm of possibility," Kevin allowed, unshaken. "But so is the risk that residents will organize a social media campaign against you. Is that what your boss would want? Bad press?" He handed the list back to Cray. "We aren't suggesting you support everything on this list. But we are suggesting you make an effort to say you're willing to become part of our community."

"To buy our membership," Cray grumbled.

"It'll be worth it in the long run," Kevin promised, hoping that was true.

Cray got to his feet. "Gentlemen, I can't say it's been fun…but it has been real." He folded the list, stuffed it into his jacket pocket, and left.

Kevin and Everett listened to him walk down the stairs.

Everett stood. "What are the odds they'll take our suggestions?"

Seventy-thirty. Against.

Kevin knew Everett didn't want to hear the truth so he said, "Fifty-fifty."

"I was thinking it was more like seventy-thirty." Everett stood, looking grim. "Against, that is."

Even his right hand man thought they were on the ropes? "We may have council votes but we don't have popular support."

"Given that," Everett said matter-of-factly, "I don't like your odds for re-election."

Kevin didn't like them either. Once Everett left, he called his contact at the state political party's office and set up a time to meet.

He couldn't wait to see how the distribution center shook out. Every career politician had to have an exit strategy.

※

"Ladies, this is your new choreographer and dance instructor." Ned introduced Mary Margaret to the rest of his dancers.

The seven women lounged around the stage at the Hanky Panky. None seemed happy to see her. Mary Margaret wasn't all that happy to be there, so she supposed they were even.

"Why do we need a dance lesson?" Crystal sported black acrylic nails nearly as long as Mary Margaret's thumb. "You wouldn't have hired us if we didn't already know how to dance."

Doubt pressed against Mary Margaret's chest, propped up by the balance owed to the online casino.

"You see what I'm dealing with?" Ned straddled a chair and shook his fist at his dance crew. "If you want to earn better tips and keep this place open, you'll listen to what Roxy has to say."

"I'm in." Didi pushed her thick glasses up her nose. "The place went wild for her on Saturday."

"How much did you earn in tips?" Crystal was going to be a hard sell.

Mary Margaret didn't like to talk money with anyone but she shrugged as if it were no big deal. "Around five hundred."

The dancers gaped at her.

Validation made.

Mary Margaret knew she didn't look like an exotic dancer. She was dressed like an FBI operative in the field. Her hair was in a low bun beneath a black knit cap. After the tutoring incident, she'd changed into black leggings, black boots, and a black turtleneck. She shrugged out of her jacket. "Ned, you should leave."

Ned protested.

"Go." Mary Margaret waited a beat before adding, "Or I will." More than four years as a kindergarten teacher had helped her learn a lot about how to deal with doubters and rebels. She waited to say anything more until she heard his office door close, and then she looked at the women. "Crystal is right. You're all good dancers.

I can't teach you how to groove any better than you already do."

"I told you," Crystal said but with less ire than before. The dollar figure Mary Margaret had mentioned was obviously still on her mind.

Mary Margaret went to the sound system tucked in the far corner of the stage. "But that's not what I'm here for." She turned on the stereo. Christmas music filled the room. She quickly punched up some classic George Michael and faced her dance team. "I'm here to put together a burlesque revue that people get excited about. I'm here to make sure we all walk out of here every night with a wad of cash. But mostly, I'm here to dance because I love it."

Mary Margaret did a slow bend, back arching, followed by a quick spin and snap. "If you don't love to dance…If you're just here because you need the money…the audience knows."

The women shifted but said nothing, watching Mary Margaret work.

Except it wasn't work. It never had been.

Dancing was joy. Dancing was power, a way to take back that bit of herself that her father's strict upbringing had tried to squelch. She and her mother used to dance in the kitchen while making dinner. The day they were caught, a light had gone out in her mother, one that was never rekindled.

"My grandmother and I dance in the kitchen like this." Mary Margaret turned up the music and did a rendition of the Mom Dance.

The women laughed.

The tension inside Mary Margaret eased. Dancing

always loosened up the stress, shook it off, made her feel free, moved her beyond her worries and fears. How could this be wrong?

Mary Margaret hadn't seen Laurel and Hardy today. They made her so afraid and at the same time so angry— *Beyoncé move, Beyoncé move, Beyoncé move.* She tossed her knit cap aside and let her hair down, claiming the pole for a free, unfettered spin.

The lightness in her limbs. There were no cares on her shoulders. No concern about what would happen tomorrow. No questions about making rent, being fired for dancing, or what Laurel and Hardy might do if she couldn't put together a bigger payment than last week.

The chorus swelled, and Mary Margaret shifted into burlesque dance mode, sleep walking through the moves, teasing the crowd.

In this case, her hands ran down Didi's back before she stutter-stepped away, at one with the beat, the highs and lows, the power of the electric guitar. She knew she'd been making eye contact with the other women. She knew she had their complete and utter attention when they joined in. Not because of promises of more tips.

But because of the love and power of dance.

✳

"Your two o'clock is here." Yolanda poked her head in Kevin's office. Her shoulder-length gray hair swung forward around her dangly Christmas tree earrings. "I put them in the conference room downstairs."

Kevin looked up from his potential list of honorees for Citizen of the Year.

"Boss." Yolanda came in and closed the door behind her. "They didn't give me their names or their business cards but I can tell political party muckety-mucks from inconsequential muckety-mucks. Are you going to do it? Are you going to run for higher office?"

Kevin grinned. How could he not? He'd only been working toward this opportunity since he'd first declared himself a candidate for mayor. And after Barb's infidelity, this was a shot to his ego. "I plead the fifth."

"My lips are sealed." She gave him a once-over. "You should have worn your best suit."

He shook his head. "The last time I wore a suit I found out my wife was cheating on me." He'd made a conscious decision to lay it out honestly. He was a polo and khaki kind of politician now.

"I get it." Yolanda hugged herself happily. "I can say I knew you when."

"Let's not get ahead of ourselves." Kevin gathered a fresh notepad and a pen.

"I'll be able to call for tours of your state office? The state house? The *White* House?"

"Slow down. The starter pistol hasn't gone off." He headed toward the door. "No races have begun."

"But if you leave…" Yolanda stood in his way, a frown marring her middle-aged face. "Do you remember when you found insurance so our farmers market wouldn't close?"

"Yeah." Without insurance, the town couldn't allow one of their local traditions to continue.

"Without it, my mother would've given up her honey

business. She supplements her social security because you were open to Sunshine taking the lead. That wasn't popular at the time."

"You don't need to remind me of the good I've done as mayor." Kevin edged closer to the door.

"Don't I? I know Barb would say it's a popularity contest. But I don't want you to forget that it's making a difference in people's lives by degrees that's important. No matter where you serve, you have to remember that communities are like marble and those in power need to delicately chip away at that marble to keep the heart of the stone intact. Sometimes I think folks around here would prefer their marble to stay a lump of clay."

It was a bad metaphor. He hugged her anyway. "I'd give you a raise, if I hadn't approved a raise for you come January first."

Yolanda still didn't move.

"What is it?"

"It's just that... If you run for state office, you won't be my boss anymore." She looked mournful. "I started here working for your dad. It'll be eons before Tad's ready to run the show."

"Yolanda." He gently gripped her shoulders. "They may not like me. My timing might be all wrong."

"Never." She sniffed and escaped, mumbling something about Victor Yates running for office.

Victor wasn't the successor Kevin would've chosen. His was the one holdout vote on the town council Kevin had been unable to earn.

Kevin descended the stairs, thinking about who would take the reins of Sunshine after he'd left rather than mentally organizing his past accomplishments in case anyone asked.

He paused outside the conference room door to wipe his palms on his slacks. This was it. His dream. Coming true. His father should have been there, acting as his wingman. His mother should have wished him luck. And they would have, if he hadn't wanted to do this his way.

Kevin drew a deep breath and opened the door.

The state party representatives consisted of a man and a woman. Their names? Paul and Paula. They both wore blue suits and the assessing expressions of seasoned pollsters.

Kevin needed something grounding, something to hold on to. He leaned back to catch Yolanda's eye but she'd already read his mind and set a mug of coffee in front of him and then left, sniffing and closing the door behind her.

"Kevin, we're excited to be here." Paul's haircut and bearing hinted at a military past. He smiled just enough to be friendly, and not enough to concede power. "You've done wonderful things with Sunshine, and we think you can do wonderful things for the state of Colorado."

Kevin murmured his thanks and sipped his coffee. *Calm. I'm as calm as a spring breeze on Sunday morning.*

Paula shifted in her seat. With shoulder-length brown hair and minimal makeup, she was pretty in a pleasant, non-threatening way. Yin to her partner's yang. "As you know, in today's climate, community servants are put under a microscope. You should be commended on the life you've led. Captain of football teams in high school and college. A history of service from an early age. Frankly, despite the divorce…you seem too good to be true."

And that would only solidify with Mary Margaret at his side.

Paul's smile didn't change. "Do you have anything you want to tell us?"

Both party representatives chuckled, as if it was beyond the realm of possibility that Kevin would have a skeleton in his closet.

"Frankly, Paul and Paula…" *Don't say it. Don't say it…* "I'm a little boring." Kevin clutched his coffee cup. Where was his polish?

"Boring is nice." Paula gave Kevin a clinical once-over. "Never apologize for boring."

Kevin didn't want to apologize. He didn't want to *be* boring.

"Boring gets re-elected when your constituents are satisfied with you," Paul echoed. "Of course, if you have any stories of personal triumphs, we can use that to unify voters around you." He paused, waiting for Kevin to share a motivating story.

Here's your chance, said that odd little whisper in his head. *Speak up. Sell yourself.*

With what? Kevin scratched a spot behind his ear. He drained his coffee. He wiped his palms on his slacks once more. "I'm afraid I have no motivational material for you." That was the problem with being boring. "The closest thing to change in my life right now is…Well, I'm just about dating." *Dang, that was lame.* "She's a lovely woman. An elementary school teacher. Kindergarten. You know what a handful kids are at that age." He couldn't seem to keep his mouth shut. He stared at the bottom of his empty coffee cup. "She's seen some hard times in her life. Abused by her father." *Stop there. Please, stop there. This is wrong on so many levels.* "Lost her husband last year to a cancerous brain tumor." He drew a deep breath before he told them about her husband's debt. "Sorry. I've suddenly realized I'm a bit nervous."

A bit of an idiot, more like.

"It's all right." Paula stopped writing, having taken notes on everything he'd said.

Kevin's shoulder twinged.

"Does this woman you're almost dating have a name?" Paul's pen was poised above the page, poised to jot down Mary Margaret's name.

"I think we should wait on formalities until things are…more formal." *Idiot.* Kevin wouldn't be surprised if they packed their briefcases and vowed never to see him again. And he hadn't even shared the real potential deal-breaker. "I feel the need to confess that we're a community divided at the moment." Kevin explained about JPM's distribution center and the reluctance of residents to embrace change. "Maybe we should reschedule this meeting in January, after we see how it all shakes out."

"I'm not worried." Paul smiled the way insurance agents did when they unexpectedly sold you full coverage. "It sounds like the right choice for Sunshine."

"You'll unify your core base over the holiday." Paula pumped her fist in the air. "That's what good politicians do."

They spent a good deal of time explaining financial guidelines for a campaign, walking him through scaling up a campaign from the local level to his district boundaries. There were rules about bank accounts and fundraisers. Advice about transparency and messaging.

"Do you have any questions for us?" Paula downshifted from pleasant to neutral.

Kevin did have questions. "I understand some state representatives operate two households. We're ninety minutes away from Denver in good weather. What if I chose to commute?"

Matching flashes of disapproving frowns were quickly replaced with reassuring smiles.

"You can commute," Paula said slowly. "But you'll miss out on networking at breakfast and after dinner. You have to be part of the political scene when in session to optimize your effectiveness."

"And move on to the next level." Paul gave an odd chuckle. "You might want to stay in the almost-dating stage. You know what they say about long-distance romances. They don't work."

Kevin didn't like the sound of that. He didn't want to live in Denver half the time. Tad was here. Mary Margaret was here.

But this is my dream.

He thanked them for their time. Yolanda escorted them to the door, where Paula asked her a whispered question.

Kevin sat back down at the conference room table, telling himself everything was okay. He'd done well.

Yolanda came to claim his coffee cup. "Was it everything you hoped for?"

Kevin smiled weakly. "You know, I think it was." And if he told himself enough times, he might believe it.

"Good. I just had to wonder..." Yolanda hesitated in the doorway. "I'm sure it's nothing."

"What?"

"I thought it was odd." She fingered one of her Christmas tree earrings. "They asked for the names of our local kindergarten teachers."

Kevin's gut clenched. He'd babbled too much about Mary Margaret—invading her privacy, breaking her trust.

What had he done?

❋

"Thank you all for coming." Kevin addressed his newly formed committee on town development.

There was only one friendly face in the assembly— Mary Margaret's. And she wouldn't be so friendly when he told her his political party might be running a background check on her.

He hadn't seen her in several days. She wore a chunky pink sweater and blue jeans. Her hair was down, flowing over her shoulders the way he'd like it to flow over his. He had to tell her carefully, gently, to prove he wasn't the wrong kind of dangerous.

But first, Kevin got down to business. "You've all got a stake or an opinion in the distribution center, and before we hold a broader town hall meeting, I thought it'd be beneficial to hear everyone's thoughts."

"No," Kevin's dad said. "That's my thought. Just say no."

"Agreed." Barney ran the convenience store in town.

The table erupted with opinions, mostly negative. Mary Margaret didn't say a thing.

Kevin's nerves jangled like he'd had too much caffeine.

"One at a time." Kevin stood, missing the calming

presence of Everett, who'd come down with a stomach bug earlier in the afternoon. "One at a time. Please. I know there are objections. I want to find out what underlies your concerns."

People shifted in their seats and wouldn't look at him. At this rate, his Sunshine political career was ending next November, if he wasn't recalled in a special election first.

Since he'd already heard his father's dead-end opinion, Kevin started elsewhere. "Barney, talk to me."

Barney didn't. He crossed his arms instead.

"Sometimes..." Mary Margaret said in a small voice from the far end of the table, "it helps to play it out."

Several members of Kevin's committee swung dubious glances her way. Of all the attendees, she was the only person new to town hall.

Undeterred, Mary Margaret gave the committee her non-threatening, schoolteacher smile. "What I mean to say is, what's the worst thing that could happen if the distribution center opens?"

"The worst *thing*?" Barney's voice rose an octave. "Another convenience store could go in by the interstate. People driving home from there or from Greeley wouldn't stop at my store."

There was a supportive chorus regarding the unfairness of commerce.

"But Barney, you'd still be the only convenience store in town," Kevin reassured him. "And the first store on the road down from Saddle Horn State Park."

Barney rolled his eyes. "I guess."

"I'm picturing the same scenario." Emory owned the town's only grocery store. "Houses will be built between downtown and the interstate. And with new homes come other stores that will cost me business."

"But won't that mean more people will move to Sunshine, increasing your sales?" Kevin asked gently. "Maybe you won't feel the pinch as much as you think you will."

Emory's mouth frumped but at least he wasn't yelling about defeating the distribution center.

"And what about you, Dad?" Kevin leveled his gaze on his father. "How will the distribution center impact your furniture business?" *Your.* He chose the pronoun on purpose. He hadn't worked in the family furniture shop since he'd been elected after college.

His father's arms were locked tight across his chest. He stared at the conference room wall behind Kevin and said nothing.

Kevin's chest felt as if someone had filled it with a smoldering cord of firewood. Whatever was going on with his father, whatever opinion he'd formed about the distribution center, it was causing a rift between them. A rift that might never heal.

Later, after most fences had been mended—thanks in large part to Mary Margaret—and the meeting adjourned, Kevin asked his father to stay behind. "Talk to me, Dad. Please."

His father ran a hand through the white hair at his temples. "You don't understand."

"Maybe I would if you put it into words."

Dad tossed his hands up, and when he spoke it made no sense. "Hadley Furniture has no future if the distribution center opens."

"How can you say that? You don't compete with them."

"Oh but we do." Dad's gaze landed firmly on Kevin. What wasn't firm was the mournful look in his eyes. "We compete for resources."

"Wood?"

"*Human* resources." Dad took Kevin by the shoulders. "If that distribution center is a success, you'll move on— the county board of supervisors, the state house of representatives. And maybe beyond that." He squeezed his fingers into Kevin's shoulders, unaware that Kevin was already actively planning to run. "You won't be around for me to pass on the mantle of Hadley Furniture."

Kevin's shoulders bunched. "Dad, I've... Well, I've already been approached about running at the state level."

The oxygen was sucked out of the room, along with any pride Kevin felt in the honor.

"How long?" Dad demanded. "How long have you known?"

"October." It shamed Kevin to admit it. "I only just had my preliminary meeting."

"Well, that's that." His father turned and walked away. But he didn't rush. His steps were slow and ponderous, the pace of a man facing certain defeat.

Kevin sank into a chair. His goal had always been to finish his grandfather's work. He'd never thought about running the family business or carrying on the Hadley furniture legacy.

He thought about it now.

Chapter Seven

✳

Mary Margaret left the town hall and walked toward the Sewing Emporium to pick up a bag of material scraps they were donating for her next arts and crafts project with her students.

A painter was decorating the craft store's plate glass windows with elves sewing Santa's costume, knitting Frosty's scarf, and embroidering names on Christmas stockings. He wished her a Merry Christmas. The Sewing Emporium was playing Christmas music, and every end cap had a display of holiday crafts. If anything was going to fill her with holiday spirit, it should be this.

With the exception of the men and women on the special panel regarding the town's development project, everyone she encountered was lighthearted and hopeful. Every song she heard was about the celebration of the season. Mary Margaret felt very little joy, very little hope, very little reason to celebrate.

No. That wasn't entirely true. She felt happy when she danced. And the money she earned gave her hope, a tiny glimmer of light at the end of a long dark tunnel. But those moments were fleeting in comparison to what she should be feeling.

A few minutes later, bag of fabric scraps in hand, Mary Margaret headed toward the Olde Time Bakery and an afternoon latte. It was the wrong thing to do. She should have gone home and napped for a few hours before driving to her second job in Greeley. But Christmas expectations were overloading her. She needed a pick-me-up. She needed to find some holiday cheer. And what better place than a bakery filled with bright holiday decorations, warm holiday smells, and festive holiday music?

The Bodine twins sat at a table near the front window, their math books open, not a pretty teenage girl in sight.

Mary Margaret paused inside the door, exchanging looks with the pair—hers with raised eyebrows, theirs with stoic expressions that gave nothing away.

One of them glanced toward the girl behind the counter. "Ms. Sneed needs a latte."

"Skinny, please." Mary Margaret moved toward the cash register.

"And a vanilla scone," said the other twin. "Give her one iced with a Christmas tree. She's not allowed to order a Grinch cookie."

Mary Margaret turned around and gave the twins a disapproving stare.

"Caffeine and carbs," said Twin One, oblivious to her annoyance. "It cures the blues."

"We should know," said Twin Two, tapping his pencil on his notebook. "We used to work here."

"We used to work everywhere," admitted Twin One.

"We don't tend to work in one place too long,"

explained Twin Two. "Just long enough to satisfy our curiosity."

The teenage cashier called Mary Margaret over to pay. Her name was Jami. One of those twins had promised to take her to a dance next month. Mary Margaret sighed.

When she had her latte and scone, Mary Margaret sat near the twins. "You're the reason I got fired from Bull Puckey Breeding. You didn't show up for work."

"It got boring." The name on top of his paper said Steve, while Twin Two's said Phillip.

Not that Mary Margaret could tell them apart. "To be clear, I'm not tutoring you."

"Nah." Steve stared at a Venn diagram. "We're bringing our grades up on our own."

Phillip looked up from his quadratic equation. "Well, Dad still thinks you're tutoring us. And if we cost you a job with Iggy, we owe you."

The twins exchanged looks and nods. And those looks seemed to say they were going to encourage their father's misconception.

"I'm not going to let your father pay me." It wouldn't be right.

"Because it's not true?" Steve closed his math book. "Dad believes a lot of things that aren't true. Lots of people do."

"Like Santa Claus," Mary Margaret murmured. Her kindergarten students were so excited about the myth.

Phillip nodded. His gaze diverted to the window. "There's the old man now."

Tom pulled into an empty parking space and honked as snow began to fall.

While the twins closed up their books, Kevin appeared

on the sidewalk, wearing khakis and a heavy blue ski jacket. He paused to greet Tom and then entered the bakery, brushing snow out of his hair. His warm gaze found hers. "I guess my reference paid off."

"Sure did." Steve darted out the door.

"Ms. Sneed is the greatest tutor." Phillip followed him. "Merry Christmas."

Kevin ordered an Americano and joined Mary Margaret, shedding his coat and pushing up the long sleeves of his black turtleneck sweater. He had strong arms, the kind a woman would feel safe encircled by, and broad shoulders, the kind a woman could lean on. If she'd been the kind of woman worthy of either. She shouldn't encourage him. But there was that dark stubble on his chin and the mischievous look in his eyes that promised long, hot kisses on cold winter nights.

"Penny for your thoughts," he murmured, half-smiling before taking a sip of his coffee.

She dragged her gaze away from his lips. "I'm not tutoring the Bodines." She had to tell Kevin the truth, on this point at least. Where he was concerned, the rest of her life was shrouded in half-truths, deception, and longing for long, hot kisses on cold winter nights. "Those boys do fine on their own."

"Sure." Kevin sipped his coffee, unabashedly studying her. "How'd you think the committee meeting went?"

"You had people thinking." Mary Margaret stared at the wreath hanging on the bakery door. It was a beautiful circle of boughs, but she had no desire to have one like it. Her holiday cheer was as fake as the plastic wreath on her door.

"The panel had me thinking too. There's something

I need to tell you but..." Kevin set his coffee down. "What's bothering you?"

"I have no Christmas spirit," Mary Margaret blurted, which was a bad idea to say out loud. The last time she'd sat here, she'd revealed some of the truth about her father. She stared at her scone and considered shoving the entire thing in her mouth to stop divulging her secrets.

"The holidays can be overwhelming," Kevin said kindly.

"I'm not in the mindset for frivolous traditions." Last year at this time she'd been artificially cheerful for Derek's sake, and look where that got her. "I'm not in the mood for...for..." She tried to hold in the negative words but her hand started waving like she was winding it up for a snap, and that seemed to crank open the hatch on her stress. "I'm not in the mood for carols. For snowmen. For sledding and snowball fights. For shopping. And not even shopping but for thinking about making a list of who to buy for." Her in-laws, for one. "I'm not in the mood for Christmas pageants and Christmas parties. And I feel so fake when I say Merry Christmas."

Kevin took her hand. "This has to do with Derek, doesn't it? He passed away during the last holiday season."

Oh, holy gremlins. "Of course this is about him." That was a no-brainer. "I loved him." That came out like a defense attorney shouting an objection. "This is about him and his baggage and the way the Christmas tree skirt was yanked out from under me last year."

Kevin leaned forward, drawing her hand closer to him as he tried to bring her near. "It's okay to resent Derek a little but eventually you have to let all that baggage go."

"I did let it go." Mary Margaret tugged her hand free. "I forgave him those bills and those purchases last summer. And I knew coming into this holiday season I was going to feel sad. But knowing it's coming and being in the moment are two different things." She had more to say but this last came out on a hoarse gasp of air. "I'm the kindergarten teacher. I'm not supposed to be the Grinch."

Jami, the barista, was cleaning dishes in the sink. Running water covered their words but they shouldn't be having this conversation. It was too raw, too personal, and gossip-worthy if the barista had fine young ears that heard every secret confessed in the bakery and she passed them along the grapevine.

Once more, Mary Margaret considered shoving her scone into her mouth. But it was too late. Her secrets were out.

"Since we're sharing the ugly thoughts inside of us..." Kevin hadn't sat back in his chair. He still leaned over the table toward her. "I freak out a little when I see married people." He spoke in a whisper too but that didn't lessen the shock of his admission. "Since my divorce, I look, and I see they're so happy and then..."

"You wonder if one of them is sneaking away to cheat." Mary Margaret understood, having weathered a cheating spouse herself.

He nodded. "And if I look around, doubting relationships I'm not a part of, how am I supposed to trust enough to love again?" Which would have been an innocent confession if not for the sly look he gave her, as if she might be the one person who could earn his trust.

She needed to turn the conversational ship around

to safer waters. "I'm a horrible person." Disqualified as Kevin's love interest. "I'm a kindergarten teacher devoid of holiday spirit."

"I'm worse." Kevin nodded subtly toward a couple in the opposite corner who were arguing with each other. "I see bad relationships the way pregnant women see only pregnant women. They're everywhere."

Mary Margaret chuckled. After a moment, Kevin joined her.

They both sat back and drank their coffee, staring at each other as if they'd been friends for a long time and these admissions were no big deal, nothing to be shocked about. Certainly, it wasn't flirting.

And that's when Mary Margaret realized she wasn't done unburdening herself. "Derek kept thinking God owed him this huge jackpot for taking him in his prime. But even when he lost, that didn't stop him from buying all the things he'd ever wanted, all the things he didn't have enough time to enjoy. I shouldn't resent him for that. He's dead. My dad taught me how to forgive."

"Let's not bring your dad into this." Kevin waved a hand as if he were wiping that last comment off the board. "Barb didn't love Randy," he said flatly, referencing the man his wife had cheated with. "She just didn't love *me*. It's hard to look back on my marriage. Did she ever love me? Or was it the idea of Kevin Hadley, politician with a bright future, that she loved?"

"Well." Mary Margaret circled her coffee mug with both hands, blocking out whatever Christmas music was playing in the bakery. The iced scone with its Christmas tree sat untouched on her plate. "Christmas will eventually pass and I'll close out Derek's markers before the next holiday. There's hope for me and the Christmas spirit. But you, *my friend*, you will still have to wonder..."

"Nah." A glimmer of a smile cut through the grimness of the man. "Don't even go there. My first marriage was a fool-me-once episode. The next time I get married, it'll be for real. She'll be infinitely popular and highly trustworthy."

Mary Margaret ignored the ache in her chest. She wasn't going to be his next time. "What will this paragon of virtue have to do to prove herself? File an annual affidavit declaring her undying love for you?"

"Nothing that complicated." He leaned forward once more, the light in his dark eyes magnetic. "She'll have to catch fire when I kiss her."

Mary Margaret couldn't breathe, not even to reinforce that they were friends, because deep down in Lady Land something caught fire.

Kevin held her gaze. He held her gaze with eyes that were the tinder to the answering flame inside her. "She'll have to catch fire and melt in my arms."

Mary Margaret didn't know if that was a promise or a threat.

But just for a moment, she didn't care.

＊

Short on time to get to Victorian choir practice, Edith barreled out of the dentist's office and into the chest of a very tall, very solid man.

Strong arms came around her. "It must be my lucky day."

Edith vaguely recognized that deep voice, that hint

of an accent, but she breathed in Old Spice and leather and imagined, for just a few moments, that the arms encircling her belonged to Charlie. No one but Mims and Mary Margaret ever hugged her anymore.

A wave of melancholy struck. She gripped the leather lapels of the man's jacket.

"What's the matter, sweet one?" Hands claimed her upper arms and gently moved her a step away.

She had to tilt her head very far back to register that strong chin, those pale blue eyes, the shift of a crumpled red stir stick from one side of his mouth to the other.

Oh, fudge nuggets.

This was one of the men who'd vandalized Mary Margaret's car the other night when she hadn't given them money.

"Did you slash my tires?" Edith's boots slipped on a patch of ice, and she would have gone down if not for his strong hand on her arm once more. "I don't have any money."

"I don't recall asking for any of yours," he said with a sly smile.

Edith liked a man with a sense of humor. But—safety alert—she shouldn't be attracted to this man. She shouldn't even like him.

"Would you recommend this dentist?" Still smiling, he cast a thumb in the direction of the office. "I was eating a pistachio, and one of my fillings popped out."

Edith was speechless. She was never speechless. This ruffian needed the mundane services of a dentist. "I…uh…I have to go." Although at the moment she couldn't remember why, so she didn't move out of his grip.

"I like your hair." His faded blue eyes roved over her short auburn hair. "It's as wild and unpredictable as you are."

Was she wild? Her clean teeth didn't seem to belong to a wild woman.

Was that a compliment or a tease? She didn't know.

David knew how to give out compliments. She always knew where she stood with him.

David.

Edith slipped out of the man's arms. "I have to go. I'm going to be late." She turned and started walking toward her car.

"Merry Christmas," he called after her.

"Merry Christmas." She didn't look back. She had five minutes to get to the Victorian choir rehearsal at the retirement home. Five minutes to insert herself into David's life and show him how well she fit. She'd read all that magazine advice. He was going to love her. They'd date for a year or two, long enough for Edith to serve a few terms on the Widows Club board. And then she'd say yes to a very simple dress, a civil ceremony, and they'd live happily ever after in the retirement home.

Edith sped the two blocks down the street, turned into the parking lot, and found a space. Lipstick. Cheerful Christmas ornament hair clips over her not-wild hair (*what was that man thinking?*). And a check to make sure her blue eye shadow hadn't faded during her dental cleaning.

David wasn't going to know what hit him.

Edith waved to Beatrice at the reception desk as she scurried past and into the rec room. "I'm sorry I'm late." She tossed her purse and jacket on an empty chair.

Thirteen heads turned her way, ten of them female, one of them David. His white hair and mustache were like a beacon. She veered toward him.

"Can I help you?" Mr. Patrick, the high school music and drama teacher, quirked an eyebrow at her.

"I want to join the choir." Edith smiled for all she was worth, prepared to smile until they all saw she was one of them.

"Have you performed with a choir before?" Mr. Patrick was a hard sell, probably because he dealt with teenagers all day. "What are your singing credits?"

"I sing every day in my shower." *Take that image, David, and see if you can resist me.* "I'm quite good."

"We have a performance this Friday at the town tree lighting ceremony," Mr. Patrick said, preparing to let her down easy. "I'm afraid it's—"

"The perfect time to join given you'll be singing well-known Christmas carols." Edith's cheeks began to hurt from smiling. As a child, her mother had been late signing Edith up for everything. Edith had had to smile her way onto every club, team, and special project she'd ever wanted.

Mr. Patrick hesitated.

"You aren't seriously considering letting her in." That was Patti Potter. Thin nose in the air, she clung to David's arm.

A pox on her.

Patti was in the Widows Club but she'd never gone to a board meeting and she wasn't a vice president.

"Technically, I have to give everyone a chance." But the music teacher didn't look happy about it.

Edith wasn't here to make him happy. She was here to

show David how much they had in common. Mission accomplished. She thanked Mr. Patrick and surged forward to David's side.

"We'll offer you a tryout with 'The Twelve Days of Christmas.'" Mr. Patrick clapped his hands twice. "Places everyone."

The original twelve choir members formed ranks. Edith elbowed Patti aside.

"Oh, darn. This lacks symmetry." Mr. Patrick scurried to Edith. "We're going to have to put you over here." He took Edith by the arm and positioned her five bodies away from her man.

I can work with this.

Edith leaned over to smile at David. She had to smile past Alise, Karen, Maya, Kirk, and Patti, but smile she did.

"Edith, eyes on me." Mr. Patrick pointed two fingers at his eyes. "You'll be singing the opening line—*On the first day of Christmas*—and then each soloist will sing the gift while you're silent." He made a pinching gesture in front of his mouth. "When we get to the second and subsequent days, you'll sing the countdown—with the exception of the golden rings line. That's Patti's part."

"Gotcha."

Mr. Patrick blew into a little harmonica, and everyone hummed his note, even Edith.

This is going to be fun.

They chorused the introductory line, "*On the first day of Christmas…*"

They led up to David singing, "*A partridge in a pear tree.*"

Edith moved to the other side of Alise.

They all belted out the second day of Christmas line.

"*Two turtledoves*," sang Alise.

Then came the partridge part, and then as they chorused the third day line, Edith made her move, squirming past Karen.

"*Three French hens*," sang Henry from the back row.

Mr. Patrick gave Edith a sideways look but she thought that might be because he was surprised by the quality of her singing. In any case, she got around Maya as the choir chorused about the fourth day of Christmas. She made her move past Kirk between French hens and turtledoves.

Success!

The only thing standing between Edith and her man was Patti.

"On the fifth day of Christmas…"

Patti had turned her head and was singing into Edith's ear. And then she belted out, "*Five golden rings!*"

It was Edith's moment.

Except Patti began flapping her elbows like she was a calling bird, a French hen, a turtledove, *and* a partridge in a pear tree.

Edith flapped back, assuming it was part of the performance.

Mr. Patrick clapped twice. Everyone stopped singing. "Edith. There are rules in our choir, the first of which is what I say goes."

"And I say she goes," Patti said in a nasty voice.

"I'm afraid so." Mr. Patrick led Edith over to her things. "You can try out again after the holidays."

"What?" Edith's insides tumbled. She hadn't been refused admittance in anything, anywhere, since she hadn't gotten into college, since Daddy had called her stupid and she'd believed him. She always outlasted every obstacle, every objection, every door slammed in her face.

"You're out," Patti said in that snarky voice of hers.

Snooty Patti was right. Edith was out. She was too short, too round, too brash. Edith's throat burned with the truth. Why would David want someone like her when he could have Snooty Patti?

"That's rather harsh." Mr. Patrick put his arm around Edith. "You have a lovely singing voice but it's just not convenient at this time. We've rehearsed for weeks. I'll let you know when we have tryouts for next year's choir."

"Out." Patti smirked.

"Until tryouts." Edith smirked back, recovering some of her confidence. It wasn't a complete save. But she couldn't give up David completely. She caught his eye and made the call me sign.

He smiled back, a pearly white, genuine kind of smile without crowns or silver fillings. Her tummy stopped spinning with failure. And then David held up his cell phone and began tapping.

His message came through before Edith left the building.

Drinks someday soon?

Heck to the yeah!
Who needed the Victorian choir when she had a date with David?

✳

"Thanks for letting me hire you as Mrs. Claus on such short notice." Rosalie placed a red velvet beret on the white wig Mary Margaret wore.

"Isn't that what you do in a small town?" Mary Margaret had agreed despite her admission to Kevin that she had no holiday spirit. She'd been going through the motions this year. What was one more motion? "You pitch in."

She and Rosalie stood in the cramped restroom of the pet store, preparing for the Santa & Friends Photo Experience that preceded the town's annual Christmas tree lighting ceremony. Rosalie's dogs, a Saint Bernard and a scrappy little terrier, patiently watched Mary Margaret's transformation.

"Yep." Rosalie took in Mary Margaret's appearance with a critical eye. "The Mr. and Mrs. Claus I booked from Greeley came down with that stomach flu that's going around. This is the second year in a row I've scrambled for a Santa."

"I'm glad to help." Mary Margaret had been recommended for the job by Kevin and had seen it as something of a challenge to accept. Besides, every little bit of money helped. "How do I look?" Mary Margaret turned to look in the small mirror over the sink. "Oh."

Her red velvet dress was made for a much plumper Mrs. Claus. It gathered and hung limply. Her wig of white curls needed a trip to the salon. She looked down at her hemline, which hit her mid-ankle, and realized her wire spectacles were actually prescription bifocals. Her head gave a little spin.

Compared to Mrs. Claus, Rosalie was stylin' in slimming green trousers, a red cropped sweater, a green

Santa hat and green pointed sneakers. Her short dark hair curled playfully at her neck.

"I think you look more like a suffragette after a march to obtain the vote than Mrs. Claus." Rosalie was spot on. "But it was the best costume I could come up with in one afternoon. Mims had these outfits in her closet." She sighed. "What would we do without the Widows Club?"

Mary Margaret nodded. "Be prepared. That's their motto." It wouldn't be the end of the world to join their ranks.

Rosalie fluffed Mary Margaret's velvet skirt. "The kids won't care how you look. They'll be more interested in the baby animals and the big man on the throne, making sure they tell him exactly what they want for Christmas. Are you sure you'll be okay ushering them on and off stage?"

"I teach twenty-six kindergartners every day. I'll be fine as long as my students don't recognize me." And as long as the fashion police didn't storm the pet store. She lowered her glasses to the end of her nose so she could see over the rims without falling sideways. "Let's do this."

They stepped out of the ladies' room and into chaos. The line to have a picture with Old Saint Nick was out the door and the crowd noise ear-stuffing. Most had brought pets to be included in the photo. Cats meowed in carriers. Bunnies twitched nervous noses at dogs of every breed, shape, and size. Rosalie's Saint Bernard and terrier trotted toward the sales counter, plopping on a large red and green dog bed that was situated to one side.

Kids pointed at Mary Margaret and called out, *"Mrs. Claus!"*

She waved back, tension easing because none of the children called her Mrs. Sneed. The parents smiled indulgently. No one seemed to care that her dress barely reached her ankles or that she was nearly six feet tall.

Rosalie knocked on the storage room door. "Santa? Are you decent?"

A masculine voice behind the door told them to come in. At the same time, a young woman's voice called to Rosalie.

"I've got to help my cashier." Rosalie craned her neck to see what the problem was. "Are you okay helping Kevin?"

"But... I thought your husband, Everett, was Santa," Mary Margaret whispered furtively, suddenly as dizzy as if she'd been looking through her glasses.

Rosalie clutched her stomach. "He's got the bug too."

"Come in," Kevin repeated from the storage room. "Mr. Claus is decent."

Mary Margaret had no choice but to help her pretend husband. To hesitate meant to risk a riot in the store. She opened the door and then shut herself in with temptation—a man dressed in red and a bushy amount of fake white hair.

"I'm having trouble with my bowlful of jelly." Kevin stood in red velvet pants held up by suspenders. His pillow padding hung high on his broad chest, right under his fake white beard. He looked a mess, and, to her, kind of sweet. He made a mopey face. "Help me, Mrs. Claus."

"Turn around, Santa." Mary Margaret adjusted his straps in the back, reached around his chest with both hands, and yanked the quilted padding down.

"That was some hug." Kevin looked at her over his shoulder, a tease in his eyes. "Are you feeling the Christmas spirit?"

"Are you prepared to greet a slew of happy children and their pets?" she shot back.

"Ho-ho-ho. Looking good, Mrs. Claus." He had a wicked smile despite that white beard.

She wouldn't let herself fall for it. "We're friends, remember? We were pathetic together. That's not sexy." *Oh but it was.* She'd looked for him in the audience at the Hanky Panky all week. She took his jacket from the hanger and helped him into it. "We need to hurry, Santa. The natives are getting restless. Fair warning. I saw the requests my students wrote to Santa. Most were longer than my arm."

Kevin stopped buttoning his velvet jacket and took her forearm with both hands. "That's long, even for kids who don't deserve coal."

"And another thing." Mary Margaret drew her arm back into the neutral zone, resting her hand on her stomach in the hopes it would squelch the flutter of attraction caused by his touch. "I saw a student from my class out there. Louise tends to need the bathroom when she gets excited. And when she's startled, she's a nervous vomiter."

Kevin's eyes widened in mock horror. "I'll try not to scare her or hype her up." He gave a practice *ho-ho-ho*. "Anything else I should know?"

That she found him attractive? That despite the challenge she'd thrown at him at the bakery, she feared she'd never find her holiday spirit again? That she was deathly afraid Laurel and Hardy would be disappointed with whatever money she made this week and do more than slit her tires?

"Mary Margaret?" Kevin's brows lowered in a look of concern.

"Nothing." She forced a smile. "I'm filled with holiday cheer."

"And I feel great joy at seeing other couples walk arm in arm. Not a doubt in my mind that they aren't happy and won't be forever and ever." Kevin joked as he threaded the black belt through the thin loops at his sides. "Scrooge and the jaded bachelor. We were made for each other."

If for no other reason than they were poor choices for anyone else. She no longer had to force her smile.

A child shrieked on the other side of the door. A dog barked, which set off several more in the line.

"Let's go, Santa." Mary Margaret picked up his bulky green bag and handed it to him. It was loaded with photo frames made and donated by his father, frames that would presumably be filled by the pictures they were about to take.

Kevin slung the bag over his shoulder, clattering wrapped frames in the process. "Mrs. Claus." He held out an arm, a twinkle in his eye beneath the shaggy wig, bushy white brows, and thick beard. "Shall we?"

"We shall." Unable to resist his charm, Mary Margaret took his arm. They were married, after all, at least for the next two hours.

Rosalie and Everett had set a chair fit for the King of the North Pole. There were two steps up to the stage where the large chair awaited. A backdrop of green velvet curtains had been hung behind it.

They walked to the throne to the enthusiastic cries of

children. It didn't matter that Kevin and Mary Margaret were tall or that they didn't fill out their costumes. They were like K-pop stars to teenage girls.

Kevin stopped at the sight, spread his arms and said, "Is that my throne?"

The kids let out shrill, enthusiastic affirmations.

Rosalie stepped behind the camera mounted on a tripod. She had some high school kids working the register and standing guard over the litter of puppies in the store window.

Kevin turned, playing to the crowd. "That's where the magic happens, boys and girls. That's where you'll tell me what you want for Christmas." He let out a deep *ho-ho-ho*.

Won over, Mary Margaret giggled, along with the forty or so children who'd squeezed into the store.

Maybe there was hope for her yet.

*

While Rosalie took care of some last minute details, Kevin stared into Mary Margaret's bespectacled eyes.

He appreciated a good sport. Mary Margaret had come in on short notice and embraced the role as the wife to his jolly old elf. He hadn't seen her since their dual meltdowns at the bakery. They'd finished their coffees and said their good-byes without so much as a hug or a Merry Christmas. Since then, he'd been practicing smooth lines to inform her she was most likely being investigated by his political party.

Maybe he wouldn't have to tell her. It wasn't as if they'd find anything detrimental to his career in her past.

Mary Margaret self-consciously tugged at her red velvet beret.

"How's that holiday spirit holding up, Mrs. Claus?" Kevin had to raise his voice above the boisterous crush waiting to have their picture taken with Santa.

"Any progress on finding that paragon of virtue?" Mary Margaret's smile was soft, her voice uncertain.

He waggled his fake white eyebrows, the ones pasted on top of his own. "Are you interested in applying for the role?"

Before she could answer, Rosalie climbed on the dais with Kevin and called for quiet. "The second annual Santa & Friends Photo Experience is about to start. For five dollars, you'll receive a photo and a photo frame donated by Hadley Furniture. All proceeds benefit the Friends of Sunshine Animal Rescue. Let's get this photo shoot started by giving Santa a big round of applause."

Clapping, Mary Margaret moved toward the mother-daughter duo at the front of the line.

Rosalie darted behind the camera.

"Santa!" A cute little girl walked up to him holding Mary Margaret's hand. She had neat brown pigtails, big brown eyes, and a name tag that said Ella.

At the bottom step, the little munchkin dug in her pink snow boots. Mary Margaret couldn't encourage her up the stairs to Kevin's lap.

Rosalie hurried over with a small white puppy with curly hair and a shiny red bow. She set the ball of fluff in Kevin's arms and turned to the girl holding up the line. "Don't you want to pet the puppy, sweetie?"

"Oh, she's evil," Ella's mother, Tamara Whitfield, scowled at Rosalie. "We don't need another dog."

"It's not a dog." Rosalie grinned like she'd won the lottery. "It's a puppy. And we encouraged kids to bring their pets."

You shouldn't be associated with unhappy parents. That was Barb's hypersensitive voice in Kevin's head. When she'd been in charge of his schedule, she'd kept him away from events like this.

Always give the public what they want. That was his father's voice. As was, *you won't be around for me to pass the mantle of Hadley Furniture.*

The chair Kevin sat on was a Hadley product. He rolled his cramping right shoulder and shifted in his seat.

"Santa?" Mary Margaret looked concerned.

"I'm fine." Stupid shoulder injury always acted up when he was stressed. "Just waiting for Ella." Kevin pitched his voice low and waved the hesitant girl forward. "Rosalie's puppy wants to hear what you want for Christmas."

Eventually, Mary Margaret was able to coax the little girl up to the throne. She turned Ella so she faced the camera. "Tell Santa what you want, honey."

"I want... I want..." Ella's eyes glazed with fear. Her hand was on the puppy. "I want a puppy!"

Tamara frowned. Ella's eyes filled with tears, and her expression crumpled. A puppy was clearly not on her list but she was too frightened by meeting Santa to remember what she wanted.

"Ella," Kevin said and patted her head. "I know you didn't have a puppy on your list before today."

"I didn't." The little angel turned her face toward him, wonder in her brown eyes. "I asked for a Barbie Jeep with a real engine for me to ride in and a BB gun because

Dad says I'm going to be a hunter. And don't forget the rolls of colored duct tape to make friendship bracelets. They don't carry them at Emory's."

"That's a Colorado girl for you." Kevin grinned and let out a bellyful of *ho-ho-ho*'s.

Rosalie snapped pictures.

"We love Santa." Tamara gave Kevin two thumbs-up.

Ella slid off his lap and then buried her face in the puppy's fur. "But I'd love a puppy. *This* puppy."

"And Santa crashes and burns." Ella's mother rolled her eyes.

"Do you know what, Ella?" Kevin asked. "There's a rule that Santa can't bring puppies or kittens to boys and girls. Only mommies and daddies can give those as gifts."

"You never should have doubted him," Mary Margaret said to Tamara, handing her a photo frame. She turned to Ella, taking the puppy. "Come on, girlie. I bet you've got some shopping to do before the Christmas tree lighting ceremony later."

An event Kevin had promised to emcee.

The next few kids and pets were pros and didn't make a scene. And then it was Tad's turn.

"Rosalie should've given you a mask." Mary Margaret put her glasses on Kevin and slid his hat lower on his forehead.

A mask? That reminded him of Foxy Roxy. "Santa doesn't need a sexy mask," he whispered to her, causing Mary Margaret to give him a double-take. But he had no time to dissect the meaning of that look. Tad approached with Chester, Kevin's father's Labrador, in tow.

Tad's hand covered his name tag, a test to see if Santa knew his name.

"*Ho-ho-ho.* Come on up, Thaddeus."

His son turned to Kevin's mother. "He knows my name, Grandma." Tad ran up the steps and into Kevin's lap, beating Chester, who settled for resting his broad, brown head on Kevin's knee. "Santa, I bet you know what I want for Christmas too. I sent you a letter."

"*Ho-ho-ho.*" Not wanting to disappoint his son, Kevin lifted his gaze to Mary Margaret's in a plea for help. "Sometimes Mrs. Claus opens the mail."

Mary Margaret hurried to Kevin's side and whispered in his ear. "A fire truck, a drone, and a gift card to the Saddle Horn."

"So, little Thaddeus, you like the Saddle Horn, do you?" Kevin's low pitch was building a scratch in his throat. "Don't your mom and dad take you there often enough?" He was teasing. Barb took Tad there every Sunday.

Tad shook his head and said in a furtive voice, "Mommy says mile-high whips make me fat. When we go, I get an egg with yucky cheese and a water."

Kevin's heart contracted, leaving him breathless. Depriving Tad of a hot chocolate when other kids had one? His ex-wife had gone too far.

"I'm not supposed to tell Daddy." Tad faced the camera, fingering the snaps on his jacket. "If I had a gift card, I could go on my own."

"You should never go alone." Kevin held Tad like the precious, fragile person he was, silently vowing to take his son to breakfast every Sunday from now on. "I'll tell you a secret, Thaddeus. Mile-high whips don't make you fat. Your mommy doesn't know that yet." But she will, he vowed, putting his bearded cheek next to Tad's face. "Smile for the camera and say Merry Christmas."

"Merry Christmas!" Tad cried with his usual exuberance. Rosalie snapped several pictures.

Kevin helped Tad get down but he was ready for his reign as Santa to end. He needed to find Barb and put an end to this body shaming. Tad was a healthy eater. And like many kids, he bulked up a bit before he grew. Just last year, he'd put on some weight and then had grown two inches in two weeks, slimming down in the process. How could Barb forget that?

"Here comes Louise," Mary Margaret announced as she led a little blond girl up to Kevin.

Louise. The nervous wetter and fearful vomiter.

Louise stumbled to a stop at the base of the stairs and stared at Kevin as if he were the boogeyman and had just crawled out from under her bed. A small white mouse poked its nose out of her shirt pocket, sniffed, and then retreated.

"*Ho-ho-ho*, Louise."

"Santa, Louise wants to make sure you received her letter," Mary Margaret said cheerfully. "And her mother would like a picture of the three of us."

"*No.*" Louise shook her head, leaning backward against Mary Margaret's hands.

Mary Margaret glanced back at Kathy Franklin.

"Louise, baby, I was hoping to send your picture to Grampy in Denver." Kathy gave her daughter a watery smile.

"Louise, you like to have fun, don't you?" What had she been doing the other day when he'd visited Mary Margaret's classroom? Ah yes. "You like to color. I like to color too. But I don't always color in the lines." He leaned forward, resting his arm on his knee. "But you and I both know that doesn't matter, does it? Colors on the paper are pretty no matter what lines they cross."

Louise mounted the first stair. Mouth open, she nodded.

"That's why I'm going to give you lots of blank paper to color on this year."

"Ohhh." She climbed up another step. "Thank you," she breathed, twirling her thin blond hair.

"Can you coax your mouse out, turn around, and smile for Grampy?" He gently encouraged Louise to face the camera while Mary Margaret took her place on the other side of him. The mouse was nowhere to be seen.

Once turned around, Louise realized everyone in line was looking at her. She backed up into Kevin, and then glanced at him over her shoulder with a frightened expression, gagging.

"It's okay, Louise." He patted her back, urging her forward slightly. "Don't be afraid. *Ho-ho-ho.*"

Louise convulsed.

Kathy and Mary Margaret rushed for the little girl. Mary Margaret got there first, just in time for Louise to projectile vomit on Mrs. Claus's dress.

Both females froze. The people in line for photos quieted. Kevin's planned *ho-ho-ho* stuck in his throat.

"I am so sorry." Kathy produced wipes from her purse. She concentrated on cleaning up her daughter. "We stopped for a quick bite to eat before we got in line."

"It's all right," Mary Margaret said in a small voice. "Excuse me, honey. Merry Christmas." She disappeared in the direction of the bathroom.

"No worries." Unperturbed, Rosalie appeared with paper towels and disinfectant spray. "Good thing we're used to pet accidents."

"You see? It's okay." Kathy reached into Louise's pocket. "Snowflake's okay too." She shepherded her daughter toward the exit. "Come on, sweetie. Let's get you home."

"*Ho-ho-ho.*" Kevin stood and waved to kids in the back of the line, the ones who hadn't witnessed the disaster.

A few minutes later, Mary Margaret returned in her street clothes, Ms. Sneed once more. "I've been downgraded to volunteer elf."

"Are you okay?" Kevin felt traumatized.

"I'm fine." Her smile proved it. "Kindergarten teacher, remember? I'm used to accidents and upset stomachs...at least from kids, not bulls. Besides, the show must go on."

And go on it did.

Nearly two hours later, Kevin had been rejected by crying babies, growled at by nervous dogs, glared at by suspicious toddlers, and told he wasn't the real Santa by at least a dozen older kids. But he'd also been hugged, squeezed, slobbered on, and grinned at. Playing Santa was a lot like being a politician. You didn't know what you were going to get from one minute to the next. You just had to roll with the punches. Kind of like kindergarten teachers too, he supposed.

"What a turnout," Kevin said when Rosalie finally called a halt to the event. "Where did they all come from?"

"I advertised in Greeley." Rosalie was unapologetic about the crush. "It was a success, don't you think? We sent home two puppies, three kittens, and four bunnies. Plus, the cash register was ringing the entire time. And best of all, we raised over five hundred dollars in donations for the local animal shelter."

Mary Margaret accompanied Kevin to the back room

where she helped him out of his padding. Now was the perfect time to tell her he'd slipped up during his screening interview and implied they were almost a thing. But before he could say anything, Mary Margaret stepped out.

When Kevin was beardless and back in his street clothes, he joined Mary Margaret and Rosalie out in the shop.

"You guys were great." Rosalie handed them each an envelope.

Mary Margaret stared at it, then she handed it back. "Add it to the donation."

Kevin did the same.

"Really?" Rosalie gushed and hugged them. "You two are the greatest. Merry Christmas!"

Mary Margaret and Kevin walked out the pet shop door. The sidewalk was bustling with holiday shoppers. "All I Want for Christmas" was playing through the speakers in the town square.

"That was nice of you to donate your pay." Especially when he knew she needed the money.

"I'll tell you a secret I learned growing up." Her smile was tentative, as if her secret was sad. "Preacher's kid wisdom. There's always someone in a worse situation than you are. In this case, there are homeless animals worse off than me."

"I know that was a test of your holiday spirit, Mrs. Claus." He brushed a lock of red hair over her shoulder. "I don't think your Christmas batteries are as low as you originally thought."

"And you can't be as jaded about relationships as you claim." Her smile strengthened. "Anyone who saw Lola and Drew with little Becky today couldn't deny they'd found their happily ever after."

"Point taken." The couple had beaten the odds. Kevin stopped in the middle of the sidewalk, reaching for her gloved hand. "Some couples you just know will make it." Like them. He had a good feeling about Mary Margaret and him.

"Merry Christmas, Mr. Mayor!" Edith called from across the street.

Mary Margaret tried to slip her hand free.

"I've got to check in with my staff." Kevin pulled Mary Margaret out of the foot traffic to the window in front of the Sewing Emporium. "Will I see you later at the tree lighting ceremony?"

"Yes." She took a black knit cap from her pocket and pulled it on. "The Widows Club is selling hot chocolate. Make sure you bring Tad by for a cup."

His son. Hot chocolate. Kevin's shoulders tensed.

He had to find his ex-wife and have a discussion about their son and calorie counting.

Chapter Eight

✳

All I want for Christmas . . .

The song was playing on the speakers in the town square. Mary Margaret didn't dare complete that thought as Kevin disappeared into the crowd.

"Rough day, Mrs. Claus?" Mr. Hardy materialized at Mary Margaret's right shoulder. "You look spent."

"Those little angels can be hell." The tall Mr. Laurel bookended her on the left, red stir stick in the corner of his mouth.

Grandma Edith called her name. She had yet to cross the street. Mary Margaret led the men away from her.

"Gentlemen, you don't need to follow me." Unless they'd decided she wasn't able to zero-out Derek's balance owed and had decided to rub her out. "I'm gathering funds."

Fear tingled through her veins. Somehow, Mary Margaret kept walking down Main Street toward the town square, even though her legs felt like kinked pipe cleaners. Since the last time she'd paid them, she'd earned two grand. Helping Ned turn his business around was increasing her profit.

Mr. Hardy chuckled. "Given there's not much to do in this town, we're curious about where—or if—you're earning extra money."

The pipe cleaners developed another set of kinks. Mary Margaret's steps faltered. She stopped. The gathering darkness closed in. Grandma Edith's calls grew louder.

"Hope you got paid good money for that Claus gig." Mr. Hardy assumed the hip-rocking position, legs spread, hands in his jacket pockets. "'Cuz you know you need to maximize your income."

Ahead on the town square, the local Victorian choir began to sing "God Rest Ye Merry Gentlemen." Store windows sparkled with lights and gift ideas. Shoppers laughed and gave voice to snatches of carols. Sunshine was picturesque and peaceful. There should be no darkness here, no threat. Just as there should have been no darkness or threat as a child of a minister.

The unfairness of her situation shored up her shaky legs and pushed that rebellious streak she tried to contain up her throat. "If you were looking for lunch money, I donated my pay." It was the kind of comment that used to test her father's patience.

"That wasn't smart, considering your position." Mr. Laurel's expression saddened. The stir stick drooped. "We'll be by on Sunday morning for our next payment."

"And it better be a big one." Mr. Hardy broke away from her, crossing the street toward the movie theater with his tall partner following in his footsteps.

Mary Margaret shivered.

"Hey." Grandma Edith appeared at her side, panting. "Didn't you hear me calling your name?"

"No. Sorry."

Edith walked ahead a few paces and then returned to claim Mary Margaret's arm and tug her along. "Don't dally. We've got hot chocolate to sell." And then she huffed. "It's not like they're going to let us sing in the choir."

Mary Margaret's legs worked but were stiff and stilted.

"Are those new boots?" Edith admired the black boots that had escaped Louise's upset stomach. "Do they hurt your feet? Is that why you're walking funny?"

A group of teenagers crossed their path. The Bodine twins nodded a greeting.

"We love our tutor," one of them said with a laugh that made Mary Margaret grind her teeth since it wasn't true.

"You're tutoring the Bodine boys?" Edith adjusted her cream-colored scarf beneath her bright red hair and hurried to keep up with Mary Margaret. "Good. I recommended you to Tom. I was hoping he'd ask you out."

"I thought you said I wasn't ready to date." Mary Margaret's gaze drifted toward the center tree where Kevin stood surrounded by his staff. If he knew about her real second job at the Hanky Panky, he'd stop being her friend, stop trying to be something more. She wasn't sure she could bear that.

What a fool I am.

Edith followed the direction of her gaze, smirking. "*Kevin.* After some consideration, I don't think he's right for you. Why don't you come over tonight? We'll put on music, make cookies, and dance around the kitchen while we talk about our dating prospects." She turned Mary Margaret's shoulders toward the far end of the town square. "Tom Bodine is single. And you're brave enough to help his boys."

"Tom Bodine is at least a decade older than I am." And unyielding when it came to disagreements.

"Come over to dance." Grandma Edith gave her a one-armed hug. "There are other single men in town. Maybe not as wealthy as Tom but—"

"I have plans tonight." She was dancing elsewhere.

"What? You'll turn down cookies and pop music?" Her grandmother *tsk*ed. "Are we still on for our annual trip to get a Christmas tree tomorrow?"

Mary Margaret wanted to say no but she nodded. Just because her holiday spirit was at an all-time low didn't mean she had to bring Grandma Edith down with her.

Across the street, Laurel and Hardy leaned against a light pole, staring their way. Mr. Laurel's shoulders were hunched against the cold.

As they neared the hot chocolate table, Mary Margaret glanced up at the sky and its smattering of clouds. "Is it supposed to snow tonight?"

"Not until tomorrow morning." Edith stared right back at Laurel and Hardy, feet slowing, mouth drawn toward one side, a predictor of trouble.

It was Mary Margaret's turn to tug her grandmother along. "Can I borrow Grandpa's motorcycle?"

"You want to tool around on two wheels with snow on the ground?"

"There's no snow on the ground. They plowed the roads." The important ones between here and Greeley.

And like any Sunshine resident, Mary Margaret knew where there was the likelihood of black ice.

"I always thought you took Derek's passing a little too well." Grandma Edith shook her head. "This is your meltdown then? Some odd phase of grief where you date a dangerous man? Or are you testing your mortality on two wheels?"

"Don't overthink this, Grandma." Mary Margaret turned her back on the thugs in case they could read lips, which meant she faced Kevin at the podium. "I want to go somewhere, and I don't want anyone to recognize my car."

"Oh. *Incognito.* That's an entirely different story." Grandma Edith glanced toward a cluster of women standing near Kevin, a cluster which included Barbara, who held Tad's hand but stared at her ex-husband the way a hawk stared at plump, young prairie dogs. "Did the former Mrs. Mayor find out you had a drink with Mr. Mayor at Shaw's the other night?"

"Shhh." Mary Margaret drew her grandmother close. "How did you—"

"Mims had closed-circuit cameras installed at the bar," Edith said, straight-faced. And then she laughed. "That's a fib. I saw Noah at the grocery store, and he asked if you were all right. Apparently, you ordered a daiquiri and then bolted, which had him worried. The only way you'd be worried in a bar was if you were afraid Barbara might find out you and the mayor were running around *incognito.*"

"I wasn't thinking of Barbara when I ordered that daiquiri."

"Ahhh." Grandma Edith slowed to a stop, attention

drawn to the Victorian choir gathering near Kevin. "You found someone other than Kevin. That's my girl."

Mary Margaret sighed. It wasn't worth the time it would take to convince Grandma Edith otherwise. "Does this mean I can borrow the bike?"

"As long as you promise me you'll be careful on the road but a little wild in…" She giggled. "You get the idea."

Mary Margaret let her grandmother make assumptions. She faced her fellow widows. "How can I help?"

"Edith, did I hear you say Mary Margaret is dating?" Mims wore a thick brown jacket with lots of utility pockets and a welcoming smile. Her hair had been washed with silver rinse, and all her white curls had been gelled into short spikes that waved in the wind like a wheat field.

Barbara's work. Not her best.

"No, I'm not seeing anyone," Mary Margaret said at the same time her grandmother said, "She's found a mystery man." Grandma Edith made it sound exciting.

"I'm getting out in the world," Mary Margaret allowed, because the Widows Club board had been nothing but kind to her since Derek's death. "I like what you've done with your hair, Mims."

The Widows Club president blushed and glanced across the square at the Victorian choir where David Jessup was smiling at any woman over the age of sixty in his vicinity.

"I like it too." Clarice leaned on her wooden staff. "It's important to remember you're widowed, not dead."

"And to let yourself have fun once in a while." Bitsy wore a pristine white jacket with faux fur trim and a jaunty beret that she pulled off with more ease than Mary Margaret had done in the pet store.

"It's normal to feel a bit of guilt when you re-enter the dating pool," Mims said, color high in her cheeks. She stared at David, who was laughing with several widows from the general club membership.

"When a widow finds the right man..." Edith stared at David too and fussed with the fringe of auburn hair peeking beneath her knit cap. "It hits you like a slap in the face."

"A gentle whisper," Bitsy said longingly.

"A warm bath," Mims murmured.

Clarice harrumphed, making the other widows laugh.

*

"Can you give me a ho-ho-ho?" Kevin stood in front of the largest pine tree in the town square, microphone in hand, working the crowd. "That's the spirit. If there's one thing you can count on in Sunshine, it's the long list of traditions we keep alive at the holidays. Tonight, we're lighting up Sunshine and our local Christmas Tree Lane. Tomorrow, many of you will make the trek to The Woodsman's Tree Farm for your Christmas tree. In a few weeks, we've got the Christmas parade and a Christmas ball."

The Widows Club cheered, understandable since they were the Christmas Ball sponsor.

Kevin scanned the crowd, eyes lighting on Mary Margaret. "I'd like to thank our town staff for putting up the lights tonight and the Widows Club for providing us with hot chocolate to keep us warm. Shaw's is extending happy hour until an hour after the lighting." He hoped Mary Margaret would attend. "The Widows Club will have a booth set up at Shaw's with gift advice, in case anyone needs it."

"Daddy." Tad tugged Kevin's jacket. "When are the lights coming on?"

"Soon." Kevin picked up his son. "Can you lead the town in a countdown?"

Tad nodded, grinning at the crowd. His son was comfortable in the spotlight and at the town hall.

But what about at Hadley's Furniture? And what about at the Saddle Horn?

The crowd shifted, restless. Kevin had a lot to work out, and now wasn't the time to do so.

"We're going to start at five and count backward. The lights will burn bright when we reach one." Kevin jiggled Tad. "Are you ready?"

"Yeah!" Tad shot one arm in the air, so enthusiastic he made Kevin's heart ache.

He couldn't allow Barb to steal their son's joy. And somehow he had to make sure Hadley Furniture would be there if his career stalled or if Tad ever wanted to carry on the business.

Putting the microphone near Tad, Kevin began the countdown. "Five. Four. Three. Two. *One!*"

The trees rimming the town square glowed with strands of white lights.

The assembled crowd cheered, turning slowly to appreciate the contrast of greenery and light. The old brick buildings surrounding the town square were blanketed in snow, windows glowing warmly. The town had a cozy, Dickensian feel.

The Victorian choir began to sing "The Twelve Days of Christmas." They sounded really good this year.

We are so lucky.

Kevin's gaze drifted to his parents, who stood arm-in-arm at the front of the crowd, smiling and laughing with their neighbors.

This is why no one wants Sunshine to change.

"Hot chocolate time." Tad slid to the ground, waited for Kevin to give him some money, and then ran to the Widows Club table.

Kevin handed off the microphone to one of his staff and followed.

Victor Yates, town council member and all-around prune of a person, stepped in his path. "You talk about traditions like you care. If you cared, you wouldn't support the distribution center."

"Not now, Victor." Kevin must not have sounded authoritative enough because Victor only got louder.

"You'll have to add more staff to the fire and sheriff's departments." Victor's volume and upset tone drew the attention of many, including Barb. "And you know crime is going to go up. One thousand parking spaces. That's a lot of employees."

"Careful, Victor." Kevin clung to his patience with the same tenacity Victor held on to his seat on the town council every election cycle. "Sunshine residents will be considered for jobs first. You wouldn't want to accuse your constituents of being criminals."

Victor swept that argument away with one gloved hand. "What about the quality of our drinking water? They won't be dumping chemicals into the river, will they?"

"If you'd read the environmental report, you'd know that's not true." Kevin scowled. "They're storing and distributing pre-made goods, not manufacturing." He tried to push past the older man.

Victor stepped in his way again. "It's not like we need the jobs, Kevin. Our unemployment rate is less than five percent."

"That's because most folks who can't find jobs move out of town and don't get counted as unemployed." That was it. Kevin's patience was lost. In its place, he found pulse-pounding anger. "You know this. Your nephew moved to Greeley last summer for just that reason."

"Don't tell me what I should know!" Victor roared. "Or you won't be the only name on the mayoral ballot next year."

The wind shimmied through the trees, trying just as hard to unsettle the Christmas lights as Victor was trying to unsettle Kevin.

"Hi." Mary Margaret separated herself from the thickening audience surrounding them. "Kevin, can I talk to you in private?"

"Excuse me, Victor." Kevin marched toward the hot chocolate table, muttering, "*Merry Christmas*," to anyone foolish enough to look like they might stand in his way.

"You looked like a man in need of a rescue." Mary Margaret had long legs that kept pace with him. "Or maybe a spiked hot chocolate. Slip Mims an extra five, and she's got you covered."

"Thanks." Kevin's entire body vibrated with tension.

Tad darted through the crowd toward Barb, hot chocolate in hand. Kevin hadn't yet had a chance to pull his ex-wife aside and have that *our-son-is-not-fat* conversation.

Barb was surrounded by a cluster of her busybody friends. Heads turned toward Mary Margaret and Kevin as they passed. Jaws moved as they exchanged gossip and speculation.

He gave them a casual wave, stopping a good distance between them and the hot chocolate table. "I've got to hand it to you, Mary Margaret. I couldn't face Victor with as much patience and grace as you showed with Louise earlier."

"Louise innocently upchucked on me." Mary Margaret glanced back at Victor, her red hair streaming in the wind beneath her black cap. "Victor was itching to start a fight in front of all these voters." But she nodded toward Barb and her friends when she said it.

"I may have divorced her but Barb is on my side." Kevin was certain of it.

"Don't kid yourself." Mary Margaret shook her head. "The more independent you become, the louder she'll voice her opinions against you."

Kevin started to deny it but on some level he knew what Mary Margaret said was true. "I hadn't realized you knew Barb so well."

"I don't." Mary Margaret's expression blinked from carefully neutral to carefully contained hurt. "My father was just like her." She ran a hand around the back of her neck. "Controlled, civil even, until people chose independence over obedience."

Kevin wanted to take Mary Margaret into his arms and hold her until the memories of dark days receded. But everyone was watching. He held her gaze instead. "If I could, I'd soothe all the pain in your past. And I'd give you my extra holiday cheer."

"You have some?" she teased.

"Yes." Kevin wanted to tell her he could be her rock but there was something in the way she held herself, stiffly and apart, not with pride but with endurance. She hadn't let her father break her. At the moment, it didn't look like she was going to let Derek's foolish decisions snap her either.

Mary Margaret squeezed his forearm. "Be careful with Barbara, for Tad's sake and your career. You're a politician. You have to be careful with everyone about everything."

"If you say I have to be careful with you..." Kevin didn't know how to complete that sentence. Luckily, his cell phone rang. He excused himself to take the call.

"I know it's late on a Friday night," Cray said. "But can you meet me at the silos? Alone?"

The future site of the controversial distribution center? Kevin agreed.

Chapter Nine

✳

"Why does this feel like a mob meeting?" Kevin said to Cray upon arrival at the silos.

His parents had gladly taken Tad for the night, although his dad hadn't looked Kevin in the eye when he'd asked. There was a rift between them that needed mending.

His old football teammate chuckled. "Should I check you for a wire, Kev?"

"Nah." But Kevin remained uneasy.

The old grain mill looked cheerful covered in snow. A string of holiday lights in the shape of a Christmas tree on one of the silos completed the look. The current owner had put up the lights years ago. He turned them on every holiday.

In the summer, the site wasn't so cheerful. The empty silos were rusted. Weeds grew through cracks in the asphalt. The office building was covered with graffiti. Local kids for ten miles each direction came here to skateboard and get up to no good.

Kevin shrugged deeper into his jacket and turned toward the interstate. He'd gotten state funding to build a stoplight there after two town residents had died trying to pull out onto the highway. The distribution center developers predicted one day there'd be an overpass here.

An overpass.

Doubt crept between his shoulders on spiked cleats. Being at the mill, imagining the changes that would take place, it became less of a puzzle piece necessary to his political rise. The worried words of his unhappy constituents echoed through his head, making him think about happy memories of Sunshine's holiday traditions, like tree lighting ceremonies and mile-high whips.

If the distribution center moved forward, life in Sunshine would change, not just the landscape but the people. He just hadn't realized how much until now.

"I have news." Cray stood next to his truck. "I got management to approve some of your community projects."

With Cray's concessions, many residents in Sunshine would change their minds about the distribution center, or at the very least be more open to the idea. And that's what scared Kevin. This project could really happen. For good or ill, rezoning the land so JPM Industries could open would change Sunshine and the surrounding communities. "I appreciate you going the extra mile."

"Then..." Cray frowned. "Why do I get the feeling you created that list to scare us off?"

Here was the real reason Cray had chosen to meet at this location alone. He wanted to talk to his former college football teammate without others around to hear.

Kevin sighed. "Do you remember our senior year? When our safety and two defensive ends went down before the championship game? Do you remember that win or lose, everything was going to be on the shoulders of the offense? On us? I'm looking up at those silos"—instead of keeping his head down and his feet moving forward—"and I'm wondering if this is much-needed change or a soul-sucking disaster."

"Kev." Cray clapped a hand on his shoulder. "You've never shirked your responsibilities before. If this is going to be an issue, let me know now. I can jump on our alternative location."

If Kevin said yes, Victor Yates would be happy. And smug. His father would worry less about the family business. But there were people who'd be disappointed in Kevin if he lost his nerve. And he believed with everything in his being that the town needed this to survive.

Cray shoved his hands in his jacket pockets. "No one can predict the impact of the distribution center with certainty, Kev. We just set up and run the plays the best we can."

"And hope for the best." Kevin stared at the man who'd protected him through four years of ground-pounding football. "Promise me your company will look to Sunshine residents first for hires, that they'll be environmentally responsible and continue to be a good partner to the community."

"You've got a contract and my word, man." Cray's gaze lowered. He resettled his booted feet in the un-plowed snow. "But you know what corporate America is like. If you aren't mayor and a Sunshine native isn't on the management team when the terms of our initial agreement run out, someone may change the contract and do what suits them, not Sunshine."

If all went as planned, Kevin wouldn't be mayor when the initial terms expired. Things could go south if, say, someone like Victor Yates was elected mayor. Or if the distribution center failed.

They stared up at the lights on the silo.

A Christmas tree. It represented a time of year to appreciate family and tradition, to reflect upon your life and that of your fellow man, to forgive, embrace, and count your blessings.

"I admit," Kevin said quietly, "this level of change scares me but I can't let the opportunity pass. The population of Sunshine has been diminishing annually for the past ten years. If we don't do something—"

"So, let's do something." Cray raised his arms as if signaling a touchdown. "Let's go down as the men who saved Sunshine." He wrapped Kevin in a bear hug.

Kevin patted his friend on the back. "Okay. I have a couple more weeks to garner support." Until the town council meeting before Christmas. "And those donations of yours will help."

"Geez, will you look at yourself?" Cray laughed, clapping Kevin's bad shoulder. "You're so tense. Go home and have a beer."

"I'll do that." But Kevin stared at the highway. In the direction of Greeley. And Foxy Roxy. He knew a place where the music was so loud that he couldn't think. But he could feel.

If Roxy was going to perform.

Not that he was headed that way. Not that a small town politician with more than his career at stake should be seen in a place like that.

✳

Kevin hadn't meant to drive into Greeley.

He hadn't meant to park at the dance club, pay the cover—which was higher than before—and find a seat at the bar.

He wasn't impulsive. He wasn't reckless. He had a political career with hopes of moving on.

But he was curious. And he wanted to understand why he was fascinated by a woman who danced no more provocatively than she would as a backup dancer for a pop star. And perhaps he wanted to live on the edge a little before he decided once and for all to be the squeaky-clean politician who lived a predictable, practical life with his predictable, practical kindergarten-teacher wife.

Kevin ordered a whiskey and soda on the rocks, watering down his drink as much as possible and vowing to make it last all night. And then he scanned the crowd for anyone he might know. It was a more complicated task than the last time he'd attended, since there were more people and customers continued to stream in. He watched them in the bar's mirror.

There were changes to the show too. It was no longer a stream of women put forth like they were in a dance competition where they got extra points for being sexy. There was a theme for the night too—eighties music. All the women danced to it. Some of the costumes were eighties throw-backs, if leg-warming garters and shoulder pads counted. They'd added group dance numbers, and the deejay was more than just an announcer in a tacky jacket. He actually seemed to be enjoying himself, telling a joke or two.

Heck, Kevin was enjoying himself, settling his elbows back on the bar and forgetting to check to see if anyone was watching him.

Roxy came out for her first solo performance dressed as a bride in a mini-dress. Her stockings were held up by white garters. Her high heels and mask were white, and her lipstick a vivid red. Her platinum hair was covered by a short wedding veil. As before, there was a single lock of red hair amidst the platinum.

Again, she challenged the crowd to watch, to engage, to be mesmerized. They were all of that and more. This time she only danced on stage. Again, the crowd surged forward as the music neared its end. She was handed bills. Despite his determination to remain detached, to remain loyal to the idea that there was something important brewing between Mary Margaret and him, he handed Roxy a fifty.

He retreated to the bar and waited for the promised second performance, selfishly hoping Roxy would work the crowd the way she had the first night he'd seen her dance solo. He turned his back to the stage and ordered a second drink. Found himself laughing at a joke or two tossed out by the deejay. Caught himself nodding his head to the beat of the music. Wondered if this need to be here was a wild hair, a product of his divorce, or a meltdown from the stress of being mayor and having his dreams within reach.

And then he realized it didn't matter. For years, he'd chosen activities for their career traction rather than his enjoyment. Tonight, he was having fun.

An hour later, Roxy came on stage for the grand finale—this time as a biker chick in high-heeled boots, black mini-skirt, and a leather jacket zipped up to the line of her cleavage. Black mask, black lipstick, black hair. But still, there was that one slim lock of red, barely visible unless you knew what to look for.

When she was done, the crowd went wild. Kevin went wild, offering her another fifty.

You're going to burn your career to the ground. Barb's voice, sharp and accusatory.

You've always got the family business to fall back on. His father's voice, less disparaging than he'd expected.

Obstinately, Kevin lingered as the dance floor lights came on and the crowd displayed their own moves. He imagined Roxy climbing into a sleek little sports car and driving away before anyone could wait at the stage door for her...autograph. He liked the fact that she was a mystery. It wasn't as if he was going to date her. In fact, this needed to be the last time he caught her act.

He tipped the bartender and left, trudging through the thickening snow to the parking lot. Precipitation hadn't been in the forecast until morning but that was Colorado weather for you, as unpredictable as Barb's moods.

A lone figure stared at a motorcycle parked next to the Hanky Panky's back door.

A lone figure wearing a helmet and a pair of form-fitting motorcycle leathers that displayed a familiar set of curves.

Hands on her hips, Roxy glanced over at Kevin.

The air left his lungs in a *whoosh*.

This was it. His political career balancing in an intact nutshell. He could leave Roxy to fend for herself and protect his nut. Or he could walk over, offer his assistance, and risk his protective shell being broken.

Before Kevin realized what he was doing, he'd started walking, boots sinking into six inches of snow.

Roxy turned her back on him and dug in her backpack. Probably for a gun.

"Do you need any help?" He slowed, holding up his hands.

"I'm fine on my own." She'd removed her helmet, revealing a black knit cap. When she turned she'd put on her black mask, the one she wore when she danced.

The fantasy factor registered off the scale.

"Not the best night to be riding a bike." Kevin forced words past a dry throat, sounding like Mr. Claus. "I can give you a ride...*somewhere*." The flashing neon sign of the cheap motel across the street beckoned, and somehow his gaze drifted thataway.

"No, thanks." Her voice was low and gruff but her gaze traveled that way too. "My mess. My clean-up."

"I understand." Boy, did he ever. "I was a Boy Scout." Not information she needed to know. His hands were still in the air, as if she were holding him hostage, which, in a way, she was. "You probably have guys propositioning you all the time."

That neon sign was truly eye-catching.

Snow fell between them while he waited for her to kick him to the curb.

"I have rules," Roxy said in a faraway voice, gaze snagged by the same neon. "I'm a dancer, not...No one touches me unless they have permission." And then her gaze swung around to him as if she wanted to give him the go-ahead to touch but was having second thoughts.

He lowered his hands. "Those are rules a man can abide by." This man. This night.

This one time.

"I…" Her focus fell to his lips.

One night with her would last a lifetime.

The gold leaf on the dome of the Colorado state house flickered in his mind's eye.

Or ruin everything I've worked for.

He swallowed.

"No names," she continued, listing restrictions in that gruff voice. "No numbers."

"Perfect," Kevin choked out. She was just what the doctor ordered for a newly divorced man with a reputation to protect.

"All we need to do"—she closed the distance between them with a sultry walk—"is seal this deal with a kiss."

He stood very still.

Her delicate hand came to rest on his cheek and drifted around his neck, drawing him closer. Her body pressed against his. And then her lips touched down.

She kissed with abandon. With passion. As if she had nothing left to lose.

Whereas he…

Tried very hard to feel, not think. She was like a decadent chocolate snuck from the candy jar before dinner, one he simultaneously wanted to devour, yet savor.

His hand found the base of her neck, a tendril of soft hair, the line of a delicate scar.

He deepened the kiss, making a silent vow to never show his face in the Hanky Panky again in exchange for…

*

"Stupid, stupid, stupid." Mary Margaret ran away from Kevin.

From near disaster and that powerful, dangerous kiss.

She'd made a series of mistakes tonight. She'd driven her grandfather's motorcycle. She'd left the saddlebags with the motorcycle's snow chains back in Sunshine because it wasn't supposed to snow. And then Kevin had shown up and approached her with his gallant innuendos.

She'd just meant to have a little fun with him. Tease a little. Scare him off with a kiss. But he hadn't been deterred, and deep down she'd experienced an odd mix of emotions—feminine power because he wanted her, anger that he wasn't being true to Mary Margaret, and longing for the kiss to be real, not part of her deception.

And then things got dangerous.

He'd slid his fingers around the base of her neck and into the hairline at the base of her skull, touching the scar, the one made when Dad had hit her and a corner of the bureau nearly paralyzed her.

Sinner.

That scar... She'd been reminded of all the things she had to lose if Kevin discovered her identity. She'd drawn back and bolted. Slower than she wanted, because she was wearing motorcycle boots and there was fresh snow on the ground.

Now what?

She looked up. There was the all-night coffee shop on the corner. She could phone someone—although it was one in the morning—or she could spend the money on an Uber to get home. Before she entered the diner, she remembered she was wearing a mask and peeled it from her face.

Mary Margaret ordered a cup of coffee and chose a booth as close to the back as she could, half expecting Kevin to follow her, to barge through that door and let it bang behind him while he pointed at her and shouted, "*You.*"

She blinked, because it wasn't Kevin shouting in her mind's eye. It was her father.

She picked up her phone, decision made.

Nearly an hour later, Lola's new SUV pulled into the parking lot.

"Don't ask." Mary Margaret climbed into the passenger seat.

"You can't call me in the middle of the night and not tell me what happened." Lola turned in her seat, SUV still in park. She wore thick, fuzzy gray leggings and a New York Giants blue hoodie. "Are you okay? If something bad happened, I can call Drew." Sunshine's sheriff. Her husband. "He's home." But probably no longer sleeping.

Probably the only reason Drew wasn't in the SUV with his wife was because he had a young daughter at home from his first marriage.

Mary Margaret tried to smile. "I'm fine. I just…" *Bolted when Kevin kissed me.* "I should have gone back inside…" But then she'd have had to explain her situation to Ned, and he might take any slip she made as a weakness he could exploit later. "And then I was stuck here. Thank you for coming to get me."

Lola frowned. "That's what friends are for."

Lola drove slowly through the falling snow. She was a New York City transplant and clearly wasn't comfortable driving in challenging road conditions. It took them nearly thirty minutes to reach the mill and its holiday lights.

Two tall, slender men of similar height and build were on the silo catwalk too far away to identify. It looked like they were trying to spray paint. They probably didn't realize it was too cold for the paint to spray or stick if it sprayed. They probably didn't realize they were risking their necks up there on the icy catwalk for nothing.

Like I'm qualified to tell anyone they're taking too many risks.

"What's your feeling about that distribution center opening here?" she asked Lola, which was a safer topic than asking Lola her opinion of Kevin.

"If it creates jobs, I'm for it." Lola successfully completed the turn from the interstate to the two-lane road leading to Sunshine. "But like you, I didn't grow up here. I don't have fuzzy memories about the way Sunshine has always been." She reached for Mary Margaret's hand. "Emotion is a tricky thing. Emotion overrides logic every time."

Guilt tried to shake loose the truth. Lola was her friend. Mary Margaret didn't like to hide things from her but she wasn't ready to confess the truth either. "Is this where you expect me to confess I almost got carried away by a handsome man's kiss?"

"No. This is where you confess what you were doing in Greeley in a sexy leather outfit carrying a backpack. You don't even wear leather to Shaw's." Lola spared her a smile. "Why don't you save me some guesses and tell me why you were in Greeley in the middle of the night."

Mary Margaret passed her fingers over her lips, remembering the heat of Kevin's kiss. "I'll tell you some other time."

"Hey, I had parents, and I'm a stepmom. I know that *some other time* means never." Lola released Mary Margaret's hand and sighed heavily. "You can talk to me. I understand getting a bit out of control after your husband dies."

"It's not like that." But it was, in a way. Mary Margaret felt desperate, reaching for things she couldn't have—like Kevin—and didn't have time for—like Kevin. And it was all Derek's fault.

When Derek died, she'd loved him, faults and all. And then she'd discovered just how deep his faults ran but she'd continued to love him, telling herself she needed to find it in her heart to forgive him. That's what she'd been taught, even if her father was a hypocrite when it came to forgiveness. And now? Now the thought of Derek made her gut clench.

Mary Margaret faced Lola. "How did you ever forgive Randy for cheating on you?" Immediately, she regretted her question. "I'm sorry. I had no right to ask."

Before Lola married Randy, he'd slept around, including one night with Mary Margaret during the two weeks Derek had left her. But Randy hadn't stopped sleeping around after he'd married Lola, and Lola hadn't found out until a year after he died.

"It's all right, because..." Lola tried to laugh. "You know, it took a while but I finally realized Randy loved me. Well, he loved a lot of women. But I think he needed love like...like..."

"Like Derek needed to gamble."

Lola's brow furrowed. "Yeah, maybe. Maybe our dead husbands were both searching for something in all the wrong places. But when all was said and done, I still loved Randy, and I know that, in his own way, he loved and needed me." She shook herself. "You'll forgive Derek someday, when you're ready to move on."

"When I finish clearing up his debts." Which was still a long, long way off. She'd made eight hundred bucks tonight. Could she get away with dancing at the Hanky Panky for three months? "Why are you turning here?"

Lola drove through the neighborhood of streets that competed for the annual title of Most Christmas Spirit—Sunshine's Christmas Tree Lane. "Because I think you need a dose of holiday cheer. You know. Ho-ho-ho, Merry Christmas. Let's hug and celebrate life with the ones you love."

"I owe you a bottle of wine," Mary Margaret admitted, spirits lifting now that she was almost home.

Lola nodded. "And you owe me the story behind all this when you're ready."

Mary Margaret settled back to enjoy the simple beauty of Christmas.

Despite the late hour, most of the Christmas lights were still on. Some houses were decorated all in small white lights. Some homes were illuminated by big, colorful bulbs. There were homes with nativity scenes and with wooden cutouts of Snoopy and the Peanuts gang. An inflatable Darth Vader took a swing with his light saber at a Christmas tree. Santa's sleigh sat on the corner, reminding Mary Margaret of Kevin.

"Feel better?" Lola pulled into Mary Margaret's driveway.

Thankfully, there was no black Town Car in sight.

"Yes." Mary Margaret hugged her. "Thank you."

Her outdoor Christmas lights were on, cheery and welcoming, but there was a not-so-cheery handwritten note tucked in the crack between the door and the frame.

Payment Due Sunday.

Chapter Ten

Kevin picked up Tad at his parents' house Saturday morning still thinking about Foxy Roxy.

That kiss had sizzled. Had he broken one of her rules by letting the fire ignite between them? By drawing her close and wishing for a fantasy fulfilled?

It didn't matter. She'd run away, which was for the best. He'd never had a one-night stand, and he shouldn't start now while a political opportunity loomed. Mary Margaret was the one he needed. She was so much more than a one-night stand.

"We're going to pick out a Christmas tree, buddy," Kevin told Tad while greeting Chester. "Get your snow boots on."

"We'll go in my truck." Dad delivered his proclamation like a judge passing sentence.

"I guess Grandpa wants to talk to me about mayor stuff." Kevin winked at Tad, who giggled.

"Comedian," Dad scoffed, adding in a low voice, "Make sure you tell your mother how nice her miniature

Victorian village looks. She spent hours setting it up on the coffee table."

"All right." Kevin said in a loud voice so Mom could hear, "Fabulous village this year, Mom."

Dad gave him a thumbs-up.

Tad gasped and rushed closer to the village. "There's a ninja sneaking around behind this house." He raised his face to the ceiling. "Ninja Christmases are awesome!"

After Kevin's mother accepted more compliments, they all piled into his father's truck.

Dad wasted no time speaking his mind. "What does the party say your chances are in this race?"

"They didn't say." Kevin made a face at Tad, who'd claimed Kevin's cell phone and started to play a game.

"What kind of resources are at your disposal?" He caught Kevin's gaze in the rearview mirror. "Speech writers? Pollsters? Branches of the party's volunteer network?"

"We didn't talk about that. The most they got into was campaign finance law in the state of Colorado."

"In other words, they grilled you on you." The lines around Dad's eyes relaxed. "Nothing's been decided."

"Nothing's been decided." Kevin sighed, unable to stop the feeling that this was his time. And yet unable to stop guilt from gripping his bad shoulder for being disloyal to his father and meddling in Mary Margaret's life when they weren't even dating. "Worst case, this time next year I'll still be your mayor."

"Nobody's tenure lasts forever," his mother said, applying lipstick in the visor mirror. "And your father would like to retire someday. You should spend a little more time down at the furniture shop. Things have changed since you worked there."

"I'm sure they'll change a lot more before his political career is over," Dad said gruffly.

"How about we talk about our Christmas lists? You know, Mom, men's fashion socks are the new power tie. Hint, hint." Kevin rarely wore a tie, and it was his mother's standard gift.

"Ninja-ninja-ninja," Tad murmured, proving he was listening.

"How about I tell you about the new client your father landed?" His mother continued to talk about the family business during the thirty-minute drive to the Christmas tree farm.

There were several Sunshine residents' vehicles at The Woodsman's Tree Farm, including Sandy Franklin's truck. Her daughter, Elizabeth, was in Tad's class.

As soon as his father parked, Kevin grabbed Tad and a saw from the tree farm kiosk and headed for the least populated section of the tree farm—the one with the trees shorter than six feet.

He rushed around a rather broad tree and nearly tripped over Mary Margaret. She sat between two thick branches, playing a game of solitaire on her phone.

"Ms. Sneed!" Tad fell into her lap as naturally as if he used her as a chair every day. "What are you doing on the ground?"

"Hiding from holiday cheer," Kevin murmured.

"Hi." Blushing, she hugged Tad. "Are you here for a tree?" She paused. "Duh. Of course you are. I'm *not* in the market for a tree this year but my grandmother is. Except she saw David Jessup and asked me to skedaddle."

"We're hiding too." Tad rocked from side to side in her lap. "Grandma and Grandpa were talking about furniture the whole drive." He fake snored. At the sound of voices nearby, he tugged Kevin's hand. "Dad, you're too tall. Grandpa will see."

"We can't hide out forever." Kevin sank to his knees, setting the saw aside. Unlike Mary Margaret, he wasn't wearing snow pants. Almost immediately, his jeans were soaked. And then he looked into Mary Margaret's eyes over the red pom-pom of Tad's knit cap and forgot about cold banks of snow. "Although we might try."

Kissing Roxy had been one of those surreal never-happen-again moments. Mary Margaret was real. He wanted to hide out with her, test the fit of her hand in his, talk about things that mattered. But there were the approaching voices. And, of course, Tad.

His son tossed him a bone. "Let's pretend we're ninjas and have a snowball fight." He scrambled to his feet and scampered between the trees.

"Let's pretend..." Kevin began, his gaze sinking to Mary Margaret's lips. He leaned forward. "That we're Mr. and Mrs. Claus." That earned him an indulgent smile. He leaned closer. "And we're hiding from the elves under a bouquet of mistletoe."

She glanced at his mouth and gave a clear sigh of longing.

He'd show her how hot Mr. Claus could be without his beard and maybe infuse her with a little holiday spirit.

A snowy projectile glanced off his head and onto Mary Margaret's jacket.

"Ninja strike!" Tad cried, popping out from behind a tree to clench his fist in a sign of victory. And then he scurried off again.

"Hold that thought, Mrs. Claus." Kevin helped Mary

Margaret to her feet. "Ninja retaliation." He darted behind a tree, scooping up snow as he did.

A snowball hit him in the back.

Mary Margaret's laughter came to him from his left. He caught a flash of red hair streaming below her knit cap as she ran between two fir trees.

The image of another woman running through the snow came to mind, and for a moment, the two images blended together.

A snowball sailed past his nose.

"Shoot!" Tad jumped up and down. "I missed."

Kevin forgot about women fleeing the scene and tossed his snowball at Tad. It hit him square on the chest. "Ninja bull's-eye."

"Ninja vanish." Tad disappeared once more.

Kevin bent to scoop up more snow. Another snowball flew through the air, exploding in the tree behind him.

"Ninja miss," Mary Margaret called.

Crouched where he was, Kevin made three snowballs.

Tad leaped from behind a tree, arm drawn back to fire. "Ninja attack!"

Kevin fired, landing one on Tad's leg. His son disappeared, giggling.

Red hair and a broad grin appeared to the side of a nearby tree. A snowball arced through the air in a horrible miss.

"That doesn't even qualify as a ninja missile," Kevin taunted. A sound behind him had Kevin whirling and firing.

His snowball landed in his father's face. Dad wiped it away with a gloved hand. "What's going on here?"

Kevin hesitated but then he saw Tad and Mary

Margaret closing in. "Ninja free-for-all." He scooped up snow and threw it at his dad.

Tad and Mary Margaret did the same.

His father ran for cover, promising retribution.

As one, Tad and Mary Margaret appeared and creamed Kevin with snowballs.

It was all-out war for a few minutes after that.

"Can't catch me." Tad giggled and ran.

"Or me." Mary Margaret didn't giggle. She just ran.

Kevin tackled her, spinning mid-air so she landed on top of him.

"Oh." Her breath wafted over his face. Her red hair fell about his shoulders.

It's perfect. Kiss her.

Tad landed on top of both of them.

Kiss her.

Mary Margaret rolled off Kevin and to the side, sending Tad into a bank of snow.

"Seems a shame to snowball them when they're down," Kevin's mother said.

"There's no going easy in a snowball fight, Miriam." Kevin's father carried a slew of snowballs in the crook of his arm, and he wasn't shy about using them.

The downed ninjas were pelted with snow. They scrambled to their feet and laughed until their sides hurt.

"Time for a truce and hot chocolate." Kevin didn't wait for an answer. He claimed Mary Margaret's hand and marched toward the refreshment stand.

Mary Margaret chuckled.

"What's so funny?" he asked with a smile.

"Ninjas." She laughed some more. "Mr. Ninja Claus."

He looped her arm through his. "Mr. *and Mrs.* Ninja Claus."

Who needed masked exotic dancers when there was Mary Margaret?

✳

Twice.

That's how many times Mary Margaret thought Kevin would kiss her among the Christmas trees.

Twice.

That's how many times Mary Margaret had dodged a bullet.

Because as soon as Kevin's lips touched hers, she was going to have to keep herself from kissing him whole-heartedly, the way Foxy Roxy had. Because if she did, he might discover who danced behind the mask. But oh, how she longed for him to kiss her again.

In the afterglow of the snowball fight, Mary Margaret had forgotten what was at stake. She'd allowed Kevin to lead her to a picnic table and buy her a hot chocolate topped with miniature marshmallows and chocolate drizzles.

"That was fun." Richard Hadley smiled at Mary Margaret as if she was something more than his grandchild's teacher. "I haven't been in a ninja war in a long time."

"That's because Dad said no more ninja attacks on grandparents." Tad sported a hot chocolate mustache and a pleased-with-himself grin. "Because my attack broke your favorite coffee mug last year."

"What? No more ninja attacks? Why?" Richard drew

back to give his son a look of disbelief. "You think I'm old? You think I can't take a ninja war?"

"I thought it was a sign of respect..." Kevin grinned. "Old man."

A verbal ninja sparring match ensued between Kevin and his father.

Their obvious love for each other, combined with the ease with which they teased one another, created an unexpected ache in Mary Margaret's throat. She'd never had that kind of relationship with her father. And she never would.

"Come on, Tad." Richard got to his feet, drawing his wife with him and then claiming Kevin's saw. "Help your decrepit old grandfather pick out a Christmas tree."

"Okay." Tad practically tumbled off the picnic bench and grabbed on to his grandparents' hands.

It was an adorable sight and sharpened the ache in Mary Margaret's throat.

"Hey." Kevin took her hand and held it in both of his. "Where'd you go just now?"

She smiled, and the ache in her throat loosened the lock on her secrets. "I was just thinking what a wonderful family you have."

They'd removed their gloves to drink hot chocolate. His skin was warm against hers, his clasp one of understanding.

"I never had a family like this. My dad had his own church." Mary Margaret hadn't realized how much she'd missed holding hands and sharing confidences. "We were supposed to be the perfect family. Kind, giving, selfless. And we were. To others."

Kevin's gaze turned distant. "Isn't it funny how easy it is to forget to love and nurture those closest to you?"

She nodded. "I suppose to my dad I didn't fit the image of a preacher's perfect daughter. I was a chunky child, always tripping over my own two feet. They kept my hair short, and it always looked like a bird's nest. My mom made me wear Easter hats to school in the spring and fall, which did not help me in the popularity department. I think I was seven when they sent me to ballet class, hoping I'd become graceful." Besides dancing in the kitchen with her mother, that had been the one place Mary Margaret had fit in. Learning how to move to music was nirvana.

Kevin waited for her to say more.

He hadn't come after Roxy last night when she'd run but he was persistent in his pursuit of Mary Margaret in town. Her heart panged. She needed him to know she wasn't the woman he thought she was. And the only way to do that was to tell him more of her past. Not all, just enough that he'd understand. She wasn't meant to be the wife of a politician.

She drew her hand into her lap. The back of her neck felt chilled, exposed. "When he hit me, I fell onto the corner of my dorm room dresser. There were a few days when I didn't know if I'd walk again." She dredged up the unwanted memory of being in a hospital bed, of her mother kneeling next to her in prayer. "When you're a preacher's kid, your needs always come last. While I was in the hospital, a drunk driver hit a family in our congregation." The same day her father had hit her. "My father rushed home to support them." Taking Mom with him. "My grandparents came to stay with me until I was released."

"That was wrong of your father." Kevin's words were colder than the wind coming down the mountain.

"Was it? My dad thinks that I—"

"Don't say it." Kevin's smile was tender. "If you say something bad out loud, it gives the words power. And I can assure you, whatever your father thinks, he's wrong." He inched closer to her on the bench, his warmth seeping into her leg, into her veins, into her heart. "I think you're fabulous. I think fate brought us together, Mrs. Ninja Claus."

It wouldn't take much to close the distance between them and kiss. It wouldn't take much to let all those sparks she was constantly trying to put out build into a flame.

And then what?

I'd tell him the truth.

And he'd walk away, just like her father had done.

"Fate?" Mary Margaret forced a teasing note in her voice but it fell as flat as her dreams of a debt-free life. "You told Rosalie to offer me the Mrs. Claus gig."

"It was fate that her first choices were felled by the flu." Kevin gave her shoulder a gentle nudge with his own. "We make a good team. We could go places."

More than Mary Margaret's scar went cold. Her father had wanted her to be a part of a good team, to always put her best foot forward, to uphold an image that didn't ring true.

"Kevin." There was no more tease to her tone.

He ignored her. "I think we should test the relationship waters with dinner at Los Consuelos."

"Kevin, I—"

"Or some place more private, like that steak restaurant in Greeley."

She slid away from him on the bench and lifted one leg over, so she faced him squarely. "Dating me is a bad idea."

He frowned. "That's your father talking."

"You're darn right it is." She stood. "But sometimes, Father knows best."

❋

"Thank you for helping me find a tree." Edith batted her eyes at David.

He was so tall and strong, not to mention a good singer. She couldn't wait to watch him chop down a tree for her.

"It's no problem," Mims said in a hard voice. "Seeing as how *we* were already here." She put the emphasis on *we*.

Edith's smile didn't dim.

The threesome walked toward a section of tall Douglas firs. Edith sped up a few paces and then slowed down, inserting herself between David and Mims. "It smells fabulous out here, doesn't it? Like home and family and Christmas." Like husbands and wives. The competition was so fierce for David's affection she might have to give up her Widows Club membership to lock him in.

The thought gave her pause. She glanced at Mims, her face almost more familiar than Charlie's had been.

Mims shouldered her purse, bumping Edith out of the way in the process. "Home is important. A safe place you always defend." She bumped Edith with her bag again. Her big, bulky bag.

Like Edith cared that Mims was packing heat. Mims was all talk when it came to defending her turf. Why, just last spring she'd had a raccoon in her attic. Instead of shooting it, she'd trapped it, drove up to Saddle Horn Pass, and released it.

"Oh, look, David." Edith grabbed his hand and skipped away from Mims, dragging him along. "What a beautiful tree." She stopped in front of an eight-footer. "What do you think? Is it perfect?" She batted her eyes.

"Edith, you should be careful." David cradled her face in his gloved hands.

Her heart raced. She batted her eyes with more fervor. A kiss? So soon? And in front of Mims? It was all Edith could do not to stretch up on her toes and—

"There's a stiff wind blowing, Edith." David peered at her. "And it looks like you've got something in your eye."

"Oh." *Oh, shoot.* She'd forgotten he was a retired optometrist. "Did you get it? Is it gone?" She blinked some more, trying to entice him closer.

"All clear." He set her aside. "This is a gorgeous tree but it's too big for my apartment. What about you, Mims? You have that big formal living room."

"It's too big. It wouldn't work in Edith's house either." Mims managed to hip check Edith aside. "She's got *short* ceilings. We should look over here." She hooked her arm through David's and set off, leaving Edith sulking behind them.

What was she doing wrong? It had been more than fifty years since she'd flirted with a man. Surely the old rules still applied—conveniently close, an ever-present smile, and never a bad word to say about anyone.

Except for Mims. Edith narrowed her eyes. She'd break the rules for Mims.

And once she had David's engagement ring on her finger, they could go back to being best friends.

"There you are, Grandma Edith." Mary Margaret rounded a large tree. "It's time to go."

"But I haven't gotten a tree." Edith jerked her head toward David and tried to infuse her words with their real meaning: *I haven't gotten my man.*

"We'll get a tree another day." Mary Margaret latched on to Edith's arm. "I have to go."

Mims and David turned, staring at them with concern.

"Is there an emergency?" Edith asked, moving despite her reluctance.

Mary Margaret's mouth worked until she finally admitted, "Yes."

Edith didn't believe her, not completely, but she went along anyway, because something had happened to her granddaughter; something had upset her. And Edith wasn't so selfish as to put her desire to nab a man ahead of her granddaughter's happiness.

If only Mary Margaret would confess what was upsetting her.

Chapter Eleven

It wasn't enough that she'd had to turn down Kevin at the Christmas tree farm. Now she had thugs outside her door?

Merry Christmas.

Laurel and Hardy got out of their big Town Car, looking as downtrodden and sleep-deprived as Mary Margaret felt.

Desperation fueled her anger. She marched to the end of her driveway and crossed her arms over her chest. "Why is it that you say I've got a few days to gather my next payment and then you dog me constantly? I'm trying to operate in good faith, and yet here you are."

"We wouldn't be doing our job if we didn't make you nervous." Tall Mr. Laurel swiveled his red stir stick out of the way so he could push his chin to one side and crack his neck.

Mr. Hardy backhanded his partner in the stomach. "It would be nice if you gave us your payment a day early. We're under a bit of pressure from our boss."

Mr. Laurel pushed his chin toward his other shoulder,

cracking his neck once more. "He doesn't like us racking up expenses in Colorado. We spent last night at a truck stop by the interstate."

Mr. Hardy slapped his partner in the stomach once more.

They scowled at each other.

Mr. Laurel blinked first, swiveling the red stir stick in his mouth. "Besides, it's cold here. I wasn't made for the cold." He caught Mr. Hardy's hand before he was struck again.

"I'd be happy to send you payments via check or bank transfer." Not just happy. She'd be ecstatic.

"You must first establish our trust," Hardy said, still scowling at his partner. "Can we come inside and collect our next payment?"

Mary Margaret got the heebie-jeebies, the kind that skittered down her back and leaped into her throat. "You can wait on the front stoop while I write you a check." No way was she letting these men inside her house. She turned and hurried toward the door.

"No takers on your ATV?" Mr. Laurel asked.

"No takers." And boy, she'd been trying. She'd asked some kids in line at the Santa event if they wanted one for Christmas and then some people at the hot chocolate table last night.

Mary Margaret triple-locked the door behind her before she went to search for her checkbook. When she had the check written, she unlocked the front door and handed Mr. Hardy the draft. "That's twenty-five hundred dollars." All the dance money she'd deposited this week. She'd been making cash deposits at the branch in Greeley to avoid town gossip.

"Have you been holding out on us?" Mr. Hardy stared at her check. "I thought you were broke."

"Never mind how I made the money." She gripped the door handle. "You owe me three hundred for two new tires."

"I can't extend credit." Mr. Hardy walked away. "That's not how shakedowns work."

"But…" Mary Margaret sagged against the door frame. "I'm *honoring* my husband's debt. The least you can do is be honorable in return."

"She's got a point." Mr. Laurel nodded, and then an odd expression came over his face. Almost as if he was embarrassed. "How's your granny? I haven't seen her today."

"You stay away from my grandmother." Mary Margaret channeled the ferocity of a Chihuahua. "If you harm a hair on her head, you'll be sorry."

Mr. Laurel held up his hands in surrender. "It's not like that."

"Get in the car." Mr. Hardy was making a beeline for the driver's seat. "It's too cold to broker deals I have no authority to make. We'll need another payment next weekend. Try to make a bigger dent next time."

A bigger dent?

Anger made Mary Margaret scowl at them until they drove off.

Anger slammed the door.

But it wasn't anger that left her legs shaking so bad that she slid to the floor.

*

"Barb, we need to talk."

Barb took Tad's backpack from Kevin late Saturday afternoon and stood blocking the doorway to the house that used to be theirs. "For the love of Mike, Kevin." She glanced over her shoulder to where Tad was turning on the television. She moved to the porch and closed the door behind her. "If you want a booty call, phone someone who won't sell you out if things go south."

"What are you talking about?" Kevin took a step back. Did she know he'd been to the Hanky Panky?

"Sandy told me you were making moves on Tad's teacher at the Christmas tree farm." She rolled her eyes. "If that goes south, you'll turn half the school staff against you, not to mention the school board and all those parents in Tad's class. If you've got an itch, I'm right here." She ran her hands from shoulder to waist.

She was offering...

Annoyed, Kevin took another step back. "That's not an option." It hadn't been since he'd found out about her cheating last spring.

"Why are you dead set on ruining the career we built together?" Barb clenched her fists between them like a fighter. "And don't deny we were a team."

She made their marriage sound like a business deal and continued to present her case. "We used to stay up all night talking about how we'd transform things for the better here in town, at the state level, and in the White House. None of that has to end."

"Yes, it does. We need a change here in Sunshine, and we need a change between us." Kevin rubbed a hand against his pounding temple. "You know, since our marriage broke up, I've been in this fog, blindly putting one foot after another, heading in a direction people I respect told me was right. But I guess my heart was bruised from those broken vows. And now"—because of Mary Margaret, and maybe even Roxy—"I know what I believe in. And beliefs are worth defending, even if someone you used to love and respect disagrees with you."

Barb's features were colder than the wind whipping down from Saddle Horn Mountain.

"You're not going to change my mind about the distribution center," Kevin said firmly. "And we're not going to be exes with benefits. We're going to co-parent Tad on friendly terms, and…" He knew in his gut now wasn't the time to broach the subject of Barb's fat-shaming their child but…

"And?" she prompted, cold as ice.

He had to say something. "And I'd appreciate it if you stopped watching out for me. There's someone inside— *our son*—who is much more deserving of your attention." And with that, Kevin turned and walked away.

"You'll regret this," Barb said in a frigid voice.

He paused at the end of the walk, thinking about Mary Margaret's observation that Barb would be protective of him until he asserted his independence.

"I'm sorry, Barb." He faced his beautiful ex-wife, lamenting the fact that her beauty now only seemed skin deep. Tad needed his mother to have a big heart. "But it's you who'll have regrets if you keep on trying to run this town—and me—from the beauty parlor."

Kevin drove to Mary Margaret's house and knocked on her door.

When she opened up, her mouth fell open. "What are you—"

Kevin pounded the Christmas tree trunk on her porch. "It's pretty, isn't it? Nice shape. Manageable size. Tad and I picked it out for you." And his parents had been incredibly interested that they'd done so.

"You shouldn't have."

"Are you kidding me?" She looked so demoralized that he nearly dropped the tree and gave her a hug. "Regardless of how you feel about the season, you deserve a happy holiday." And he was determined to give her one.

She opened the door wider. "You better come inside before someone sees you."

Not, *Thank you, Kevin. You're so sweet.*

"You don't even need a Christmas tree stand. I had the tree farm nail one on." He carried the four-foot Douglas Fir inside. "With so little time until Christmas, you'll be fine as long as you don't put it near your fireplace." He glanced around the small living space and set it down in front of the narrow slider. "Good thing you don't have a fireplace."

"You really didn't have to do this," she said. But there was a crack in her defenses; he could feel it in the way she ran her fingers over the needles on one branch. "Thank you. It smells so good."

"I see someone dropped off a bit of mistletoe." He nodded toward a wilted bag on her counter.

"Don't get any ideas, *friend*."

He had ideas. And they had nothing to do with being her friend. "It's a shame to let mistletoe go to waste. Find me a push pin, and I'll hang it in the foyer."

She crossed her arms over her chest. "That's not happening."

"You've got some boxes in here." He bent to open one. "Are these your ornaments?"

"No!" She closed the flaps. "Those are *personal* things."

He was sorry he'd moved so slowly. Any quicker and he'd have seen what she wanted to hide. "Okay, then. I guess that's my cue to leave. But I want an invitation back to see your tree decorated." Although he'd settle for a photo via text. "I know there's holiday cheer inside you. After all, you enjoyed our snowball fight and the hot chocolate."

She made a noncommittal noise and showed him the door.

He hesitated on her porch. "I need to tell you something." His stupid slip-of-the-tongue with the political party.

"Kevin." Mary Margaret stared at him with what he'd swear was longing in her eyes. "Thank you for the tree and... and your friendship."

"Friendship is a solid basis for a relationship." *That was both boring and lame.*

"I'm closing the door on you now." True to her word, she shut him out.

Chapter Twelve

Mary Margaret had signed up for a shift in the Widows Club wrapping booth back when she'd thought it was a good excuse to get out and socialize during this difficult holiday season.

She'd had no idea how badly she'd end up wanting to be a hermit. She'd put lights on the tree Kevin had brought her and strands of tinsel, but that only made her think of Derek and burlesque costumes—the latter of which Kevin had nearly found when he'd started to open the box in her living room.

The tree made her long for some of her family traditions, like baking, planning gatherings, and giving donations to various food banks and toy drives. And it made her think about Kevin and how much she'd wanted a kiss during the snowball fight.

A table was set up in the lobby of the town's small mall, a historic brick building on the town square that was filled with quirky shops. Plastic tubs underneath the table held bins of wrapping supplies. There was a large, beautifully decorated tree nearby. Christmas music was piped in from somewhere. Mary Margaret recognized The Chipmunks.

Classic.

She hurried inside for her two-hour wrapping shift, after which she'd drive to the Hanky Panky, where she was scheduled to dance sometime after ten.

"The temperature's dropping outside," Mary Margaret told the two ladies she relieved. Both wore holiday sweaters with flashing lights. "Bundle up."

As soon as the widows left, a huge line for wrapping formed. Mary Margaret tried to wrap as fast as she could, wondering who'd skipped out on the shift by her side.

"I'm sorry I'm late," said a masculine voice.

Mary Margaret looked up from the careful folds she was making in sparkly Rudolph wrapping paper and froze. There was Kevin. "You signed up to wrap?"

"No. My Great Aunt Sophie volunteered." She was a Widows Club member. "She came down with a stomach bug, and my mother insisted I take her place." He removed his coat and set it aside, surveying the lobby. "You have a line."

"I know." Mary Margaret tried to wrap faster while sparing him a glance. "You can take the next customer."

"Actually..." He leaned in to whisper. "I'm not much of a wrapper."

"You better learn really quickly before we lose customers." She edged away from him and reassured the line. "We'll be right with all of you. Remember that all proceeds benefit the local food bank." *That ought to buy their patience.*

As would Kevin's sigh-worthy smile, which he bestowed on the ladies in line. He held up glitter-trimmed handmade tags with string ties. "If you could, just personalize a gift tag while you wait. I challenge you to be clever. My mother always gives a clue about what's inside." He gestured toward Wendy Adams, who was holding a red sweater. "Might I suggest something like, *Bright and cheerful winter snuggles*?"

Mary Margaret snorted. "My grandmother does that so she remembers what's inside." But it seldom worked. Last year, Grandma Edith had unwrapped two of Mary Margaret's gifts because the not-remembering had killed her. Mary Margaret plastered the ends of the box she was wrapping with tape. No one was peeking at that present. "Can you fluff a bow for me, Mr. Mayor?"

Mr. Ninja Claus, bringer of trees and holiday cheer.

Her gaze drifted his way, and she released a kiss-induced sigh.

This kind of thinking isn't helpful.

Kevin hadn't moved.

She had to assume he didn't know what she'd asked him to do. "Do you know how to fluff a bow?" She spared a moment to hand him the spool of curling ribbon and a pair of scissors. "Curl ribbon with the scissors."

Kevin blinked the way Tad did when he wasn't sure what crayon he wanted to use to color.

"I'll do it." Louise's mom, Kathy, stepped out of line to volunteer. "At the rate you're going, we'll be here until Christmas."

"Surely it isn't that bad." Kevin returned to the here and now, no longer a male deer in mostly female head-lights. "Look how our tight-knit community chips in to work toward a common goal—full pantries and pretty presents."

"Is it okay to groan?" Mary Margaret handed Kathy the wrapped package of socks.

"I'm groaning," Kathy said, curling a long length of green ribbon. "You aren't going to approve that distribution center, are you, Kevin?"

"I have a very special announcement to make regarding the distribution center." Kevin hung on to his smile while Mary Margaret searched for a box that was the right size to wrap a pair of leather driving gloves. "JPM Industries is donating to several causes in town. We're finally going to upgrade the high school stadium snack bar. And make that war memorial bench at the cemetery a reality. And—"

"This sounds like a plan to buy your vote." Kathy refused to be appeased.

"Or it could be them establishing a place in our community." Kevin handed her a filled-out gift tag to go with the bow she was making, sprinkling glitter on the table in the process.

"I'm a bit excited about the distribution center opening." Mary Margaret swathed the gloves in white tissue paper and laid them in the thin cardboard box. "I'm hoping more families will move to Sunshine. There will be more kids in school. And more kids in school means we can maintain school property without raising taxes."

Kathy made a noise just like Louise did before upchucking.

Reflexively, Mary Margaret took a step back.

"Thanks for the support, Mrs. Ninja Claus." Kevin handed out gift tags to those in line. "I knew adding you to the development committee was the right idea."

"You didn't add *me* to the committee," Kathy said.

"Do you want to come on board?" he asked.

"No." Kathy handed Wendy her completed package. "I'm still against the project."

"Kevin?" Mary Margaret dug into a tub for a box the right length to hold the rose-colored bud vase Eileen Taylor wanted wrapped.

"What?"

"If you can't make yourself useful in this production line, I'm going to have to break up the band." She caught his eye. "No more Mr. and Mrs. Ninja Claus. No more discussions about distribution centers."

Her threat worked. Kevin began making curled ribbon bows while continuing to charm the customers, even the occasional one who expressed their disapproval of new development in town.

In no time, the stores began closing. Their line dwindled to nothing. Patti from the smoke shop, another Widows Club member and part of the Victorian choir, took their cash box for the night.

"You like the notoriety of being mayor." Mary Margaret's back ached from bending over the table to wrap. "You were comfortable with all the small talk, the fawning, the oh-you-poor-boy-who-can't-wrap teasing."

"I suspect there's a question in there somewhere that I don't want to answer." But he smiled when he said it.

"I don't think it's a question." She shoved the table sideways and out of the way. "You like leading the pack, whether it's a pack of ninjas or a group of ladies worn out from shopping or a committee of residents talking through the pros and cons of commercial development."

"I like people." A frown clouded his handsome features. "I think I forgot that after my divorce. In fact,

I forgot a lot of things." His gaze pivoted to her. The frown disappeared. And then all the charm and attention he'd paid their customers was directed her way. "You're part of my remembering what makes me happy."

She wasn't sure she should be part of his journey at all. It felt too similar to being a part of her father's ministry. Teams and committees. Common goals that required appearances and sacrifices.

"Have dinner with me tonight." Kevin wasn't asking. When she would have protested, he rushed on. "Don't think about this in the context of you, my son's teacher, and me, the mayor with the prickly ex-wife. If we didn't live in Sunshine, you'd go out with me. At least once." His voice dropped to a whisper. "Maybe twice if you liked the way I kissed you."

She was horrified that someone might hear him, petrified that Derek's mess might bounce off her and stick to him like glue.

"I know." He held up his hands, using that charming tone and winning smile that had won over all the ladies in the wrapping line. "No kisses until the third date. But isn't that rule outdated? Isn't that rule for people who weren't friends beforehand?"

Her heart beat a rhythm that urged capitulation while the pounding in her temples urged caution. She should do the right thing for both of them and turn him down. "Did you ever know to the depths of your heart that something was the wrong option to pick?" she asked instead.

"When it comes to matters of the heart, you shouldn't listen to what your head says."

Mary Margaret had fallen for Derek on a winter night like this. He'd walked her to her car after a holiday party at her principal's house and kissed her under a starry sky. Despite her best efforts to convince him a homegrown girl was a better choice for him, he'd persisted in his pursuit, as if she was worth the effort.

Which in his case, she had been. She was nothing if not loyal to a fault.

Kevin didn't need loyalty from someone like her, someone with a prickly past and a thorny present.

But the fact that Kevin wasn't deterred by her doubts and her caution...It meant something to her. Kevin was the kind of man who stood by his woman until she betrayed him. And Mary Margaret's dancing her way out of debt would be a betrayal. She didn't follow national politics closely but she knew enough about the profession to know people didn't vote for men who openly dated exotic dancers.

"I need to be somewhere." She needed to be where she could make money. "It was fun watching you in action tonight though."

"If you ever need someone to fawn over, you know where to find me." That glint in his eye promised mischief.

She put on her jacket and tugged a dark knit cap over her hair, eager to be gone, to be anonymous, to leave without sullying his reputation.

"Mary Margaret, I..." Kevin cupped her shoulder. "Is that what your friends call you?"

"It's my name." Where was this line of questioning going?

"It's a long name."

"It's two names." And he couldn't have annoyed her more if he'd made a pass at her. She marched toward the door.

"Would you mind if I called you—"

"I don't do nicknames." Her father had hated them.

"—Maggie."

Mary Margaret hesitated, one gloved hand on the cold glass door.

"Maggie," Kevin said again, hot on her heels. "Have a good one, Maggie."

Jim, the school janitor who moonlighted as a security guard downtown, came in the door as she was heading out, slowing her exit. And then Kevin held the door for her, resulting in the two of them standing on the sidewalk staring at each other like a couple on their first online date who couldn't decide if the attraction they felt was worth a second one.

"Maggie," Kevin began.

Her heart melted at his nickname.

He smiled. "You haven't heard my question. I was going to say I have some steaks marinating at my place. I'd love to cook you dinner." He chuckled. "That wasn't a question either." He moved closer, lowering his voice. "Will you have dinner with me?"

She desperately wanted to say yes.

Perhaps he could recognize the longing in her eyes. She'd kissed him, and she wanted to kiss him again. How could she hope to project the appearance of neutrality?

Kevin must have sensed her hesitation. He took her arm, leading her to the corner and Los Consuelos, the local Mexican restaurant. "We'll share fajitas."

"Why?"

"Because I want to learn more about you."

"And?"

"Are you asking me my intentions?"

"I shouldn't…We shouldn't…" Her cheeks felt hot enough to melt chocolate. "We can't just have dinner in town. We have to have a reason. Or Barbara is going to…"

"You're on my development committee, remember? Alibi covered." He opened the door for her at the restaurant. "Not that we need one. I told Barb to back off."

"*What?*" The splash of bright colors in the restaurant combined with this news was dizzying.

But Kevin's touch steadied her.

A margarita and a shared basket of chips later, and Kevin had switched gears to the standard dating questions. "Why did you decide to move to Sunshine?"

"My grandparents collected me from the hospital." The scar on the back of her neck tingled. "I was looking for a small, out-of-the-way community." To prove to her father that she could lead an exemplary life.

How's that working out for you?

"If you're determined to defend your father, why don't you reach out and attempt to mend fences?"

Oh, heavens no. "To my father, I'm a lost cause."

"But…you're a kindergarten teacher."

"Go ahead and say it." She rolled her eyes. "You mean, kindergarten teachers live exemplary lives and never do anything interesting."

"That's not what I meant." He glanced around the restaurant. "Okay, yes, you have two names like you're a nun. And yes, you teach the town's budding little angels. And all right, no one ever has anything bad to say about you."

"I'm ho-hum." That was relief coursing through her veins and a blind eye she was turning toward her part-time job for the evening.

"I don't think you're humdrum."

"Why not?"

He leaned forward, expression serious. "Because I find myself wondering what it would be like to kiss you."

It'd be hot. Too hot for Mary Margaret, squeaky clean kindergarten teacher, to handle.

She lowered her eyes so he wouldn't see the longing there. "You shouldn't say things like that to me."

He sat back with a weary sigh. "Would you like me better if I said things like, 'I'm wondering how to keep Sunshine's youth from moving away after high school'? Or 'I'm wondering how much is too much in the road repair budget'?"

"Now, those things are truly boring." But they were safely boring. She smiled.

"Why is it that when you say it I don't feel so bad?"

He paid the bill and opened the door for her when they left. They walked along the sidewalk toward their vehicles, not speaking.

"Hang on a minute." He dragged Mary Margaret into the shadowy alley between the movie theater and the mortuary. And then he kissed her as if she were break-able, his arms looped carefully at her waist, his lips pressed gently against hers.

It was nothing like the way he'd kissed Roxy.

And it inspired nothing much in return. At least, nothing but anger. That kiss told her exactly what Kevin thought about Maggie, despite his arguments to the contrary. She wasn't sexy enough for him.

"*Oh.*" He released her. And then he seemed to reconsider. "Let's try that again."

Mary Margaret pressed her palm to his chest, stopping him. "Let's not press our luck." She scurried back into the light.

"*This time,*" he said, following her. "We won't press our luck *this time.*"

She shivered, calling out, "Good night."

Luckily, he let her escape.

Speaking of luck, she needed some. And she needed to bring Grandpa Charlie's motorcycle home. If she borrowed Grandpa Charlie's truck and some tie-downs, she could bring the bike back tonight after her shift. But she needed to hurry if she was going to pull that off.

On the way to her grandmother's house, she tried to tell herself she was relieved that there had been no sparks in that kiss, no chance for Kevin to realize Mary Margaret and Foxy Roxy were one and the same.

She tried to tell herself she was relieved. But that was a lie.

She wanted Kevin to know she was more than the ho-hum kindergarten teacher.

If only the truth wouldn't make him walk away.

Chapter Thirteen

Y ou started drinking without me?" After escorting Mary Margaret to her car, Kevin sat down next to Jason at the bar at Shaw's, wondering where that kiss had gone wrong.

Noah slid him a beer and a bowl of unshelled peanuts.

"You're late." Jason was in a mood, scowling into his drink instead of at Kevin.

"It's not like you and I had a *date*," Kevin said. "I worked the wrapping booth and then took Mary Margaret to dinner."

"*Man*." Jason groaned. "You had a date. How can it be that you've got a better social life than I do? You're the guy in town who never has sex."

"What's the matter with you?" Kevin looked from Jason to Noah.

"Judge *and* Mrs. Harper came in for a drink earlier." Noah shed light on the matter.

"The judge tottered over and asked me how I was doing." Jason pounded his plaster cast with his fist. "He married *my* girl, and he's asking *me* how I'm doing?"

"Dude." Kevin put a hand on Jason's shoulder. "You kissed another woman on national TV after a bull ride, and you expected Darcy to forgive you." Kevin experienced a twinge of guilt. He'd kissed two different women in two days. No wonder his kiss with Mary Margaret had been a dud. He needed to choose a woman.

But there was no choice. On paper, it was the kindergarten teacher all the way. And in his heart too. He could talk to her, laugh with her, feel safe in a relationship with her. There would be no surprises.

"Darcy didn't have to dump me *and* marry a man with one foot in the grave." Jason drained his beer.

"Maybe you couldn't give her what she needed," Noah said, surprisingly blunt.

"Long distance relationships don't ever work," Kevin added. Although he'd stayed true to Barb while he was in college. And oh, that stomach churn was him realizing she probably hadn't been faithful to him.

"I have a legitimate company here in town," Jason groused. "A thriving business. I'm a good catch."

"Are you still living above Iggy's garage?" Noah arched his brows. "That bachelor pad?"

Jason blinked. "Yeah. I hop up those stairs every night—*alone*."

"Are you still driving that jacked-up pickup truck?" Noah was having fun with this. "The one you need to lift women into because it's so high off the ground?"

"Yeah. I mean, I own it but I haven't been driving it since my accident."

"Let me spell it out for you." Noah placed his elbows on the bar. "Women like stability. They like boring. They may fall for your charm and your dangerous profession but they stay for the guy who pays the mortgage on a three-bedroom house, the one with flowers he planted for her in the yard. They stay for the guy who helps their dad tune up his car on Saturday and drives their mother to church on Sunday in their minivan."

"That's it!" Jason sat bolt upright, as if struck by lightning. "I need to win over Darcy's parents. They never liked me."

"I think he missed the point," Kevin murmured.

Jason clambered off the bar stool and reached for his crutches. "The Joneses always go to a movie on Friday night after they go to dinner. Thanks, guys."

"Where are you going?" Kevin asked.

"The movie theater. I'm going to buy some popcorn and sit next to Darcy's parents and offer them some."

"Whoa, whoa, whoa." Noah ran out from behind the bar and steered Jason back to his seat. "You smell like a brewery."

Jason resisted, shrugging his arm free and nearly toppling over backward. "Are you saying I'm drunk?"

Noah sent a pleading glance Kevin's way. "Help me out here."

"Has he had more than two beers?" Kevin asked Noah. At the bartender's nod, Kevin said, "Yes, Jason. Noah's saying you're a stinking drunk. If you hobble into the movie theater during a show, Avery's going to toss your butt out on the street and Darcy's parents will continue to hate you."

"You might be right." Jason ran a hand over his face. "Avery runs a tight ship at the theater." He hobbled back to his stool. "Maybe I could help Mr. Jones string his house lights. He hasn't put them up yet."

"I'm vetoing that idea." Kevin pointed toward Jason's crutches. "If you can't climb into your own truck, you won't be going up on a ladder."

"Right." Jason stared at his cast. "I need to talk to my doctor about getting this cast off."

Kevin caught Noah's eye and mouthed, *Change the subject.* Because knowing Jason, he'd talk himself into cutting off his cast in another minute.

While Noah and Jason talked football, Kevin replayed Noah's assessment of what women wanted in his head. Except for the minivan, he was what women wanted. Except for that uninspired kiss, he might be what Mary Margaret wanted.

At times like these, a man could hope.

✳

"Why are you borrowing all my vehicles?" Edith demanded of her granddaughter while putting on a second coat of *Kiss Me, Stupid* red lipstick. "Have you been getting speeding tickets in your car?"

"Remember me?" Mary Margaret seemed in a hurry. "Miss Incognito? I need a stealth-mobile."

Edith spared her granddaughter a glance. All this subterfuge and urgency had Edith worried. A little stalling was in order to encourage Mary Margaret to confess.

They stood in Edith's cramped bathroom. Edith peered at her eyeliner and then puckered her mouth to make sure the lipstick remained smooth. She rearranged the girls in her reinforced-cup bra. It was a garment designed to defy gravity, one she took out only on special occasions.

Lipstick. 18 Hour Bra. Waist cincher. Church heels.

She was going all-out for drinks tonight with David. She'd even glued on false eyelashes.

Eat your heart out, Mims.

"Why are you all dolled up?" Mary Margaret picked up an eyebrow pencil and filled in Edith's freshly plucked, gray brows. "It's close to your bedtime."

"If you're going to treat me like a child, I'm not going to let you play with my toys." Meaning Charlie's truck. Edith snatched the eyebrow pencil back, checked her look in the mirror, and re-tucked her left tata. "If you and Mims had your way, I'd be home in bed every night at seven and out fishing on the river at five." She hated fishing. She only went because Mims made her. And when she went, they laughed all morning. They hadn't laughed a lot together lately, but then again, with all the snow, they hadn't been fishing. "You haven't returned the motorcycle yet. Why do you need the truck?" She squinted in the mirror. Her top end was still lopsided.

At this rate, the neckline of her blouse was going to be stretched out of shape, as saggy as her boobage.

"I'd rather you didn't ask me questions." Mary Margaret seemed to register Edith's activities for the first time. "What are you doing with your bra?"

"Isn't it obvious?" Edith tucked her lipstick in the small black sequined clutch she normally only used for weddings and funerals. "I've got more sag on one side than the other." She gave one of the girls another boost. "Should I tape it in place?"

Mary Margaret had backed into the hallway, eyes nearly as wide open as her mouth.

"Don't look so shocked. Your tatas aren't the same size either. No one's are." Edith swiveled to check that she was level and square. "And it gets worse as you age, which is why I always sleep with a bra on." But not a constricting bullet bra like the one she had on now. "Admittedly, now that your grandfather's gone, I don't wear my black underwire." Mims had convinced her to switch to a more relaxed sports bra.

Mary Margaret made a strangled sound.

Edith spritzed perfume at her cleavage. "Don't dodge the issue. Tell me what's going on with you. Why do you need the truck?"

"I told you, I don't want to be recognized." From the hallway, Mary Margaret blushed, which wasn't a good look on a redhead. "Plus, it snowed last night, and I didn't have the motorcycle's chains with me. I left the bike in Greeley, and I need to go get it. Then there will be no more motor vehicle borrowing...On second thought, I can't promise that. The next few months aren't looking good for me."

Edith stopped fussing and focused on her granddaughter—the blush, the fidget, the need for secrecy. There was only one conclusion. "You're in love with a married man." She rubbed her forehead. "This is a disaster."

The Widows Club is going to kick me off the board.

I need to elope with David first.

Saving her the embarrassment of being stripped of her title.

"I'm not having an affair with a married man." Mary Margaret put her hands on her hips. "Do *not* go spreading that rumor to your friends."

"When I encouraged you to date, I thought you were ready. Well, maybe not as ready as I am, but I hoped you wouldn't have a crisis like...like...like Lola did last spring. She nearly ran her life off the rails. And for what? Because she discovered her dead husband had cheated on her?" Edith paused, as another thought entered her head. "Did Derek cheat on you again? Is that what this is about?"

Mary Margaret blocked the bathroom door. "Could you just tell me where you hid the truck keys?"

Edith hid everything of value and rarely in the same place twice. "You didn't answer." Edith's back went rigid. "That means yes. If Derek wasn't dead, I'd kill that cheating rat turd."

Oh, heavenly days. Edith never used to use such strong language. What was happening to her?

"Grandma Edith—"

"And I felt sorry for Derek too. Dying of cancer. That's no way to go. Unless you're a lying cheat. In which case—"

"Derek didn't cheat on me!" Mary Margaret's hands fluttered in the air. "Except that time in Vegas. But Grandma Edith, just slow down and stop worrying. I should be worrying about you. You're dressed up for a night on the town, and it's almost nine o'clock. What's happening here?"

Edith lifted her chin. "I'm going out." She could be cagey about her personal life too. "What do you care? You never come over anymore. We never just cook and dance."

"First off..." Mary Margaret's blush returned. "Neither one of us has wanted to dance in a long time."

The doorbell rang.

Mary Margaret startled. "Who's that?"

"Your lover's wife. She's tracked you down." Edith drew a calming breath. All they had was each other. And hopefully soon they'd have her husband-to-be, David. "Actually, that's my date. And don't you say anything about doubling. I won't tolerate whining. I gave you your chance, and you decided to meet your married man *incognito*."

She opened the front door to the most sought-after bachelor in town. "Hello, David. I'm so glad we're going out this evening. Did you enjoy your game?" She'd swung by the retirement home mid-afternoon and found him playing Mahjong with three widows. He was truly all the rage, and the sooner she took him off the market and away from the competition, the sooner she'd be able to sleep at night. "Look." She pointed to the ceiling, posturing like a pin-up, because that's what men liked. "Mistletoe."

David glanced up and then down at Edith with a sexy smile. "Can't buck tradition." He swooped in with a kiss.

To her cheek.

But still, Edith's heart tripped through the matrimonial tulips.

"I'd like her home by ten." Mary Margaret stood behind Edith, frowning.

"Such a kidder." Edith turned and gave her granddaughter a look of intense disapproval.

Edith ushered David inside and went to retrieve the truck keys from behind the cable box. Charlie had purchased the truck two years ago and paid for an on-board support system that could be used like a cell phone to call for help or as a tracking system if someone stole the truck. A waste of money, if you asked Edith.

She dangled the key fob in front of Mary Margaret. "Last chance to tell me where you're going." *And with whom.*

Mary Margaret wasn't talking, other than to say thanks.

Suddenly, all Edith's battle gear constricted her airflow. The motorcycle. The Christmas tree farm. The lack of dancing. Mary Margaret was in trouble.

"Is something wrong?" David asked when Mary Margaret was behind the wheel of the truck and Edith stood at the window watching her drive off.

Edith should turn, roll her shoulders back, and smile. Men liked women who were no trouble and had no cares. Especially older men who didn't wear orthopedic footwear. They were in the minority and had their pick of women.

Normally, Edith had no problem putting herself first but Mary Margaret had been her rock when Charlie died. She'd held her hand through all the funeral arrangements, despite the fact that she'd just buried her own husband. They supported each other through thick and thin.

Mary Margaret needs me.

Behind Edith, her date shifted on his feet.

If I let this chance slip away, Mims will get David for sure.

And Edith hated to lose. But there was the welfare of her flesh and blood to consider.

"David." Edith faced her date but didn't thrust her 18-hour assets his way. "How would you like to go on a little adventure?"

His smile was slow growing but gratifying. And if she squinted, his smile was reminiscent of Charlie's, whose framed picture was on the mantel.

"We'll need to gas up your car." Edith checked her cell phone to make sure it was fully charged and then opened the app that tracked the location of Charlie's truck. The one and only time she'd done so. "And I can't promise you I'll behave when we arrive at our destination."

If Mary Margaret was silly enough to get involved with a married man, Edith was going to put a stop to it, no matter the cost.

Chapter Fourteen

We need to have a talk about your mask."

"My mask?" Mary Margaret blew past Ned toward the exit. The show was over. The evening had been another uptick in the Hanky Panky's success. But she'd pulled something in her neck during her second performance, causing a kink that felt as large as a lump of dried Play-Doh in her neck. She couldn't hold her head up straight without causing a muscle spasm.

"You should take the mask off at the end of the show." Ned lumbered behind her, breathing heavy. "Throw the audience a bone. You've got a nice face. They might tip you more to see it."

They were still inside the club but they might just as well have stepped outside because Mary Margaret was suddenly as cold as ice. "The mask is part of Foxy Roxy's mystique."

"I like her mask." Didi trailed behind them. "I was going to ask to borrow one."

"The last thing you need is to cover up more," Ned snapped.

"The customers like it." Mary Margaret turned stiffly, mindful of her twinging neck muscle. "In fact, your clientele is changing. You should probably consider adding male dancers too. I've seen bridal shower parties in here every time I dance."

"Me too." Didi smiled, looking weary.

"Male dancers?" Ned was horrified. "What would my regulars think?"

"The guys who order the two-drink minimum?" The ones who tipped one-dollar bills? Mary Margaret shrugged, not the wisest of moves given her physical condition. She needed a heating pad and some Tylenol. "They won't fund your retirement. Don't cling to loyalty at the expense of profit."

"Roxy, you forgot to take your mask off." Didi pointed at her face.

"Oh, geez. I forgot. I'll take it off when I get home." Truth was, Mary Margaret had left her mask on in case Kevin was waiting for her outside, not that she'd seen him in the audience, but the bigger the crowd, the harder it was to make out individual faces. "Can someone help me put my motorcycle in the back of my truck?"

"Not it," Ned grumbled, returning to the bowels of the club. "Bad back."

"Oh, shoot." Didi glanced over her shoulder. "I forgot my biology flash cards in the dressing room. If you wait a minute, I can help."

"I'll lower the tailgate and bring the bike over." Mary Margaret opened the back door and froze.

Grandma Edith stood a few feet away.

Mask. Knit cap. Hoodie. There was a chance her grandmother wouldn't recognize her.

Mary Margaret ducked her head and started to walk past.

"This is the reason you've been sneaking around?" Grandma Edith's low heels clacked on the snowplowed pavement as she fell into step with Mary Margaret.

So much for wishful thinking.

Mary Margaret pulled up short. "How did you find me?"

"The truck is one of those smart cars that you can track on the internet." She eyed Mary Margaret up and down. "I suppose you're going to tell me you've got a second job at this place." She sounded betrayed. "I suppose you're going to tell me you're waiting tables here ... with a mask on."

"That sounds about right," Mary Margaret fibbed. After all, Grandma Edith would never go inside a club like this. "Why are you here?" At her age, waiting in the cold couldn't be good for her.

Grandma Edith's brow furrowed. "I was worried about you. I thought you were in trouble. I had to pick you up from the hospital once, you know."

She knew. Mary Margaret rubbed her neck, trying to loosen up the muscle and the guilt. Instead, she felt relief that her grandmother hadn't watched her dance. "What about your date?"

"David's at the coffee shop. He thinks I went to the ladies' room." Edith turned and headed that way. "I can't think with this girdle on. We'll talk tomorrow. Meet me at the Saddle Horn for breakfast."

Mary Margaret drew a deep breath.

At least she didn't call me a sinner.

But still, guilt raked at Mary Margaret's insides. She wanted to tell her grandmother the truth but she couldn't risk it. Grandma Edith was a leaky sieve when it came to secrets.

Mary Margaret sighed and headed for her grandfather's truck.

Laurel and Hardy came around from the front, looking grumpy and cold.

"I was wondering how you could make your payments." Mr. Hardy rested one arm on the truck bed and used his free hand to make a *gimme* motion. "We'll take whatever you made tonight."

Mary Margaret flinched, and the pinched nerve in her neck nearly caused her to fall over. "How did you find me?" She dug in her purse and handed over her cash. "I need a receipt for that."

"We followed your granny," Mr. Laurel said while his partner counted her money. "You're a good dancer. Even your granny thought so." He put a fresh red stir stick in his mouth.

"She saw me?" Mary Margaret's neck twinged once more. She'd hoped to dance without being found out until spring. She hadn't lasted until Christmas. "She came inside?"

"I bought her and her date tickets," Mr. Laurel said with a rare grin. "It was the least I could do after she led us here."

Mary Margaret wheezed. It was worse than she thought.

"My man here tried to steal your granny from her date." Mr. Hardy removed an envelope from his pocket and tucked Mary Margaret's bills inside. He *tsk*ed. "Always thinking he's a Romeo."

Mr. Laurel shrugged, practically blushing. "I like my women seasoned."

"I think I'm going to be sick." Mary Margaret bent over and tried to breathe through the nausea.

The tall thug bent to her level. "You don't think I'm good enough for your granny?" His question came bullet fast.

"I'm afraid you..." She drew herself up and swallowed back bile. "I'm afraid you'll hurt her if I can't make money fast enough."

Mr. Laurel spit out his stir stick, scowl deepening. "I would break *your* legs before my woman's."

"That's comforting." *Not.* Mr. Laurel was in a questionable profession. She preferred not to call him Grandpa someday.

Laurel and Hardy turned to go without having given her a receipt. Not that she'd actually expected one.

Didi still hadn't reappeared—which kept her safe, Mary Margaret supposed.

"Hey, I need help." Mary Margaret thought she was about as low as she could get, asking Laurel and Hardy for assistance.

The men faced her with closed-off expressions.

"I need to get my motorcycle in the back of the pick-up." She tried smiling but it felt more like a grimace. "Do a girl a solid."

Surprisingly, they did.

Maybe they were starting to like her.

Or perhaps they pitied her.

Mary Margaret didn't know which was worse.

Chapter Fifteen

What are you doing here?" Barb scowled at Kevin
when he showed up at her house on Sunday morning.
It was only seven-thirty but she was dressed and had
makeup on. Odd, since she didn't go to church. "You
need to call before you come over."

"I need to talk to you about Tad." He should have
talked to her before this.

"Babe?" A deep, masculine voice carried from inside
the house.

Barb flinched.

"Is that..." Kevin stepped closer and lowered his
voice. "Is that a man? Did you...while Tad was here?"

Barb had a really good poker face but her expression
cracked, showing her derision. "If you remember, you
turned me down."

"Babe?" That voice.

Kevin knew it from somewhere.

"So...what?" Kevin craned his neck to see past her.
"You just called the next guy on your list?"

A man in a blue terry cloth bathrobe appeared in the hallway. "Oh, hey, Kev. How's it going?"

"Iggy," Kevin said in a hard voice, hoping Paul and Paula didn't find out about this. "That robe looks better on you than it ever did on me."

Barb very carefully kept her back to Iggy but her cheeks were turning red.

"Thanks, buddy." Iggy apparently had no qualms about Kevin finding him in his old house and his old bathrobe. "Want some coffee?"

"No, thanks." Kevin felt more like starting his day with a stiff shot of whiskey.

"Daddy!" Tad ran into the foyer wearing ninja jammies. "We had a sleepover."

"Goody," Kevin murmured. So much for wondering how Barb had explained her lover's presence.

Tad grabbed on to Kevin's hand. "Do you want to go to the Saddle Horn?"

"I'd love to. Put some clothes on. I'll wait." Outside, where the temperature was warmer than inside.

Tad ran back to his room.

"Coffee's ready." Iggy headed for the kitchen. "I'll just grab myself a cup."

"You have Tad three nights a week, Barb." Kevin said in a hard, low voice. "We agreed there would be no *sleepovers* during those nights."

Barb's scrutiny was intense. "Are you jealous?"

"No." He meant it too. Their divorce had been hard enough on Tad without him seeing Mommy sleep over with a man she had no intention of dating, much less marrying. "I never broke the rules when we were married. And you've been doing it nonstop. I came here this morning because I wanted to talk about Tad. A five-year-old shouldn't be on a diet. Kids pack on weight, and then they grow. He's the child of divorce. He doesn't need you giving him a complex about food too, in addition to *that*." Kevin waved a hand toward the kitchen.

"Childhood obesity is a serious issue, Kev." Barb grabbed the edge of the door as if prepared to shut him out.

"Agreed, but that isn't Tad's problem."

"I disagree." Apparently, she and Kevin didn't see eye to eye on much anymore.

"I'll make him an appointment at Dr. Arnett's." The town doctor. "He'll be the judge."

"Fine."

"Fine."

Tad ran out the door and didn't stop until he reached Kevin's SUV. "Come on, Daddy. This ninja needs breakfast."

Without another word, Barb shut the door in Kevin's face.

Kevin stalked back to the SUV, knowing it would take more than a hot chocolate at the Saddle Horn to diffuse his mood. "Let's invite Grandma and Grandpa along."

"Sweet!" Tad was already buckled in.

His parents were happy to accompany them so Kevin swung by to pick them up.

Tad ran to the door and rang the bell like it was a button on a video game controller.

Ding-dong, ding-dong, ding-dong.

"Who's there?" Kevin's dad opened the door and stared over Tad's head as if he didn't see him.

"It's me! It's me!" Tad jumped up and down, waving his arms.

Dad opened the door and welcomed them in. He did a double take when he saw Kevin's face. "I can tell you've had words with the ex this morning. How about an Irish coffee before we go to breakfast?"

"I'll just take the Irish." Meaning a shot of whiskey.

"Coming right up." True to his word, Dad went straight to the wet bar in the living room. "Have you heard anything else after that political meeting you had?"

"No." Kevin bit back a frustrated growl. "It's the holiday season. They're probably busy." Investigating his almost-girlfriend, who he still needed to inform of that fact.

"No need to rush." His father sounded upbeat, maybe even relieved.

Kevin's head hurt.

"Daddy! Come look at their Christmas tree. It's all silver and black." Tad danced around it. "And look! There's a ninja!"

"It looks great." Kevin made the appropriate sounds of approval. His mother always had a theme or color scheme for her tree. He'd never seen black on a Christmas tree but it fit his mood.

Tad gasped. "Look. There's already a present under there." He dropped to his knees. "And it's to me!" He glanced up at Kevin. "Can I open it?"

"No. It's a *Christmas* present. Not an everyday present." Kevin pointed out the Santa-themed wrapping paper.

Tad fell onto his back and held his fists to his stomach as if he'd been stabbed. "But it's *forever* until Christmas."

"Isn't it funny how some things in life seem like

they last forever." Dad handed Kevin a double. "But it's actually only one small moment in a lifetime. I wouldn't stress." He looked from his son to his grandson.

"Wise words, old man." Kevin drank half of the whiskey, letting it burn its way down his throat. "Tad, the wait will be made easier because you're getting a mile-high whip today."

Tad sat up with a dramatic gasp. "I never get mile-high whips."

"And pancakes." Kevin finished the last of his drink and drew a deep breath. "I'm ready to face the world."

Dad clapped him on the shoulder and took the tumbler to the kitchen.

"How did the wrapping go last night?" Mom came down the hall, putting her jacket on. "I felt bad about sending you but we'd made plans with the Reeds."

"I fluffed bows and encouraged people to get creative with their tags while Maggie wrapped."

Mom picked up her purse from the table in the foyer. "Who's Maggie?"

"Mary Margaret." Kevin realized he probably shouldn't be calling her that in front of anyone else.

"Oh, so now she's *Maggie*." His mother's voice took on that knowing tone.

"She's the perfect girl for a second go-round." Dad returned and took his jacket off a hook near the door. "When you marry her, she'll become ineligible for the Widows Club fashion show. And then everyone would forget…"

Kevin and his mother stared at him.

"Forget what, hon?" Mom demanded sharply.

"Nothing," his father mumbled.

Mom swung around to face Kevin, slim eyebrows raised.

"No clue." Kevin held up his hands.

But then he remembered why his father had stepped in it. Kevin had emceed a few Widows Club fashion shows over the last few years. Maggie had participated last spring. She'd strutted down that catwalk like she'd owned it.

Like Roxy.

Kevin smiled. There was hope for that kiss yet. "What's wrong with the way Maggie was in the fashion show?"

"Never mind," Dad mumbled.

Mom swatted Dad's arm.

Kevin shepherded them out the door and into his SUV, his mood considerably lightened.

✳

Mary Margaret dressed conservatively for breakfast with her grandmother at the Saddle Horn.

A gray tunic sweater. Jeans. Boots. Her hair in a thick braid covering her kinked neck.

She was working on her second cup of coffee when Grandma Edith came in. She waved to her cronies on the Widows Club board. They sat in their usual corner booth in the back.

"Mornin'." Pearl appeared at their table with the coffee pot and a holster with a can of whipped cream, ready to make mile-high whips.

Grandma Edith fished in her purse for several little containers of flavored creamer. "I'll have coffee, Pearl. Room for cream."

"And..." Pearl only filled Grandma Edith's cup halfway.

"And I'll have the special, only without the blueberries and whipped cream." Grandma Edith leaned over her mug and whispered toward Mary Margaret, "My undergarments last night gave me the fumes. I've decided to lose a few pounds." She busied herself doctoring her coffee.

"Hence the pancakes and creamer," Pearl deadpanned, staring at Mary Margaret. "And you?"

"I'll have two eggs scrambled." Mary Margaret swiped one of her grandmother's flavored creamers and added it to her own coffee as Pearl left them. "Didn't Pearl used to give you French vanilla creamers?"

"Yes." Grandma Edith sniffed. "But they started charging me for them. I can get them cheaper at Emory's Grocery."

Over at the counter, Laurel and Hardy were eating breakfast. Mr. Laurel gave Mary Margaret a narrow-eyed stare before beaming at Grandma Edith.

Who beamed back.

Mary Margaret's stomach slid to the floor. "You don't talk to that man, do you?" She nodded toward Mr. Laurel and then used her commanding kindergarten voice. "The tall man who's at least twenty years younger than you."

"Who cares how old he is?" Grandma Edith executed a little shoulder shimmy, accented by an eyelash flutter. "He paid my cover last night."

"And how did David feel about that?" Trying to garner her grandmother's attention, Mary Margaret shifted her torso back and forth—stiffly, given her neck issues.

Meanwhile, her grandmother had her own style of fidgeting. *Flutter. Shoulder roll. Coquettish smile.*

"Grandma." Mary Margaret snapped her fingers in the air between them. "Grandma Edith. I asked you a question."

"What?" Her grandmother returned her attention to Mary Margaret. "You know, there's a ritual to catching a man. Haven't you ever watched *National Geographic*?"

Mary Margaret considered thunking her forehead on the Formica. "I wanted to know how your date was last night."

"David thought I was interesting and adventurous given I took him…" Grandma Edith leaned forward once more.

Mary Margaret had a feeling this was going to be a whisper-laden breakfast.

"…to a strip club. As he should. I am interesting and adventurous. I'm starting to get my feminine mojo back."

"It's burlesque." Mary Margaret massaged her neck. "Not stripping. Nothing comes off."

"Never?" Grandma Edith looked more shocked at this than at Mary Margaret's part-time job.

"Never," Mary Margaret reassured her.

"That's not quite as adventurous." Grandma Edith pursed her lips in disappointment. "I assumed the stripping part came during the late show. David had to get home. He had an early breakfast appointment."

"That was the only show of the night. And from what I hear about town, it's more likely David had an early morning date, not a breakfast appointment." Mary Margaret glanced around, surprised that David wasn't here with another woman.

Kevin entered the diner with his parents and Tad. His glance was warm and made Mary Margaret want to flutter her hands, roll her shoulders, and bat her eyes. But then she noticed his parents. They scrutinized Mary Margaret as if they were bartending and she was underage and trying to buy a drink with fake I.D.

What had Kevin told them about her? That she was a dead-fish kisser? Mary Margaret frowned.

"I was shocked last night," Grandma Edith was saying. "I didn't let David see I was but still..."

The Hadleys were seated in the back dining room, where families with kids let them order hot chocolate topped with four to six inches of whipped cream. The topping wasn't for eating. Kids dunked their faces in it, creating white beards and mustaches. Mary Margaret had been told it was a tradition started by Pearl decades earlier to keep her daughter, Bitsy, busy while she worked. Today, gray-haired Pearl topped off the whip to the delight of several children. As a grown up, Bitsy sipped tea in the corner booth.

Kevin stared at Mary Margaret over the top of his menu, smiling like he wanted to coax her into another kiss.

If only his kisses could wipe away all her debt.

"I was torn while I watched you." Grandma Edith paused to sip her coffee. "On the one hand, I wanted to storm the stage and throw my coat around you. Is this an addiction of yours? Should I get you in counseling? You can't tell me that's normal."

Tad fairly trembled with excitement when Pearl brought him his mug and topped it with inches and inches of whipped cream. He dunked his entire face in it and then turned to Kevin, grinning and dripping and having a wonderful time.

Something inside Mary Margaret panged. Not being a child of Sunshine, she'd never had a mile-high whip of her own. She'd never be a part of that ritual, never a part of the Hadley family.

"On the other hand..." Grandma Edith leaned forward to whisper, "Tell me everything. How did you start? I couldn't sleep last night for wondering if—"

"Stop right there." Mary Margaret recognized that tone. It was her grandmother's *I-can-do-that* octave. "Mom would kill me if you started an exotic dance career. You know... You have to know. That's why we don't talk." She confessed how she'd paid her way through college.

"And here I thought he'd caught you with a boy. *Pfft*. Dancing. They talk about dancing in the Bible, you know." Grandma Edith smiled conspiratorially. "I'm going to need a stage name."

Mary Margaret shook her head once, stopped by the pulled muscle. "It's not going to happen. And it's not safe." Not when reputations were at stake.

Reality was, Ned would never allow Grandma Edith on stage. He was so uptight that he wouldn't allow men, much less older women.

Reality was, Mary Margaret couldn't keep her side gig a secret forever. Her livelihood and Kevin's reputation, if she didn't keep him at arm's length, were at stake.

Reality sucked.

"Not safe?" Grandma Edith's eyes narrowed. "Are you undercover? Is that why those two men slashed your tires the other night?" She didn't wait for Mary Margaret to answer. "It is. No one would ever expect a kindergarten teacher to go deep undercover. And sticking your tires throws the real baddies off the scent. I knew there was a reason I liked that tall man."

Kevin was giving his order to Pearl but his eyes were on Mary Margaret, stealing her breath, depriving her brain of much-needed oxygen to follow her grandmother's logic, to register her grandmother's shoulder roll, eye flutter, and coquettish smile for what it was. And then her words sank in.

She thinks I'm undercover. She thinks Mr. Laurel is a good guy.

Mary Margaret drew a deep breath, prepared to argue, when it hit her. The undercover alibi worked perfectly for her grandmother. If Grandma Edith slipped and said anything about this, no one would believe her. Mary Margaret would have to figure out a way to clarify that Mr. Laurel was *not* on the right side of the law, but the ruse could work.

"You're right." Mary Margaret tried to look contrite. "I'm undercover. Someone contacted the sheriff looking for recruits who could dance."

"It's why you don't want to drive your car," Grandma Edith surmised.

"Yes." It wasn't hard for Mary Margaret to look like this was serious business, because it was. Just not the serious business her grandmother made it out to be.

"Are you in danger?" The spoon Grandma Edith had been using to stir her coffee clattered to the Formica. Her eyes teared up. "I can't lose you too."

"I'll be fine." Mary Margaret gave her a reassuring smile, hoping it was true.

"No." Grandma Edith sat back and placed her hands on the tabletop. "I can't let you do this. Not alone."

What?

"We're a team, you and I." Grandma Edith's head wobbled. "Except on dates. I've decided doubles aren't my thing because..." She leaned forward, gaze drifting to her admirer at the diner counter. "I got a kiss good-night." She smacked her lips. "And there's more where that came from."

Grateful for the diversion, Mary Margaret played along. "David has skills?"

"David has the touch." She preened, gaze drifting to Mr. Laurel. "Maybe your FBI fella has the touch too?"

Holy Gone-to-Your-Head.

"Should you risk your relationship with David with a wandering eye?" Lame. But what the heck was Mary Margaret supposed to say? Grandma Edith never did anything halfway. She always dove all-in on the deep end.

"Well, David..." Grandma Edith withdrew what she was putting out, glancing toward the Widows Club booth.

"Hey, you didn't tell me. Did the girls stay in place?" Mary Margaret blurted, gesturing in the general direction of her grandmother's secret weapons.

Grandma Edith grinned. "They don't call it the 18 Hour Bra for nothing, honey." She framed her breasts and gave them a supportive squeeze. And then she frowned. "I should take you shopping. You needed more support beneath your flapper costume last night."

And just like that, they were back in the trouble zone.

"David didn't notice, did he?" Mary Margaret tried to steer the ship back to safer waters.

"He might have. He's very detail oriented. One of the other gals wore those harem pants. I didn't notice they were slit up the sides until he pointed them out."

Mary Margaret had a sudden dislike of David.

"And that one girl...*Crystal*? He liked her ripped costume." Grandma Edith sipped her coffee. "I'd like a dress with flapper fringe, if only to see him smile when the tassles shake. Maybe I'll get a pole at the house so we can practice."

"No." Mary Margaret sucked in a breath.

"Good morning, ladies." Kevin came to stand near Mary Margaret. With the familiarity of more than friendship, his hand slid back and forth across her shoulders before landing in his rear jeans pocket. The gossip grapevine was going to love that.

"Kevin..." Grandma Edith's brow furrowed. "You don't know how to dance, do you?"

A pit of apprehension formed in Mary Margaret's stomach, waiting for the other stiletto to drop. "Of course he does. Remember, he's my partner when I teach dance the hour before the Widows Club Christmas Ball." She would have liked to have forgotten that fact.

She could see the wheels doing a slow turn in Grandma Edith's head the moment she'd said *teach dance*.

Kevin grinned, oblivious to the undercurrents. "We should get together and practice."

"Oh, no. If I can't have a pole, you can't have lessons," Edith said.

"Pole?" Kevin's brow furrowed.

"Time out. Time out." Mary Margaret made a T with her hands. "There's some confusion here. *We*"—

she gestured between Kevin and herself—"are teaching *ballroom* dancing at the request of the Widows Club." She fixed her grandmother with a firm stare. "If you've forgotten this, maybe you should head on over to the board meeting in the back."

Edith made a choking noise and glanced toward her cronies. "I was here to support you and now..." She turned back around. Smiled. Shook her finger at Mary Margaret. "I get what you're doing. You're trying to protect me."

Mary Margaret stared up at Kevin and sent him a telepathic message: *Save me.*

Kevin didn't disappoint. "If you're worried about your skill on the dance floor," he said to Edith, "you have nothing to worry about. Patti told me David has two left feet, *and* I know that Maggie is a patient teacher, whether it's kindergartners or regular folks like you and me."

"He's clueless." Grandma Edith's brows lowered. "Handsome but clueless."

Kevin smiled at Mary Margaret as if he hadn't heard. "Tad and I were wondering if you wanted to go to the movies this afternoon."

"She's very busy," Grandma Edith said before Mary Margaret could say anything. "*We're* very busy." She nodded knowingly toward Laurel and Hardy at the counter.

"I'd love to go." Mary Margaret ignored the warning bells in her head because, right now, Kevin seemed to be the lesser of her problems. Right now, Grandma Edith needed a cool-down period.

"Great. I'll pick you up around twelve-thirty."

Mary Margaret plastered a smile on her face and shooed him off with one hand.

She waited until Kevin had returned to his family. And then she waited until Pearl delivered their breakfast. And then Mary Margaret reached across the table to clasp her grandmother's hands, gave them a squeeze, and said, "Undercover means you can't tell anyone. Undercover means no one will understand references like 'pole.' Undercover means in order to keep me safe, you have to zip your lips."

Edith tugged her hands free. "You don't have to talk to me like I'm the weakest link." She stared at her plain pancakes. "Why do they list the special as special? There's nothing special about this plate."

Mary Margaret sighed and wondered what dollar figure she needed to reach before Laurel and Hardy could leave town.

Chapter Sixteen

✳

It's done." Grim as death, Edith sat with the Widows Club board, resigned to her fate. This was it; they were going to kick her off the board.

"Yes." Bitsy nodded. "We're canceling the Christmas Ball. Fifteen tickets sold."

"That's not what…" Edith grimaced. "I'm sorry, Bitsy."

"That's not what you wanted to announce?" Clarice looked up from her mile-high whip, a white goatee sliding down her chin.

"Mary Margaret has a date with Kevin." Edith hated to admit it but her failure was like a Band-Aid. It had to be ripped off. "They're going to the movies and taking Tad."

"Oh, Edith." Mims didn't look happy. "Even Iggy would be better than Kevin at this point."

"Or Tom Bodine." Bitsy set down her tea. "He's grumpy but stable."

"Or Jason Petrie." Clarice wiped her face clean and then stared at her whip as if determining whether she should take another go. "I think he learned his lesson about how to treat women when Darcy dumped him.

Although, did you hear he's writing a dating advice column? One that includes advice for the...*boudoir*?"

Her statement was met with open-mouthed bewilderment. Edith was simultaneously shocked and intrigued.

"Anyway." Clarice cleared her throat. "I take back my pick of Jason and replace him with David Jessup."

Mims's and Edith's mouths continued to hang open. Bitsy chuckled.

"Why would you put David's name in the mix?" Mims recovered first, fluffing her spiky hair.

"I saw him coming out of Prestige Salon with Barb the other day." Clarice dipped her chin in the white foam. "They were doing the head nod and hug, as if they'd made plans to meet. If David's interested in a younger woman—and we all know older men usually are—why wouldn't we see if there are sparks between Mary Margaret and David?"

Bitsy picked up her teacup and tried to hide a smile, gosh darn her.

Mims and Edith stared at each other, neither one willing to admit they had David in their own gun sights.

"Edith." The tall man who'd paid her cover last night captured her hand and brought it to his lips. "I've been meaning to ask you to share a drink with me." His blue eyes were full of masculine appreciation. "I noticed you like piña coladas."

Edith held her breath and then...giggled. She'd had one last night.

"Who is he?" Clarice asked, loud enough for the man to hear.

Bitsy and Mims shrugged, perplexed looks on their faces.

"My apologies, beautiful ladies." He bowed slightly. "My name is Francisco but my friends call me Paco."

"I thought you were Laurel and..." Edith turned to look at the other man, as short as Paco was tall. "Oh, I see. It's one of Mary Margaret's jokes."

"You didn't give me an answer, sweet one." Paco's eyes sparkled like sapphires.

"Isn't he a little young for you?" Clarice asked, wiping her chin again.

Edith hesitated. Mary Margaret had cautioned her against playing the field. But David seemed to be dividing up his eggs by the retirement home busload. And then there was Mary Margaret, who needed backup on the job.

On the job? Hot diggity.

Paco was one of those feds who'd put Mary Margaret undercover at the dance club.

"Yes, I'd love to have that drink with you. At our usual place?" She'd pack one of Mims's handguns just in case things got ugly at the Hanky Panky. Of course she'd have to swipe one first.

"*The usual place*?" Mims's eyes bugged.

"The usual place isn't open tonight, sweet one. Shall we say Tuesday?"

Edith nodded.

"I'll pick you up at your house at nine."

"Nine p.m.?" Mims couldn't believe it.

"I look forward to it." Edith extended her hand to Paco for another kiss.

He obliged, leaving Edith feeling like the cat's meow.

There was no way the board was stripping her of her vice presidency now. She was a woman of mystery.

And enigmatic females were powerful beings to be reckoned with.

*

"Hey." Kevin stood on Maggie's stoop, unable to stop staring.

Her hair was gathered over one shoulder. Red curls tumbled in one unruly wave that led his eye over gentle curves beneath a pea green turtleneck and black leggings.

He was speechless because she was beautiful. And he was speechless because he didn't want to say anything to scare her off. Things weren't going as he'd planned.

"I want to be clear." Maggie met his gaze squarely. "This doesn't qualify as a date since Tad is along." And then she stepped out, locking the door behind her.

Now Kevin couldn't say anything. He walked her to the SUV and opened the door for her.

She climbed in and he closed the door, trying to walk to his side as if this was no big deal.

"Where's Tad?" she asked before he'd climbed behind the wheel.

"Yeah, about that..." Kevin sat next to her, scratching the stubble on his chin. This close, he could smell her flowery perfume. "Tad got an offer to go to the movies with his very good ninja friends, Jose and Eric. I was disinvited. And if I can't go..."

Maggie crossed her arms and gave him a look of disapproval she'd probably perfected as a teacher.

Unlike at his interview with his political party, he refused to crack. "I thought I'd take you somewhere we can talk without being interrupted." So he could understand why she seemed to like him but didn't want to date him. He wanted to tell her about mentioning her to Paul and Paula during his preliminary interview. And he'd love a second chance at a kiss.

"If you say your place"—her blue eyes flashed a warning—"I'm jumping out now."

"Not my place." He started the engine.

"Okay, but..." Maggie seemed relieved, although still hesitant. "Not anywhere in town."

"You want to sneak around with the dangerous mayor?" he teased as he backed out of her driveway. "I like the sound of that."

"What am I going to do with you?"

"I have an idea or two." When he had the SUV in gear, he took her hand, learning the texture of her smooth skin with his thumb. "I have two lattes in my center console and some sugar cookies from Olde Time Bakery in the back." Because he knew how much she liked caffeine and sweets.

She stared at their hands but didn't pull away. "I'm listening."

"I want to take you somewhere important to me." A place he rarely visited anymore. "And then we'll talk and drink coffee like civilized couples who live in towns where few people know their true identities."

"*Incognito,*" Maggie murmured, smiling but holding her neck stiffly.

"You have a kink in your neck. How did that happen?"

"How does any muscle strain happen? You move cold muscles too fast." Maggie sank back against the leather seat and closed her eyes. "Wake me up when we get there."

"Hey." He gently shook her hand. "We're on a date. You should be talking to me."

"You tricked me." Maggie didn't open her eyes but her lips turned upward. "I was planning on napping during the movie but I need to steal a couple *z*'s now. You don't mind, do you?"

"If I did, you'd only have me drive you home."

"Smart man. You'll probably make something of yourself someday, like mayor."

He grinned, taking the back streets. It wasn't long before he parked behind a large building south of the convenience store.

Maggie opened her eyes and glanced around. "I thought we were taking a drive out into the wilderness, like to Saddle Horn Pass or something." It had a romantic lookout.

He took her assumption as a positive.

"This is Hadley Furniture." He'd parked in one of the delivery bays in the back of the warehouse.

"And we're here because..."

"I'll show you." He got out, making sure to bring the coffee and cookies.

Once they were inside, he turned the warehouse lights on. There were several workstations throughout this end of the building with couches, chairs, tables, and headboards in various states of finish.

"This is the end of the line." He took a newspaper and laid it on a walnut coffee table before setting the coffee and cookies on top. "This is where all the finished furniture sits before it gets shipped out or put on the showroom floor." He offered her a seat on a loveseat with burgundy flowered cushions.

Maggie looked around. "Did you ever work here?"

"Yeah. When I was a kid, I came here after school and cleaned up the work areas." He'd come home with wood shavings in his hair and upholstery strings on his clothing, so proud of his contribution to the family business. "But my dad and grandfather...They were ecstatic to have me here. They'd bring me in on weekends and teach me how to run the saws and the lathes." He ran a hand over the beveled edge of the coffee table. "I liked it but I loved driving the forklift better. I was operating the heavy equipment before I could legally drive." And then after his grandfather had died, he'd fallen in love with sports and his work at the shop diminished.

Maggie chose a plain, round sugar cookie, one without holiday embellishments, and settled back against the cushion. "When was the last time you made a piece of furniture?"

"I made a crib for Tad." His throat threatened to close the way it always did when he thought about his little guy. "I built it out of ash. It's a sturdy wood. And sometimes...More often lately, I lie awake at night thinking about making a piece of furniture again. Maybe a bunk bed..." His voice trailed off.

"Kids love bunk beds. Do you think Tad could help?" She catalogued his expression. "What's wrong?"

"The problem is...I don't think I'm going to have time." He explained about his opportunity at the state level of politics.

Maggie chewed her cookie, working her neck and shoulder between bites, occasionally flinching. "You're going places. Don't forget folks in Sunshine when you serve in Washington."

Kevin was reminded of the party's implication that he'd need to establish two households. He stared at his parents' offices, frowning.

She sipped her coffee, studying him intently. "I can tell you're worried about something. Why don't you tell me what's on your mind? Maybe I can help."

"It's just..." What would it hurt to tell her? "When I was growing up, my dad and grandfather missed out on a lot of my games because they were here. Working. If I'm lucky enough to achieve office at a higher level, I'm going to miss out on some of Tad's milestones."

"Isn't that the dilemma all working parents face?" Maggie rolled her head in a circle. "Don't all dreams come at a cost?"

"Is it wrong to want it all?" Kevin set down his coffee. "Turn around. Let me work the kinks out."

Maggie hesitated before putting her back toward him and turning the cowl of her turtleneck up toward her hairline. "Okay but keep a layer of turtleneck between us, because you're—"

"Dangerous. Yes, I know." He placed his palms on her shoulders and worked his thumbs in the muscles between her shoulder blades and her neck.

"Gosh, that feels good." Her head lolled forward and she sighed. "Would it be the end of the world if you stayed here and were mayor for twenty years or so? Would you consider yourself a failure if you turned down the opportunity?"

His gut clenched. His fingers stilled. "You mean quit?"

"I mean *choose*." With her chin to her chest, her voice was muffled.

"Everyone expects me to move on, even my father."

Even if his father didn't want him to go. He blew out a breath, which happened—completely by accident—to waft over her neck.

She made a soft mewling sound.

He found that kink and kneaded it ruthlessly.

Maggie groaned. "Oh, yeah. Right there."

It was all Kevin could do not to draw Maggie back into his lap and kiss her objections to a relationship away.

Somehow, she still had the ability to speak, even if he didn't. "So what you're saying is you don't want the town to see you as a failure. This is where Ms. Sneed, kindergarten teacher, would tell you that what matters is inside you, not what others see. What is it you hope to get out of higher office?"

"I want to make a difference in people's lives." Kevin cleared his throat, trying to sound like a man who wasn't dying with desire. "I want someone to say it all started here."

"You want to live forever," she teased.

"Nobody ever said going down in history as a positive game changer was a bad thing."

She made a noncommittal noise.

"Let's say I do serve in Denver, first as a state representative and later as governor." He wanted to knock wood but that would mean taking his hands off her. And that wasn't happening. "I want to prove I'm more than a Hadley from Sunshine, that I can succeed outside this small town. Would that work for you?"

Maggie drew a breath and straightened, rolling her shoulders. "I'd vote for you if that's what you mean."

"That's not what I mean." Kevin sat back and gave in to temptation, easing her head into his lap so he could stare down into her eyes. "I mean…" He couldn't explain. He had to show her.

Lifting her head, Kevin bent down to kiss her. Sideways. It was nothing like their first aborted kiss. This time there was heat and longing. Her arms came up around his neck, drawing him closer.

Sideways.

It should have been awkward.

It should have been uncomfortable.

But sideways worked. And why not? Sideways was his life. Nothing was in alignment. Not his career, not his future, not his love life.

And in that moment, he liked it like that.

*

There'd been moments in Mary Margaret's adult life where she'd felt like everything was right with her world.

The joy of dancing on the stage. The pride of supporting herself through college as a dancer. The early years of her marriage to Derek, when just being with him had filled her with happiness. The hour she'd spent in Kevin's arms this afternoon, so languid and at peace she'd forgotten the debt hanging over her head.

She lay on her couch staring at the Christmas tree Kevin had given her. It was a lovely little tree, subtly bringing cheer and the smell of Christmas to her home, much as Kevin's presence tried to bring warmth and joy to her heart.

Mary Margaret knew this window of everything being right in her world would close, just as surely as the Christmas tree would shrivel and die.

She'd learned to take what life offered because there was no guarantee happiness would last. In the case of Kevin, there was no guarantee that love would last. He needed to decide on a career path. If he ran for state representative, he'd have no time for a small-town teacher, much less the inclination to love her.

But she loved him.

The thought wrapped tightly around her chest. It should have inspired anxiety—that wrong-place, wrong-time, gut-churning feeling that doom was about to strike. Instead, it held her still, as if her very heart wanted to revel in this moment before it disappeared.

I love Kevin.

She loved his touch, his tenderness, and the passion in his kiss. She loved his commitment to the community, his willingness to volunteer, the way Tad meant the world to him. She loved that they'd grown up along parallel paths but in different universes—he in a small town with great expectations in him, she in a small ministry with great strictures placed on her. She loved that he was willing to put on a Santa suit so that children wouldn't be disappointed.

She couldn't ask to love a better man. But she'd never ask for him to love her.

Mary Margaret flopped onto her back, letting her arm fall out to the side where it banged into a cardboard box. This one was filled with Christmas decorations. She rolled back over and sat up. She might not feel so melancholy if she put an ornament on the tree. One ornament, not several. She opened the box. A photo sat on top of a package of red glass ornaments. It was a picture of Derek after his last round of chemo, sitting on the quad and wearing a broad grin. He was bald, practically toothless, his face swollen from the drugs he'd been taking to keep him alive. Mary Margaret couldn't help smiling back.

Her gaze went to their wedding photograph on the wall. A stranger might have had trouble recognizing Derek in both pictures. She didn't. The smile was the same. The joy was the same.

Her love for him was the same.

Oh, Derek.

She ran a finger over the picture of Derek and the quad. He'd lived life on his terms, making mistakes but making apologies as well. He'd suffered enough in life. She was letting go of all his recently discovered baggage so he could be at peace in the afterlife.

Someone knocked on her front door.

Mary Margaret's heart raced. "Kevin?" She hurried to open the door. But the man standing there didn't inspire love. She clutched the door handle. "What do you want?"

Mr. Laurel pushed his way inside and closed the door behind him, red stir stick in his fist, not his mouth. "I don't have much time. You're making a big mistake."

Mary Margaret's heart nearly stopped beating. "You're here to warn me about Mr. Hardy, aren't you? Do I have time to leave town?" How quickly her world dipped back into dangerous territory. "What about my grandmother? Is she safe?"

"She's in no danger." He made a derisive noise. "I'm talking about you dancing."

Mary Margaret's jaw might have dropped to the floor. She took a moment to pick it back up. "I'm dancing because you're demanding money from me."

"Listen. I hear people talk around town. Tradesmen stopping at the convenience store or the burger place. Guys at the bar. Women at the dentist's office and salon." Mr. Laurel touched his graying hair, which appeared to be freshly cut. "And there's buzz building about a dance club in Greeley. This isn't Miami with thousands of places to choose from for entertainment. Just on the way over here, I heard some teenagers talking about using their fake I.D.s to get into the Hanky Panky."

That was just the kind of prank the Bodine twins would pull.

"Your point?"

"Somebody is going to put two and two together." He gestured toward her legs. "Those are kind of unique, you know. You'll be found out. Quit now before you lose your life here." He gestured toward the door and downtown. "And that mayor you like so much."

Her head spun.

Somehow, Mary Margaret kept from fainting. "You have to realize what a huge irony it is that you—*Mr. Collection Agency*—are telling me to stop making the money I need to pay off a debt. If I don't dance, how am I supposed to pay you?"

He shrugged and left her.

Left her with nothing. Nothing but more danger and more risk.

Chapter Seventeen

✳

I don't like gingerbread." Tad slumped over his gingerbread math worksheet. "I like chocolate chip cookies."

It was mere minutes before the end of a long day. In addition to teaching Monday through Friday, Mary Margaret was dancing five nights a week, Tuesday through Saturday. Her neck was still bothering her, and all she wanted to do was go home, nap, and try to ignore Mr. Laurel's warning.

She had two choices. Let Tad's remark slide and release the class to gather their things and bundle up. Or use this as a teaching moment. Responsibility tugged at her conscience. "Class, Tad brings up an interesting point. Do you remember our discussion about friends?"

"Oh." Elizabeth's hand shot up. "We can be friends even if we don't like everything about our friends."

"Yes." Mary Margaret nodded. "The same applies to worksheets and homework. You may not like everything about it but it still has to be done."

"Shoot." Tad let his head drop to his desk just as the bell rang.

There was a flurry of activity. Several students tried to hurry out without cleaning up their desks. Mary Margaret tried to have eyes in the back of her head.

Barbara showed up at the door with a box filled with gift bags for their holiday party. She was the perfect example of Mary Margaret's teaching moment. There were things Mary Margaret didn't like about her but she was always willing to volunteer. And she was excellent at layering Mary Margaret's thick hair so that it fell in natural, manageable waves.

"I was wondering…" Barbara faced Mary Margaret as children flowed out the door past her. Despite having come in during a gentle snowstorm, her blond hair was immaculate. "Would you like to do something with me this weekend?"

"Uh…" Mary Margaret's lunch quivered in her stomach.

"My friends and I have been hearing good things about that new club in Greeley." Barbara smoothed a lock of Mary Margaret's hair.

It was all Mary Margaret could do not to flinch. "The Hanky Panky?"

"That's the one." Barbara slid her hands in her jacket pockets. "It'll be a fun girls night out, don't you think?"

The room was suddenly too empty.

Mary Margaret managed to mumble some excuse about promising her grandmother she'd help wrap presents.

"I still don't like gingerbread," Tad grumped, dilly-dallying with his ninja-themed backpack. And then he beamed. "*Daddy!*"

"Tad!" Kevin picked up his son and swung him around. His gaze locked with Mary Margaret's. And it was the kind of look that said, *You are my person, and I'm glad.*

I'm glad too.

She just wished Barbara wasn't here to witness their gladness.

"I have homework, Daddy." Tad resumed his petulant expression. "Gingerbread homework. Yuck."

Mary Margaret reminded Tad about finding something to like about his assignment.

"Are you ready for the town council meeting on the development project?" Barbara's normally cool voice was tinged with interest as she moved closer to Kevin. "Do you need any help?"

"I'm not talking about my career with you, Barb."

"Ms. Sneed, did Louise get crayon on your cheeks?" Tad pointed at her face as he wriggled out of his father's arms. "Daddy, look how red she is. Like Santa's suit." Tad laughed and ran into the bathroom that separated the two kindergarten classes.

Mary Margaret busied herself hanging Jose's forgotten backpack, picking up the pieces of a broken black crayon, and closing her lesson plan book. Tad was still in the bathroom, and his parents were still in her classroom.

Barb tossed her head and gave Mary Margaret a side-eye. "If you're going to date, Kev, make sure you vet this woman."

This woman inwardly cringed. Mary Margaret's secrets wouldn't stand up to vetting of any kind.

Tad flushed the toilet and banged the stall door open.

"'Vet this woman'?" His words may have parried Barbara's thrust but Kevin sounded as smooth as a fresh layer of snow on a softly slanting roof. "Like you vetted Iggy?"

"If you don't do it, I will," Barbara said coolly.

Uh-oh. Mary Margaret vowed to call in sick at the Hanky Panky on Friday.

Tad ran out of the bathroom and to his cubby.

"Go right ahead. She's got nothing to hide." Kevin joined his son at the wall of cubbies. "Let's get your snow boots on, Tad. We can tackle your gingerbread homework together before my next meeting."

"Somebody's got to watch out for you, Kev." Barbara glided toward the door, because stomping was beneath her.

Mary Margaret was frozen, trapped with no way out.

Tad's broad brow clouded. "Mommy's mad. She's madder than I am at gingerbread."

"But she's not mad at you," Kevin said firmly.

Tad's expression cleared, and his signature grin returned. He wrapped his arms around Kevin's legs. "I love you, Daddy. That's why I'll do gingerbread worksheets."

Kevin clung to his son a little too long. Something was wrong. Did he realize Mary Margaret wouldn't pass Barbara's inspection?

"Is everything okay?" Mary Margaret wanted to soothe the worry lines furrowing his brow. But she also wanted to lean into the strength of his embrace and hear him say everything was going to be all right.

"I don't want you to feel threatened," Kevin said.

Mary Margaret's breath caught. "I don't want you to be hurt."

"I'm hungry." Tad stomped in a circle in his snow boots.

"We'll pick up something before we go back to town hall." Kevin's gaze hadn't left Mary Margaret. "But before we go, Ms. Sneed needs a hug." He led Tad over and put his arms around her. "I'll take care of this."

"I love my teacher." Tad hugged her leg. "But I still hate gingerbread."

"Wait for me in the hall, Tad. I'll be right out." Kevin didn't say anything more until his son had left the room. "I've been meaning to tell you something."

That you love me?

Mary Margaret swallowed her question.

Kevin moved closer, holding her arm above her elbow. "When the party came to interview me... Well, your name came up."

"My name?" Mary Margaret sat on top of the nearest desk, which happened to be Tad's. "Why?"

Kevin shifted his feet the way Tad did on the rare occasion he considered his words carefully. "They need to do background checks on everyone close to me."

"You mean..." She pressed her hand to her throat. "They're going to investigate... me?" Run a credit report? Employment history?

He nodded.

Time slowed. She drew in a shaky breath. "You're saying that, not only is Barbara going to pry around my life, but your political party as well?" It was over. Whatever window she'd had to be with Kevin had been closed. She'd never survive this level of scrutiny.

"Daddy, come on." Tad clomped back into the classroom.

"I'm sorry." Kevin framed her face with his hands. "I know it seems like an invasion of privacy, but it's really nothing for someone like you."

Mary Margaret couldn't manage so much as a nod.

Kevin and Tad left. Mary Margaret sat at her desk and tried to work on a lesson plan, a futile effort. All she could think about was the corner she'd backed herself into. It was only a matter of time until everyone knew she was dancing at the Hanky Panky. Why quit now? She had to make as much as she could while she was still able.

"We had an agreement." Tom Bodine marched in with his two teenage boys in tow. "You were going to tutor my sons. I just found them ordering milk shakes at the Burger Shack. They were supposed to be with you." His scowl was as dark as his black cowboy hat.

"I never agreed to help them." And the sly dogs were smart enough to bring their grades up on their own. What they needed was discipline, not academic attention.

Tom waved an impatient hand. "You never said no. Boys, sit down and show Ms. Sneed your work." He waited until his sons each squeezed themselves into a small chair at the front of the classroom. "They'll be here after school every day until the end of the term." He stomped out.

One of the twins fell over in Tad's chair. Mary Margaret was sure he did it on purpose because his brother did the same thing. They lay sideways on the floor, chuckling.

"Whatever game you're playing with your father isn't going to work with me." She walked over to the door and closed it, shutting them in.

The twins stood. They wore hoodies underneath their thick jackets. They flipped the hoods up and then faced her, black jackets contrasted against the white board behind them.

There was something familiar about their silhouettes. Her tired, stressed-out brain made a connection. "I'll give you two choices. Confess why you're pretending school work is beneath you or I'm going to call the sheriff and report you for vandalizing property."

The twins exchanged a long look. She'd read about twin-speak but these two were masters of it.

"You've got nothing on us," Twin One said.

"Don't I?" She *tsk*ed. "I saw you trying to spray paint the grain silo by the interstate. That was stupid in itself, but you did it while it was snowing. You were on the catwalk forty feet above the ground. Your dad may be loud and bossy but he loves you. He wouldn't bother trying to straighten you out if he didn't care. How do you think he'd feel if either of you had fallen and been paralyzed or worse—*killed*?"

Her words were met with silence.

"Do you know how many children I see in this school who have parents who don't care that they can't read? Who don't want to acknowledge that their child has a learning disability? Do you know how many kids don't have enough to eat over the weekend? Who don't have snow boots and walk to school in the snow with sneakers that are duct taped together?"

"We should start a charity," Twin One said, regaining his snark.

"We'll do that." Twin Two righted Tad's chair. "After we pass this term and Ms. Sneed gets paid."

"We heard you need money." Twin One pushed Louise's chair beneath her desk.

Mary Margaret lost all appreciation for Sunshine's grapevine. "I'm not going to take your dad's money when I haven't helped you." She should have saved her breath.

They were gone.

⁕

"What are we doing here?" Tad looked around the furniture shop.

"I thought we'd talk to your grandpa about making you a bunk bed." Kevin had Tad by the hand and was headed toward his father's office. He had to raise his voice above the sound of the planer and lathe.

"Cool." Tad began to skip. "Bunk beds are good for sleepovers and ninja forts."

The family's office space was in the corner of the building and had windows on two walls. Paper cutouts of Santa and Frosty were taped to the windows. His parents each sat at a desk inside, where the doors and windows kept out much of the woodworking noise.

"What a surprise." Mom hugged them both.

The back wall was covered with awards and photographs of the family working with wood.

Dad noticed the direction of Kevin's gaze. "Remember this?" He removed a framed photograph from the wall. "You must have been eight or nine when this was taken."

In the photo Kevin held a push broom, grinning from ear to ear. His father and grandfather stood behind him, each with a hand on his shoulder.

Tad peered at the photo. "Daddy, you look like me."

He was right. Kevin had been a chunk-o-monk. He'd forgotten he hadn't been slim and athletic all his life, possibly because his parents hadn't made a big deal about his weight.

"Some family traditions are meant to be passed on," Kevin said. "Tad and I want to build a bunk bed. And we'd be thrilled to have Grandpa's help." He nodded to his father.

Kevin's parents were ecstatic with the request.

"First we have to choose a design." Dad was old school. He produced a binder filled with ideas, examples, and plans, and lifted Tad into his lap.

"Is there a ninja bunk bed?" Tad asked.

Mom glowed at the pair, clearly pleased with this turn of events.

Kevin pulled up a chair next to her desk. "I need some advice about Barb."

"She found out about you and Maggie." It wasn't a question. His mother looked grim. "I'm assuming you've already told your ex-wife to stay out of your love life."

Kevin nodded. "And my career."

"Who's Maggie?" Tad asked.

"It's a style of bunk bed," Kevin's mother said without missing a beat. "Rich, give your grandson a candy cane." They filled a pencil cup on his desk.

Between the candy cane and bunk bed photos, Tad lost interest in their conversation. He flipped pages and hummed a tune.

"She's going to make Maggie's life miserable. And it's all my fault."

"Ah, honey." Mom rubbed his arm. "Barb's so used to running the town that she needs a special project."

"Her and the beauty shop posse," Kevin muttered.

Mom *tsk*ed. "Those women are Barb's support group.

Maybe you need to call in the Widows Club. They could recruit Barb to help with one of their fundraisers. I hear the Christmas Ball isn't living up to expectations."

Kevin shook his head. "I need something a little bit more immediate and preferably time consuming."

"You could offer a truce," Mom suggested. "She can help you with the state political campaign."

"No. No chance." He'd just succeeded in extricating Barb from his life. He wasn't letting her back in again.

"This one." Tad tapped a diagram of a bunk bed. "It has a desk and a ladder."

"With a few blankets hanging over the rail, it could be a ninja cave," Dad told him. He opened the binder and handed Tad the diagram. "Can you run this out to Pete? He's taking inventory in the wood storage room. He'll know just what wood to pick."

"Yeppers." Diagram in one hand, candy cane in the other, Tad scurried out of the office.

"Son." Dad turned to Kevin. "If Maggie is the girl for you, she's got to be made of stern stuff."

Mom frowned.

"You mean she should weather whatever storm Barb brings." Kevin shook his head. "That's not fair."

"Barb is enthralled by power. You've taken that away from her." Dad closed the binder and set it aside. "Have you considered dropping out of politics altogether? That way there'd be no excuse for your ex-wife to protect you, so to speak."

"She's not protecting me," Kevin insisted.

"But she is. In her way." Dad's gaze was steady. "Let the state opportunity pass. Settle down here with Maggie." And by here, he meant the furniture operation.

"Way to work this around to your agenda, Dad." And make Kevin feel guilty at the same time.

His father shrugged. "You came here looking for advice. That's my two cents."

Kevin shook his head and went to find Tad. Give up his political aspirations?

There had to be another way.

A promotional poster for the chain of stores Dad had landed as a client caught his eye. The headline read: FANTASTIC BED FOR THE NEWLYWED.

Kevin paused. *Marriage.* Barb would have to ease up on Maggie if Kevin married her. There would be nothing to vet.

He cared for Maggie. She felt like the right person for him. And Tad loved her. Why waste time dating when they could make a commitment and put Barb in her place on the sidelines?

The idea of marriage to Maggie calmed him. She understood the importance of his dreams. She was kind and caring, not to mention beautiful and sexy in an understated way. But after what her father had done to her and the mess Derek had left her, she needed to feel special, which meant a very special proposal. A truly romantic proposal.

And because of Barb, a proposal delivered as soon as possible.

Chapter Eighteen

✳

Tad tugged on Mary Margaret's hand Monday morning in class. "Ms. Sneed, are you a zombie?"

"No, Tad."

"But you're walking like one." He tilted his head to one side and walked stiffly. "I watch a lot of Scooby-Doo. They chase after zombies all the time."

The class laughed.

"You shouldn't make fun of the way people move." Mary Margaret rubbed her neck, wishing for another of Kevin's massages. "I hurt a nerve in my neck." She hadn't danced professionally since she'd received that scar. She was using muscles she didn't normally use. And she'd danced her heart out this weekend, as if it was her last set of performances. "Did everyone practice their lines for the Christmas pageant last weekend?"

A few girls raised their hands enthusiastically. The rest of the class avoided her gaze.

"All right. Let's spend a few minutes practicing. You wouldn't want to stand up in front of the whole school and blink like an owl, would you?" She widened her eyes and blinked, making sure every child saw her. "Let's line up in order."

More giggles as her little charges scurried into position.

"Tad, aren't you supposed to be Z?" And therefore, at the end of the line.

He scuffed his feet on his way to the end. "I just wanted to stand by Louise." His crush.

"You can stand by Louise at recess."

Tad huffed and sat in Elizabeth's chair, kicking out his feet in rebellion.

"First off, you'll be introduced." Mary Margaret faced an imaginary audience. "Tonight, my kindergarten class has come up with twenty-six reasons to celebrate the holiday season. Take it away, Elizabeth."

Elizabeth tugged her dark curls. "A is for all the pretty lights." She curtsied and walked primly to the back of the line and then crossed her arms in disgust. "Ms. Sneed, I can't get in line behind Tad because he's not in line."

"Tad." Mary Margaret made his name into a warning. A gentle warning but a warning nonetheless.

He got to his feet, slouching and letting his arms sway like two elephant trunks. Mary Margaret didn't have the heart to reprimand him today.

The alphabet progressed. Predictably, Louise was too shy to speak her line.

"T is for shiny tinsel, honey," Mary Margaret prompted her.

Louise repeated the line in a whisper and headed toward the back, earning her a moon-eyed stare from Tad. He considered himself her ninja protector.

Finally, they came to the last letter.

Tad was still slouching but his dangling arms were banging together like seal flippers now. "Z is for the zest we feel when Christmas presents are revealed."

Mary Margaret bent down and stroked his soft brown hair. "A zombie couldn't have delivered that line any better." She straightened everything but her neck. "And now we all hold hands. Swing them up. Swing them down. And bow. And then off the stage we go."

"Can we do it again?" Hector asked.

"You really should." Barbara appeared in the open doorway. She wore a black sweater dress, black boots, and a black stadium jacket. Two guesses as to her mood. "That performance was—"

"Inspired," Mary Margaret cut her off. "Normally, I'd say let's do it again, but if we don't finish our holiday party placemats, we'll have nothing to put our plates on. And if we can't put plates down, we can't fill our plates with cookies and cupcakes."

Twenty-six five-year-olds scurried into their seats and began coloring their holiday placemats.

Mary Margaret joined Barbara at the back of class.

"Are you all right?" Barbara rubbed her neck in solidarity.

"Pinched nerve, I think." Mary Margaret grimaced. "I'm headed to the doctor after school."

"It looks painful." Barbara nodded toward her son. "They need to practice. Tad's delivery was flat."

"He was having fun with me. He'll be fine at the pageant." She hoped Barbara wouldn't take that as a promise. Tad was unpredictable, as his mother well knew.

"I've been trying to have him practice at home but you know Tad." Barbara's gaze softened, as it sometimes did when she was feeling charitable toward her son. "The only thing he takes seriously is being a ninja."

The children were talking quietly. A few were almost coloring inside the lines. Others, like Tad and Louise, made broad strokes to fill their placemats.

"Can I talk to you for a moment in private?" Barbara held the door open and smiled.

Barbara didn't smile often. That was twice in just a few minutes.

Mary Margaret's neck stiffened as they stepped into the hallway. She hadn't seen Barbara at the Hanky Panky this weekend but that didn't mean she hadn't been lurking in the shadows. Was that what this was all about?

"I just wanted you to know that Kevin and I..." There was Barbara's smile again. "Well, we're having our challenges but I'm going to be his campaign manager when he runs for state office. We'll be working very closely together, which means he won't have as much time to spend with you."

Mary Margaret's neck convulsed as if she'd stuck her finger into an electrical socket. "I'm not sure I'm the appropriate person to tell this to. I mean, I'm just Tad's teacher?" Had that come out as a question? She pressed her lips together lest she confess she'd used them to kiss Kevin more than once.

Barbara rubbed Mary Margaret's arm consolingly. "I wanted you to know because someone saw the two of you together coming out of Los Consuelos recently."

"Oh, that?" Fake laughter. Fake smile. Fake bravado. "We grabbed a bite after our stint as volunteer gift wrappers. Just as friends." Friends who were hot for each other.

Barbara's expression didn't change. "And I heard you had a drink together at Shaw's a time or two."

"My friends hang out there. But... Well, there was that one time I had car trouble after the poetry slam." Mary Margaret forced a chuckle that sounded like she was throwing herself on the mercy of the court. "Two flats. Can you believe it?"

"And someone saw you having a snowball fight at The Woodsman's Tree Farm." Her smile was chilling.

"Barbara, I am *not* dating your husband." Mary Margaret's head was tilted at an awkward angle. She wished it'd just roll off and down the hall. "Er, your estranged husband. Ex-husband. I mean, Kevin. There's no reason to poke around in my life."

"I just wanted to make sure you understood where I'm coming from," Barbara said in that frigid voice of hers, accentuated by that ice queen countenance. "I don't lose."

She turned and took a few steps toward the principal's office before changing her mind and coming back for what could only be a knockout in round two. "Oh, and don't forget your hair appointment this Saturday." She gently brushed a lock of hair from Mary Margaret's shoulder. "I see we need to touch up your gray again." She pivoted and walked down the hallway, a spider having eaten the fly.

✳

"Sir, you have to be at the doctor's office in ten minutes." Yolanda didn't just show up in Kevin's doorway to remind him. His assistant marched around behind his desk and tugged his arm upward. "If you miss this one, Dr. Arnett will drop *me* from his patient list."

"But we're still working on my press release concerning JPM's charitable contributions." He and Everett were wordsmithing the document and had been emailing it back and forth. He couldn't find the right words to make the announcement, just like he couldn't find the right words to ask Maggie to take a chance and marry him.

But Yolanda had the grip of a boa constrictor. Her fingers closed around Kevin's bicep and dragged him out of his chair. "It's just a flu shot. You're supposed to be the shining example to the town."

"Nobody knows I haven't gotten the shot." Kevin dragged his feet down the stairs after her. "Nobody except you and Dr. Arnett's office."

Yolanda *tsk*ed. "I asked the *Sunshine Weekly News* to do an interview with you. You have to get the shot or they'll write something about you being scared of needles."

"A complete fabrication." Besides, who liked needles?

"Don't come back until you've been jabbed." Yolanda pushed him out the door.

Thankfully, he had his cell phone in hand. He sent Maggie a text to say he was thinking of her.

A few minutes later, Dr. Arnett's nurse Bridget led him down the hall toward an exam room.

His phone rang. It was Everett. Kevin stopped in the middle of the beige hallway. "I've got to take this."

"No go, sir. You need to step outside to use your phone." Bridget paused in front of exam room three, backing toward the door.

"It's just a quick call." Kevin flashed her the display.

Bridget gave him the stink eye. "That's what they all say. Out with you, then."

Kevin answered Everett in a whisper and walked down the hall.

"Mr. Hadley. Kevin." The nurse dogged his steps. "The lobby is the other way."

Everett wasted no time in pleasantries. "Someone spray painted a No Distribution Center sign on one of the silos."

Groaning, Kevin darted into the medical office's kitchen. This was a disaster.

Bridget walked up to him and said, "I need you in room—"

Kevin looked away and gave her the wait-one-minute sign. "I'm going to get someone out there to clean it up."

"No." Everett's answer surprised him.

"What do you mean, no? Cray's people aren't going to like it." They could back out. And then all the flack he'd been taking from the community would have been for nothing.

"They already know we have opposition." Everett was calmer than Kevin was. "JPM will show up at the town meeting and see it. We need to be up front to both sides."

Someone called for Nurse Bridget. She left Kevin alone in the break room.

"People need an outlet, Kevin. I say leave it up."

"I suppose it's the right thing to do but it still sucks." Kevin hung up and hurried back down the hall, throwing open the door to room three, which was where he and the nurse had stopped earlier, the room he'd assumed he was supposed to be in.

Maggie sat on the exam table with her back to him. She was holding up her hair so the doctor could see her neck. A thin scar climbed from the top of her shoulder blade and disappeared into her hairline.

Kevin slammed the door shut, stunned.

"Why are you always trouble when you come in?" The nurse marched down the hall and opened the door to room two. "I'm going to use the biggest needle I have. We have rules to protect people's privacy. Canceling appointments and taking phone calls. That's just rude."

In a fog, Kevin let her ramble. His sweet, innocent Maggie wasn't sweet and innocent at all!

He rubbed his thumb across the tips of his fingers. Those same fingertips had traced the length and shape of that scar when he'd kissed a masked Roxy behind the Hanky Panky. Now he understood why Maggie hadn't wanted his hands near her neck when he kissed her.

Bridget jabbed Kevin with a needle like he was a piece of tough meat and she was inserting a cooking thermometer. She covered the injection site with a Band-Aid. "Get out of my office."

Kevin was happy to comply. He walked slowly back to town hall, numb. The wind swirled snowflakes around him, tugging at the open ends of his jacket. He didn't care.

He found it hard to believe that Roxy and Maggie were one and the same, just as he'd found it hard to believe that Barb had been cheating on him. But he couldn't deny the truth. Maggie was Roxy.

He washed a hand over his face, steps slowing as he rounded the corner and neared the movie theater. He'd told the party's screening committee about Maggie. He'd sung her praises. He'd thought she was going to be a great asset to his life, his career. What an idiot he'd been.

He'd bought an engagement ring. He'd made proposal plans. He'd told his parents! His mother had probably already told everyone who worked in the furniture shop. They'd think he was a chump.

He still wanted her. He shouldn't but he did.

Kevin wasn't a prude. He knew Maggie hadn't taken off her clothes in that club. In theory, there was nothing wrong with her taking on a second job. But he was willing to bet there were voters who would care that she danced suggestively in skimpy costumes, not to mention private investigators who'd eat that information for lunch.

His heart was breaking for the second time that year, and he was angry. Limb-shaking, sweaty-palmed angry.

Betrayed!

What if he'd married her before he'd found out? It would've been his first marriage all over again. The deception. The lies.

But with more passion, more of a connection, more truth.

He took back that last word, thank you very much. He'd been looking at other couples and seeing flaws in their relationships. He hadn't looked at his own relationship. He hadn't looked because...

He stopped dead in the middle of the sidewalk, standing in front of the pet shop window where the sole remaining poodle puppy stared back at him with unconditional love in her eyes.

He hadn't looked at his own budding relationship with Maggie because he didn't just care for her. He loved her.

I love Maggie.

He loved her big heart. He loved the way she strived to forgive Derek his flaws. He loved her honesty. Sure, she'd kept her Roxy-ness from him but 'she'd told him several times that he shouldn't date her. He loved the way she clung to him when he kissed her deeply. He loved the way she commanded a crowd when she danced. She'd earned his respect time and again.

But love…

Love didn't change the fact that she was dancing on the back of his dreams.

His feelings didn't matter. Love didn't matter. If he continued to pursue any kind of relationship with Maggie, his political career was over. His dreams unfulfilled.

✳

Mary Margaret took muscle relaxers, called in sick on Tuesday to both jobs, locked her doors, and turned off her phone.

Kevin had left a voicemail and text, as had Grandma Edith, wanting to talk to her. Still feeling languid, she dutifully showed up at the evening rehearsal for the Christmas Pageant Tuesday night without having answered either one. In her state, she wasn't up for in-depth conversations.

"Ms. Sneed!" Her kindergarten charges surrounded her.

They all wore white, adult-size T-shirts that fell below their knees. Each shirt was decorated with the glittery letter they were to recite. Sparkly angel halos made of pipe cleaners shimmered in the light. They shouted questions concerning her health.

"Are you okay?"

"Did you throw up?"

"Did you get a shot?"

"Is your neck broken?" Tad asked.

"I'm better. I'll be back at school tomorrow." She herded them into their line, straightening the occasional slipping halo. "Remind me…Who is M?"

"Mari!" several students cried, guiding Mari to her spot.

"I don't know how you keep track." Barbara materialized beside Mary Margaret, like a deadly spider you hadn't noticed building a web above your back door.

Mary Margaret chalked up her overactive imagination to the muscle relaxers and gave Tad's mother a benevolent smile.

"I brought candy canes for after the performance." Barbara patted her pink leather purse, which was large enough to carry a cuddly dog had she been the type to have one.

But when Tad shouted, "Hurray! Candy canes!" Barbara countered, "Not for you, Tad."

Tad looked crestfallen but not surprised.

"Barbara." Mary Margaret couldn't let that injustice slide. "We're not supposed to hand out treats unless they can be consumed by everyone." Not that this year's class had anyone on a gluten-free or peanut-free or dairy-free diet.

"Who says?" Barbara leveled her gaze on Mary Margaret. "That isn't a school board rule."

"Principal Rogers." And anyone with any sense of fairness.

Kevin entered the gym. Because Barbara was with her, Mary Margaret pretended to be enthralled by the upper grade choir. Still, she managed to note his progress in her direction.

"I swear that man is overexposed." Barbara crossed her arms and tapped a booted foot impatiently. "Don't tell me you were asked to emcee this event too, Kev."

"I'm not the emcee." Kevin bypassed his ex-wife and came to a stop in front of Mary Margaret. But he didn't regard her with tenderness in his eyes or heat in his gaze. He looked at her as if he were Tom Bodine and she were one of his twin boys.

Maybe I should have answered his messages.

"Tad will be glad you could make it tonight." Disappointed and blushing under his scrutiny, Mary Margaret turned away. Clearly, she shouldn't take muscle relaxers when she went out in public. Her heart had escaped to her sleeve. "Louise, do you need to go to the bathroom?"

"No." Louise spun back and forth, making her skirt float like an upside-down tulip.

"No?" Mary Margaret asked, just to be sure.

"No."

"Daddy! Did you come to see me?" Tad ran toward Kevin, tripped, and fell to his knees. He rolled into a ball and began to cry.

Kevin scooped his son into his arms before Mary Margaret could reach him.

"You're fine, Tad." Barbara hadn't moved. Talk about tough love.

Mary Margaret brushed Tad's hair from his forehead. "Anything broken, little ninja?"

Tad must have been tired because he wailed through his tears. "Everything!"

Kevin patted Tad's back. "Give us a minute." But

instead of moving away, he said to Mary Margaret, "I need to talk to you. In private." There was an unfamiliar note to his voice, a distance he didn't normally use with her.

She brushed it off. The auditorium was loud, and she might have imagined it. She'd taken muscle relaxers, after all.

"Whatever you have to say in front of our son's teacher about Tad, you can say in front of me." Barbara had dropped into their conversation like the territorial spider she was.

"I'm not discussing Tad." Kevin raised his voice over his son's wails. "What I have to say to Mary Margaret is none of your business."

Mary Margaret? But...I'm your Maggie.

The distance in Kevin's gaze said otherwise.

Mary Margaret spun back to her milling charges before she threw her medicated self at his feet and asked what was wrong.

On the stage, Wendy was coaching the third graders in their skit. She instructed them to speak up and start from the top. At this rate, Mary Margaret's class wouldn't be done until nine.

The Widows Club board entered the auditorium with Grandma Edith, but upon seeing Kevin and Mary Margaret, they seemed to huddle together like a college basketball team talking strategy after a foul. She watched as, instead of heading their way, they worked the room.

Mary Margaret had no idea what was going on.

"Test-test." Wendy turned on the microphone. "Will Ms. Sneed's kindergarten class line up on the side steps to the stage." She repeated her instruction twice.

Mary Margaret led the way, hoping that Barbara would stay behind with Kevin and a still crying Tad. She marched her class up the side stairs single file.

"Elizabeth!" Sandy called out to her daughter. She wanted a picture and told Elizabeth to stay put so she could take one.

Elizabeth, who was to recite the letter A, obeyed her mother and stopped the flow of traffic.

The take-charge little girl smiled dutifully as Laurel and Hardy entered the gym. Elizabeth looked beyond her mother to the crowd of parents, who all seemed to be staring at her, or at least at the little angels of Ms. Sneed's kindergarten class.

Caught in the spotlight, Elizabeth's expression crumpled. And then she began to cry, walking to center stage with her arms outstretched toward her mother.

It wasn't unusual for one of Mary Margaret's students to break out in tears but it was unusual for the crier to be Elizabeth. She was usually an overbearing Lucy to their tenderhearted gang of Peanuts.

Then, from the second step, Elizabeth's best friend Ariceli also burst into tears. A ripple of tears raced through the line like the spread of chicken pox—that is, until the ripple hit Louise.

Louise didn't cry, but she did look stricken.

"No, baby. It's okay." Kathy ran for her daughter but Mary Margaret knew she was too late. Louise had wet her pants.

A deluge of kindergarten parents rushed the stage as if they were storming the Alamo. Halos fell off in the midst of comforting pick-ups and hugs.

"Attention," Wendy said into the microphone. She

wasn't the school secretary because she was faint of heart. She might have been soft-spoken, but she could've made the mighty General Patton fall in line. "Mrs. Sneed's kindergarten class will proceed to the backstage dressing room immediately."

There was a lull in the sobs and wails and words of comfort.

"That means now," Wendy clarified, still using her military tone.

The class mobilized, including the parents. Everybody went up the short flight of stairs to the stage. Around stage left and the thick black curtains hanging in the wings. Down the back stairs into the dressing room beneath the main stage.

Mary Margaret stood at the door, ushering in her students and parents, righting halos, wiping tears, doling out reassuring smiles. She counted heads. Three students were missing. Leaving Barbara in charge, she left to find Louise, Mari, and Tad.

Back in the auditorium, Mary Margaret plotted a course for a family sitting on a blanket in the back. Mari was the oldest of four children. She held her baby sister, rocking her from side to side.

Mr. Hardy blocked Mary Margaret as she tried to pass him. "I had no idea kindergarten teachers led such exciting lives."

"Me either. That's the beauty of our job, isn't it?" Mr. Laurel made googly eyes at Grandma Edith as he chewed on a red stir stick. "You get to meet a variety of interesting people."

Mary Margaret forgot about Mari and the alphabet recitations. "You are not to date my grandmother."

"Why can't I date her?" Mr. Laurel demanded. "She reminds me of my first wife."

"You see what I have to put up with?" Mr. Hardy might have been making a joke. Since he never smiled, it was hard to tell.

Mr. Laurel gave Grandma Edith a jaunty wave that sent the entire Widows Club board into a tizzy. "Your grandmother is unpredictable, speaks her mind, and yet—"

"She has a kind heart," both Mary Margaret and Mr. Hardy said together.

There was an uncomfortable silence, during which Mary Margaret remembered her mission.

"You are *not* dating my grandmother." Mary Margaret repeated, then continued on her way. Upon reaching Mari and her family, she plucked Mari's halo from her younger brother's hands. "It's time to go backstage, sweetheart." She placed the halo on Mari's head, transferred the adorable little baby into her mother's arms, and sent Mari skipping toward the stage.

Louise and her mother emerged from the bathroom. Louise had removed her skirt and changed into a pair of red leggings decorated with Christmas trees. Mary Margaret caught Kathy's eye and pointed toward the stage. The pair headed in the right direction.

Mims tapped Mary Margaret's shoulder. "Do you know those gentlemen?" She pointed to Laurel and Hardy, who were talking to Grandma Edith. Well, Mr. Laurel was talking. Mr. Hardy rolled his eyes.

"I've seen that pair around town." Clarice leaned on her walking stick. "They must be visiting someone for the holidays."

Bitsy looked just as concerned as the rest of the

board. "We're worried about your grandmother dating Paco."

"Who?" Mary Margaret was scowling at Mr. Laurel.

"The taller man," Bitsy clarified. "Paco asked her on a date."

Annoyance and fear melded into a fast dance step with dizzying spins. "Is that so?" Was that what Grandma Edith had wanted to talk to her about? Had she given up on dating David and moved on to Paco/Laurel?

"We'll take care of her," Mims promised, and then hesitated, touching Mary Margaret's arm. "Are you all right? There are rumors that you're dating Kevin, and we... Well, frankly, we're worried about how Barbara will take it."

Mary Margaret went with her standard rebuttal. "I'm not dating Kevin. He asked me for some help on the development committee. And since I had time..." She could tell by the looks on their faces that they didn't believe her. "Look, the truth is we've hung out once or twice but I'm not at a place in my life where I can date."

And there was that look in his eyes before Tad had fallen and cried. That was a break-up face if she ever saw one.

"I'm so proud of you." Clarice gave Mary Margaret a hug. "It's important to know your limits."

"Yeah, well." Mary Margaret nodded toward her grandmother. "I don't think Grandma Edith knows hers. Could you take care of her?"

"We're on it," Bitsy reassured her.

Mary Margaret noticed that Kevin and Tad were going up the stairs on stage right. The third graders were still blocking their scene, with their parents congregating just beneath the front of the stage, phones at the ready for photo ops. She hurried after Kevin and Tad, who lingered in the wings on the wrong side of the stage.

"It's dark, Daddy, like a ninja cave."

"Tad," Mary Margaret said, "you need to hurry around the back and down the stairs on the other side, like we practiced. The rest of the class is waiting underneath the stage."

Tad raced off.

"Hey." Kevin caught Mary Margaret's arm, still wearing break-up face. He drew her deeper into the shadows of the wings where no one else could see them. "I need to talk to you."

The trouble with being a realist was that reality sucked. She'd known getting involved with Kevin was a risk while she was dancing and dealing with Paco and Hardy. And yet, she wasn't ready for a break-up.

"Mary Margaret..." His touch on her arm was gentle, respectful.

He touched her the way a mayor touched the kindergarten teacher when the whole town was watching. Worse, he'd called her Mary Margaret. Not Maggie. She wanted him to touch her the way he'd touched Roxy. She inched away from him, drawing him deeper into the shadows where Roxy lived.

Instead of following, his grip loosened. "I can't... Roxy."

Her stage name disappeared on her gasp. She wished the black curtain could swallow her up. "How..."

"It doesn't matter." His voice. So low. So intimate. "You know why."

She did.

Sinner.

The snide criticism of her father echoed in her head, but this time in Kevin's voice. The words cut her breath to ribbons, made her hands numb and her scar ache. Her father had been right.

"I thought you were different," Kevin said in a quiet voice that still managed to ring in her ears.

Wendy released the third graders. They cheered and rushed to the edge of the stage and their parents.

The commotion didn't stop Mary Margaret's heart from breaking, her hopes from being crushed. *Not now*, she told her crumpling self. There was still the rehearsal to get through. She forced herself to draw breath, to hold her head high, to count her blessings—few though they might be.

And then—because she was the black sheep in her family—she reached for what she couldn't have. *Kevin*.

She surged into his arms the way Roxy had that one fateful night, kissing him like he was the balm to her lonely, rejected soul.

Kevin didn't hold back or hold her gently. He dragged her against his body and returned her kiss with the heat and passion she'd come to expect from him. He didn't kiss her like they had all the time in the world. He kissed her as if they stood on the gangplank leading to the *Titanic* and one of them was leaving. He took what he wanted.

As good-bye kisses went...She thanked her lucky, tree-topping stars.

Sinners burn in hell, Mary Margaret.

Someone ran across the stage, footsteps echoing on the wood.

"Ninja Angel wishes you a Merry Christmas!" Tad's shout had Mary Margaret and Kevin breaking apart but moving as one toward center stage.

"Tad." Kevin reached him first. "What are you doing?"

"I'm photo-bombing." The pipe cleaner halo tilted jauntily over one of his eyes.

The parents of the third graders chuckled, lifting their noses from their cell phone screens.

"Mrs. Sneed." Wendy pointed toward stage left and the staircase to the dressing room. "Take your ninja photo bomber downstairs."

Mary Margaret led the way.

"We need to talk," Kevin said. "Now more than ever."

"Why? You're breaking up with me."

Chapter Nineteen

✳

Edith stewed the entire day after the Christmas pageant dress rehearsal about her impeded love life.

The Widows Club board had run a blockade around Edith at the school rehearsal, chasing Paco off. And then they'd whisked Edith out the door because they'd carpooled. The reason? Bitsy claimed she'd forgotten to take her evening medicine.

Edith didn't buy that for a minute. The board clearly didn't approve of Paco. Did Edith care? After stewing all day long, she decided she did. The fate of her position on the board might depend on it. Which meant David was back to being her number one option for romance.

She hadn't had a chance to talk to Mary Margaret to see if everything was all right. And her granddaughter hadn't returned her calls. Neither had Mims or David. At five o'clock, Edith got in her car and drove around town.

Mary Margaret wasn't home nor was she downtown with the mayor. Edith spotted him walking Main Street alone. David and Mims weren't home either. Edith drove the now-familiar circuit around town. The last place she stopped was Shaw's. Bingo. A dinged-up Subaru and a pristine Mercedes SUV sat in the parking lot. Mims and David.

Edith parked near the door and stared at herself in the rearview mirror. Her face was lined like rings in an exposed tree trunk. She wasn't a spring chicken, and no amount of makeup or slimwear could disguise that fact. She didn't have the hourglass curves of Mary Margaret. She didn't have the brass of Mims. It was time to face facts. She wasn't a serious contender as the next Mrs. David Jessup.

The thought gave her an unexpected measure of relief.

Someone knocked on her passenger window. Edith jumped.

It was Mims, wrapped in her camouflage jacket, her short, spiked hair flattened by the wind. She rapped on the window again. "Unlock the door."

"Is your date over so soon?" Edith asked when Mims was settled beside her. She tried not to sound bitter but the sting of loss was still fresh.

"David told me he had another engagement." Mims sighed. "I'd barely finished my beer and peanuts." She turned to Edith. "Do you love him?" That was the thing about Mims. She wasn't put off by Edith's direct nature. She had one of her own.

But the question took Edith by surprise. She didn't know what to say other than, "I barely know him."

"Me too," Mims admitted on a sigh.

And as they sat there, Patti pulled up in her shiny red car. She applied a coat of lipstick with the aid of a lighted visor. Then she headed toward Shaw's, oblivious of her audience.

"You don't think..." Mims leaned forward.

"He wouldn't dare..." But Edith remembered Patti singing about those five golden rings and realized the truth: David was a player.

David opened the door to Shaw's before Patti reached it. He said something to her and then swept her into his arms for a hot kiss.

Slack-jawed, Edith turned to look at Mims.

Slack-jawed, Mims turned to look at Edith.

And then they both began to laugh.

"I've never thanked you for being my friend," Edith said when she caught her breath. "My only friend, especially in school."

"You've always been a bit much but my kind of much." Mims touched the top of her spiky hair. "I got a new hairdo for him."

"I glued on false eyelashes." Edith looked down at her blouse. "And got a new bra."

"I bet Paco likes that look," Mims said slyly.

Edith huffed. "Haven't you been trying to discourage me from dating him?"

"When have you ever followed my advice?" Mims countered.

"Doesn't mean I don't like to hear it." Edith smiled softly. "Paco has more important things to do than woo me. He and Mary Margaret are undercover somewhere."

"When you say 'undercover,'" Mims said slowly, "do you mean law enforcement undercover? Or under-the-sheets undercover?"

"Paco isn't interested in Mary Margaret like that." Edith explained about her granddaughter's cover as a dancer. "Which reminds me. I need to borrow a gun from you. I shouldn't have been so selfish. Mary Margaret needs me to watch her back."

"And who's going to watch yours?" Mims sniffed. "I'll pack the heat. You've suffered enough with those false eyelashes. I don't want you to accidentally shoot yourself."

※

Two days after the fateful good-bye kiss, Mary Margaret was getting ready to leave for work in Greeley when there was a knock on her door.

"Hello, hello." Edith entered using her key. She was wearing a flirty red dress and a black demi-mask. "I've thought a lot about it, and I've decided it's too dangerous for you to go undercover without me."

"No." Mary Margaret gently removed her grandmother's mask. "You can't come as my sidekick."

"I thought you might say that." Grandma Edith put her fingers in her mouth and whistled. "Therefore, I brought my own sidekick."

The front door opened. "I feel silly." Mims entered the living room. She wore white leggings beneath a red flowery tunic and a black plastic demi-mask. "Your security detail is here, reporting for duty." She patted her bulky pleather purse.

"No." Mary Margaret scowled. "That's a hard no. Mims, I'm disappointed you'd let my grandmother talk you into this. Don't one of you have a date with David?"

"David is a player, and we've decided not to play along." Grandma Edith fluttered her false eyelashes.

"Let him make a fool of every other woman in

Sunshine." Mims held out the hem of her tunic and frowned. "We've decided to be fools where no one knows us."

"I forbid this."

Mims and Edith exchanged glances and then started to laugh.

"You can't stop us. We have our own vehicle. Our own masks." Grandma Edith snatched hers from the counter. "What good is being a widow if you can't kick up your heels every once in a while? And who knows? We might meet a man in Greeley."

"Adventure and potential love connection aside"— Mims patted her purse again—"you need protection. I can't believe you were called to serve. Are we after a crime syndicate? Drug dealers?" She gasped. "Human traffickers?"

"Get me backstage." Grandma Edith had her mask back in place. "This will end tonight. And just in time for Christmas. There aren't very many shopping days left, and I don't see any wrapped gifts under your tree."

"You're not coming backstage." Because if Mary Margaret admitted she'd bamboozled her grandmother about the undercover story, Grandma Edith would be hurt. So she improvised. "If anyone sees us together, they'll know who I am. You'll ruin everything." There was still a possibility Barbara would show up at the Hanky Panky, although now that Kevin had decided she wasn't good enough for him, that was highly unlikely.

"But..." Grandma Edith's expression crumpled. "You need me."

"I'm sorry." It hurt to burst her grandmother's bubble. "You can't help me with this."

"Honey." Her grandmother was hurt. "You're all I have left."

"Family, you mean," Mims murmured. "My condolences, Mary Margaret. I heard you and Kevin broke up."

The town grapevine... She much preferred listening to the gossip, rather than being part of the gossip itself.

"We were never really together. It was more of a test-the-waters kind of thing." Mary Margaret tried to shrug but Kevin's rejection made her heart heavy. He'd texted her, asking to talk, but why would she submit herself to his judgment? She couldn't live up to the high standards he needed to help him achieve his dreams. "Excuse me. I have to get ready." She stepped into her bedroom.

"Is this what you're wearing tonight?" Grandma Edith pushed past her. "A purple and black corset with a matching tutu?"

"It's a flounce skirt, not a tutu." Mary Margaret fingered the stiff lace.

"Surely you're not wearing this to dance." Mims picked up the holiday sweater laid out next to the corset costume. "The Grinch?"

"I dug out a tacky holiday sweater for school tomorrow." She'd promised little Elizabeth, and the kids would enjoy it. "I'm wearing the polka dot raincoat for my second dance." She gestured toward the jacket hanging from the back of her bedroom door. She'd already packed her group dance costumes in a small travel bag.

"Do you need to take your grandfather's truck?" Grandma Edith asked, still staring at the corset dress.

"No. I was more concerned with keeping my dancing a secret from Kevin." Mary Margaret tried to smile. "But he found out, which is why we're not seeing each other anymore."

"Oh, honey." Grandma Edith moved to her side and wrapped an arm around her.

"I can understand why he did it," Mims said, moving to Mary Margaret's other side and curling her arm around her. "But it's disappointing nonetheless."

Mary Margaret hugged Edith and Mims. Three widows. Two grandmothers. And one much needed dose of the feels.

Mary Margaret sighed and released the pair. "If you want to protect me, protect what's left of my anonymity. I don't need your gun for that. Can you do that for me?"

"Can we at least go to the show?" Mims removed her mask. "I've never seen a dance act like yours. I promise to pretend you're a stranger to me. Oh, and I promise to chaperone Edith if Paco shows up for drinks like he promised."

"Can I ask the manager if he'll consider an amateur night?" Grandma Edith shimmied. "I want to shake my booty but I don't want a job."

Mary Margaret sighed. "I can't stop you two from coming, can I?"

"Nope." Grandma Edith pointed her bullet bra toward the door.

Chapter Twenty

✳

I don't understand why you broke up with Maggie."
Kevin's mother put a huge helping of au gratin potatoes
on Kevin's plate. "You bought that beautiful ring and
then you didn't even propose."

"Isn't Maggie a bunk bed?" Tad asked, smashing his
potatoes.

"This is why we only tell rugrats the truth, Mom,"
Kevin teased, nodding toward his son. "Tad, if you're
very careful, you can take your plate to the coffee
table and watch television while you eat." Which would
provide Kevin with some much-needed privacy because
his mother couldn't seem to stop asking him about Mary
Margaret.

Tad carried his plate into the other room and then
returned for his glass of milk.

"You discovered a flaw in your perfect girlfriend,
didn't you?" Dad was loading up on comfort food with
a double side of potatoes and a homemade biscuit. All
those carbs brought out the *shoulda-woulda-coulda*'s of
the Advice Train. "There was something in Maggie's

past you thought would harm your political career. If you were in the furniture business, none of that would matter."

"Rich…" Mom began but then she stared at Kevin. "Tell me that isn't true." She paused, waiting for Kevin to refute the accusation. When he didn't, she shook her head. "We've all made mistakes in our pasts, honey. Personally, I don't want reporters digging around in mine."

"Lucky for me, you two are squeaky clean." Lucky for him, he'd found out about Mary Margaret's dance career before it was too late. Still, he mourned the loss of her in his life. He missed talking to her. He missed her laughter and the way she blushed when their conversation turned personal. He missed the warmth of her hand in his. She'd settled something restless inside of him. And now…

It took Kevin a moment to realize his parents were staring at each other and saying nothing.

"What? No." Kevin shook his head. "You can't have anything bad in your pasts. If you were convicted felons, you'd have told me when I was younger."

"It's nothing like that," Dad grumbled. Then he swiped his biscuit through his potatoes and took a big bite.

"Then what is it?" Kevin set down his fork. "If this is something a reporter is going to bring up one day, I need to be prepared. I need to know how to answer."

"It's nothing by today's standards," his mother said in a low voice. "And therefore none of your business."

"Like Mary Margaret is none of yours?" he challenged.

Mom glowered at him. "Maggie. Her name is Maggie. And my heart breaks for her because you were so good together. You laughed more in that one afternoon at the Christmas tree farm than I'd seen you laugh in a long time. But you've tossed her aside, like one of those ties I've given you for Christmas because ties and politicians no longer go together. Can you imagine how she feels? Can you?"

Kevin swallowed his shame. "She understands. She knows I've always dreamed of serving at the state level and beyond."

"Understanding and being hurt are two different things." His mother stabbed a bite of pork chop. "Your father had higher aspirations too, you know."

"Miriam," Dad warned.

"But he was told he couldn't move past being mayor because of me." She popped the pork chop in her mouth and glowered at both men.

"You?" Kevin shoved his plate away.

"Do we have to go into this?" Dad mopped up potato remnants with the remains of his biscuit. "I made a choice a long time ago. It doesn't matter to me. *You* matter to me, Miriam."

"Would somebody please tell me what's going on?" Kevin's mind was reeling. What had his mother done? He couldn't, and didn't, want to imagine.

"I was married when I fell in love with your father," his mother said hotly. "And I'm older than he is by five years."

"Who cares?" Kevin picked up his fork.

"Exactly." Dad's gaze was fiery. "The important people who care are sitting right here."

"Who cares?" Tears filled Mom's eyes. "Who cares how dedicated your father is to public service if he fell in love with an older woman before her divorce was final? He gave up his dreams because of me, because I wasn't good enough for *them*."

"I didn't give up anything," Dad said gruffly. "I *chose* you and made new dreams."

"You see?" Mom wiped away a tear. "You can help a community, or the world, in many ways. You don't have to hold office. And you shouldn't ever trade-off someone you love for the approval of someone else."

"Do you love her?" Dad stared at his plate.

"Yes." Kevin's scowl deepened. "But—"

"Then your priorities are all messed up." Dad didn't raise his voice, perhaps out of concern for Tad in the next room, but his words echoed in Kevin's head as if he were shouting. "No job is worth sacrificing love. I want you to work in the family business but I understand if you choose another path. Just make sure you're choosing it for the right reasons."

❋

A few hours later, Kevin parked his SUV at the Hanky Panky, having left Tad with his parents. He was determined to talk to Mary Margaret, determined to float the idea of her quitting the stage and becoming his Maggie full-time.

The crowd was bigger than he'd ever seen before. Kevin found a spot at the end of the bar in a dark corner. Shortly thereafter, he was joined by Mims and Edith. They wore masks and outfits inappropriate for their age.

Maggie's grandmother gave him a once-over. "Should

you be here?" She slurped her piña colada. "You spent so much time with Barbara that her judginess has rubbed off on you. You don't deserve my granddaughter."

"Unless you're here to get down on your knees and beg her forgiveness." Mims carried a tumbler of whiskey.

"There's no easy answer to any of this," he said, dumbfounded by their honesty.

"He's not here to grovel." Edith frowned.

Ordering her friend another drink, Mims shouldered up to Kevin. "This is outside all of our wheelhouses but we're here to support our girl, regardless. And you should do the same."

Before Kevin could give another wrong answer, Maggie came on stage for her first solo number.

Kevin reconciled the two images of the woman he was attracted to. Maggie wore clothes with a casual sophistication. Most of the time her hair was down or bound in a thick braid that hid her scar, while her blue eyes were framed in light makeup. Roxy had every curve on display and moved with a sexy confidence kindergarten teachers weren't supposed to have. She swung her platinum blond hair like it was a fifth appendage. Beneath her superhero mask, her eyes were heavily lined with electric blue and fringed in thick, false eyelashes.

Edith tried to mimic Maggie's moves, getting to her feet once or twice to shimmy. "What's wrong with you, Mims?" she demanded when her friend sat and watched.

"I'm shocked and mesmerized and feeling my age." Mims took a healthy swig of her drink. "I could throw out my back trying that." She glanced at Kevin. "I take it this isn't your first time here."

Kevin shook his head.

He waited for the grand finale before escorting Mims and Edith to their vehicle. And then he located a familiar car parked on the motel side of the street. She emerged from the back door a short time later, dressed all in black with a knit cap pulled low over her hair. He stopped her before she reached her car.

"Maggie."

She glanced up at him, fear turning into relief.

That's when he saw them. The two men who'd scared her in Sunshine after the poetry slam. He'd seen them around town too. At the bakery having coffee a couple of times. At the Saddle Horn having breakfast. But Sheriff Drew had assured him they'd broken no laws, so as mayor, he could do nothing but glare.

He wanted to do more than glare now.

"Mrs. Sneed." The heavy-set man planted his feet wide, as if he was going to drop one hand in a lineman's stance.

Kevin stepped in front of Maggie. "Don't touch her."

"It's okay." Maggie came around in front of him. She offered the thug a wad of cash.

Kevin pushed her arm down and held it at her side.

The heavy-set man frowned.

"There were a couple locals from Sunshine in the audience tonight." The tall, thin man sized Kevin up. "Besides your biggest fan here and your granny."

Kevin hadn't noticed any Sunshine residents. Why hadn't he noticed?

Because I was lulled into the normalcy of it all with Mims and Edith.

"There are a lot of people who'd be shocked to learn

Sunshine's mayor is a regular at the club," the heavy-set man said in a sour voice.

"Are you threatening me?" Kevin pushed Maggie behind him. Anger knotted his fingers into fists.

"Step aside, lover boy." The shorter man narrowed his eyes. "We'll have our money."

"Kevin, wait for me at the car." Maggie tried to step around him.

"Don't give them a cent." He'd known she owed money, and he was all for paying off one's debts but this…These men didn't seem like legitimate collection agency employees. And he could practically smell Maggie's fear.

"Kevin, please wait by my car."

"Do as the lady says." There was an *or else* hidden in the words of the taller man.

"No." Kevin had never backed down from a fight in his life. "You do as the mayor says."

The slighter of the two men shook his head. And then it was game on. Punches thrown. Voices raised. Maggie screaming at them to stop.

A car skidded across the road toward them, high beams blinding them all.

Kevin jumped to the sidewalk, pulling Maggie with him. The two men hurried in the opposite direction. The car careened off.

"Your nose is bleeding." Maggie dug in her backpack for a tissue.

Kevin wasn't feeling like her knight in shining armor. Not because he hadn't given as good as he got but because Maggie was radiating annoyance.

"You have to stop coming here to watch me," she said.

"Are you kidding?" He pinched his nose. "If you insist upon doing this, I'm going to drive you out here every night. Those guys are—"

"None of your business." She straightened his jacket, yanking on his sleeves. And then gingerly placed her palms on his cheeks. "Just like your political career is your own to navigate." She sighed. "You're going to have a black eye. How are you going to explain that tomorrow?"

"It was worth it. And I'd do it again." Even if she never told him the truth about those men. "Are they blackmailing you?"

"To dance, you mean?" She shook her head. "Derek made some bad decisions." She tugged Kevin toward the coffee shop on the corner. "Come on. You need to calm down before you drive back."

"Wait." He pulled her into his arms. "Tell me you're all right." He brought a hand to the back of her neck and the scar her father had given her. "I know I let you down but—"

"Shh." She kissed him the way she'd kissed him that first time when he'd thought she was Roxy, the way she'd kissed him the other night in the stage wings. There was longing and need and desperation in that kiss.

I love her. How can I let her go?

He drew back. "Your father labeled you unworthy of his love. You're not unworthy of mine. It's just—"

"Love is unconditional." Maggie stepped out of his embrace, shaming him with the truth. "Come on. They'll probably have a bag of ice for you in the coffee shop too."

She was treating him better than he deserved. "If you

offer to follow me home and make sure I'm safely tucked in tonight, my masculinity may be in jeopardy." Unless she planned to spend the night in his bed.

"You have nothing to fear in that department." She stayed two steps ahead of him in the snow. "What am I going to do with you?"

"I have so many ideas."

"I mean..." She faced him as she opened the restaurant door for him to pass through first. "You made the right decision the other night by breaking it off. Don't drag it out."

The coffee shop was crowded with customers from the strip club who needed to sober up or get a bite to eat before calling it a night. Kevin and Maggie sat in a booth across from each other. Christmas carols played from a transistor radio in the kitchen. There were paper Christmas decorations scattered around the diner.

Maggie ordered him a cheeseburger, fries, and an ice pack, and ordered herself a slice of pumpkin pie. "Before you ask again, I can't stop dancing. Not until Derek's debt is paid off in a few months."

"Tell me more about these guys and the company they represent." If there was a company. "I don't want to sound like a character in a movie but they don't seem legit."

She sighed. "They gave me all the proper documentation. There was a government certified letter confirming the balance owed."

"What if I made all that go away?" He hadn't gone looking for love but there it was staring at him with deep blue eyes and a heart so true it hurt. "Would you stop dancing then?"

"And what if I did?" Her gaze hardened. "Would you

find something else I do that your voters or political party wouldn't approve of?"

He thought of the engagement ring tucked in a bureau drawer back home. "I'm in a career where there are restrictions."

"I grew up as a preacher's kid," she chastised gently. "I don't want to live my life second-guessing every choice I make." When he would have argued, she reached across the table and touched his hand. "I don't want to be the person in your life you sweep under the carpet."

"You wouldn't be. Not if you stopped dancing." She'd only been doing it for a few weeks. How damaging could that be?

She withdrew her hand, sat back, and stared out the window. "Do you know what's so hard about being a kindergarten teacher?"

He shook his head.

"It's teaching my students to abide by the rules and respect the choices of others, the choices they wouldn't make." Maggie leveled her gaze on him. "You'd choose not to dance. You'd choose to default on a debt. You'd choose to declare bankruptcy. But you aren't living in my shoes. I make the decisions about how I live, what I value, and what I honor."

"I understand." And yet he loved her, damn it. "I don't want to lose you."

"I don't want to say this but..." She swallowed, reaching a hand gingerly behind her neck, probably touching that scar. "I think you've already lost me. You've chosen a path and a set of rules you want to live by. And I...I can't be the person who walks with you down that road."

"Don't say that." He couldn't get the words out quickly enough. "I can find a way. After the development project passes." He'd pay off those goons and propose to her.

"What am I going to do with you?" she whispered, teary-eyed.

He'd said it before, and he'd say it again. "I have lots of ideas."

Chapter Twenty-One

The high school auditorium was packed.

The town council sat on either side of Kevin at a table on the stage. To one side, the committee he'd formed to talk about town development sat on chairs. His father sat next to Maggie. Cray and some officials from JPM Industries sat in the audience, standing out in their suits, as did Paul and Paula.

The good news was no one had asked Kevin about his black eye. It seemed the topic at hand took more precedence.

Kevin called the meeting to order. "We've talked a lot in recent months about the future of Sunshine. And by we, I mean everyone in town. There's fear that change will strain the fabric of our town's character— more people means less personality and heart. There's concern that in the wake of one large employer, other new businesses will arrive and negatively impact existing ones."

"We vote no!" someone in the back shouted, their cry taken up by others.

The contingent from JPM Industries frowned. Paul and Paula frowned.

"Please. Calm down," Kevin said into the microphone. He waited until the crowd quieted. "Every decision has a flip-side. There are positives to change." He had to raise his voice over erupting objections. "Hear me out. We'll open the floor up to comments and questions once everyone on the council weighs in."

They'd placed a microphone on a stand at the head of the center aisle for that purpose.

"What does Sunshine get for opening its arms to new commerce?" Kevin asked. "I'll tell you what I see. We'll gain another business leader in the community, one willing to give back." He read the list of donations JPM had agreed to provide. "We'll gain another employer, increasing the chance that our children can work here if they choose rather than leave town for jobs elsewhere. We increase our town's revenue without increasing taxes to individual residents, which means improvement in the quality of life. Roads repaired. Services expanded."

Everett sat with Kevin's committee, nodding his approval.

Kevin felt heartened. "And now, I'd like to turn over the microphone to the town council and our resident committee, people who've studied this issue from different angles. They'll tell you where they stand. Please listen with an open mind. As I said, we have time to hear from everyone."

Everyone on the stage had a chance to speak. Victor made an impassioned speech about rejecting the issue. Mary Margaret talked about the benefit to schools. Kevin's dad admitted he hadn't supported the project initially but had changed his mind because the benefits outweighed the risks. And then, Kevin opened the floor to questions and statements by other residents.

Things were going well until Barb stepped up to the microphone.

"This question is for Mary Margaret Sneed." Barb was petite, but standing at the microphone just then and hearing the note of superiority in her voice, Kevin felt that she was huge and hugely threatening.

"You can direct all questions about the development project my way," Kevin said briskly as his father passed the wireless microphone to Maggie.

In the second row, the Widows Club board watched Barb closely. Edith had been knitting what looked like a long red scarf. She paused, needle ends pointing in Barb's direction.

"It's all right." Maggie's smile didn't reassure Kevin. "Ask away."

"It's come to my attention that you've taken on a second job." Barb knew how to tease an audience. People cocked their heads and shifted in their seats, wondering how this pertained to the development issue at hand.

"Of course she has. Mary Margaret tutors my boys," Tom Bodine said impatiently. He sat in the front row, arms crossed, a supporter of the distribution center.

Warning bells rang in Kevin's head. But Maggie? Her smile never wavered.

"I'm sorry, Tom." There was nothing apologetic in Barb's tone. "I'm referring to Ms. Sneed's job as a *stripper* in Greeley." She smirked.

The crowd erupted. Kevin's shoulder twinged. In

the back, Paul and Paula frowned at Kevin. Near the front, the Widows Club frowned at Barb. Maggie looked pale.

Tom Bodine got to his feet, jamming his cowboy hat on his head. He pointed accusingly at Mary Margaret. "You're fired!" And then he walked out.

Fortunately, or unfortunately, no one else followed him out the door.

Kevin called for order. "This isn't an issue under the town council's jurisdiction, Ms. Kaine." He used his ex-wife's maiden name, not giving her the satisfaction of an association with him.

But Barb was getting satisfaction elsewhere. She held up a sheaf of papers like a minister holding up a Bible. "All school personnel sign an agreement to conduct themselves appropriately and in a way that—"

"Excuse me, Ms. Kaine." Kevin was practically shouting into the microphone. "Are you bringing these allegations against my *fiancée* now, tonight, instead of at a school board meeting because you hope I'll back down in my support of the distribution center?" So much for romantic holiday proposals.

Barb's mouth dropped open, as did Maggie's. They were speechless. The crowd quieted, on the edge of their seats, reluctant to miss a word of the drama playing out before them.

"I..." Barbara seemed shaken. "I've seen her dance." She held up her cell phone. "I have pictures." She passed her phone to the school superintendent, an ancient gentleman with thick glasses.

Maggie's cheeks were beet red, and she wouldn't look at Kevin.

"Who's the blonde?" the superintendent asked. "I can't see her face. Everything's dark, and she's wearing a mask."

"And clothes," Edith piped up from behind him. "That woman's got all her clothes on."

"I think it's clear what's going on here." Kevin spoke into the microphone. "My ex-wife is jealous of my soon-to-be wife and trying to abuse her power."

The crowd ate that statement up alive.

Barb snatched her phone back from the superintendent. Her parting shot—"This isn't the end of this"—was swallowed by the chatter of residents happy to have witnessed the long reign of Queen Barbara end.

In a way, Kevin felt sorry for her.

But not as sorry as he was to see Maggie grab her things and hurry down the stairs.

He'd botched his marriage proposal. He wasn't going to lose her too.

＊

The roar in Mary Margaret's ears didn't come from the crowd.

Fiancée? He'd done it now. Kevin had attached an anchor to his career hopes and tossed it overboard.

A woman in a business suit toward the back of the auditorium grabbed her arm as Mary Margaret tried to pass. She smacked of self-importance. "Excuse me. You never denied any of those allegations."

A man stood behind her in an equally fine wool suit, wearing an equally concerned expression. The pair's appearance and demeanor said Important Political Party

Member more clearly than any button pinned to their lapels.

They hold Kevin's political fate in their hands.

Or rather, Mary Margaret did.

"I'm in a dance troupe," Mary Margaret said, aware that everyone nearby hung on her every word.

The woman nodded but her brow didn't clear. "And you're engaged to Mayor Kevin Hadley?"

Don't lie to me. Her father's voice snuck beneath the near-deafening crowd noise.

Mary Margaret opened her mouth to deny being Kevin's fiancée but he appeared at her side, took her hand, and drew her close.

"It was a spur-of-the-moment thing," Kevin lied swiftly, his case not helped by the shiner underneath his eye. "I had a ring, but when the moment is right, the question just pops out."

There had been no question. And Mary Margaret doubted there was a ring anywhere outside of the circle of Kevin's lies tonight.

Across the room, Barbara's gaze captured hers. There wasn't viciousness in her eyes. There was a plea. After all, practically Barbara's entire life—outside of the bedroom, the salon, and the school board—had been devoted to supporting Kevin's career. She knew Kevin would succeed on a bigger stage if given a chance. And to do that...

"Okay," Mary Margaret capitulated to the pressure to explain. "I'm a dancer in a burlesque revue at the Hanky Panky in Greeley." She swallowed thickly. "I don't take off my clothes when I perform. I don't do lap dances or disappear with men into back rooms. I dance solo and with a group of women I respect and admire. I dance because I love it, and—"

"She's undercover." Grandma Edith shoved her way through the crowd using her knitting bag as a battering ram. "It's part of a sting operation."

Uh-oh.

"That's not true." Mary Margaret met her grand-mother's gaze squarely, fighting back tears when the realization that she'd been lied to dawned in Edith's eyes. "I'm not dancing to help the police or the FBI. I dance because…" She didn't want to cast stones on Derek's reputation but what choice did she have? "I dance because my husband left me with over a hundred thousand dollars in debt."

That caused a stir in the immediate vicinity, including the suited pair with Kevin's political fate in their hands.

"Mims and I have seen her dance." Shaking off the disappointment of Mary Margaret's deception, Grandma Edith pushed her shoulders back and glared at anyone foolish enough to meet her stare. "Shame on you and your dirty minds. It's not one of *those* places." She shook her finger at the crowd. "My granddaughter is an upstanding citizen."

There were chuckles and looks of doubt.

"Excuse us." Kevin hustled Mary Margaret out the door, whispering, "Best quit while we're ahead."

"Ahead?" Mary Margaret laughed mirthlessly.

"Yes, ahead." He didn't stop when they went through the doors and into the snowy night. He dragged her toward the parking lot, slogging through the snow. "That might have salvaged my career but it put an end to your dancing."

"You don't have to sound so happy about it." Besides, she still had all that debt hanging over her head. "Now what am I going to do?"

"Marry me? I'll take out a loan to pay off those loan sharks."

She broke free of his hold. "Thanks for taking me under your protective superhero shield but you know that's not the answer. I won't let you take out a loan, and I won't marry you. You don't even love me."

He frowned.

Does he love me? Her heart *ka-thump*ed. Then again, it had been a nerve-wracking few minutes with lots of *ka-thump*ing. "The club is going to be filled with Sunshine residents tomorrow night. I'm not going to back down. I have nothing to be ashamed of."

Sinner.

The label pressed down on her.

Kevin shook his head. "You can't dance again, not after this. Barb will bring the school board. Even with the mask, you'll be recognized. Fired."

"You forget." She pointed toward Laurel and Hardy, taking a smoke as they leaned against the fender of their car at the far end of the high school parking lot. "I have obligations."

"And you forget I'm the mayor. I'll fix this." He stepped to the side and made a phone call.

But he couldn't fix the fact that he was ashamed of how he felt about her dancing.

"I like a man willing to risk it all for his woman," Grandma Edith said as she arrived and hugged Mary Margaret, banging her with her knitting bag. "He wouldn't be a bad addition to the family."

"Grandma Edith, you know as well as I do that I'm not marrying Kevin."

"You could do worse," she said cryptically, gaze drifting to Laurel and Hardy.

"I'm sorry I lied about being undercover," Mary Margaret said in a voice as shaky as her knees. "Paco isn't a good guy. At least now you know the truth."

"The truth doesn't always set you free, honey." Grandma Edith hugged Mary Margaret again.

Mims and the rest of the Widows Club board surrounded them.

Clarice leaned on her walking stick. "I've waited years for Barbara to be put in her place."

"Hopefully, she'll learn a lesson from this," Bitsy said kindly. "I know she's got a heart in that regal demeanor somewhere."

The older women laughed, clearly doubting it. Mary Margaret stayed silent. She knew bitter Barb cared for Kevin.

People streamed out of the auditorium and toward their cars. Some called out greetings. Some gave Mary Margaret speculative glances.

Kevin rejoined them, staring at Mary Margaret. No one said anything.

"I should be going." Mary Margaret dug in her purse for her keys.

"Wait just a bit more." Kevin turned toward the center of town.

A siren sounded in the distance. The sheriff's cruiser sped around the corner. Drew parked behind Laurel and Hardy's vehicle and got out. "Gentlemen, we have a law against loitering. I'll need to see some identification."

Laurel and Hardy reached in their pockets for their wallets.

Mary Margaret tried not to get her hopes up.

Deputy Wycliff pulled up across the street in the department's SUV. He hurried over, palm on the handle of his revolver. He was young and a little trigger-happy.

"Florida?" Lola's husband, Drew, held Laurel's and Hardy's identification cards up to their faces, as if checking to see that the photographs matched. "What brings you to Sunshine? Or should I ask what keeps you in Sunshine?" He followed the direction of their gazes to Mary Margaret.

When they didn't answer his question, he asked them to turn around and then handcuffed them. "You're not being arrested, just detained. Do you have any weapons on you? Illegal substances? Anything sharp in your pockets that might stick me?" When they answered in the negative, he patted them down. "Is there anything in your car that's illegal in the state of Colorado?"

Deputy Wycliff shined his flashlight into their vehicle. "Are those bullets in your cup holder, sir?"

Mary Margaret gasped.

In short order, Laurel and Hardy were loaded into the back of the deputy's SUV.

Kevin was on the phone again, probably talking to Barbara or perhaps with Darcy, who'd gotten the news last week that she'd passed the bar. He'd promised to fix things. *He'd better not be talking to his banker about a loan.*

"You know, if you need to pay those two gentlemen off, I can loan you money." Grandma Edith put her arm around Mary Margaret's waist. "Although I'm loath to pay Paco. Do you know he stood me up? He was going to buy me a piña colada at the Hanky Panky."

Kevin rejoined them. "Come on." He took Mary Margaret's hand.

"Where are we going?" She had no choice but to follow, looking back over her shoulder, relieved to find her grandmother scurrying after them with the Widows Club.

"I'm taking you to jail," Kevin said in a flat voice. "We're going to get to the bottom of this."

Chapter Twenty-Two

✳

Sunshine's sheriff's office was the size of a small living room. It housed two small jail cells in an addition in the back.

Kevin, Edith, Mims, and Mary Margaret waited outside the office in the lightly falling snow while Laurel and Hardy were booked. Every time Edith or Mary Margaret tried to start a conversation, Kevin held up a hand and told them to wait.

Darcy and her husband, Judge Harper, pulled up. The judge looked like he'd had a hard day. His thin white hair hung limply about his ears, and his complexion seemed sallow under the streetlights. Mary Margaret was reminded of Lola saying the judge had ordered a coffin last spring. Was he seriously ill? Was that why he'd married the much younger Darcy?

"Thanks for coming out so late, Judge." Kevin shook his hand. "The gentlemen I asked you about are inside. I think they were booked on possession of illegal bullets. Hollow points."

Mary Margaret shivered. She watched enough television to know those did more damage than a regular bullet.

"These men have been harassing you about your husband's debts?" the judge asked Mary Margaret in a gravelly voice.

"Yes." Given his tone, Mary Margaret suddenly felt foolish. "They said Derek owed their online casino. They had a letter of validation." All of Derek's business creditors had provided one.

"Did they produce any other documents proving their claim?" The judge leaned against the metal railing on one side of the ramp leading up to the building's entrance.

Darcy held on to his arm as if afraid he might collapse.

Mary Margaret nodded. "They showed me a receipt of his transactions." It was sitting in her pile of bills back at the house.

The judge narrowed his eyes. "And you didn't sign anything at the time your husband created this account? Anything that authorized him to borrow? Any agreement that you'd be responsible for the obligation?"

"No." Mary Margaret was horrified. He thought she'd have allowed that? "I didn't even know he was gambling online." What kind of person did the judge think she was?

Sinner.

She wanted to go home.

Perhaps sensing she needed moral support, Kevin put his arm around her shoulders.

Judge Harper blew out a breath. "I hate bullies." He leaned on Darcy. "Let's go see these reprobates."

They all traipsed in, including Mims and Grandma Edith, who was wide-eyed and silent for once.

"And here I thought our guests might have to wait until morning to see you." Drew escorted them down a narrow hallway to see his prisoners.

Judge Harper asked for a chair. When he was seated, he introduced himself. "Gentlemen, forget for a moment that you had armor-piercing bullets in your vehicle."

Mary Margaret's blood ran cold.

"Forget for a moment that I suspect our mayor's face might bear a bruise that matches that ring on your pinkie." Judge Harper gestured toward Paco. The judge may have been old and not feeling tip-top but it seemed hard to get anything past him.

"I'm here to tell you about a federal law. The Fair Debt Collection Practices Act. Now this law...this *federal* law...It states that no family member may be held accountable for a debt they did not create or authorize with their signature. Which means, gentlemen, that unless you can produce Mrs. Sneed's signature on her husband's account—which I doubt you can—insisting she owes you money is against a federal law. The sheriff tells me you had over eight thousand dollars in cash and checks in an envelope labeled Mary Margaret Sneed. I'm sure that money came from Mrs. Sneed. Am I wrong?"

The imprisoned men chose silence over an admission of guilt. Paco stared at Edith apologetically.

"I'm the law of the land here." Judge Harper raised his gaze to Darcy. "And while I could recommend the sheriff charge you with blackmail or extortion, I'm reluctant to keep the taint of you in our fair town at Christmas. Therefore, I'm going to cut you a deal. If you return the money in that envelope to Mrs. Sneed, you'll be cited and fined for illegal possession of armor-piercing bullets, and I'll let you drive out of town tonight. But if you choose silence, in addition to the bullet charge, you'll be referred to the federal prosecutor for blackmail and extortion charges."

The old judge cleared his throat. "If you need time to make your decision, I'll most likely see you in my court-room tomorrow morning, but I have to warn you, I'm not a morning person, and items on my morning docket are dealt with more severely than issues addressed at other times." He got to his feet and made his way slowly down the hall, leaning on Darcy.

There was a law to protect her? Mary Margaret stood frozen in disbelief.

"We accept your conditions," Mr. Hardy said.

"Good. I hate the snow," Mr. Laurel added mournfully.

Kevin swept Mary Margaret into his arms.

"Thank you," she whispered, trying to plant this moment in her memory because, even if Kevin didn't realize it now, the representatives from his political party would make it clear.

Despite having Derek's gambling debt taken off her shoulders, she was the wrong woman for him.

✳

"I'm proud of you, son," Kevin's father said to him the day after the town hall meeting.

They sat in the Olde Time Bakery having coffee.

"Thanks, Dad. That means a lot." Kevin nodded a greeting to each constituent who came in.

"But the problem isn't resolved, is it?"

Kevin frowned. "We held a special council meeting this morning and approved rezoning and development of the old mill." Victor had been the one vote against.

"I'm not talking about that." Dad leaned forward and lowered his voice. "I'm talking about your Maggie."

Kevin drew a deep breath, not wanting to have this conversation. Maggie had left last night with her grandmother and Mims. Kevin hadn't had a chance to talk to her alone. "I got her out of debt. What more needs to be done?"

He knew what needed to be done, all on his end. Humble apologies. Groveling. Declarations of love. Promises of faithfulness. A formal request for her to marry him. Except... it felt as if she wanted none of that.

"You wanted to help her," Dad said.

"Yes."

"More than you wanted her to stop dancing?" Dad asked.

Kevin closed his mouth.

"Son, you say you love Maggie but part of being a man is knowing how to love someone without clipping their wings. If you want to be with Maggie, you have to accept who she is and that her being in a burlesque revue is something to be proud of."

"I'm proud of her." But Kevin's voice was gruff and unsure.

"From what I hear, she's a good dancer. From what I know, she's a wonderful teacher and a great person." Dad sat back and sipped his coffee. "Is your dream of higher office more important than your opportunity to love a woman like that for the rest of your life?"

"No."

Dad's smile was slowly building. "Then you need to win her back with a grand gesture so she knows you have no regrets being her man."

Chapter Twenty-Three

"Mary Margaret!"

Darcy, Avery, and Lola greeted Mary Margaret at the back door of the club when she arrived for her shift.

"Kevin told us you'd be here." Lola hugged Mary Margaret. "Why didn't you tell me about all this the night I picked you up?"

"Well, I—"

"It doesn't matter." Darcy shook her head. "We came to warn you that Barbara is bringing the school board. You know she's like a bulldog. She won't let things go until you're fired."

"Why are you here?" Avery shrugged deeper into her coat. It wasn't snowing but the wind was blowing. "You don't need to dance anymore."

"Yeah." Lola knotted her scarf more firmly around her neck. "Kevin said you got all your money back. And Drew said those men who were shaking you down left town."

"I like to dance. Besides, I can't let my girls down and

not show up for the group numbers." But it looked like she'd have to if she wanted to protect her teaching job. She'd suspected as much but she'd shown up anyway, hopeful.

"Are you still engaged?" Avery asked.

"No." Mary Margaret's voice was strained. She had to clear her throat twice before she could say more. "Kevin only said we were engaged to throw Barbara off the scent. He doesn't love me."

"Successful marriages have been based on less than love at first," Darcy said, a statement which was worrisome given her hasty marriage to the judge.

"Mary Margaret deserves love," Lola said firmly. "We all do." But she didn't look Darcy in the eye.

A horn honk drew their attention. Mims's familiar, older model Subaru pulled up next to them.

Mary Margaret bent down to look inside. "Grandma Edith, what are you doing here?" And why had she brought the rest of the Widows Club board?

Edith rolled down her window and huffed. "If those closed-minded ladies back in Sunshine want to see what it takes to get out there on the stage and dance, Mims, Bitsy, and I are going to show them."

"I'm here to support freedom of expression, bad knees and all." Clarice patted said joints. "This is just like the time I marched in Washington, DC."

"Oh, snap." Avery smiled at Grandma Edith. "We can dance too? Do you have an extra mask? Or three?"

"Do I?" Mims laughed. "I ordered a package of ten back when I thought Mary Margaret was undercover."

Avery and Lola held out their hands. Avery nudged Darcy until she held out her hand too.

"And do you have an extra costume?" Avery asked Mary Margaret. "Or six?"

Mary Margaret held up her hands. "I don't want to rain on anyone's parade, but this isn't my dance club."

Ned opened the stage door and surveyed the women. "Ah, I'm assuming these are the women interested in performing on Amateur Night."

Mary Margaret's jaw dropped. "We have an Amateur Night? Since when?"

"I might have made a suggestion about it the other night when we were here," Grandma Edith admitted, grinning.

"I've received other requests about it." Ned directed the women inside. "Besides," he told Mary Margaret as they walked down the hall, "it's the holidays and my regulars expect special shows at the holidays."

Mary Margaret smiled. "You remembered."

"Seriously, *Roxy*?" Ned called all the dancers by their stage names although he had their real names and social security numbers on file. "You've never steered me wrong. I remember everything you've told me. Although Amateur Night..." He shrugged. "We'll see."

"Amateur Night is going to be a hit." She hugged her boss. "And then you're going to bring in classy male dancers, who are going to be a hit as well."

"Things are moving fast, Roxy, thanks to you." Ned stopped at the dressing room door. "Merry Christmas."

"Merry Christmas, Ned." For the first time this holiday season, when Mary Margaret said Merry Christmas, she felt the joy of the holiday deep in her broken heart.

Ned held her at arm's length. "Now, you aren't going to like this but..."

✳

"I can't believe Barb dragged the school board here." Kevin sat at a table near the stage nursing a beer.

"I can't believe it's Amateur Night," Jason groused, which he'd been doing since the host had announced the special program a few minutes prior—newbies mixed in with the regular show. "It's going to be like the first night we came here all over again. Except for your woman's quality performances."

Kevin didn't explain that the show was ten times better than when they'd first attended. He'd let Jason be surprised.

The Sunshine school board sat in the corner. Barb lorded over them all. Arnold, the school superintendent, put his hands over his ears when the music began.

The lights dimmed. A spotlight swung around the red velvet curtains and then settled on the emcee.

"Ladies and gentlemen, the Hanky Panky is proud to host our first Amateur Night. It takes a lot of nerve to get out here on stage, so let's give a big Hanky Panky welcome to our first group of dancers—the Old Ladies Still Got It!"

The opening chords of Madonna's "Like a Virgin" filled the air as the curtain was drawn back.

"Oh." Jason jerked back in his seat, holding a hand in front of his eyes. "I can't unsee that."

"Clap your hands," Kevin commanded, taking his own advice as three of the Widows Club board took the stage in dominatrix wear, masks, and blond wigs.

Jason clapped but he squeezed his eyes shut. "I paid ten dollars for this?"

"What did you expect on Amateur Night?" In costume, Clarice hobbled by and snapped her riding crop close to Jason's head.

Since the cowboy had his eyes shut, Kevin pushed him back in his seat.

"What happened? What'd I miss?" Jason peeked again. "Ack!"

"Suck it up, man." Kevin was used to emceeing or judging unusual events. He went back to clapping as Mims stumbled around the pole at the end of the runway. She'd be lucky not to fall and break a hip.

Thankfully, the song ended, and the Widows Club made their exit. The red velvet curtains fell back into place.

"Wow," the host said, smoothing his blue velvet lapel. "Way to go, ladies. You can cross that off your bucket list. And now for a younger take on Amateur Night. I bring you the Ladies of Shaw's!"

The deep bass of "I Kissed a Girl" shook the room. The curtains came back. Three younger women in blond wigs, masks, and fringed flapper dresses began dancing center stage.

"Shoot me." Jason drank half his beer. "That's Darcy. I'd recognize those legs anywhere."

The Ladies of Shaw's were brave enough to take the stage but stayed main stage. Far, far away from the pole.

"If Darcy woulda danced down here, I would've tipped her," Jason said when the dance was over.

"She's married." Kevin shook his head.

"If the judge saw this..." Jason shook his head. "She'd be widowed."

The Widows Club board, minus Edith, now sat at the reserved table next to theirs, crowing about their success on stage. A group dance opened the main show, saving Jason and Kevin from commenting too much. The Ladies of Shaw's sat down with them next. Jason gaped at Darcy, robbed of all speech. The show went on. Maggie had yet to appear on stage.

"And now...the act you've all been waiting for..." The host was drawing his introduction out longer than an announcer in the WWE.

Kevin caught a glimpse of Maggie in the wings. Something about her seemed out of place.

"Here for her last engagement...*Fox-xy Rox-xy!*"

The crowd applauded enthusiastically. Maggie had built quite a following.

Edith leaped out from the curtains in a purple spandex gown, a white demi-mask, and Mary Margaret's platinum blond wig.

The air was sucked out of the room.

What Edith lacked in choreography, she made up for with enthusiasm. She earned every hoot of appreciation and every thunderous beat of applause. That woman had been born for the spotlight.

The song ended. Edith blew kisses to the crowd and skipped off.

The school board looked to be having angry words with Barb. They left in a pack.

Kevin stood.

"Where are you going?" Jason found his voice.

Kevin didn't answer. He headed for the side door leading backstage.

✳

Mary Margaret and Edith joined the Ladies of Shaw's and the Old Ladies Still Got It in the audience as the main troupe of dancers did a throwback ode to "Step Up" in sneakers and street clothes.

"Where's Kevin?" Mary Margaret didn't want to ask but couldn't stop herself. She'd seen him from the wings while her grandmother danced as Foxy Roxy.

"He went looking for you." Jason watched Darcy, ignoring the performance. "I could tell he was wondering why you weren't dancing."

Ned had told Mary Margaret he wasn't going to allow her to dance anymore, although he was keeping her on as a consultant and choreographer.

"Hey." Grandma Edith, who was still wearing her mask, nudged Jason and shouted over the music. "I've always wanted to ask you about your animal magnetism."

Jason's gaze swung to Mary Margaret's grandmother and turned wary.

"What would happen if you used your magnetic charisma for good?" Grandma Edith noticed something on stage she liked and hooted. "I want to hear more about your dating advice."

Jason looked like he regretted showing up this evening. "You want me to advise you?"

"No." Grandma Edith hooted some more. "I want to make sure your column isn't full of bull."

The dance ended, the performers ran off stage, and then Ned appeared.

"We've got one more brave dancer coming on for Amateur Night," he said.

Mary Margaret and her friends all exchanged confused glances and shrugs. The women from Sunshine had been the only ones on the roster for the event.

"Let's give it up for The Mayor and 'Stayin' Alive.'" Ned cued the music from his remote.

"The Mayor?" Mary Margaret froze. It couldn't be.

The Bee Gees song filled the room as the curtains were drawn open. Kevin stood on stage in a powder blue tuxedo with a matching ruffled shirt. His hips and shoulders were moving, and then he lifted his face revealing no mask. His gaze found Mary Margaret's as he strutted down the runway, owning it like John Travolta.

The Sunshine contingent erupted in appreciation and glee.

"Dude, have you lost your mind?" Jason shouted as he passed.

Unable to move, Mary Margaret stared at Kevin. This was the same man who'd wanted her to quit dancing burlesque to protect his career? What was he doing?

Kevin swung around the pole nearly as gracelessly as Mims had done. And then he held the lapels of his jacket to the sides and moved his jacket back and forth as if he'd just gotten out of the shower and was toweling off.

As dancers went, he was bad. The crowd loved him anyway.

And Mary Margaret... She'd never loved him more.

Kevin struck the classic John Travolta pose, and then he extended a hand toward Mary Margaret.

Everyone turned their attention toward her.

"Go on," Grandma Edith shouted. "He's doing this for you."

Mary Margaret's heart swelled with love. She reached

up, clasping Kevin's hand. He drew her to the stage. There wasn't much left of the song but they danced together anyway.

The song faded away. The audience filled the void with applause and shouts of "More!"

With a firm grip on her hand, Kevin sank down on one knee, silencing the crowd.

If Kevin thought she was going to run away, he had another think coming. She couldn't move. She could barely breathe.

His gaze softened to a warm smile. "Maggie, you're a far better dancer than I'll ever be. But you're not one-dimensional. You don't run from responsibility. You honor your commitments, even when you sometimes shouldn't." The corner of his mouth tilted up in a half-smile. "You have a big heart, one able to forgive the frailties and imperfections of others. I know I haven't always made the right decisions to show you how much I care or chosen the right words to tell you how very much I love you but…"

Kevin held out a blue velvet box and opened it to reveal a solitaire diamond ring. "I love you with all my heart. I love you so much I'll give up my political career for you. Just say the word. But first say one word. Say you'll do me the honor of being my wife. Say yes, Maggie. Say yes."

"Yes," Grandma Edith shouted.

Others took her cue and shouted their encouragement.

Instead of capitulating, Mary Margaret had to point out the obvious. "You dancing here tonight probably ruined your chances at higher office."

"I don't care. It'll mean nothing without you." His

gaze didn't waver. His smile didn't slip. "They have to want me unconditionally, the way I love you unconditionally."

She loved him but this wasn't wise. "Someone probably took your picture or—heaven forbid—a video." Her gaze roamed the crowd but all she saw were supportive faces. "You've got to protect your dreams."

"If it means losing you, I'll make new dreams. I had fun dancing with you." He squeezed her hand. "I love you, Maggie. Let's change the way we see the holiday and married couples. I'll get you a real wreath for your door and you can promise to love me no matter what I do for a living."

A smile worked its way past her defenses because she loved him so very much.

Kevin got to his feet, sliding his arms around her. "All I need is for you to say you love me too. Say yes, Maggie."

The crowd began to chant. "Yes. Yes. Yes. Yes."

Mary Margaret swallowed her worries for Kevin's dreams and let tears of joy clog her throat instead. "Yes. I love you so much. Yes."

"I could tell you loved me," he said, drawing her close. "By the way you catch fire in my arms whenever we kiss."

And then he proved how combustible they were together with a kiss that had the audience applauding and Mary Margaret burning.

As promised.

Epilogue

✳

I think we found a new charity event—The Foxy Roxy Amateur Dance Revue." Mims was more serious about her idea than the sugar cookies she was frosting. Green icing dripped down the sides of many a tree. "It'll be like Amateur Night. Maybe we can rent the club in Greeley."

"No more dancing. We're all retiring," Mary Margaret said firmly, taking a sheet of cookies from the oven at her grandmother's house. There was no way she was letting Kevin near the dance floor again.

"But it was empowering." Grandma Edith swiveled her hips as she rolled out more cookie dough.

"I hadn't realized I had an inner dominatrix." Bitsy chuckled and sprinkled more silver beads on star cookies.

Clarice snorted. "I hadn't realized how mortifying it was to be on stage in such a skimpy costume."

They all reassured her she'd looked beautiful.

Mary Margaret finished transferring her cookies to a cooling rack. Kevin had given her back her holiday spirit. And Derek's actions at the end of his life had led her to a place of love and understanding. Christmas was in two days. She couldn't have been happier.

"Hello! Merry Christmas!" Kevin called from the front of the house. "We thought we'd stop by with lunch. I've got a hungry ninja and enough sandwiches for my gorgeous fiancée and the board of my favorite club in town."

He and Tad appeared in the kitchen holding a large bag filled with sandwiches from the deli at Emory's Grocery. They were bundled up for the gentle snowfall outside.

"Cookies!" Tad rushed forward.

Mary Margaret gave him one with a promise of another after he ate his sandwich. For her kindness, she received a kiss on the cheek from both Hadley males.

Edith dusted the flour off her hands and went to give Kevin a hug. "Every time I look at you two, I realize how much our club made a difference in your lives. If it wasn't for the four of us…" She gazed fondly at her friends before returning to her rolling pin duties. "You two wouldn't be engaged."

Kevin and Mary Margaret exchanged glances and tender smiles. The Widows Club was always trying to take credit for their impending nuptials. They knew their love had nothing to do with the Widows Club but they were too fond of them to refute their claims.

"Edith." Mims set her frosting knife aside. "We're going to hold an election in January. The board voted to officially add a vice president position."

Grandma Edith gasped, smooshing her rolling pin into the cookie dough.

"You should know," Clarice said, "Patti already signed up to run."

"Not Miss Five Golden Rings?" Edith huffed and set about smoothing out her dough. "Aren't she and David a thing? Is there any hope she'll get engaged and drop out of the club?"

"Nope." Bitsy selected a small container of red sugar sprinkles. "She got smart and realized David's playing the field. But no matter the club election outcome, we need to think ahead. January's around the corner, which means..."

"A new poker game." Grandma Edith gasped again. "Can we match Patti?"

"No." Clarice pounded her walking stick. "The game has to be played. There are rules, Edith."

"Can I play your game?" Tad smiled at them angelically.

The Widows Club assured him there were other games he'd prefer more. Edith snuck him a cookie, clearly trying to distract him.

"Rules. Games." Kevin's arms came around Mary Margaret, his breath warm across her ear. "Add in a mask and it sounds like my kind of fun."

Mary Margaret reached back to touch his wickedly stubbled chin with her palm. "What am I going to do with you?"

"I have ideas," he whispered. "Plenty of ideas."

About the Author

Melinda Curtis is the *USA Today* bestselling author of light-hearted contemporary romance. In addition to her Sunshine Valley series from Forever, she's published independently and with Harlequin Heartwarming, including her book *Dandelion Wishes*, which is currently being made into a TV movie called *Love in Harmony Valley*. She lives in Oregon's lush Willamette Valley with her hot husband—her basketball-playing college sweetheart. While raising three kids, the couple did the soccer thing, the karate thing, the dance thing, the Little League thing, and, of course, the basketball thing. Between books, Melinda spends time with her husband remodeling their home by swinging a hammer, grouting tile, and wielding a paintbrush with other family members.

For a bonus story from another author that you'll love, please turn the page to read *I'll Be Home for Christmas* by Hope Ramsay.

After ignoring the dating advice of local matriarch Miz Miriam Randall, Annie Roberts expects another humdrum holiday in Last Chance, South Carolina. But when a stray cat arrives in the arms of Army sergeant Matt Jasper, a calico named Holly just may be the best matchmaker of all.

FOREVER

Baby Jesus wailed loud enough to be heard in the next county. His floodlit manger rocked back and forth while a group of gaily painted plaster wisemen looked on. Staff Sergeant Matt Jasper took a few hesitant steps toward the crèche and wondered if PTSD had finally found him. He peeked into the wobbling manger.

A pair of golden eyes stared back.

He let go of the breath he'd been holding. It was a cat, not a baby. Thank goodness. He knew how to handle a cat. A baby would have scared him silly.

"What're you doing in there with Jesus?" he said as he scooped up the animal and cradled it against his chest. It sank its claws into the fabric of his combat uniform and ducked its head under his chin.

It started to purr, its body shaking with the effort.

He looked down at the animal. The markings on its face weren't quite symmetrical—a little patch of brown fur by its white nose made its face look dirty. The cat stared back at him as if it could see things beyond Matt's vision.

Then it let go of its claws and settled down into his big hands as if it believed it had found a permanent home.

Stupid cat. It should know better than to settle on him. He didn't have a permanent home. He was as much a stray as the animal in his hands.

He didn't need a cat right now.

He just needed to deliver Nick's present—the last one he'd bought for his grandmother. And once Matt finished that errand, he could think about the future—preferably without any animals in it.

Annie Roberts sang the closing lyrics to "Watchman, Tell Us of the Night," her solo scheduled for tomorrow night's Christmas Eve service. Dale Pontius, the Christ Church choir director, sat in the back pew listening and nodding his head.

Pride rushed through her. She had a very good singing voice, and she loved this particular carol. She was looking forward to singing it for everyone at tomorrow night's services. Singing on Christmas Eve was one of Annie's greatest joys. She'd been singing in the Christ Church choir since she'd returned home from college, almost fifteen years before.

Just as the closing notes of the guitar accompaniment faded, a soldier in fatigues with a big pack on his back entered the sanctuary through the front doors. He strolled down the center aisle a few steps, the sound of his boot heels echoing. He stared up at the choir and Annie in particular.

He had forgotten to take off his dark beret, and a shadow of day-old beard colored his cheeks. He looked hard and worn around the edges.

"Who the dickens are you?" Dale said from his place in the back pew.

The soldier looked over one broad shoulder. "I'm Staff Sergeant Matt Jasper, sir," he said in a deep voice. "I was wondering if anyone had lost a cat. And also I need some directions."

It was only then that Annie noticed the ball of orange, white, and brown fur resting in Sergeant Jasper's hands.

"Good heavens, get that mangy thing out of here. I'm allergic." Dale stood up and gestured toward the door.

Millie Polk, standing behind Annie in the alto section whispered, *sotto voce*, "Maybe he'll have a sneezing fit, and we'll all get to go home to our gift wrapping and cooking."

This elicited several chortles of laughter from the vicinity of the sopranos. Annie loved choir practice, but she had to admit that Dale was a real taskmaster this time of year. And, like Millie Polk, she had a long list of Christmas errands she needed to get done before tomorrow afternoon.

"You think a cat in this sanctuary is funny?" Dale said, turning toward the soprano section. "Did ya'll have any idea how lacking your performance of the 'Hallelujah Chorus' was this evening? There is nothing funny about this situation."

Dale turned toward the soldier. "I am very grateful for your service to the country, but this is a closed rehearsal. I would appreciate it if you would leave and take the cat with you."

It was almost comical the way Dale managed to stare down his nose while simultaneously looking up at the sergeant holding the kitten. The situation was sort of like a Chihuahua playing alpha dog to an adorable collie.

Matt Jasper wasn't intimidated by Dale though. He simply stared down at the choir director out of a pair of dark, almost black eyes. His eyebrows waggled. "Sorry to bust up your choir practice, sir, but I found this cat in your manger. If I hadn't picked it up, it probably would have broken your baby Jesus. So I figure the cat's yours. I need to get going. I've got an errand to run, and I—"

"Well, it's not *my* cat." Dale turned to the choir. "Did any of you bring your cat to choir practice?" There was no mistaking the scorn in Dale's voice.

The choir got really quiet. Nobody liked it when Dale lost his temper.

"See? The cat doesn't belong to anyone." Dale gazed at the bundle of fur in the soldier's hands and sniffed. "It's probably a stray. Why don't you leave it outside and get on with your errand?"

"He can't do that," Annie said, and then immediately regretted her words. She did not *want* a cat, no matter how lonely she felt sometimes.

On the other hand, she wasn't going to stand by and let Dale Pontius and Sergeant Jasper drop a stray in the churchyard and walk away. That was inhumane.

Dale turned toward Annie, his displeasure evident in his scowl. Dale could be a tyrant. She should keep her mouth shut. But for some reason, the little bundle of fur in the big soldier's hands made her brave. "It's cold outside. It's supposed to rain."

She pulled her gaze away from Dale and gave the soldier the stink eye. She wasn't intimidated by that uniform or his broad shoulders. He needed to know that she frowned on people leaving stray cats in the neighborhood.

Jasper's full mouth twitched a little at the corner. "Ma'am," he said, "you can rest easy. I'm not going to leave it outside to wander. I'd like to find it a good home." His gaze never wavered. His eyes were deep and dark and sad, like a puppy dog's eyes.

She didn't need a puppy either.

The cat issued a big, loud meow that reverberated in the empty sanctuary. The church's amazing acoustic qualities magnified the meow to monumental proportions.

"Get that thing out of here." Dale was working himself into a tizzy.

"Uh, look," the soldier said, "can anyone here tell me where I might find Ruth Clausen? I went to what I thought was her address, but the house is all boarded up."

The choir shifted uneasily. "Ruth's in a nursing home," Annie said.

The soldier's thick eyebrows almost met in the middle when he frowned. "In a nursing home?"

"Yes, she's very old and quite ill," Dale said. "Now, if you don't mind, I have a choir practice to get on with." Dale strode past the man in the aisle and back to the front of the church.

"That was very nice, Annie, Clay." Dale turned toward Clay Rhodes, the choir's main instrumentalist. "I'd like one more run-through on the Handel."

Annie resumed her place with the altos, and Clay put his guitar in its stand and took his place at the organ. He flipped through a few pages of music and began the opening chords of the "Hallelujah Chorus."

Annie sang her part and watched as the cat-packing

soldier ignored Dale's request and took a seat in the back pew. Halfway through the choir's performance, Sergeant Jasper must have remembered that he was in a church, because he finally took off his beret. His hair was salt-and-pepper and cut military short.

For some reason, Annie couldn't keep her eyes off him. She wondered if he might have been one of Nick's friends.

It seemed likely, since he'd come in here asking after Ruth, Nick's grandmother. She didn't want to be the one to tell him that he'd come on a fool's errand.

Matt settled back in the pew and listened to the music. This little town was way in the boonies, but the choir sounded pretty good. Not that he was a student of religious Christmas music. Matt had never been to church on Christmas. In fact, he'd pretty much never been to church in his life.

Not like Nick Clausen. If Nick's stories were to be believed, his folks had practically lived at church.

That's why Matt had come here to the church after he'd discovered that Ruth's house was boarded up. He'd known that someone at this church would know where to find Nick's grandmother.

Just like he'd known that the altar would have big bunches of poinsettias all over it, and the stained-glass window would have a picture of Jesus up on his cross.

It struck him, sitting there, that Nick had gone to Sunday school here. Nick had been confirmed here. He'd come here on Christmas Eve.

Matt took a deep breath. Boy, Nick sure had loved Christmas. Matt could kind of understand it, too, listening to the choir.

Matt's Christmases had been spent in a crummy apartment in Chicago while his mother and father got drunk.

He closed his eyes and let the music carry him away from those memories. He'd gotten over his childhood. He'd found a home in the army. He'd made something of himself.

He buried his fingers in the stray's soft fur. It licked his hand with a rough tongue.

He needed to find the local animal shelter, followed by the nursing home. Then he planned to get the hell out of Dodge before the urge to stay overwhelmed him. Because a guy like him didn't belong in a place like this. This was Nick's place, not his.

The music ended, and the choir director finally let everyone go. Matt stood up and slung his pack over his shoulder. Maybe the brown-haired woman with the amazing voice could help him. He'd heard her singing from out on the lawn, after the cat had stopped howling. The sound had called to him, and he'd followed it right into the church.

The choir members seemed thrilled to be dismissed. Probably because the choir director was a jerk, and they had shopping, and cooking, and a lot of other holiday crap to do. People in Last Chance would be busy like that, cooking big meals, wrapping presents, decorating trees, and stuff.

He found the brown-haired woman who'd spoken up in the cat's defense. "Ma'am, I was wondering, could you help me, please?"

She was shrugging into a big dark coat that had a sparkly Christmas tree pin on its collar. She gazed at him out of a pair of dark blue eyes. She had very pale skin, a long nose, and a thin face.

"I'm not taking your cat," she said in a defensive voice. "But if you're looking for Ruth, she's in the Golden Years Nursing Home up in Orangeburg."

He frowned. "Where's that?"

"You're not from around here, are you?"

"No, ma'am. I'm originally from Chicago. Since I joined up, I'm from wherever they station me." Except, of course, that wasn't true anymore. He hadn't re-upped this time, and he had nowhere permanent to go. He'd come to deliver Nick's present, and then he had some vague plans for spending New Year's on a beach somewhere—maybe Miami.

"Well, Orangeburg is about twenty miles north of here. But I need to warn you, Ruth's been in the nursing home for the last year, and she's pretty ill. I know because I work for her doctor."

"I see."

"Are you a friend of Nick's?" she asked.

He smiled. "Yes. Did you know him too?"

"I went to high school with him. I had a bit of a crush on him." She blushed when she said it.

"And you are?"

"I'm Annie Roberts."

He blinked and almost said *I know you.* But of course he didn't know Annie, except from the things Nick had told him. Annie had been Nick's girlfriend in high school. They had broken up the night of their senior prom.

"You studied nursing at the University of Michigan," he said.

"How did you—Oh, Nick told you that, didn't he?"

He grinned. "He told me you were looking forward to going someplace where it snows."

She frowned at him. "Why are you here? Nick died more than a year ago."

"I know. I was with him when it happened."

"Oh."

He shouldn't have said that. People always got that look on their faces when he spoke about this crap. No one back home really understood.

She squared her shoulders. "I'm so sorry. Are you a member of the Army Engineers K-9 team too?"

He continued to stroke the cat. "I was. As of yesterday, I'm officially a civilian."

The words came out easy. It took everything he had to hide the emotions behind them.

"And you came here? Right before Christmas? Don't you have a family someplace?"

He shrugged. "I have Nick's last Christmas present— you know, the one he intended to send home to his grandmother. I need to deliver it."

Her gaze pierced him for a moment. It was almost as if she could read all of his thoughts and emotions. A muscle ticked in her cheek, and she seemed to be weighing something in her mind.

She must have decided that he wasn't a threat because she let go of a long breath and gave the kitten a little stroke. "Poor thing. She looks half starved."

"How do you know it's a female?"

"How do you know it's not?"

He shifted the animal so he could actually inspect it. "Well, you were right. It's a girl. Means she'll have to be fixed. Is there an animal shelter somewhere?"

"Yes. In Allenberg. But it's probably closed."

His frustration with the situation mounted. "Uh, look, Annie, I just got in on the bus from Charlotte. I don't have a car. And now I need to find a home for this kitten, as well as a place to stay for the night. It's probably too late to go visiting at a nursing home twenty miles away."

She buttoned up her coat. "Boy, you're in a fix, aren't you?"

"Is there a hotel somewhere?"

Her cheeks colored just the slightest bit. "Well, the only place in town is the Peach Blossom Motor Court. They would probably allow you to keep the cat."

"I've heard about the Peach Blossom Motor Court," he blurted and then remembered the story. "Oh, crap. That was stupid."

Annie's cheeks reddened further. "I guess guys in the army have nothing better to do than talk."

"Yes, ma'am. And believe me, being in the army can be really boring at times. Guys talk about home all the time. I'm sorry. I should have kept my mouth shut."

"Don't be sorry. What happened between me and Nick the night of senior prom happened almost twenty years ago."

"I guess he never told you about me, did he?" Matt asked.

She shook her head. "Why would he? He and I parted ways that night. He went off to join the army and see the world. I went off to college to see the snow. I guess I saw him that Christmas right after he went through basic training, but I wasn't speaking with him at the time." She hugged herself, and Matt noticed that she wasn't wearing a wedding ring.

So the girl Nick had never forgotten was unmarried.

She gave him a smile that didn't show any teeth. A few lines bunched at the corner of her eyes. She wasn't young. But she was pretty.

And Matt knew that she was sweet. He had a lot of Nick's stories filed away in his head. Nick had been a real good storyteller when things got slow.

Annie studied the cat sleeping in his hands and then nodded her head as if she'd come to a decision. "Look, you can't stay at the Peach Blossom. It probably has bed bugs. It's just an awful place. So you might as well come on home with me. I've got a perfectly fine guest room where you can sleep, and in the morning, we can figure something out. I'm sure I can find someone to run you up to Orangeburg, or I can do it myself."

"How about a friend who wants to adopt Fluffy?" He held up the cat in his hands.

"Fluffy?" She gave him a funny look. "That is a stupid name for a cat."

"Why? She's kind of fluffy."

"Yeah, but everyone names their cat Fluffy. There must be five Fluffys living here in Last Chance, and they all belong to single women. Please don't name the cat Fluffy."

"Okay, I won't," Matt said. "I thought you didn't care about this cat."

"Well, no, but you found it in a manger a couple days before Christmas, didn't you?"

"Yeah."

"Well, then, it needs a better name than Fluffy. Something holiday-related, like Noel."

He looked down at the slightly scruffy kitten. "That's

a pretty pretentious name for this particular cat, don't you think? Of course, if you were going to adopt it, you could name it anything you wanted."

She scowled at him. "I'm not adopting any cats, understand?"

"Yes, ma'am."

Annie should have her head examined. She could almost hear Mother's voice outlining all the reasons she should send Sergeant Matt Jasper off to the Peach Blossom Motor Court. Mother would start with the fact that he was male, and then move right on to the worry that he was secretly either a pervert or an ax murderer.

Mother had trust issues.

But Annie could not, for the life of her, believe that a man with Matt's warm, dark eyes was either a pervert or a murderer. And besides, he knew how to handle the cat. His hands were big and gentle. And that uniform seemed to be tailor made for him.

She led him down the aisle and out the door and into the blustery December evening.

"Feels like snow," he said.

She laughed. "I don't think so. We don't ever get snow here."

"It seems like you should." They headed across Palmetto Avenue and down Julia Street.

"Snow in South Carolina? Not happening."

He shifted the cat in his arms. "Nick used to talk about Christmas in Last Chance all the time. I always kind of imagined the place with a dusting of snow."

She snorted. "Nick sure could tell stories. But I can only remember one year when we got a dusting of snow. It was pitiful by snow standards. And it didn't last very long."

"Well, I'm from Chicago, you know."

"So I reckon ya'll have snow on the ground at Christmas all the time."

"Yeah. But in the city it doesn't take very long for the snow to get dirty and gray. I always kind of imagined Last Chance covered in pristine white."

"Well, that's a fantasy." She reached her mother's house on Oak Street. The old place needed a coat of paint, and a few of the porch balusters needed replacing. Annie ought to sell the place and move to Orangeburg or Columbia. A registered nurse could get a job just about anywhere these days. And her social life might improve if she moved to a bigger town.

But she'd have to leave home. She'd have to leave friends. She'd have to leave the choir and the book club, not to mention Doc Cooper and the clinic.

No wonder Miriam Randall had told her to get a cat. If she wanted to deal with her loneliness in Last Chance, a cat was probably her best bet.

She pushed open the door and hit the switch for the hall and porch lights. Her Christmas lights—the same strand of large-bulbed lights that Mother had used for decades—blinked on.

"Oh," Matt said. It was less than a word and more than an exhalation.

"I'm afraid it's not much of a display. Nothing like the lights the Canadays put out every year."

She looked over her shoulder. Matt was smiling, the lights twinkling merrily in his eyes. A strange heat flowed through Annie that she recognized as attraction.

Boy, she was really pathetic, wasn't she?

She shucked out of her coat and hung it on one of the pegs by the door.

"It smells wonderful in here," Matt said. He strolled past her into the front parlor. His presence filled up the space and made the large room seem smaller by half. He made a full three-sixty, inspecting everything, from the old upright piano to Grandmother's ancient mohair furniture.

Crap. Her house looked like it belonged to a little old lady. Which, in fact, it had, until last spring, when Mother died. Suddenly the cabbage rose wallpaper and the threadbare carpet made Annie feel like a spinster. The cat would complete the picture.

Matt stopped and cocked his head. "You have a tree."

"Of course I have a tree. Mother would—" She cut herself off. The last thing Matt wanted to hear about was what Mother expected out of Christmas. This year, Annie planned to make a few changes.

But she'd still put out Mother's old Christmas lights. And she had still bought a Douglas fir instead of a blue spruce.

And she'd made the annual climb up to the attic for the ornaments. But when she'd gotten the boxes down to the front parlor, she'd lost the will to decorate. One look at her mother's faded decorations, and she'd felt like her life was in a big rut.

She'd done the unthinkable—she'd carried all those old boxes right back up to the attic. If she'd been a braver woman, she would have carried them to the curb for the trash man.

Of course, she hadn't done one thing about replacements. She had been putting all of that off. And suddenly, she realized that if she was going to take Matt up to Orangeburg tomorrow to visit Ruth, and still host a party for her friends from the book club, she was going to have to get her fanny in gear.

Matt pulled in a deep breath, drinking in the Christmas tree aroma. He squeezed his eyes closed and could almost hear Nick's voice, talking about how he'd helped his grandmother trim her tree.

Annie's tree was naked.

He put the cat down on the carpet. She darted under the sofa, where she crouched, looking up at him as if he'd abandoned her.

Stupid cat. She should realize that she had found a better home than he could provide. Annie's house was like something out of a picture postcard. If Matt had had a grandmother, this is precisely the way he'd want her house to look.

Matt had a feeling that Nick's grandma's house had been like this too.

He turned back toward Annie. She looked like a picture postcard too. Like Mom and apple pie. Like home.

"So," he said on a deep breath, "your tree needs help, Annie Roberts."

She gave him a bashful smile. "I guess it does."

"I'm willing to work for my room and board. Just point me in the direction of the lights."

She laughed. "Everything is up in the attic. Wait a sec, and I'll go get the boxes."

She scurried away up the stairs in the main hall, and he amused himself watching her shapely backside, clad in a pair of blue jeans, as she climbed to the second story.

Oh yeah, Annie Roberts was more than pretty. She was built. He could understand why Nick had had trouble forgetting her.

"No, cat!" Annie tried to pull the feline away from the string of lights that Matt was hanging on the tree.

"Maybe we should call her Pouncy," he said with a deep, rumbling laugh.

He stood rock steady on the stepladder. He'd taken off his army jacket and wore only a tan-colored T-shirt that hugged his torso. He looked fit.

Okay, she was understating the fact. Matt looked gorgeous, and ripped, and competent standing there hanging tree lights.

The cat, on the other hand, looked like a menace on four feet. The kitten had gotten over her fear of the new environment and had decided that the Christmas tree and anything associated with it was her personal play toy.

Matt was no good at discouraging her either. He kept tugging on the string of lights, making them move suddenly in a way that the cat found irresistible. The kitten pounced ferociously on them and then backed up and pounced again.

The cat was growing on Annie.

But not as much as the man.

"So, you said you have a Christmas gift for Ruth?" she asked, purposefully raising the specter of Nick. She really needed to remember that Matt had come to do something that was going to make Ruth unspeakably sad. And then he would go away, just like Nick had done. Best to keep her distance.

"Yeah. Nick bought it for her a year and a half ago."

"What is it?"

"I have no idea. I don't even know where he bought it. I just know that I found it with his stuff after he died. I took it before the CO could lay his hands on it. Not exactly regulation, I know, but I kept thinking about Ruth getting Nick's effects and finding it there. I thought it would be really crummy to get a gift and not have Nick there, you know? I thought it would be better to bring it myself."

She studied him for a very long time. He was a pretty sensitive guy for a soldier. Her opinion of him rose a little more. "You waited a long time."

He finished putting the lights on the tree and stepped down from the stepladder. "I was in Afghanistan. It was a long deployment."

Annie unwrapped the angel that Mother always put on the top of the tree. The angel wore yellow velvet with gold trim, and her halo had been broken years and years ago. She handed the tree topper to Matt, and their fingers touched. Heat flooded through her, and the look of longing in Matt's eyes told her that the reaction was mutual. Matt let go of a big breath, as if he'd been holding something inside. They stood there for the longest moment, their fingers touching across the angel. Eventually Annie let go, and Matt turned, stepped up the ladder, and put the angel in her place.

For some reason, the angel, even with her bent wings and broken halo, looked beautiful up there. Once, a long time ago, Annie had thought the angel was the most beautiful Christmas ornament ever. How had she forgotten that?

Matt turned back toward her, his eyes filled with joy. "I love doing this," he said. "I haven't had much experience trimming trees. My folks used to put a little fake tree on the kitchen table when I was a kid. We always lived in a pretty small apartment."

Annie turned away, suddenly overcome by emotions she couldn't name. Who was this stranger who had walked into her house with a cat and a heaping dose of holiday spirit?

He was the man who'd come to give Ruth a present she didn't need or want.

But Annie could hardly explain that to Matt, could she? He'd come here first thing after the army let him go. Like delivering his gift was a kind of obligation.

She held her tongue and picked up a cardboard box filled with slightly tarnished glass balls. "Here, make yourself busy."

He took the box and immediately set to work. She watched him for the longest moment before she said, "You know, Ruth isn't in her right mind."

He stopped. Turned. "No?"

Annie shook her head. "Hasn't been since those army men came to her door with the news."

He pressed his lips together. "I'm sorry."

"What do you have to be sorry about? It's just the way it is. She's been in a nursing home for more than a year. And according to what I heard from Doc Cooper, she's not expected to live past New Year's. She's got congestive heart failure. It's only a matter of time. But, you know, she's alone now and almost ninety."

He startled. His hands reflexively squeezed the box of ornaments.

Annie stood up. "Can I get you something? A cup of coffee? Some hot chocolate?"

He stood there, looking a little confused, his eyebrows

cocked at a funny angle. "Uh, yeah. Some hot chocolate would be great."

What was he doing here? He looked up at the little angel atop the tree. She didn't seem to have an answer.

Just then the cat attacked his bootlace. He bent down and picked Pouncy up.

Annie was right. Pouncy was a stupid name. One day the kitten would grow up and quit pouncing on everything in sight.

He cuddled her closer and sat in the big armchair facing the front window. The lights on the tree looked festive. The cat curled up in his lap.

"Poor little stray, born out of season. Were you abandoned?" he asked the cat.

The cat only purred in response.

He let go of a long sigh. He wondered what was in that gaily wrapped package at the bottom of his knapsack. Maybe it would be better if he left town tomorrow and didn't bother.

"Here you go." Annie came into the room bearing a tray and a bright smile. "Hot chocolate, made with real milk."

She bent over to put the tray down on the coffee table, giving Matt a great view of her backside. Unwanted desire tugged at him with a vengeance.

He shouldn't be getting the hots for Nick's old high school flame. Even if she and Nick had broken up twenty years ago. It seemed forbidden somehow.

And yet attraction was there as clear as a bell. Annie was everything Nick had said she was, and more. And her home was...

Well, he didn't want to delve too deeply into that.

Especially since he felt like he'd walked right into one of Nick's Christmas stories.

Annie handed him a cup of chocolate, their fingers touched again, and the heat curled up in his chest.

He took the mug from her and lifted it to his mouth. The chocolate was warm and rich and sweet. A lot like the woman who had made it.

She turned away and put her hands on her hips. "We still have a lot of work to do."

She picked up another box of ornaments and began digging through tissue. "These are my mother's birds," she said.

She pulled out a delicate red glass bird and clipped it to a branch.

"I take it your mother is gone?" he asked.

She nodded, her shoulders stiff. "Yeah, she died last spring. This is my first Christmas without her."

"I'm sorry."

"Well, she's in a happier place. She was always sick, and she missed my father." Annie stopped and turned and gave him a very serious stare. "Sort of like Ruth these last few years."

"You think I shouldn't deliver my present?"

"Depends on the reason you want to deliver it."

Before he could answer, the kitten got up and stretched, then bounded off Matt's lap. It pranced over to a box laden with decorations and dived right into it. Pouncy stalked and jumped and pussyfooted while Matt and Annie watched her and laughed.

Finally she lifted her "dirty" face over the lip of the cardboard as she ferociously batted at the red ribbon she'd managed to entangle herself in.

"I think we should name you Holly," Annie said on a laugh.

"Holly's a good name for a cat that was found two days before Christmas," Matt agreed.

Annie turned her head, and they gazed at each other for the longest moment. She finally blushed, and an answering heat rose like a column right through him. He stood up, drawn to her by some force he didn't quite understand. "Annie Roberts," he said, "I feel like I've known you all my life."

She blinked at him. "Uh. That's not possible. It's probably just because Nick talked about me."

"Maybe, but that's not quite it. Do you believe in love at first sight?"

She blanched. "No. No, I don't." She turned a suddenly nervous gaze on the kitten who had curled up under the coffee table.

She stepped back toward the hallway. "Uh, I'm going to go check the guest bedroom—make sure the bed in there has clean sheets."

She turned and escaped.

Matt stood by the tree watching her run.

Boy, he was an idiot. He should have kept his feelings inside. He glanced around the room, filled with Christmas decorations that had been carefully handed down through the generations.

Annie was like Nick. She had traditions and a place where she fit. Matt wanted all that. He could tell himself he'd come to deliver a Christmas gift, but that would be a lie.

He'd come to Last Chance in the hope that Ruth might invite him in and give him a taste of what Nick had known growing up. The truth was, Matt envied Nick's childhood.

But Matt was just a stray, like the cat. And Annie had made it clear that she wasn't interested in taking in any strays.

Christmas Eve day dawned gray. Annie awakened just before seven. She snuggled down under the covers and listened to the rain pinging against the tin roof.

She didn't realize she had company until Holly pranced across Grandmother's quilt, her little claws pulling at the fabric. Annie started to scold and then held her tongue.

The old quilt was nearly a rag anyway. She slept under it only as a matter of habit. For months now, she'd been telling herself that she'd make a run down to Target and buy herself something new.

Why had she been putting that off? Why hadn't she gone down to Target earlier in the week and purchased new ornaments for the tree?

Why had she run away from Matt last night?

The kitten wormed its body up against her chest, curled itself into a little ball, and started to purr.

If she was going to keep it, she'd need to get a litter box.

She stopped herself in midthought.

She was not keeping this cat. No matter what. The cat was like an emblem for everything that was wrong in her life. If she took responsibility for a cat, like she'd taken responsibility for Mother all those years ago, how was she ever going to escape and find her own life?

She was getting old. She wanted children. She wanted a family of her own—someone she could hand the old ornaments off to. But if she accepted that cat, she was accepting the end of that dream.

No way. She pushed the cat aside. It didn't get the message. It came right back at her, cute as a button and looking for love.

Matt looked up from his cup of coffee as Annie stepped into the kitchen. She looked like something out of a Christmas movie in a red-and-white snowflake sweater, her hair in a ponytail with a red ribbon.

"Thanks for all your help last night," she said, as she leaned in the kitchen doorway. "I just checked in with the nursing home. They open for nonfamily visiting hours at ten a.m. I've got an early appointment at the beauty shop, and after that, I can run you up to Orangeburg. I've got some last-minute shopping to do; then I have to get back here to cook before my friends arrive for Christmas Eve dinner."

"I've been an imposition, haven't I?"

"No, it's all right." She seemed so nervous with her arms crossed over her breasts, as if she were trying to shield herself from him.

He came to the decision he'd been mulling over for most of the night. "Look, I've been thinking about what you said last night, about Ruth's present."

"Oh? What did I say? I don't remember saying anything in particular."

"You asked me why I wanted to deliver a present that's probably going to make her very sad."

"I asked that? I mean, I think you should think about what you're doing. After all, Ruth is ill and she's not entirely with it, you know."

"Okay, maybe you didn't. But it's still a good question, isn't it? I've been trying to decide why I wanted to come here and deliver that stupid gift. And well, the thing is, I'm not sure I came here for the right reasons."

"What do you think are the right reasons, Matt?" Her gaze seemed to focus on him, as if she really cared about his answer.

He shrugged. "When I took that present from out of Nick's effects, I told myself I was going to do his grandmother a favor. I thought it might be hard for her to get a Christmas present from a person who had died. I thought maybe I could come and say a couple of words to her, you know, about what a great buddy Nick had been."

"That seems like a good reason, Matt."

He nodded. "Yeah, but there was something else. I realized it last night while I was helping you with the tree."

"What?"

"The thing is my Christmases as a kid were crummy. They sucked. But Nick used to talk about Christmas all the time. He used to tell stories about how his grandmother made a big roast with mashed potatoes. He used to talk about his parents kissing under the mistletoe, before they died." Matt's voice wavered, and he stopped and took a big breath.

"So you thought you'd come and experience that?" Annie said.

He turned away and looked out the window that opened on to the back yard. The window had lacy curtains, and outside the rain was pouring down.

"My dog died three weeks ago," he said in a voice that he could barely control. "They shipped me home, and because the dog died, they let me out a little early. I had already told them I wasn't going to re-up. Now I just want..." He shook his head and pressed his lips together.

"Oh, Matt, I'm so sorry. I didn't know."

Then he turned back toward Annie. "Losing the dog was hard. He wasn't killed in action. He just got sick and had to be put down. He was getting old anyway, and I had planned for the two of us to retire together. But now I'm alone. And being a soldier is the only thing I know how to be."

"Matt, every returning soldier has an adjustment period."

"I know. But I came here looking for Ruth. I thought maybe she would have some wisdom for me, or at least maybe a slice of her apple pie. God, Nick used to talk about that pie all the time, especially when we were stuck eating MREs. And then I found her house all boarded up, and I was lost. I went to the church because I knew she was a member there. To be honest, I heard the cat yowling, and Holly kind of led me right there."

"Really?"

He gave her a short nod. "And then I heard you singing, and it was like, for an instant I felt like I'd...well, hell...I don't...like I'd come home. And that's ridiculous because I don't belong in Last Chance. I'm a street kid from Chicago."

She blinked down at him but didn't say a word.

"I've scared you again, haven't I?"

"No, it's more like I'm a little surprised. What was your dog's name?"

"Murphy. He had liver failure. He'd been a pretty

hard worker for six years. He saved a whole lot of lives over there, sniffing out IEDs. He was a good, hard-working, war dog." Matt swallowed before the emotion ate him up.

"I'm sure he was. You know, you should take Holly. She'd be a comfort to you."

He nodded and took a calming sip of his coffee. Annie really didn't want that cat, did she?

"So, uh," Annie said, "I have an early appointment at the Cut 'n' Curl. I won't be more than an hour at most." She turned on her heel and strode out of the room like she was trying to escape his toxic emotions.

Matt watched her go. He really needed to get a grip. He probably needed to put that stupid gift under Annie's tree and go see about taking a bus to someplace warm and sunny.

Annie's appointment at the Cut 'n' Curl was for nine in the morning, and even at that early hour several members of the Christ Church Ladies Auxiliary were already present and accounted for. It being both Saturday and Christmas Eve, Ruby Rhodes, Last Chance's main hairdresser, had opened up an hour early.

Thelma Hanks was having her roots touched up. Lessie Anderson was in Ruby's chair getting a wash and set, and Jane Rhodes, Ruby's new daughter-in-law, was giving Miriam Randall a manicure.

"Hey, Annie," Thelma Hanks said after Annie had hung her coat in the closet. Thelma had just looked up from one of those romance books Ruby kept on a shelf at the back of the shop. This particular book had a cover featuring a naked male torso.

"How are you doing, honey? Everything okay?" Thelma's voice was laden with concern. All the women in the shop stopped what they were doing and watched Annie as she sat down in one of the dryer chairs. "What?" she asked, flicking her gaze from one woman to another.

"We're just concerned, sugar," Ruby said.

Ruby and her customers had been Mother's friends. Mother had been an active member of the Auxiliary. She had a standing Wednesday appointment at the Cut 'n' Curl, so it was just natural that they would be worried about Annie this Christmastime.

It was her first Christmas alone. And everyone seemed to be working hard to make sure she didn't have a minute to be sad about it. She'd received invitations to Christmas Eve and Christmas Day dinner from Ruby, Lessie, Thelma, Miriam, and several of Mother's other friends. She had declined them all and had invited some of the members of the book club to dinner instead.

Mother had not fully approved of the book club. She was living in the last century and looked down her nose at Nita and Kaylee, because of their race. But Annie had always counted them as friends, even in the face of Mother's disapproval. And now Annie could invite whomever she wanted to dinner, without hearing Mother's ugly complaints.

"I'm fine," she said to the ladies in the beauty parlor. "I've got my tree all trimmed, and I'm going up to the Target in Orangeburg for some shopping this afternoon, and then Nita and Jenny and a few other friends from the book club are coming over for dinner before midnight services."

"I'm so glad to hear that," Ruby said, "what with Nita's daughter being off in Atlanta this year. It's nice the two of you are spending time together."

"So, honey, have you taken my advice yet?" Miriam asked from her place at the manicure station.

Everyone turned to stare at Miriam. Today the little old lady was dressed in a pair of red plaid slacks and a red sweatshirt with a big graphic of Rudolf on its front. She had a pair of dangly Christmas tree earrings in her ears. Her eyes twinkled behind her 1950s-style trifocals.

Miriam was about eighty-five years old and widely regarded as Allenberg County's premier matchmaker. Not that Miriam considered *herself* a matchmaker. She always told folks she was a match *finder*. She said God made the matches, but sometimes He would clue her in.

Her matchmaking advice sometimes resembled the messages you might find inside a fortune cookie. But the weird thing about Miriam's marital forecasts was that they almost always came true.

"I declare," Ruby said to Miriam, "when did you give Annie any advice?"

"Oh, I think it was last week after church."

"And what advice did you give Annie?" Thelma leaned forward, her romance book forgotten.

"I told her to get a cat."

"What?" Lessie turned her head, and the roller Ruby was trying to secure came undone.

"And I told her that I wasn't so lonely that I needed a cat." Annie folded her arms across her chest. "I need to get out and have a social life now that Mother's gone. I don't need a cat."

"Miriam," Ruby said, "you didn't really tell Annie she needed a cat, did you?"

"What's wrong with suggesting that she get a cat?" Miriam looked honestly surprised.

"Because you don't tell a single lady of a certain age that she needs a cat. It's, well..." Ruby's voice trailed off.

"It's pitiful," Annie said into the silence. "It's bad enough that I'm sleeping under a quilt my grandmother made and living in a house with old-fashioned mohair furniture. Getting a cat would be like sealing my fate."

"Yes, exactly," Miriam said.

Ruby, Lessie, and Thelma stared at Miriam as if she'd lost her mind. Miriam was a little quirky, but she'd never been mean.

Jane pulled Miriam's hand out of the soaking solution and said, "Clay said something about a big soldier finding a cat in the manger down at the church last night. This guy came strolling into the sanctuary with a little kitten, interrupting choir practice, and Dale almost had a stroke."

"Really?" Miriam asked. Somehow Miriam didn't sound very surprised.

Everyone turned toward Annie. Her face flamed. "His name is Matt Jasper, and he did find a cat in the manger. He came in on the bus from Charlotte last night, and he was looking for Ruth Clausen."

"Oh dear," Ruby said. "Is he one of Nick's army friends?"

"Yes, he is. He's come here to deliver Nick's last Christmas gift."

"What?" the women asked in unison.

"Evidently, Nick bought Ruth's present before he died last year. Matt has been carrying it around Afghanistan for a long time."

"Oh my," Thelma said. "He has no clue, does he?"

"No, he doesn't."

"Did you tell him about Ruth?" Thelma asked.

"Well, I told him that she'd been sick and a little out of it. But I didn't say anything else. He's committed to making this delivery. It's kind of sweet, actually. His heart's in the right place."

"So he didn't spend the night at the motel, did he?" Jane asked.

"Uh, no, he didn't."

Miriam snorted. "See, I told ya'll. Annie needed to get a cat. The Lord was very specific about that part."

While Annie went to her appointment at the beauty shop, Matt showered and shaved and put on his civies. Holly kept him company, trailing after him like a little lost soul.

He and the cat were kind of alike. If anyone could understand how a man could come looking for a warm place by a holiday fire, it would be a stray cat.

But he didn't really belong by Annie's fire, did he? And what was the point of delivering Nick's gift to his grandmother if she was senile and sick? How could that possibly brighten her day?

He'd come for his own selfish reasons, not to do any favors for Nick. And now, here he was, staying at Annie Roberts's house, thinking things about her that he had no right to think.

He should leave, right now, and take the cat with him

as a consolation prize. He started packing his bag. He had just brought the bag downstairs and set it in the corner when Annie's key slipped into the front door.

She came prancing into the foyer like a young girl. She stopped just a few feet from where he was standing and gave him the biggest grin. She was red cheeked from the cold outside, and there was a spark of something in her eyes that hadn't been there last night or even this morning. Something had changed. She seemed lit up from the inside.

"Uh," he said, suddenly tongue-tied, "I was thinking that with Ruth so ill, it might be best if I just..." He couldn't finish the sentence.

Holly pussyfooted across the floorboards and meowed a welcome. She rubbed up against Annie's legs and tried to wrap herself around both of them simultaneously.

Annie laughed. The sound was so merry and full of life. She bent down and picked up the kitten. "You need some cat food and a litter box," she said to Holly. "I hope you're housebroken."

She glanced up at Matt, and he had a feeling Annie was talking about something other than the cat.

"I understand your hesitation about Ruth," she said, her blue eyes darkening with some emotion he couldn't quite fathom. "But there's no rush. The Ladies Auxiliary always visits up there on Christmas morning, and you could tag along with them. I offered to drive Miriam Randall and the rest of the ladies up there, since I don't have a big family. So, if you want, we can all go together tomorrow morning. In the meantime, if you came to Last Chance for a Christmas like Nick loved, you're free to stay here at my place. In fact, I could use some help with my errands."

The tension he'd felt all morning suddenly eased. He'd been given permission to live out his deepest fantasy and let tomorrow slide. War had taught him the benefits of living in the moment. He didn't have to think very hard about her offer.

"I'd be happy to help. But I'm warning you, I'm really inexperienced in this whole Christmas thing."

"It's okay. There are plenty of people in Last Chance willing to give you pointers on how to celebrate the season."

Annie held out her hand, and he took it. It was small and warm, and it seemed to fit in his like it had been custom made.

They went to Orangeburg and practically bought out the Target there. Annie seemed to be hell-bent on taking advantage of every cut-rate deal on Christmas decorations. It being Christmas Eve, she made a few spectacular bargains—especially on a glow-from-the-inside snowman that had caught Matt's fancy. She had refused to let him buy it for her. She told him she needed to spruce up her lighting display before the neighbors complained about her lack of imagination.

She also bought some new sheets and a blanket—a move that made Matt just a little bit uncomfortable, since she asked his opinion on every choice. When he'd wrinkled his nose at the girly flowers on one set of sheets, she'd changed her mind about them.

Shopping for sheets with Annie was definitely sexier than it probably should be. He kept thinking about what it might be like to lie down on those new sheets with this amazing woman.

He needed to watch it. She had been Nick's girlfriend, and he was already perilously close to losing his grip on the real world.

Annie was brimming over with good cheer. Her day with Holly and Matt had been so happy. But then she could hardly fail. Miriam Randall hadn't been speaking literally last week in church. She'd been finding Annie a match.

And Annie couldn't be more pleased with the way things were going. Matt was tall, dark, and handsome. He was kind, and he seemed to understand the inherent problem associated with his grim chore. And yet she got the feeling he still wanted to deliver that present, even if he wondered whether it was the right thing to do. His conflict made him all the more loveable. And she knew she was falling for him. Maybe she did believe in love at first sight after all.

When they got home from shopping, she put him to work finishing the decorating and setting up the big glow-in-the-dark snowman they had purchased.

The snowman was silly and a little tacky. But it reminded her of the few years she'd spent in Michigan at college. Those had been happy years, before Mother had come down with rheumatoid arthritis. Before Dad had died. Before her future had been hijacked by circumstances beyond her control.

Matt had fallen in love with the snowman too. He said if he couldn't have real snow in Last Chance, he'd go for the fake kind.

Of course, Mother would never have approved of the snowman, the cat, or the soldier, which made all of them welcome additions to Annie's holiday. Nothing about this Christmas was going to be like last year.

And having Matt around, lapping up all the holiday cheer, made everything seem a little more joyful. He had so many reasons to be sad, having lost his dog this year and his best friend last year, but he seemed determined to let the joy of Christmas in. And his joy was infectious.

Nita Wills was the first member of the book club to arrive at Annie's dinner party, with Cathy close on her heels. Both of them seemed more impressed and surprised by the snowman than the cat or the soldier.

"Well, Annie," Nita said as she put a plate of gingerbread cookies on the buffet table, "it sure does look like Santa has been good to you this Christmas."

Annie didn't have a minute to respond before Elsie and Lola May arrived, followed very closely by Jenny Carpenter. Jenny, of course, came bearing apple and shepherd's pies. Jenny's pies were to die for, and Matt seemed more than a little interested in both of her offerings.

Annie stifled the strange, unwanted wave of jealousy. And she was soon busy playing hostess when Kaylee and Nomi arrived each bearing matching bean casseroles.

The women gathered around the buffet and filled their cups with eggnog and Christmas punch—two things Mother would never have allowed in her home at holiday time. They laughed and chatted about Barbara Kingsolver's latest book. All in all, the house hadn't seen so many people in years, and Annie was feeling happy and free and flushed with Christmas spirit.

Then Nita scooped Holly up from the easy chair and

sat down. She held the kitten up for inspection. "Well, aren't you just the cutest, dirty-faced matchmaker in Last Chance?" she said aloud.

The women of the book club collectively laughed, and Annie felt suddenly stripped naked. She glanced over at Matt to see if he'd heard what Last Chance's librarian had said.

Apparently he had, because Nita hadn't used her librarian voice. Matt's dark stare zeroed in on Nita, and his eyebrows bunched up in the middle.

Elsie gave him a pat on the back. "Don't you mind Nita, now. She's just talking about how Miriam Randall told Annie that she needed to get a cat."

Matt's frown deepened.

"See," Cathy explained, "Miriam has a pipeline to the Lord, and when she gives advice, it's always right."

"Exactly," Lola May said. "And that just means that you and Annie are a match made in heaven."

Matt turned his dark gaze on Annie. Her heartbeat raced, but whether in embarrassment or desire she wasn't sure. It was insane to think that Matt was destined to become her lover, just because he'd found a cat in a manger.

But hadn't she been behaving like that all day?

"Uh, ladies, I think there's been some kind of mis-understanding," Matt said. "I just came here to deliver a gift to Ruth Clausen."

"And have you delivered it yet?" Nita asked.

Matt scratched the back of his head and glanced at Annie. "Uh, no. I kind of got involved with a bunch of errands. I'm going up to Orangeburg tomorrow for that chore."

Nita spoke again. "Do you think that's wise?"

"I don't know. But I've been lugging that thing all over Afghanistan. I think it needs to find its way home."

Nita nodded. "Well, I guess I can understand that. And I admire you for bringing it to Ruth personally. You didn't have to do that." She gazed at the kitten. "Well, one thing is for sure, this cat is cute," she said.

The members of the book club went back to chatting and grazing at the buffet.

Matt strolled over to where Annie was standing, his dark eyes filled with emotions that weren't very merry.

"I can explain about the matchmaker," she said. "See—"

"I know all about Miriam Randall," he murmured.

"What?"

"Nick told me all about her. He seemed to think she was infallible. He told me once that he was very sorry Miriam hadn't matched him up permanently with you. You should know that Nick really regretted what happened between the two of you."

"He wanted to be a soldier. He wanted to leave this town, Matt. That's all he ever talked about. And I wasn't sure I wanted to be in love with a soldier or a man with wanderlust in his soul."

"I know all about what happened. I know how you guys fought that night at the motel. I know how he walked away in a huff. He told me everything."

"He told you all that?"

"He told me a lot of things. You talk about things when you're getting shot at. And God knows, we got shot at a lot when we were in Baghdad on our first deployment. You were the girl he never forgot, Annie. You're the girl he regretted. The one he missed. He never married, you know."

They stared at each other for a long emotion-filled moment; then he leaned in to kiss her on the cheek. She saw what was coming and turned her head to meet his lips. It was a pretty brazen thing to do, given the fact that Matt had been talking about how Nick had loved her. But Nick had walked away twenty years ago and never come back.

Annie tried, for all she was worth, to take the kiss a little deeper, but Matt pulled back. He looked up. "So, ah, that's what mistletoe is all about, huh?"

Annie followed his gaze. Sure enough they were standing under a sprig of the stuff. Disappointment swallowed up her Christmas merriment.

"Sorry, I couldn't resist," he said in a voice loud enough for everyone in the room to hear, "seeing as you were standing there under the mistletoe."

"Do you remember what you said last night?" she whispered.

"Yeah, I remember. I was insane last night. I don't know what came over me." He let go of a long breath and turned to look at Mother's parlor, filled with the members of the book club.

"I don't belong here. This is Nick's place, not mine."

"But—"

He turned and held up his hand. "I'm a guy from Chicago, Annie. And they don't have snow here. I'll probably go back to the Midwest and see if I can get a job as a dog handler someplace like Milwaukee or St. Louis. There isn't anything for me in Last Chance. I just came here because I wanted to see if Nick's stories were true. I wanted to meet his grandmother. So I'm going to go up there to the nursing home tomorrow. I'll pay my respects, deliver Nick's present, and be on my way."

"But—"

"Annie, I'm not your soul mate, no matter what Miriam Randall says. And don't you go mistaking me for Nick Clausen either. Because I'm not him. If you believe in what they say about Miriam, you should keep the cat. I'm guessing that there's a handsome veterinarian in your future."

Matt went to midnight services along with all the members of the book club. He sat in the back of the church. He wasn't a believer. He was out of step with the people who came to celebrate the birth of Jesus that night.

The only thing that kept him in his place was the choir.

When they sang the "Hallelujah Chorus," Matt's skin prickled. But that reaction was nothing compared to what happened when Annie sang her solo, especially when she got to the last couple of lines.

> *Traveler, darkness takes its flight,*
> *Doubt and terror are withdrawn.*
> *Watchman, let thy wanderings cease;*
> *Hie thee to thy quiet home.*
> *Traveler, lo! the Prince of Peace,*
> *Lo! the Son of God is come!*

There seemed to be a message in that song, even for an unbeliever. He needed to firm his resolve, push his own needs aside, and visit Ruth tomorrow. Nick had wanted his grandmother to have a Christmas gift last year, and

Matt had kept it from her. He needed to go and let her know just what a good friend Nick had been.

Early the next morning, after a night of very little sleep, Matt found himself in the Christ Church van, sandwiched between Miriam Randall and another, equally ancient church lady. Making good on her promises, as Matt suspected she always did, Annie took the wheel of the van and drove everyone up to Orangeburg.

The church ladies came laden down with gifts like the wisemen. They carried cookies and gingerbread and a bundle of quilts the size of pillowcases that they called prayer blankets. He was literally surrounded by a bevy of ancient angels of mercy.

Within an hour, he stood alone on the threshold of Ruth Clausen's room at the nursing home, holding a brightly wrapped shirt box in his hands. The box wasn't very heavy, nor did it rattle. It was surely something to wear—something Ruth Clausen, now consigned to this small room, didn't need anymore.

He stepped up to the bed. The old lady looked pale and tiny, her gray hair thin. She had an oxygen tube hooked over her ears. She seemed to be having trouble breathing.

"Ruth," Matt said gently.

She opened a pair of hazel eyes, the exact same color as Nick's. Man, staring into those eyes threw him for a loop. They seemed clear and aware and alive.

A little smile quivered at the corner of her lips. "Nicky, you're home," she said.

Matt opened his mouth to correct her. But just as he was about to speak, something came over him. He flashed on the sound of Annie's voice singing that carol from the night before. He said not one word.

Instead, he pulled up the chair and took Ruth's hand in his. Her skin was paper-thin, her hand cold. He rubbed it between his.

"I've missed you so much," Ruth said.

"Me too, but you didn't expect me to miss Christmas, did you?"

"Christmas?" Ruth's voice sounded frail and confused. Her eyes dulled a little.

"Yes, Grandma, it's Christmas. The best time of year. You remember that year when we had the snow?"

She nodded, and her lips quivered. "It wasn't really snow, Nicky, just a dusting."

"I made a snowman."

"It was three inches tall."

"It was still a snowman. Size is not that important, Grandma."

She laughed and squeezed his hand. "I love you, boy, you know that?"

"Yes, ma'am, I do," Matt said; then he launched into one of Nick's favorite Christmas stories that involved a dog named Gonzo and an apple pie that disappeared when no one was looking.

Ruth enjoyed that story, and the five other Christmas stories Matt told her as if they belonged to him.

At some point, just as Ruth was beginning to fade off into sleep, he became aware of someone behind him. He turned and found Annie and Miriam standing in the doorway of the room. He had no idea how long they had been there listening. Both of them had tears in their eyes.

"So," Miriam whispered, "you going to give her that present or not?"

Matt realized that he hadn't said a word about Nick's present. It still rested on his lap.

Suddenly the present seemed kind of stupid. Ruth didn't need or want a present like this. All Ruth wanted for Christmas was Nick. And in a way Nick lived on, in the stories he'd told when the bullets had been flying or the boredom had set in. Matt knew them all by heart.

He couldn't bear to look at Annie or Miriam because his own eyes were overflowing with the tears he'd been holding back for a long, long time.

Annie strode into the room, bent over, and put her arms around his shoulders. Her hair spilled over him like a veil. "You're staying, of course," she murmured in his ear. "I couldn't imagine Christmas without you."

"But—"

"But nothing. You aren't Nick. I know that even if Ruth doesn't. You're kinder than Nick ever was. And you came home, when all Nick ever wanted was to wander the world. He may have told great stories, Matt, but he left Ruth alone. He walked away from me and everyone he loved in Last Chance. He never came back to visit, even when he wasn't on deployment. Instead, every year, he sent Ruth a Christmas present, as if that were enough. They came like clockwork. She always put them in the charity box. She never even unwrapped them."

"You knew this all along and you didn't tell me?"

"We all knew it. Why do you think I asked you about your reasons for coming? Why do you think Nita questioned your motives last night? I guess once you explained yourself everyone understood that you'd come

here looking for something Nick had thrown away without really looking back. No one wanted to dash your
illusions. Not after what you'd been through."

"And," Miriam said, "it sure does look like Nick's last
present was maybe the best one he ever sent home."

Matt closed his eyes and leaned in to Annie. Miriam
was wrong. If there had been a gift given this Christmas,
it had been what Annie had given him the last few days—
a Christmas he would never forget.

And a warm, welcoming place to come home to.

About the Author

Hope Ramsay is a *USA Today* bestselling author of heartwarming contemporary romances set below the Mason-Dixon Line. Her children are grown, but she has a couple of fur babies who keep her entertained. Pete the cat, named after the cat in the children's books, thinks he's a dog, and Daisy the dog thinks Pete is her best friend except when he decides her wagging tail is a cat toy. Hope lives in the medium-sized town of Fredericksburg, Virginia, and when she's not writing or walking the dog, she spends her time knitting and noodling around on her collection of guitars.

You can learn more at:
HopeRamsay.com
Twitter @HopeRamsay
Facebook.com/Hope.Ramsay

Fall in love with these charming contemporary romances!

A VERY MERRY MATCH
by Melinda Curtis

Mary Margaret Sneed usually spends her holiday baking and caroling with her students. But this year, she's swapped shortbread and sleigh bells to take a second job—one she can never admit to when the town mayor starts courting her. Only the town's meddling matchmakers have determined there's nothing a little mistletoe can't fix...and if the Widows Club has its way, Mary Margaret and the mayor may just get the best Christmas gift of all this year. Includes a bonus story by Hope Ramsay!

THE TWELVE DOGS OF CHRISTMAS
by Lizzie Shane

Ally Gilmore has only four weeks to find homes for a dozen dogs in her family's rescue shelter. But when she confronts the Scroogey councilman who pulled their funding, Ally finds he's far more reasonable—and handsome—than she ever expected...especially after he promises to help her. As they spend more time together, the Pine Hollow gossip mill is convinced that the Grinch might show Ally that Pine Hollow is her home for more than just the holidays.

CHRISTMAS ON REINDEER ROAD
by Debbie Mason

After his wife died, Gabriel Buchanan left his job as a New York City homicide detective to focus on raising his three sons. But back in Highland Falls, he doesn't have to go looking for trouble. It finds him—in the form of Mallory Maitland, a beautiful neighbor struggling to raise her misbehaving stepsons. When they must work together to give their boys the Christmas their hearts desire, they may find that the best gift they can give them is a family together.

SEASON OF JOY
by Annie Rains

For single father Granger Fields, Christmas is his busiest—and most profitable—time of the year. But when a fire devastates his tree farm, Granger convinces free spirit Joy Benson to care for his daughters while he focuses on saving his business. Soon Joy's festive ideas and merrymaking convince Granger he needs a business partner. As crowds return to the farm, life with Joy begins to feel like home. Can Granger convince Joy that this is where she belongs? Includes a bonus story by Melinda Curtis!

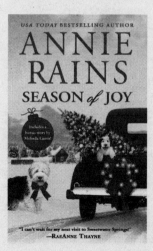

HER AMISH WEDDING QUILT
by Winnie Griggs

When the man she thought she would wed chooses another woman, Greta Eicher pours her energy into crafting beautiful quilts at her shop and helping widower Noah Stoll care for his adorable young children. But when her feelings for Noah grow into something even deeper, will she be able to convince him to have enough faith to give love another chance?

THE AMISH MIDWIFE'S HOPE
by Barbara Cameron

Widow Rebecca Zook adores her work, but the young midwife secretly wonders if she'll ever find love again or have a family of her own. When she meets handsome newcomer Samuel Miller, her connection with the single father is immediate—Rebecca even bonds with his sweet little girl. It feels like a perfect match, and Rebecca is ready to embrace the future...if only Samuel can open his heart once more.

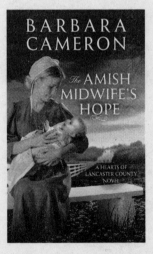

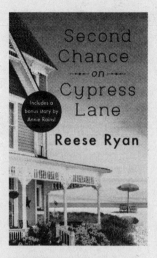

SECOND CHANCE ON CYPRESS LANE
by Reese Ryan

Rising-star reporter Dakota Jones is used to breaking the news, not making it. When a scandal costs her her job, there's only one place she can go to regroup. But her small South Carolina hometown comes with a major catch: Dexter Roberts. The first man to break Dakota's heart is suddenly back in her life. She won't give him another chance to hurt her, but she can't help wondering what might have been. Includes a bonus story by Annie Rains!

FOREVER WITH YOU
by Barb Curtis

Leyna Milan knows family legacies come with strings attached, but she's determined to prove that she can run her family's restaurant. Of course, Leyna never expected that honoring her grandfather's wishes meant opening a second location on her ex's winery—or having to ignore Jay's sexy grin and guard the heart he shattered years before. But as they work closely together, she begins to discover that maybe first love deserves a second chance...